Scratch Moss

David Barnett is an author, journalist and comic book writer based in West Yorkshire. He writes in a range of genres for various publishers, works for a wide variety of press outlets including the Guardian, Independent and BBC, and in comics has written for DC, 2000AD and more.

Also by David Barnett

Withered Hill
Scuttler's Cove
Scratch Moss

SCRATCH MOSS

DAVID BARNETT

CANELO

Penguin Random House

First published in the United Kingdom in 2026 by

Canelo, an imprint of
Canelo Digital Publishing Limited,
20 Vauxhall Bridge Road,
London SW1V 2SA
United Kingdom

A Penguin Random House Company
The authorised representative in the EEA is Dorling Kindersley Verlag GmbH. Arnulfstr. 124, 80636 Munich, Germany

Copyright © David Barnett 2026

The moral right of David Barnett to be identified as the creator of this work has been asserted in accordance with the Copyright, Designs and Patents Act, 1988.
All rights reserved. No part of this publication may be reproduced or transmitted in any form or by any means, electronic or mechanical, including photocopy, recording, or any information storage and retrieval system, without permission in writing from the publisher.
No part of this book may be used or reproduced in any manner for the purpose of training artificial intelligence technologies or systems. In accordance with Article 4(3) of the DSM Directive 2019/790, Canelo expressly reserves this work from the text and data mining exception.

A CIP catalogue record for this book is available from the British Library.

Print ISBN 978 1 83598 319 5
Ebook ISBN 978 1 83598 315 7

This book is a work of fiction. Names, characters, businesses, organizations, places and events are either the product of the author's imagination or are used fictitiously. Any resemblance to actual persons, living or dead, events or locales is entirely coincidental.

Cover design by Sarah Whittaker

Printed and bound in Great Britain by Clays Ltd, Elcograf S.p.A.

Look for more great books at
www.canelo.co | www.dk.com

For my grandad Charlie and all those who dug the coal.

'The enemy within... just as dangerous, in a way more difficult to fight...'

— *Margaret Thatcher's notes for her speech on the miners to the 1922 Committee, July 19th, 1984*

PART ONE

2025

1

There was something in the earth beneath Scratch Moss, something darker than the coal they dug there for more than a century, something that burned with the malevolent glow of the fires of hell. Something that just wouldn't let you go...

Stop dreaming up first lines, Joe reprimanded himself, forehead pressed against the train window, watching the countryside flash past. *You're not going home to write a book. You're going home to lay your father to rest.* Still, would it be such a bad thing, if he did get a book out of it? That was one of the steps on the literary author's journey, wasn't it? Go back to your depressed little Northern hometown, so dull and squalid and small after London, and write something important about the noble savagery of the working classes. He jotted some lines down on the notes app on his phone, and leaned back on the window.

Joe's ears popped as the train rushed into a tunnel, displacing air, and he was suddenly confronted by his reflection, up close, in the black mirror of the window. Never introduce your main character through them looking at their reflection, he thought. Never start your story with someone waking up, or by describing the weather. He knew all the rules. And how to break them, as well. He was Joe Collier, the occasional darling of Grub Street, twice-longlisted for the Booker, once wrote a novel with no commas in it, when he could be bothered with that sort of thing. The last couple of books... well, they'd been nicely reviewed, but hadn't sold many. He glared at his reflection, as though it was all the fault of that Mirror Joe. Or maybe it was because he was in his fifties now, and had just run out of things to say that couldn't be said better by younger writers. This time it was his reflection's turn to glare, or so it seemed. The train rattled out of the tunnel, into the cottony spring sunshine, and the window was a window again and not a mirror.

There was a lone taxi standing on the apron of the railway station, and when Joe opened the door and told him he wanted to go to Scratch Moss, the driver shook his head and said he was booked. Joe stood against the wall of the ticket office, smoking and trying to get an Uber. It was a bright, clear afternoon, still a slight chill in the air, but something offering the promise of spring. He looked up as two women came out of the station and went to the cab, loudly announcing their destination. The driver told them to get in. So, not booked after all. Just didn't want to go to Scratch Moss. Joe didn't have any better luck with the Uber app; nobody accepted his fare, even though he saw three or four Ubers driving past the station, and two more stopping to pick up passengers.

He was just about to give up and start Googling bus timetables when his phone pinged and announced he had a ride after all. A battered Volvo pulled up five minutes later and Joe threw his bags into the boot and got into the rear passenger seat.

'Scratch Moss,' said the driver, a broad, bull-necked, bald man. Joe couldn't see his face apart from his eyes, hooded and rimmed with dark circles, glancing at him in the rear-view mirror. The car smelled of stale cigarettes.

'Don't get many for Scratch Moss,' said the driver, looking at Joe in the mirror as he negotiated the one-way system of the town centre and then past a single-storey pub, its windows shuttered with steel plates, and a sprouting of a trio of tower-blocks, the concrete walls covered with fading graffiti. Joe watched the landscape slide past the window, at once recognisable and yet unfamiliar. Old landmarks had gone, replaced by new ones: a budget supermarket for a pub, a small estate of box-like houses for a school, a factory demolished and given over to austere rewilding by dry grasses and knotweed.

Scratch Moss squatted on the black ribbon of an A-road, Warrington at one end of it, Wigan at the other. Neither town was particularly keen to claim the red-brick terraces that lined the road on either side, with council estates and cemeteries and former mining land spooling out behind. There was at least two miles on either side of Scratch Moss to the next communities, as though other places shrank away from it.

Joe had never understood that, growing up. Scratch Moss had never been what you might call rich, never posh, but everyone seemed to... do all right. There was always food on the table and jobs – albeit at the pit – for everyone. People seemed to have enough money in their pockets. But tell someone you were from Scratch Moss and they seemed to pull away, something crossing their faces, even for a moment, even if they didn't understand it themselves. There was just something about Scratch Moss that made people feel... Joe didn't know what.

The road was quiet. In fact, they were almost the only vehicle on it. The driver, as though reading his mind, said, 'They built the bypass finally, like they'd been threatening to. About ten years ago. Not much uses this stretch now.'

There was some traffic ahead of them, though. Flashing blue lights. Two police cars and an ambulance, a knot of uniforms gathered around a tree set back just a few feet from the road. Police officers were erecting some kind of tall barrier around the tree. The driver slowed and Joe caught a glimpse of a body hanging by the neck from one of the sturdy branches, head lolling on one side.

'Fucking hell,' he breathed.

The driver accelerated. 'Poor bastard. What drives a man to do that? Wouldn't catch me topping myself, no matter how bad things got.'

Joe craned his neck to watch as the officers covered up the body. He could still see the thick rope hanging taut from the branch above the screens.

Joe turned back, felt the driver's gaze resting on him in the rear-view mirror, and looked up to meet it. The driver said, 'Do I know you?'

Joe looked out at the wasteland that, in any other place, would have been filled with overpriced family homes by now. Not within half a mile of Scratch Moss, though. Grey, anonymous clouds had gathered overhead. He said, 'I grew up here.'

The eyes narrowed in the mirror. 'You're not Terry and Mary Collier's lad, are you?'

Joe sighed and nodded. 'Yes, I am.' *Lad*. He was fifty-three years old.

They passed some allotments, set back from the road, and then another closed-down pub. They were in Scratch Moss. 'Sorry about your dad. I suppose that's why you've come back.'

Joe nodded, and the man said, 'He never deserved what happened to him.'

Joe stared at him. 'He kicked a man to death.'

The driver flicked the indicator and pulled up on the main road, in front of a row of terraced houses with tiny front gardens. 'This do you? Well, in my book, Terry Collier was a bloody hero. They should have given him a medal, not a life sentence.'

The driver flipped the boot catch and got out with Joe, getting his bags for him. He was tall but with a huge belly, a polo shirt with curling collars stretched over it. With a shock, Joe finally recognised him. Gary Grady. He was five years or so older than Joe, lived a couple of streets away, and in truth Joe had always looked up to him a bit. He'd thought Gary cool back in the Eighties, when he rode a Vespa and wore a fish-tail parka during the Mod revival. He was slim and good-looking and always had girlfriends. Now he looked closer to seventy than the sixty he must be approaching, pale and fleshy and faintly grimy, as though the cloud that hung over Scratch Moss was infused with the ghost of coal dust from long ago.

'You went away, after it happened, didn't you?' said Gary. Was there a subtle note of accusation in his tone?

'I went to live with my auntie in Leeds for a bit,' said Joe. 'Then went to university. Did a few jobs. Worked on a couple of local papers in the Midlands and down south. I've lived in London for twenty-five years now.'

Gary shrugged. 'What do you do? Do you work for newspapers still? The local one's crap. Nothing in it. And the bloody ads on the website...'

Joe hesitated. Saying you were a *writer* was all well and good in London. Up here... it felt wanky and show-offy. Gary had worked at the pit before they closed it down, for a couple of years. He'd been on the picket lines during the strike. *A proper man's job.* The words rose unbidden in Joe's mind. He said lamely, 'I still write stuff. Books, mostly.'

Gary nodded. 'You were always into your books, and that.' He closed the boot. 'Say hello to Mary for me. I always liked your mum. Do you know when the funeral is?'

'Next Thursday,' said Joe. 'You'll come?'

'Yeah,' said Gary, and he got back in the car. Joe watched him drive away, towards the trees that overhung the road a little way down as it turned a sharp bend between the blackened stone walls of what used to be a railway bridge.

He stood on the pavement across the road from his mum's house for a while, outside the end-terrace that used to have a plaque beside the door with an amalgamation of the names of the husband and wife who lived there, like *Brangelina* but decades ahead of its time, and seeming equal parts audacious and sophisticated to the young Joe. They were the first people he knew who went to Benidorm, which – after his holidays in North Wales and the Lake District – seemed impossibly exotic to him. *Getting peas above sticks*, his mum would probably have said about their aspirations. Joe glanced behind him; an unfamiliar face peered through the window from behind the edge of a heavy brown curtain. The aspirational family – he couldn't even remember their names – must have moved up and on, taking advantage of some property boom or other. The face was hidden in shadow and seemed bloated and greasy, pinprick rat eyes shining in the gloom of the house, then the curtains rippled queasily and the face was gone. Joe stared into the blackness of the window for a long moment, at the desiccated flies dotting the sill, at the brown curtains, until he realised what he was doing, and blinked, then turned away.

But not before he caught a movement in the house next door, a pale moon passing across the window, eyes boring into him. Then the curtains in all the windows seemed to flutter as though a stiff breeze was blowing through all the houses, as if the stout red-brick walls and wooden doors of the terrace were nothing but a facade, propped up as though on a movie set and home to sickly-white balloon-faced people who stared half-timidly, half-malevolently at passing strangers.

Joe forced himself to smile and finally looked away from the houses, the back of his neck itching like mad, something like anxiety bubbling in his gut. Don't be ridiculous, he told himself. This is where you grew up. This is where you lived for the first thirteen years of your life.

He paused at the kerb, waiting until a dirty white van sailed past him along the road, the occupants pale with cement dust and bloated with processed food, fixing their tiny eyes on him until they passed. The van followed the bend out of view, swallowed by the trees that hung over the road, their tips almost touching in a way they had never done when Joe was a child, and they seemed to shudder and rustle as the van passed beneath them and from sight, like they were welcoming back something that was part of them.

Joe took one more look over his shoulder, ignoring the sudden swishing of curtains in concert all along the terrace, then crossed the road and opened the wrought-iron gate into the tiny front garden of the house next-but-one to the end.

Crisp packets blossomed on the bare twigs of the bushes that clung to life in the rubble-filled soil of the tiny plot and there were already empty milk bottles on the step in readiness for the milkman's pre-dawn rounds. Milk in glass bottles… he didn't even know they did that anymore. A sudden memory surfaced of his dad trying to surreptitiously drink milk straight from the bottle while Mum scolded him from the kitchen door. Joe felt side-swiped, suddenly dizzy, and put his hand on the red-brick wall for support. He jumped, startled, as a shape suddenly flapped and rose with a ratcheting squawk. A magpie, sitting on the wall. He hadn't noticed it. He watched it take to the sky, frowning. There had been something about magpies, hadn't there…?

He turned back to the door and dug into his pocket, just as the grotesque-seeming silhouette of his mum loomed behind the frosted glass and opened the door before he could fish out his old set of keys.

Joe Collier was home.

2

'I saw you standing across the road like you were lost,' said his mum, frowning at Joe on the doorstep. The frown seemed like a permanent fixture on her face, the lines carved into her cheeks and chin as though by a sculptor. 'Did you have a bad journey?'

'No, it was fine, all on time,' said Joe, bending awkwardly to kiss his mum on the top of her dyed blonde hair, cut short. She was barely up to his chest now, and he doubted he'd been growing much now he was well over fifty, so presumed she must have started shrinking with old age. 'There was a man... at the tree... the police.' He stopped. Why was he telling her this?

'I know,' she said. 'Poor bugger. I saw it. Went out for a few bits from the shops earlier.'

Joe didn't know what to say. 'Poor bugger,' he repeated.

'Come in, then.' She sighed. 'You're letting all the heat out.'

He shouldered his bag and stepped over the threshold, and for want of something to say he nodded back across the road. 'What happened to...' He couldn't remember the family's name. 'Them across the road. That always went to Benidorm?'

It was as though the act of stepping into the house had started the process of shucking off his adopted London airs, and Joe almost shocked himself with how easy he slipped back into the monotone, flat-vowelled dialect of home. Mum stared at him as though, as she'd say, he'd *gone soft*. 'He died five years ago. She hooked up with some bloke from work, moved in with him in one of the new houses, where the playing fields used to be.'

Joe glanced back across the road one more time, the curtains rippling in all the houses like a pale wave, as though the occupants had stepped back in unison at the weight of his stare. Then Mum shut the door and said, 'You'll be wanting a cup of tea.'

He followed her down the short hall to the foot of the stairs and left into what they had always rather grandly called the dining room, though their meals – dinner at noon, tea at five – were invariably eaten from plates balanced on their knees in front of the television. Save for Sunday dinner, which his mum refused to allow to be consumed anywhere other than the table.

'The Little Woods has got big, hasn't it?' Joe said, thinking of the green darkness sucking in the white van and its sickly-pale passengers. That's what they always called it. The Little Woods. He frowned again, something half on the edge of his memory. Something to do with magpies.

Mum stared at him even as she helped him off with his jacket, folded it and placed it over the back of one of the dining room chairs. 'Is that all you've got to say? He's dead. Your dad's dead.'

Joe concentrated on the whorls in the pattern of the dining room carpet, finding the face hidden there that always used to terrify him as a child, then finally met her eyes. 'It wasn't my fault, you know. I never asked him to do what he did.'

She sighed a ragged, old woman's sigh. 'No. No, you didn't. I've only got PG Tips. You're probably used to something posher.'

Joe followed her into the tiny kitchen, the saucer on the windowsill holding a half-smoked cigarette, the grinning Toby jugs on the shelf over the work surface, the plaster above the grill dark with years of grease. 'PG Tips is fine.' He paused, then said, far too chirpily, 'You could decorate now. I could come home for a bit, help you out. We could do the whole house.'

She filled the kettle and plugged it in, then lit the half-a-cigarette from a box of Cook's Matches. 'What, now that he's gone?' she said, blowing smoke out with the words. 'Cover over him, like he was never here?' She took another drag from the cigarette then stubbed it out, viciously, in the saucer. 'I've been doing that for forty years.' She nodded at something on the worktop, by the breadbin. 'Besides, I made a start.'

Joe picked up the ancient drill. Must have been one of his dad's. It was plugged into the socket, and on the wall over the bin he could see plaster gouged out where his mum had tried to drill holes.

'Not got the strength to hold it properly,' she said. 'Maybe that's something you could do while you're here.'

Joe looked at the long, thick bit protruding from the drill. 'This is too big,' he said, exasperated. 'It's a...' He paused, grasping for the name, and felt the weight of his dad's amused stare from beyond the grave. 'A masonry bit,' he finished, with relief. 'For drilling holes in brick and stone, outside.' Joe looked at the holes in the wall again. 'What were you trying to do, anyway?'

'Put our wedding pictures up,' said his mum quietly. 'Thought it was about time again. Now it's over.'

His mum made tea from three tea bags in the cracked old brown pot Joe remembered her buying new on a holiday on the south coast, from a factory shop in a little harbour town famous for its pottery. It was expensive and everyone was worried it would never make the journey back in one piece. As his mum stirred the tea bags around in a whirlpool of darkening water Joe was suddenly transported back there, waiting on the softening tarmac in the baking sun as his mum clicked and clucked and ummed and ahhed over it, until his dad finally told her to get on with it, if she was buying it, or he'd melt. Then they went to buy ice creams, his mum cradling her tissue-wrapped teapot. She linked arms with his dad as they walked along the harbour, licking their ice creams. Joe had been embarrassed and happy all at the same time. She'd said, 'If we come back here next year I'll get four cups, if we can afford it.'

'Four?' said his dad. 'There's only three of us, and he doesn't drink tea.'

She'd slapped him playfully on his broad shoulder. 'Do you think we'll come back next year?'

'Don't see why not, if you like it down here.' He'd taken a lick of his ice cream. 'So long as they don't close the pit down.'

Joe's mum slapped him again, a little less playfully. 'Don't joke about it.'

His dad ruffled Joe's hair. 'What about you? Would you like to come back down here next year?'

Joe vividly remembered looking out at the white yachts bobbing at anchor on the glistening waters of the harbour. He'd loved that holiday. He'd just turned twelve. Endless hot days and ice creams and comics bought from a rack in the beach-shop. Joe had loved being in that town.

They wouldn't ever go back.

'I'll buy you a new teapot,' he said, pushing the memory away as his mum poured out two cups.

She stared at him. 'There's nothing wrong with this one.'

'It's old. It's cracked. You can see where you glued the spout on.'

Her lips – suddenly thin and bloodless, as though her vital organs were calling back all her body's resources for the final push into old age – quivered at the corners. 'I can remember buying this pot,' she said. 'You were—'

Joe picked up both mugs and shouldered his way through the saloon doors that separated the kitchen from the dining room. 'Come on, let's drink them in the front room.' He didn't want to talk about that holiday. Didn't want to remember being happy. For all his adult life, and a handful of years before, he'd never associated this place with happiness. It didn't even feel right to contemplate it in here. Not now his dad was dead, and perhaps they were supposed to feel free, and allow themselves to be happy again. Joe glanced at his mum as he sat down on the sofa. Her eyes were hard and grey, like granite. Had she cried herself out, or was she simply unable to weep now?

She settled herself in the chair under the window and took the cup of tea from Joe, then sat back and watched him expectantly. His eyes avoided hers and landed on a lump of plastic chewed beyond all recognition, stuck in the corner by the TV. For one awful moment he couldn't even remember whether the old dog was still alive. Joe dimly remembered some phone call, talk about a vet, an operation. He'd nodded and made noises at what he imagined were the right moments, as though he was listening. Probably writing, or emailing, or scrolling through his phone, or Netflix, which seemed far more important at the time. She might have been telling him the dog had died, he realised. He honestly had no idea.

Joe nodded at the ravaged toy. 'Um. Shep…'

'In the yard,' she said, blowing on her tea. 'He's getting on a bit now. Just likes to sleep most of the day. Still needs his walk, though. I'll take him in a bit.'

'I'll take him,' Joe said, a little too quickly. She furrowed her brow at him. 'I've been cooped up all day on that train, could do with some fresh air. See what the old neighbourhood's like these days.'

She frowned at the word *neighbourhood*, and Joe winced at it slightly himself, now he was back in the cocoon of the old house, the rarefied atmosphere of Scratch Moss. It sounded too folksy, too much like what they'd say on one of those saccharine old kids' TV shows with puppets and down-home philosophy, all friends together, all colours and creeds holding hands around the world.

She shrugged. 'If you like. Don't let him off near roads, though.' She paused, and clicked her tongue. 'Funeral's next Thursday. I told you, didn't I?'

'Good God,' Joe said, looking over her shoulder through the window. 'Is that Ellen Dowd?'

His mum twisted in the chair and looked at the woman, almost shapeless in jogging bottoms and an anorak, bending over a buggy and extracting what looked like a mashed-up pie from the fingers of a tiny child. Her hair was dragged back over her head into a tight ponytail, her face pinched and red and ageless.

His mum turned back to stare at him. 'That's her daughter. That's Hannah. Ellen's daughter, with her little boy. Korben, I think she called him. Something like that.'

Joe stared at the woman. 'Her daughter. Christ.'

Mum tutted and shook her head. 'You should remember how old you are. Normal people like Ellen Dowd grew up and had families of their own. She's a grandma.'

'Christ,' he said again. A grandma at fifty-three. Ellen Dowd had been in his class at school. And that summer, Ellen Dowd...

His mum finished her tea and stared into the tannin stains in the bottom of the mug. 'Your problem is, you go away and you think everything stays the same.'

Joe scrutinised his mum as she stared out of the window. Something seemed to lift around her, a cloud thinning if not dissipating totally. A hint of a smile quivered at the corners of her lips. There were other people on the road now, mainly young women, pushing buggies and holding hands with small children. Joe glanced at his watch. Must be school finishing time.

'I like to watch the little kiddies going to and from school,' she said with a small sigh. 'Makes me forget how old I am.' A small child squinted at the window and waved, and his mum waved back. 'This is what I mean, Joe. Life goes on. Even here. Even in Scratch Moss.'

3

Shep walked with weary resignation the length of the chain-link lead behind Joe, looking up at him with rheumy eyes reddened with loathing at the prospect of the walk. Joe led him along the length of the dirt track that ran between the rears of the terraces – The Backs, they always called it, unconsciously capitalising it as though it were a place in its own right, not just a gap between pre-war houses snaking along in red-brick processions, somewhere to put out the bins.

At the end of The Backs was a metal gate that brought him up short. A security measure, obviously, and not something he liked to think about too hard. Presumably there was one at the other end of The Backs, keeping the rears of the houses safe from marauding gangs and crack-addicted burglars. Shep nosed at the gate and it swung inwards, unlocked. Joe barked half a laugh, his cheeks flushing at the same time. He was beginning to sound like his dad. The thought sobered him as Shep dragged him through the gate, sniffing the ground and pulling Joe towards the main road.

'Where d'you want to go, boy?' he murmured, knowing full well that the dog, a brown and white cross of too many breeds to count, was taking him unerringly towards the dark arch created by the trees of the Little Woods that overhung the main road. There was no traffic and he let Shep lead him across the highway, past the low wall that bordered a builders' merchants, set back and below the road. He wondered who lived in the row of houses opposite now, perusing the blank eyes of the windows as they walked along the pavement. Joe paused, dragging Shep to a tongue-lolling halt as he peered at the houses. Like before, on the main road when he first arrived, it was as though a subtle movement, an almost indiscernible Mexican wave, had started at one end and rolled through the houses, keeping pace with them. He had the sudden, crazy thought that the terrace was a mere facade, shored up by braces and poles, like a cheap B-movie set, and that behind was... what? But Shep was impatient, pulling him on, and the shadowy mouth of the road ahead beckoned.

Stepping into the shade of the green canopy was like hopscotching from an even number to an odd one; the same thing, obviously, but forever different, strictly demarcated. Shep ploughed on, oblivious, even as Joe's pace slowed. He glanced back along the road as it started to bend away in front of him. Why was it so quiet? Where was all the traffic? The bypass, he remembered. They'd finally built the bypass so people didn't have to drive through Scratch Moss anymore. He could hear the distant whisper of cars. Ahead the trees that grew in the landscaped bankings on either side of the road, behind faded wooden fences, clasped branches high above the road, creating a dense canopy that glowed faintly with the lancing sunlight that it refused to allow through.

Joe zipped up his jacket; it was cold in the shade. Shep was sniffing at the gap in the fence that opened on to a rough, overgrown path, and started to pull Joe inside, off the pavement. The trees were closely packed together, their branches thick and full, blotting out any light from overhead. The path had once been a single-track railway line that connected the old pit to the main line, over the road and a couple of miles beyond. You could still see, in places, the remains of the wooden sleepers and hints of the rusted track occasionally emerging from the dirt.

Joe let Shep off the lead and the dog trotted forward, sniffing at a nettle, then cocking its leg to piss on it. Joe peered into the darkness ahead. Not just gloomy and shadowed, but *dark*. The trees rustled in a sudden, cold breeze. Joe had never liked the

Little Woods. Before the Scratch Moss pit had closed for good, the operations had scaled down over the years, and this land had all been allowed to... well, Joe supposed they'd call it *rewilding* now. Back then, it had just been pretty much abandoned, after the local council had planted trees to shield the road and the houses from the remaining mine workings. The Little Woods never felt *natural* to Joe. It wasn't like a proper woods, that had grown organically, part of the ecosystem, or even the London parks, that had been landscaped and planted for leisure and recreation. The Little Woods had always felt like it was covering something up. Hiding something. Pretending to be what it wasn't. Trees grown in industrial dirt, nurtured by slag and fly-ash, breathing in chimney smoke. The Little Woods always felt like a sick place.

Joe stopped, and peered into the thick darkness of the trees. Shep had disappeared. He called his name, and whistled, then listened for the sounds of the old dog panting in the trees. There was nothing. Not even birdsong. Just black, heavy silence.

And then he heard it.

A sharp, hard sound of something being struck, like two hard stones bashed together. But more... metallic. It cut through the darkness and the dead air, from dead ahead of him, beyond where he could see. There it was again. It was a familiar sound, but where did...

And then he was suddenly assaulted by a memory, being thirteen years old, in this very spot, more or less. There were three or four of them, finding sticks to strip the bark from and use for sword fights later on. Joe remembered the sound, the very same sound, that made them all fall silent and wide-eyed, and he remembered what Daz Twist had said.

'Red Clogs is coming to get you.'

Then Daz had struck the heel of his Kicker boot on the bit of exposed rail track, the metal seg on the bottom of his boot sparking against the steel. And they'd all laughed with nervous relief, and run back towards the main road.

Joe stood alone, shivering at the memory. How had he forgotten?

It's Red Clogs.

How had he forgotten Red Clogs?

He's coming to get you.

And then the sound came again, issuing from the undergrowth ahead of him, distinct and clear, like a bell ringing. Joe felt the hairs on the back of his neck stand up, and his legs began to quiver.

It's Red Clogs.

Where the hell was Shep? Joe wanted to get back to the main road, back to the house. Not be standing here in the sick Little Woods, the trees sucking away all the light, that sound coming from the blackness ahead.

'For fuck's sake,' muttered Joe. 'Pull yourself—'

Then he cried out, screamed really, as something barrelled out of the trees to his left, clattering through the branches, a black shape that skimmed past him with a guttural squawk.

'Fuck!' exclaimed Joe, his heart pounding, as the magpie flew up to the canopy of the trees, alighting on a high branch and calling out with consternation. Shep came stumbling through the trees, in vain yet hopeful pursuit of the bird. Joe allowed himself a long breath, then bent down and fixed the lead to Shep's collar. Shep panted his agreement, and the magpie cried again. A shaft of sudden sunlight pierced the branches overhead and abruptly the Little Woods sounded full of life again, birdsong and the distant bark of another dog, and even the faint suggestion of traffic noise coming from the road far behind.

Joe glanced up at the magpie – what was it about the magpies? He couldn't remember – then back at the path disappearing into the trees, and gave a little laugh. Red Clogs. He'd forgotten about Red Clogs. He should get back and write that down. 'Come on,' he said, dragging on Shep's lead, and headed back towards the road.

Joe's mum had made him a plate of beige food, potatoes and butter beans, cauliflower cheese and a wizened pork chop, tough as boot leather. They sat on the sofa with their dinner – tea, Joe reprimanded himself. It's tea in Scratch Moss – on their knees, watching a TV show where celebrities had to buy antiques and then sell them at auction.

'Your gran used to have one of those,' said Joe's mum, pointing with her knife at the screen where a man was holding a multicoloured glass fish. 'Threw it out when she died.'

The mention of death raised the spectre of his dad, and Joe glanced at his chair, the cushion indented with his absence. He felt like he should say something, but he wasn't quite sure what. In the end he just said, lamely, 'I'm sorry.'

His mum looked at him. 'What for?'

Joe shrugged. 'For Dad. Dying.'

She sighed and let her knife and fork clatter to the plate. 'It comes to us all. Just happened to come to your dad in jail.' She paused, and said, 'They'd have let him out, you know. By now. If he'd said the right things at the parole hearings. He'd done his time.'

Joe looked at her curiously. 'If he'd said what sort of things?'

'That he regretted it, that he was sorry, that he was a changed man.'

'So why didn't he?'

'Because he wasn't,' said his mum tightly. 'He wasn't any of those things. He did what he did and he'd have done it again in a heartbeat.'

Joe forced the rest of his food down in silence. His mum said, 'You don't know. You weren't here. You don't know what it's been like, these last forty years.' She shook her head, as though she couldn't quite believe the gulf of time that lay between this moment and that one. 'Forty years.'

'I'm sorry,' said Joe, which seemed the right thing to say. 'Was it hard? After what Dad did...?' For the first time, he wondered what his mum had done for money after his dad went to prison.

His mum shook her head. 'They think he's a bloody saint round here. You don't know. You weren't here. Everybody looked out for me. That's what people do in Scratch Moss. We got some money from your grandad just before... before it happened. It was just... the loneliness, really. It's been a long time on my own.'

'I didn't want to go away,' said Joe quietly. 'It wasn't my idea. You made me go and live with Auntie Linda in Leeds.'

'I did,' agreed his mum, standing up and taking the plate from him. 'It was for the best. Get you away from Scratch Moss. At least have a chance at a decent life. Do you want some Angel Delight?'

Joe followed her to the kitchen, where she lit a cigarette and opened the back door on to the yard. Dusk was settling, and there was a chill in the air. He got the Angel Delight out of the fridge. 'I missed you, you know. When I went to Leeds. I was only thirteen.'

'Best thing for you,' said his mum, blowing smoke out into the gathering gloom. 'You'd have gone anyway, eventually. University and that. Best you got out and didn't have to deal with everything after what happened. Best you went away and forgot Scratch Moss, like our Linda did.'

She smoked the cigarette halfway down then pinched the end and put it into the saucer on the worktop. 'Shame about you and that Jenna,' she said, closing the door, a perfume of cigarette smoke around her.

'I thought you didn't like her,' said Joe.

His mum shrugged. 'She didn't like me, more like. Thought I was too common.'

That was true. Jenna had been appalled when Joe brought his mum to London that first time. She was from rich farming stock in Gloucester. Lots of money, airs and graces to match. Joe had done a good job of reinventing himself after he'd left Leeds for university. Too good, perhaps. He was erudite and charming and handsome and kept himself in shape. He was, for brief moments that came and went, the darling of the literary world. He never mentioned his upbringing in Scratch Moss, but always said he was from Leeds, which at least sounded more cosmopolitan. When Jenna finally met his mum, Joe could almost see her turning up her nose.

'Anyway, it's over,' said Joe. Jenna was ten years younger than him, and they'd been together a decade. She'd left because she 'wanted more'. Joe suspected that, once he'd turned fifty, Jenna had in fact wanted *younger*. Last he heard, she was seeing her personal trainer. He was thirty-five. Maybe if Joe had been more successful and less given to long periods of doing nothing – with the income to match – he would have been enough, despite the age difference. But he knew as well as Jenna that the older he got, the less of an attractive proposition he was to publishers. Everyone wanted coruscating, pin-sharp debut novels by young people with things to say about modern life. Editors just weren't that interested in the latest dour, bile-filed polemic written by an increasingly irrelevant middle-aged white man who still traded on the fact that he had been long-listed for the Booker Prize when most of the people he was trying to persuade to publish him were still in nappies.

Realising he was sounding bitter, even if only in his own head, Joe made a pot of tea and they watched TV in companionable silence until he felt his eyes drooping in the warmth of the little living room, and said he was going to get an early night, after his long day travelling.

His old room had been stripped of his posters and books, of course, and decorated with a floral wallpaper. His old single bed was still there, though, and he changed into his Calvin Klein lounge pants and T-shirt – pyjamas, he said to himself. Call them what they are – and slid under the duvet. In the darkness, aside from the pale-yellow glow of a streetlight in the road at the side of the terrace, he thought about seeing Ellen Dowd's daughter, and thinking it was Ellen. That summer before he left, before what happened happened... he'd thought he was in love with

Ellen Dowd. She was his first proper crush. And then, the day he left for Leeds, he heard that she'd been fingered by Neil Hall behind the Working Men's Club, and that settled it for him. It broke his heart and he got into his Auntie Linda's car with his suitcases and drove away from Scratch Moss and never looked back.

Joe wondered what Ellen Dowd was doing now, just before he drifted into an uneasy sleep, the image of the man hanging from the tree bobbing up in his mind.

Joe dreamed of his dad. Of that night. Of sitting, legs drawn up, between the bins in the yard in the dead of night, whimpering, then stifling his breathing as the latch on the gate went. He shrank inside himself, trying to become smaller than nothing, and by the light of the full moon he saw two booted feet march past him, slick with dark, shining blood. His dad. And, later that night, in the very bed he was sleeping fitfully in now, Joe awoke to see a figure looming over him, and his dad looking down, his face serious. *I've got to go, Joe. I'm sorry, lad. I'm sorry.*

Joe started awake from the dream, disorientated in the darkness, momentarily not knowing where he was, until he remembered he was in his old bed, in his old room, in Scratch Moss. Then he gasped as a figure moved in front of the glow of the lamppost from outside. A slight, small, stooped figure.

'Mum?' said Joe blearily, fumbling for the switch on the bedside lamp. In the pale light his mum stared down at him, but with almost unseeing eyes. Her face was drooping, her eyes half-closed, as though she was half-asleep, or sleepwalking. Joe said again, 'Mum?'

'He's back,' she said, her voice thick, slurring the words. Then she turned around and shuffled out of the room.

4

Joe awoke to a commotion outside his window, the sound of Shep barking and a frantic squawking, accompanied by shouts from his mum. He ran to the window and dragged back the curtains to see her in the yard, wielding a long-handled brush as though it was a sledgehammer, while Shep ran around in frenzied circles.

By the time he got down to the kitchen and the back door, his mum was leaning on the brick wall that separated the yard from next door's, breathing heavily, while Shep sniffed around the battered and bloodied corpse of a magpie.

'What the fuck?' Joe said, stepping out barefoot onto the stone flags, surveying the carnage.

His mum gave him the same blank-eyed stare she had when standing over his bed – *Did I dream that?* he thought – then looked down at the dead bird, her bony hand flying to her mouth.

'Mum?' said Joe more gently, taking hold of her elbow. She was shaking her head, her eyes filled with tears, as though she'd just awoken from a trance. 'Mum, why did you kill the bird?'

'I don't know,' she said hoarsely. She looked around, wild-eyed. Joe followed her gaze, at the blank windows of the terrace behind them. He couldn't see anyone, but felt that they were being observed. Then his mum got the shovel from beside the door, scooped up the magpie, and deposited it in the wheelie bin. Joe saw a flutter of curtains in the upstairs window of the house directly behind them. 'Oh, God,' said his mum. 'What have I done?'

Joe made tea while his mum smoked, standing at the door and staring at the black stain of blood and feathers on the flags. He stirred the pot, brow furrowed. What was going on with his mum? Perhaps she'd been holding things together for so long while Dad was in prison, and now he was dead... maybe she couldn't hold on anymore. He glanced at her. He needed to get her to a doctor.

She closed the door and stared at him. 'You should never kill a magpie,' she said.

'Is it bad luck?' said Joe, trying to sound jovial and untroubled, as though battering a bird to death with a yard-brush was the most normal thing in the world.

'It is in Scratch Moss.'

OK, then, if they were going there. He said, 'So why did you do it?'

'I don't know,' said his mum quietly.

'Did you come into my room last night?' asked Joe.

She looked at him. 'Did I?'

'Yes. You said, *he's back*. Who did you mean?'

Then she started crying, and Joe didn't quite know what to do. He put his arm around her thin shoulders, somewhat awkwardly. 'Why don't you go and have a lie down?' he suggested. 'I'll bring you a cup of tea up. Do you want some breakfast?'

'I had some toast,' she said. 'Yes, I might do that. Do you mind?' Then she frowned. 'Shep needs walking.'

'I'll take him,' said Joe, suddenly relieved to have a focus, something to concentrate on. 'And shall I get us something for dinn— tea? Are the shops still on the parade?'

His mum nodded. 'The butchers and the greengrocer's. And the corner shop has stuff.'

'Surprised they're still going,' said Joe, steering her to the stairs. 'Most little independent shops like that have been put out of business by the supermarkets and express chains.'

'Nobody like that ever wanted to come to Scratch Moss,' she said. Joe watched her mount the stairs, then went back to make the tea.

Joe took Shep along the road under the arch of trees, but didn't turn off into the Little Woods, instead crossing the road and heading down the Donkey Lane towards the open fields and the old branch line. In any other place this would have been snapped up for housing by now. Maybe there just weren't enough people who would consider moving to Scratch Moss, especially after the pit closed down. The Donkey Lane was a wide dirt track that passed a stagnant, weed-choked pond, the Tenchy, where they used to swim and fish and make rafts, then carried on to the disused branch line. Beyond that lay a flooded quarry, which in the summers of his youth was almost a local tourist attraction, with families sitting on blankets and having picnics, overlooked by the Rabbit Rocks, a small, long hill studded with grey boulders. Sitting on top of the Rabbit Rocks was a squat concrete shape with horizontal slits in its five sides. It was an old pill-box, left over from the war, in place to defend the coal mine in the event of a German invasion. When Joe was a kid it was the haunt of glue-sniffers and the less-than-salubrious location where many a virginity had been surrendered.

'Up to a walk up the rocks?' said Joe, letting Shep off the lead. The dog scampered ahead, slowing as the path winding up the hill steepened, until Joe overtook him and waited for him at the top, taking in the views of Scratch Moss as white clouds scudded across the blue sky.

From the Rabbit Rocks Joe could see along the Donkey Lane and over the Little Woods that shielded the road. Beyond the trees was where the Scratch Moss pit used to be, now landscaped into grass covered fields and hillocks. To the right, the housing estates sprawled. To the left, the cemetery. And just visible beyond the treeline, on the road, the old church. It had never been a working church while Joe had been alive, and not for more than a century, as far as he knew. Like the housing developers and the supermarkets, the church didn't come to Scratch Moss. It had at one point, obviously, but not any more.

Joe had seen a painting once, probably a view from this very vantage point, created more than 150 years ago. Before the pits, before Scratch Moss was even a community. Close to where the mine stood there used to be a big old stately home, Scratch Moss Hall. He vaguely remembered being told at school it had burned down in the 1940s, maybe even been bombed.

Joe turned away from the view at a sound from Shep. The dog was scratching at rotten wooden boards that had been placed against the entrance to the old pill-box. Shep started whining and Joe patted his thigh, calling him to heel. The five-sided concrete shape was up to his shoulders, and even as a kid he remembered having to stoop to get inside. Joe felt no desire to recreate the childhood memories. All he remembered about the pill-box was that it had a perpetually damp earthen floor and smelled of piss and stale beer, and probably bodily fluids he was too young to recognise. He put his head to one side and considered it, while Shep continued to scratch at the wooden boards. It was an ugly thing. He couldn't believe nobody had demolished it.

But then, Scratch Moss is full of ugly things.

He didn't know where the thought came from. His writer's brain, he supposed. Which reminded him. He was going to make notes about Red Clogs after his walk in the woods yesterday, and had forgotten. If he was ever going to write about Scratch Moss — which meant writing about his dad, and what had happened — then Red Clogs would have to be a part of it.

'Red Clogs,' he said out loud, words he hadn't spoken for forty years. Shep whined again, and a cloud passed over the sun, painting the Rabbit Rocks in dark shadow. A chill breeze whipped Joe's hair, and he zipped up his coat and told Shep to come on, then headed down the hill.

Joe took Shep home and quietly looked in on his mum, who was sleeping in her darkened room, still on her side of the double bed, though his dad hadn't slept in it for decades. He let himself out of the house and walked along the main road to the shops. At the butcher's he picked up some lamb chops, and some salad leaves, potatoes and tomatoes at the greengrocer's. He bought some cream at the corner shop, to make dauphinoise potatoes, and was leafing through the local paper when a voice behind him said, 'You won't find any Scratch Moss news in there.'

Joe turned around and looked at the woman standing in the aisle. It took a second for her dyed red hair, brown eyes and dimpled cheeks to pierce his memory and assemble themselves into someone he used to know.

'Ellen!' he said. 'Ellen Dowd!'

'Joe Collier,' said Ellen, smiling. She had a diamond stud in her nose. 'I heard you were back. Sorry about your dad.'

'You're looking well,' said Joe. He always said that when he saw someone he'd not seen for a while. It always seemed a nice thing to say, without any real meaning.

Ellen laughed. 'If by *well* you mean about four stone heavier and forty years older than the last time you saw me, then thanks.' She looked him up and down. 'You are actually looking well. London life must suit you.'

Joe was suddenly a teenager again, dry-mouthed and tongue-tied. Ellen smiled again and pushed past him towards the till. 'If you'd looked like that when we were kids, I'd never have let you leave Scratch Moss. Hope to see you around while you're back, Joe.'

Joe stared at her back as she unloaded her shopping basket at the till, his brain a swirling storm of memories. Ellen Dowd. Funny how you forgot all about people. And he'd had such a crush on her, that summer. He dithered as she paid with cash, wondering what to do. It had been a long time since he'd... since he'd what? Ask for her number, he thought. No, give her yours. Ellen turned around with her shopping and gave him an amused smile. 'Let's make this easy for you,' she said. 'Black Diamond at eight?'

When Joe got home his mum was up, watching TV. He unloaded the shopping and told her what was for tea, then put the kettle on. When he carried the pot and cups into the living room, she was kneeling on the sofa, looking out of the window. It was school home-time again. He felt a pang of misplaced guilt as he put the tray down. She would have loved grandkids, he expected. She never said anything, though. Never asked him if he and Jenna were going to have children, nor when he had a few steady relationships in his thirties. Joe felt bad about denying her that, but then… he did think about kids, sometimes, but it always ended with a son or daughter asking about their grandad and Joe having to say, well, you see, he's in jail because he viciously murdered a man.

His mum said something, and Joe coughed a half-laugh at what it sounded like. 'What was that, Mum?'

She turned away from the window. Her face was slack and heavy-eyed again. 'I said, little cunts.'

Joe stared at her. 'What?'

'Little cunts.' She gestured towards the window, at the stream of children with their parents. 'Little cunts little cunts LITTLE CUNTS.'

Then she was kneeling up, banging on the glass with her bony fists, shouting it over and over again until Joe rushed to grab her, pulling her away from the confused faces staring at the old woman furiously pounding the window and shrieking obscenities at the top of her voice. Joe grabbed her and she turned at him, and he drew back with a yelp. For a split second it seemed like her eyes, her entire eyes, were black. As black as midnight. Then it was gone and she looked at him tearfully, confused.

'Fucking hell, Mum,' said Joe, hugging her on the sofa until she stopped fighting and wriggling and started to sob into his shoulder.

'I don't know what's happening to me, Joe,' she said snottily.

He put her back in bed and while she dozed he searched local dementia services on his laptop, and then made tea. His mum got up while he was dishing it up, seemingly completely fine. It was as though she had totally forgotten about the episode, or it had never happened.

'That was delicious,' she said when they'd finished. 'What do you call those potatoes?'

'Dauphinoise,' said Joe.

His mum giggled. 'Ooh, posh.'

Joe washed up while his mum smoked at the door. He said hesitantly, 'I was going to pop out for a bit, but I can cancel if you're not feeling well...'

'What are you on about?' she said. 'I'm fine. You go out. Do you good. I've got my Netflix show to watch.'

'Erm, OK,' said Joe, perplexed. He was almost beginning to think he'd misheard her, imagined it all. But he knew he hadn't. And there was the magpie that morning, and Mum standing over his bed in the night...

He showered and put on a shirt and some jeans, and gave himself a liberal spray of aftershave. 'You've got my number, call me if you feel...'

His mum sighed and paused the TV. 'If I feel what?'

'I don't know.' Joe kissed her on top of her head. 'I won't be late. Just call me if you want anything.'

Then, stomach flipping like he was thirteen years old, Joe went out to meet Ellen Dowd.

5

The Black Diamond was pretty much how Joe remembered it from when he was a kid. A drinker's pub, brewery ales on tap, a carpet that still had the ghosts of spilled beer and long-smoked cigarettes clinging to it. There had been, of course, the addition of a wide-screen TV since the Eighties, and a chalk board showing the timings of upcoming football matches. The one-armed bandits were more hi-tech and flashy, as was the jukebox, now just a small unit on the wall, not the big heavy affair filled with vinyl seven-inch records. Joe had a sudden memory of him and his mates being allowed in the pub's upstairs function room on quiet weekdays, where they could drink raspberry cordial and play darts, while feeding the jukebox 10p pieces. One time his Nana Nora had lived in the pub, when she was young and her dad was the landlord. She'd stopped working there when she met Grandad Arthur, and got pregnant with Joe's dad, Terry.

It was quiet. The current landlord, a broad, bald man with a tattoo on the back of his neck that Joe couldn't quite make out, was jabbing at a remote control he was pointing at the wall-mounted TV, with evident simmering resentment. There were two lads in their twenties in joggers and hoodies sitting at the bar, talking in low voices, and off to the left, sitting in an alcove, was an ancient, weathered man in a battered tweed jacket that had seen better centuries, never mind days, who cast his lined face towards Joe when he walked in the door.

And there was Ellen, sitting by the frosted window on padded seating worn smooth by generations of Scratch Moss backsides. She was wearing a pair of pink joggers and a zip-up top, her hair falling in fresh curls over her shoulders. She watched him approach with an amused smile.

'Not quite Covent Garden, sorry.'

Joe laughed. 'And not Covent Garden prices, I hope. What can I get you?'

'Whatever's the palest, driest rosé Barry has in the fridge,' said Ellen. She tugged at the leg of her joggers. 'If it's pinker than this, I don't want it, because it'll taste like Domestos with honey.'

Joe gave a little salute. 'Understood.' He went to the bar, the two young lads giving him sidelong glances, and waited until the landlord, Barry, gave a satisfied sigh and managed to get the desired channel, two men and a woman standing around pitch-side ahead of an imminent kick-off. He ordered Ellen's wine as instructed and scanned the pumps, opting for a pale ale. He hoped Barry took cards because he didn't have any cash.

When Barry presented the drinks he looked at Joe from beneath his heavy, tombstone brow. 'You're Joe Collier? Terry Collier's son?'

Joe took a deep breath and nodded. Barry said, 'On the house. Sorry to hear about your dad.'

'Quite the local celebrity,' said Ellen, a smile playing on her lips as Joe set down the drinks and pulled up a stool to sit across the round table from her. She picked up the glass and took a sip, and didn't pull too much of a face. 'Cheers.'

Ellen looked at him with a critical eye, and Joe glanced away, feeling suddenly awkward, like a teenager again. She said, 'You do look good, you know. Healthy. Slim. Do you go to the gym?'

'Couple of times a week,' said Joe, scratching his head. 'You look great, too.'

Ellen laughed. 'You don't have to say that. I know I'm carrying a bit of timber.' She patted her belly. 'What can I say? I'm a slave to fish and chips and cream doughnuts. I gave up bothering years ago.'

This time it was Joe's turn to scrutinise her. 'No, I mean it. You look great.' He held her gaze and she raised one amused eyebrow as she took another drink. Joe laughed as well. 'I used to fancy you like mad.'

'I know,' said Ellen, and it was her turn to look awkwardly away. 'I liked you as well. But I was a bit of a cow back then. And not just me... do you remember Julie and Jan and all them?'

Joe did. The cool girls in school. The fit ones. Ellen had been part of their gang, but also somehow on the periphery of them. Ellen gazed into her glass. 'I wanted to be one of them so much. I'd do anything to impress them. Things I'm not proud of now.'

Joe was about to say something, but Ellen looked up, and smiled, and changed the subject. 'I've read your books, by the way.'

'Oh, God, have you? Really? Did you hate them?'

'No! I really enjoyed them. Except...'

'Except?' Joe sipped at his drink, waiting.

Ellen took a deep breath. 'You can't really write a proper ending, can you?'

Joe burst out laughing. 'What do you mean?'

'Well, that one with the guy who goes over to the Middle East with the landmine charity... I mean, what's supposed to happen to him at the end? He steps on the landmine on purpose and you just leave it.'

'Well, it's meant to be am—'

'Ambiguous, I know,' agreed Ellen. 'But for fuck's sake, did he blow himself up, or not?' She raised a hand. 'And I know it's meant for me to decide. But sometimes, when you've followed a character all the way through three hundred bloody pages, you deserve to know what happens at the end.'

Joe blinked, and finished his pint. 'Right.'

'And the other one,' said Ellen, warming to her subject. 'The serial killer. Or she might not be.'

'She's an un—'

'Unreliable narrator, yes,' said Ellen. As she deconstructed the ending to the book, Joe looked at her with renewed... interest? Respect? Surprise?

'You know your stuff,' said Joe slowly, when she'd finished.

Ellen said, 'I'm not thick, you know. I can see why you might think so. I used to read all the time at school. Just never let on. You didn't want to raise your head above the parapet, did you? Didn't want people to think you were different. God, they might have thought I was a bookworm like you, or even worse, Freddy. That wouldn't have done me any favours at all.' She paused, and waggled her empty glass at him. 'I did a degree, you know. Only Open University, but still. English Literature.'

Joe gaped at her, then stopped, then took the hint and went to the bar. 'Same again,' he said to Barry. 'And I'm paying this time.'

'On the house,' insisted Barry forcefully when he put the drinks down.

'God, you mentioned Freddy,' said Joe when he sat back down. 'Freddy Blackwood?'

Ellen nodded as she took a drink. 'If you thought he was an oddball at school, you should see him now. He's the local weirdo. I feel sorry for him sometimes. The local kids give him hell, especially round Halloween. He lives in the same house. They say his mum was dead in bed for a month before he reported it. I don't know if it's true. He lives like a tramp, though. And smells like one. Always muttering to himself. Big piles of papers and books in his front room, like a nest, with him in the middle. You can see it all through his window.'

The conversation flowed easily after that, Joe asking about everyone they'd been at school with, Ellen regaling him with tales of Scratch Moss's characters and life over the past forty years. Forty years which seemed to drop away from him with every sip of his beer. Joe couldn't remember when he'd laughed so much, or so easily. He asked Ellen about her work; she did four shifts a week at The Grange, an old people's home that had been built at the back end of the estates since he'd left. 'Wiping arses and listening to stories of the past from people who can't remember what they had for breakfast,' she said.

Then Ellen interrogated him about his life, the five years he'd spent in Leeds before heading to Oxford, and then to London to embark on his writing career. She probed him about his love life, leading up to – and concluding, so far with – Jenna.

'Is it weird to come home?' she said.

Joe thought about it. 'It is. But thinking of Scratch Moss as home is weird, too. I only spent thirteen years here. Then I went to live with Auntie Linda. To be honest, by the time I got to Oxford I'd generally tell people I was from Leeds.'

'At least they'd have heard of that. Not like Scratch Moss. And if they had heard of us it wouldn't be for any good reason.'

Joe decided to turn the tables on the interrogation. 'So. You're married?'

Ellen laughed. 'No. And not with anyone. I was for a while. Pete Brown. Remember him? Used to be the captain of the rugby team.'

'What happened?'

Ellen shrugged. 'I decided I was happier on my own than with someone who thought a good time was drinking cheap lager all day, spending half of the money I brought home in the betting shop, and slapping me around when he didn't like what was laid out for his tea.'

'Christ,' said Joe. 'Where did he go?'

Ellen smiled tightly. 'First to the infirmary for twenty-eight stitches after I smacked him round the head with a coal shovel one night when I'd had enough. Then to live with his cousin in Manchester. Then Strangeways for a bit. After that, I don't know, and I really don't care.'

'Right,' said Joe. 'The coal shovel.'

'We didn't even have a coal fire,' said Ellen, bursting into laughter. 'It was the first thing to hand in the yard that day. If he'd tidied stuff up once in a while he might have got off more lightly.'

'I saw your daughter yesterday,' said Joe. 'Hannah? She's Pete's?'

Ellen shook her head. 'Hannah's thirty-three now. Korben, her little lad, is seven. You do the maths. When I was nineteen I went to Magaluf on my first-ever holiday. Brought home two hundred Marlboro and a bottle of Tia Maria from the duty free, and a baby I didn't find out I was growing until three months later. Got knocked up by some bloke from Birmingham on the first night. Can't remember his name and not sure I even knew it.' Ellen raised her glass. '*Y Viva España*, eh? Here, I've got a photo of our Hannah and Korben.'

Ellen held the phone in front of her face and jiggled it, then swore. 'That bloody face recognition thing never works. I must look like a bag of spanners since I got this phone.'

'You don't,' said Joe quietly.

Ellen jabbed at the screen with her finger and muttered, 'One... nine... seven... two...'

Joe laughed. 'You not only use the year of your birth as your passcode but say it out loud when you put it in.'

Ellen laughed too. 'Ooh, yes, and all those secrets on this phone. I'd hate anyone to see the sexts from Tom Hardy.'

Joe looked at the photo of Hannah and her son and made what he hoped were appreciative noises. He sloshed the dregs of his beer around the bottom of his glass, feeling strangely cheered that Ellen wasn't married, or with anyone. He said thoughtfully, 'You asked me if it was weird coming back to Scratch Moss. It is. But I can't put my finger on why.' He looked at Ellen. 'Sometimes I feel like everyone's watching me. As though they're... expectant. Waiting for something. And watching in secret. From behind curtains.' He sighed. 'That sounds nuts, I know.'

Ellen didn't say anything. Joe asked, 'Do you see my mum much?'

Ellen shrugged. 'I see Mary around. Chat to her sometimes. She's always looking out at the kids if I have to pick Korben up from school. Why? Are you worried about her? I mean, it's been a long time...'

A long time since you abandoned Scratch Moss, Joe couldn't help hearing. But his Mum had said everyone had been fine with her, hadn't they? Besides, it wasn't that.

'I'm not sure. She seems... strange. Only sometimes.' He dropped his voice to a whisper. 'She killed a magpie in the yard this morning.'

Ellen seemed to visibly pale. 'Fuck.'

'I know, right?' Joe frowned. Ellen's reaction seemed stronger than he was expecting, somehow. 'I mean, what is it with magpies? I can vaguely remember *something*, but...' He shook his head. 'There's so much I can't remember, or don't want to. After that night, I sort of blanked everything out. I can't really recall even the days and weeks before it happened. My therapist says it's a form of PTSD. When I went to Leeds, my mind just kind of shut it all out, and reset my life.' He glanced over at Barry. 'And everyone seems to be treating my dad as though he's some kind of hero.'

Ellen opened her mouth to say something but then a dry, raspy voice sounded from behind Joe. He turned around to see the old man in the corner staring at him. Joe said, 'What?'

'I said, Terry Collier *was* a hero,' said the old man.

'Leave it, Jack,' said Ellen. 'We're just having a quiet chat and catch-up.'

Joe gaped at her, and then at the old man. Jack? He remembered a Jack who used to prop up the bar in the Black Diamond from when he was a kid. He'd seemed old then; he must be... Christ, he must be a hundred now. Joe was going to just smile and turn away, then thought better of it.

'My dad murdered a man,' he said. He felt the weight of Barry's stare on him from the bar, and furtive glances from the two lads. 'Not really what most people would call a hero.'

Barry called from the bar, 'Johnny Crowe was a nonce. A predator. He deserved everything he got. Your dad did us all a favour. God knows what might have happened if he hadn't.'

Joe was about to say something when Jack piped up again. 'Terry Collier wasn't a hero because he kicked Johnny Crowe to death,' he said, standing up and putting his empty pint glass down on the table. 'Not just that, anyway. He was a hero because he went to jail for it, and didn't come out even when they'd have let him.'

Joe watched Jack walk creakily to the door. He said, 'What do you mean?'

Jack looked at him. 'You young ones don't remember what it was like before. You were only kids when it happened. Now Terry Collier's dead. And it's all going to start all over again.' He opened the door, then paused one last time. 'People say that they ripped the heart out of Scratch Moss when they closed the pit down. But they forget that this place had already lost its soul a long, long time ago.'

6

They sat in silence for a while after Jack had left the pub. Joe looked at his watch. 'Have you got work tomorrow morning?'

Ellen shook her head. 'I'm on the night shift, start at eight.' She gave him a crooked smile. 'Why, going to take me clubbing? Chaplin's?'

Joe grinned. 'Oh, God, is that still open? Remember when they used to have the under-eighteens night on Wednesdays? We all used to get the bus into town. I remember getting the courage up to talk to a girl once, and as soon as I said I was from Scratch Moss she scarpered.' Joe felt suddenly deflated. 'What is it about this bloody place?'

'It's always been odd,' said Ellen. 'You've forgotten because you went away. The rest of us stayed. Scratch Moss is a place on its own. It's got its own ways. Traditions.'

'Like the magpies,' agreed Joe.

Ellen seemed to hesitate, then unzipped her hooded top, sliding it off her left shoulder. There, on her exposed fleshy upper arm, was a tattoo. It was a magpie, wings outstretched, with a banner winding around it that bore the name *Danny*.

Joe admired the ink for a moment, then said, 'Danny?'

'After Hannah was born I got pregnant again, two years later. He was stillborn. I called him Brian, after my dad.' She gazed curiously at Joe for a long moment. 'Don't you remember, Joe? The graves in the cemetery?'

Something was popping in his memory. Yes. The graves. But he couldn't quite...

'Show me,' he said.

'What, now? You want to go to the cemetery? It's dark!'

'I'm sure there are no ghosts or ghouls,' said Joe, drinking up. 'Come on, it's only ten minutes' walk.'

Ellen shook her head wonderingly. 'Is this what writers do, then? Go off on mad jaunts to the graveyard after dark? OK, let's do it.'

—

The night was clear and holding on to the last gasp of a chill, with the promise of warmer weather tangy in the air. They walked along the main road, their arms brushing, and Joe had that strange, exciting, sickening feeling he used to have when he was a teenager and in close proximity to a girl. He'd noticed his accent had begun to slip back into that of the Scratch Moss of his youth, that had moulded him. As they approached his mum's house on the other side of the road, Ellen said, 'Do you want to call in and check up on her?'

Through the closed curtains Joe could see the glow of the TV in the living room. 'I'm sure she's fine,' he said. 'She won't thank me for interrupting whatever she's watching on Netflix. She hasn't got the hang of the pause button yet. Last night she kept sending it skipping backwards and forwards every time she needed to go for a wee.'

They walked on, as the road bent towards the overhanging trees of the Little Woods. Joe said, 'So how come, if you did an Open University degree...'

'Why am I wiping arses at The Grange?' Ellen shrugged beside him. 'I never meant to use it to get a career or anything. I just wanted to prove to myself I could do it. After hiding my light under a bushel at school all those years. Besides, I like working with the old people. Most of them can actually wipe their own arses, as it happens.'

The green darkness swallowed them, no streetlights on the stretch of road covered by the trees. As they passed the path where Joe had walked Shep, he suddenly remembered the chill he'd felt, the memory of youth that had surfaced. 'Do you remember Red Clogs?'

Did Ellen sharply breathe in, or was he imagining it? 'It was a thing when we were kids,' he went on. 'Maybe not for girls. I don't know. Kind of a bogeyman.'

'It was a thing for girls, too,' said Ellen quietly. She leaned in more to him, and Joe peered ahead to where the road would emerge from the trees, and pass by the old church and the sprawling graveyard behind it.

'I wonder if kids today have Red Clogs,' said Joe conversationally. 'What about your grandson? Korben? Do he and his mates talk about Red Clogs?'

'No,' Ellen said tightly. Then she shivered, and linked her arm in his. 'Stupid old story, nobody's talked about it since we were small. Best to leave stuff like that in the past.'

Ahead of them, Joe could make out the shape of the old church against the dark sky, blotting out the stars. There hadn't been a church in Scratch Moss for as long as he could remember, not a proper one. But the building wasn't derelict. It had never fallen into disrepair, or been the target of vandals. Sometimes it was used for meetings, he remembered, or community gatherings. When the miners had gone on strike they all gathered in the yard for a rally. In fact, he noticed, as they drew closer…

'There's a light on in the old church.' He looked at Ellen. 'Was there ever a new church built in Scratch Moss?'

She laughed. 'No. And this one was closed down… what, a hundred years ago? More. Hundred and twenty, probably.'

'I wonder why?' mused Joe as they passed the old building, soot-blackened stone and tall spire. He'd never wondered about it when he was a teenager. It was just the old church, the only one in Scratch Moss, and not a church at all any more. Not a Christian church.

'I'm sure there's plenty of old folks at The Grange could tell you,' Ellen said, then glanced at him, tapping her finger on her lips. 'Actually, they might like to come and hear you talk. About your books. Local boy made good and all that.'

Joe stared at his feet as they walked on. Not that there was much to tell, these days. He was out of contract, no book deals on the horizon, and nothing published for three years. And nothing likely to be, if he didn't start writing soon. He was about to say something noncommittal about visiting the old folks' home when Ellen said, 'We're here.'

They stood outside the tall, rusted gates, once painted green, that opened onto the cemetery from the main road. A six-foot stone wall ran the length of the cemetery along the road, the double gates opening on to a tarmac path that led into a labyrinth of tracks weaving in and out of the ranked plots of graves, the older ones right at the far end of the cemetery, bordering the land that used to be Scratch Moss pit. The yawning black chasm of the cemetery entrance gave Joe butterflies in his stomach, remembering childhood capers and scampers through the graveyard in the dead of night, fear and excitement and laughter roiling around inside him.

'Come on.' Ellen took Joe's hand – her touch was like an electric shock – and led him through the gates. 'This shouldn't take long. You'll remember.'

And he did, as soon as they were inside. The nearest graves to the track were recent – as recent as this year. So people were still being buried here, despite there being no church. Joe squatted down by the headstone, still bright and pale, not yet weathered like the ones further back. There were fresh flowers laid against it, the grave of a woman who had died just a couple of months back. Her name was engraved on the stone, and the dates of her birth and death. And something else. At the top of the marker, embedded in a circle, embossed on the stone. Joe traced the intricate carving with his fingers.

'A magpie,' he said, looking up at Ellen. Joe moved to the next headstone along, and the next. They all had magpie engravings of some kind. Of course. He remembered now. It was just that as a child he'd never questioned it. Perhaps when he left Scratch Moss to go and live in Leeds he might have wondered, whenever he went into a cemetery, why there were no magpies on the headstones. But as the memory of his life in Scratch Moss had receded, so did questions like that.

'Before you ask, I don't know.' Ellen shrugged. 'It's just always been that way. Magpies and death. They're tied together in Scratch Moss. Always have been. Must be some old legend lost to time.'

Not so lost to time that you didn't get one tattooed on your arm when your child died, thought Joe, but didn't say it out loud.

'Well, if that's your mystery solved, you can walk me home,' said Ellen. 'I have an appointment with my dressing gown, a cup of hot chocolate and two episodes of my show.'

'It's one mystery solved,' agreed Joe, standing up and looking back towards the main road. 'But what's *that* all about?'

He pointed as Ellen turned to the two people walking past the cemetery gates carrying what looked like some kind of dummy or mannequin. It was small, the size of a child. Ellen frowned. 'I don't know. I remember it, from when we were kids. I can't remember what it was for, though.' She shook her head, as though trying to clear fog from her brain. 'Probably the menopause. Can't remember what I walked into a room for, half the time.'

Then, a little way behind them, Joe saw a man carrying something similar, hefted up on his shoulder like a sack of coal. He set off for the gates just as the man had gone past, and looked back along the road. Coming from the other direction was what looked like a family group, between them holding two more dummies. Ellen joined him as the people all turned into the yard of the old church. He said, 'Come on.'

When they got to the gates, the couple were leaving, followed by the man. Joe hesitated; should he ask what was going on? Then the family came out and Joe vaguely recognised the father, a grey-haired man a few years younger than him. His eyes met Joe's and he shook his head. Joe didn't know what that meant, but it stayed the words on his lips, about to ask what was happening.

The big wooden doors to the old church were open, the lights burning brightly inside. Joe peered in. Any church trappings had long since gone, save for a wide, blank altar at the far end. There were no pews, no cross on the wall, no carvings or statues to say this had ever been a place of Christian worship. If there had been stained-glass windows at one point, they had been replaced by plain panes a long time ago.

Then he saw them, propped up against the stone altar. They were mannequins, of a sort. Made from straw, bound together at the ends to form torsos and limbs and a head, dressed in children's clothes, hats shadowing their featureless faces. The four that the people had brought in joined half a dozen more, creating a grotesque, silent tableau of straw children.

He looked at Ellen and raised an eyebrow. She shook her head wordlessly. Joe beckoned her with a nod of his head and walked into the old church and towards the altar, to inspect the straw figures lined up against it. There were no cards, or flowers, or anything other than the mannequins. There was nobody else in the old church who might have been able to explain.

And then there was. Joe jumped as a dry, rasping voice cut through the silence. He turned to see a tall, thin figure in a long, shabby coat standing in the doorway, his jeans baggy and shapeless, his boots dirty. His eyes were sunken pinpricks under a mop of uncombed hair. Joe recognised him a second before Ellen said his name.

'Freddy Blackwood. What did you say?'

'I said, the straw children are back.' Freddy walked forward and stared at Joe. 'I know you, or used to. Joe. Joe Collier. You went away.'

'I did,' said Joe. 'Freddy. Good to see you.'

Freddy glanced at him. 'Is it? Nobody ever says that.' Joe caught a whiff of tangy body odour, unwashed clothes. 'You went away. You should have stayed away.'

'Don't be rude, Freddy,' admonished Ellen.

Freddy shrugged and joined them at the altar. Joe could see Ellen wrinkling her nose and not even trying to hide it. He said to Freddy, 'You know what this is about? The straw children? Why have people left them here?'

Freddy stared at the effigies. 'Yes, I know. I know everything about Scratch Moss.' He looked sharply at Joe. 'You write books. Are you writing a book about here? About us?'

'No,' said Joe. 'I've come back to bury my father. I don't know if you heard—'

'I heard,' said Freddy, bending to straighten the hat on one of the scarecrow children. 'I know everything about Scratch Moss. I told you.'

'So what does all this mean, Mr I-Know-Everything?' said Ellen.

Freddy looked Ellen up and down. 'Ellen Dowd. You should be bringing one of these here. You've got a little grandson, haven't you?'

Ellen scowled at him. 'What's that meant to mean?'

Freddy squatted, the hem of his coat pooling around him like the wings of a big, black bird. With bony fingers and dirty fingernails he stroked the blank face of one of the effigies. 'They bring these to fool the devil. So he won't take their children. Because he's back. Everybody knows it. We can all sense it. He went away for forty years and now he's back. And everybody in Scratch Moss is terrified.'

'Who's back?' said Joe, grabbing Freddy's shoulder. 'Been away for forty years? Are you talking about my dad?'

Freddy laughed, showing rotten, broken teeth. 'I'm talking about the devil of the pit, the god of dirty coal and hellfire. The spirit of the broken, blasted land.' He stopped laughing, and looked seriously at Joe, then Ellen, then Joe again. 'I'm talking about Red Clogs. He's back.'

7

Joe awoke to yet more commotion from downstairs. He winced as he lifted his head, his neck stiff from having slept awkwardly in the single bed, and listened to the barking and shouting from below. He hoped his mum wasn't killing another bloody magpie.

After they'd been to the old church, Freddy having refused to be drawn with any more questions, Joe had walked Ellen back to her house behind the parade of shops, thanking her for an evening that was interesting to say the least. She'd given him a chaste peck on the cheek, and he'd wandered home to find his mum snoring on the sofa in front of the TV. She'd seemed fine when she eventually awoke and trundled off to bed. So what was going on now?

His back twinged as he raced down the stairs, reminding him that he wasn't as young as he sometimes felt. In the kitchen he found his mum backed up against the sink, with Shep in the doorway to the dining room, hackles raised, tail wagging furiously, alternately barking and growling. At his mum.

'What the bloody hell?' said Joe, making a grab for Shep's collar. The dog turned and snapped at him, and Joe swore. If he'd been a second slower those slavering teeth would have got him.

'He's gone berserk!' shrieked his mum. Shep turned back to her, growling low and mean. 'He was in the yard and I called him in for his breakfast and he just went mad.'

'Come on, boy,' said Joe in soothing tones. 'Calm down. Come and have your breakfast.'

The old dog turned again, seemingly beginning to recognise Joe, and made a plaintive mewling sound. Joe risked putting out a hand and the dog bent his head forward, allowing Joe to first ruffle his fur, and then grab hold of his collar.

'Put him in the yard, Joe,' said his mum. Joe reached with his other hand to open the back door, as his mum hesitantly stepped forward, and then Shep, with a speed and strength belying his age, tore himself out of Joe's grip and leapt straight for his mum.

The ear-splitting scream as Shep clamped his teeth around Joe's mum's thin, bony arm was something Joe would not forget for a long, long time.

-

They were in the hospital until lunchtime, when a doctor declared the injury to Joe's mum's arm looked worse than it was, and bandaged her up with a tetanus shot. In the taxi on the way back to Scratch Moss Joe Googled the name of the nearest vet and asked them to come round as a matter of urgency. By the time they got home there was a young woman in medical-style scrubs with *Scratch Moss Veterinary Services* embroidered on the breast waiting on the doorstep.

'What's old Shep been up to, Mrs Collier?' said the woman, Lois, as they let her in and Joe put the kettle on. Joe recounted the morning's events as his mum seemed suddenly sullen and uncommunicative, which he put down to the painkillers and shots she'd had at hospital.

'Hmm, that doesn't sound good,' said Lois with a worried frown. 'Let me go and take a look at him.'

When Shep had gone for his mum, Joe had grabbed the nearest thing to hand, which was the pedal bin, and hurled it at the dog. Shep had let go with a whimper and ran straight out into the yard, Joe slamming the door on him. He watched through the window as Lois cautiously approached Shep, who seemed fine; more than fine, in fact. He rolled over onto his back and let the vet tickle his tummy.

Eventually Lois came back in and sat down in the living room with Joe and his mum. She said, 'Well, physically, there's nothing wrong with him that I can see. He's in good condition for a dog of his age.'

'But?' said Joe.

Lois bit her lip and shook her head. 'I don't know. Exhibiting such violent and unpredictable behaviour... obviously there's something mentally unsound here. I mean, he's never done this before, has he, Mrs Collier?'

Joe's Mum shook her head. Joe said, 'Could it just be a one-off? Could he be ill with something?'

Lois pulled a face. 'He's not ill, at least, not with anything obvious. The thing is...' She hesitated. 'I can't guarantee he won't do this again. And strictly speaking, vets are duty-bound to report dog attacks to the police and the local authority dog wardens.'

Joe rubbed his face. 'Shit. They'll take him off her?'

Lois put a hand on Joe's mum's knee. 'They might. They probably will. I'm sorry. It was horrible for you both this time, but Mrs Collier seems to have got off quite lightly. Next time she might not be so lucky.'

'Take it,' said Joe's mum abruptly.

Joe stared at her. 'What?'

'Take the dog. Put it down.'

Lois looked at Joe. He said, 'It's Shep, Mum. You've had him a long time...' He looked at Lois. 'I mean, maybe we should get him checked out more thoroughly? In case there's something not obvious affecting his behaviour?'

'We could,' said Lois. She turned to Joe's mum. 'Are you frightened of him now, Mrs Collier? Are you worried he'll do it again?'

Joe's mum turned and stared out of the window. 'Put it down,' she said with finality.

When Lois had gone, taking Shep with her, Joe's mum announced she was going for a lie down. Joe made himself a cup of tea and went round the house, gathering up Shep's toys and bed and putting all the tins of dog food from the cupboard in a bin bag. He felt unaccountably sad, even though he'd only seen Shep a handful of times. His mum had had the dog for nearly twelve years. It wasn't the confused look on Shep's face as Lois led him away that troubled Joe, it was the seeming coldheartedness of his mum. He wondered if it was the drugs she was on from the hospital, and if when she came round the enormity of what had happened would hit her hard.

Joe sat on the sofa, flicking through the TV, feeling unsettled and fidgety. He had to keep reminding himself that the funeral was in a few days, so it was natural his mum wouldn't be feeling herself. He wished he could feel sadder that his dad had died – that would be a normal reaction, wouldn't it? But he'd not exactly had a normal relationship with his father since he was thirteen years old. After he'd gone to live with Auntie Linda in Leeds, still shocked and traumatised by the events of that summer, he'd never seen his dad again. His mum's visits became fewer and farther between, until by the time he went off to Oxford when he was eighteen he'd begun to think of Auntie Linda as his mother. It was only later, in his twenties, that he rekindled the relationship with her. And even then, when he had begun to process what had happened ten years earlier, his dad refused to let Joe come and see him in prison.

He'd said that it was for the best.

Joe turned his attention instead to what had happened at the old church last night, those weird straw effigies, and the appearance of Freddy Blackwood and his cryptic comments. After Freddy had gone, refusing to say any more, Ellen had reiterated her earlier claims that Freddy was the town weirdo, that nothing he said was to be trusted or even listened to. But his words kept nagging at Joe.

I'm talking about the devil of the pit, the god of dirty coal and hellfire. The spirit of the broken, blasted land. I'm talking about Red Clogs. He's back.

'Just the local nutter,' Joe said to himself. But there he was again. Red Clogs. The Scratch Moss bogeyman. For a story that had been one of many campfire tales when Joe was young – Jenny Greenteeth haunted the tepid waters of the ponds by the pits, White Eyes lurked in the Little Woods – Red Clogs seemed to have a lot more traction than the usual childhood urban myths. He'd raised his head more than once since Joe had arrived home. Joe racked his brains to remember what they said about Red Clogs. He was a ghost, or a demon, a spirit that haunted the pit, or was something to do with it, at least. And the more he thought about Red Clogs, the more he thought about his dad, about Terry Collier, and some of the walls Joe had built around the first thirteen years of his life, the years spent in Scratch Moss, began to shake and crumble. Especially that final year, that last summer, when his dad was taken away and never seen again.

There was suddenly activity outside the house, and Joe realised it was school home-time. He wished his mum were up and out of bed, waving at the children. From the corner of his eye he saw movement, and turned to see Ellen waving at him, a small, blond-haired boy holding her hand.

Joe waved back and pointed to the door, and rushed out to the front to see Ellen. She smiled at him and told him she was doing the school run for Hannah, and asked how his mum was. He recounted in hushed tones, mindful of seven-year-old Korben holding his grandmother's hand, about what had happened with Shep.

'Oh my God, how terrible,' said Ellen. 'Your poor mum. How is she now? Oh, there she is.'

Joe turned to see his mum, in her dressing gown, standing in front of the sofa, staring at them out of the window. He waved at her but she didn't wave back, just continued to stare at him.

'I'm a bit worried about her,' he confided. 'She's not herself.'

'I'm not surprised,' said Ellen. 'What with your dad dying and now this with Shep.' She glanced towards the window. 'What's she doing?'

Joe saw his mum bending down by the side of the fireplace, seemingly plugging something into the wall socket. 'I've no idea,' he sighed. 'I should go and see what she wants.'

'Nana, I need a wee,' said Korben, tugging on Ellen's hand.

'In a minute, Nana's talking,' said Ellen. 'Korben, this is Nana's friend, Joe. He used to live in Scratch Moss a long time ago. Nana was at school with him.'

'Is he your boyfriend?' said Korben, giggling.

Ellen ruffled his hair with mock annoyance. 'Hey, you. What's so funny? Can't Nanas have boyfriends?'

'You're too old,' said Korben.

'And there you have it.' Ellen laughed, turning back to Joe. 'Out of the mouths of babes. Officially over the hill.' Then her face fell. 'Joe...'

Joe turned back to the window, and his breath caught in his throat. His mum was holding the drill, the one that had been lying around the kitchen, with the long, thick masonry bit still in it.

'Oh, Christ,' muttered Joe. 'I'd better go before she wrecks the house.'

Before he could move, his mum, her gaze locked on his, lifted the drill in front of her face. Joe suddenly saw that she was crying, big tears rolling down her thin, wrinkled cheeks. Then she put the end of the masonry bit into her right nostril.

Joe felt frozen to the spot. There was a roaring in his ears. He could hear Ellen saying something, screaming something, but it was like he was underwater and couldn't make it out. He started for the front door but felt like he was wading through treacle. He glanced back at the window just as his mum rammed the drill bit deep and then squeezed the trigger switch. Joe let out a formless cry.

From the corner of his eye he saw Ellen cover Korben's face with her hands as blood, bone and brains splattered over the inside of the window.

8

Joe had been at school with the policeman who came to see him. He remembered Joe, and said kind words about his mother, and made them both a cup of tea. The living room was still sealed off after a visit from two white-suited forensics officers, so they had the tea in the dining room. Joe felt detached and curious; Mike Speed had been an utter twat at school, a bully and a thief who everyone was in agreement would come to a bad end. Now he was the local copper. Poacher turned gamekeeper, Joe thought to himself. And had he not remembered Mike Speed's twattish behaviour, he might think he was a really nice guy. *It was forty years ago*, he told himself. *People change*.

'In a way, you're lucky,' said Mike, taking a sip of his tea.

Joe stared at him across the table. 'Lucky?'

'I didn't mean it like that. I meant... you've come back to Scratch Moss after forty years...'

'Because my dad died.'

'Because your dad died,' agreed Mike. 'And while you're here your mum dies as well. Leaving you the sole beneficiary.'

Joe gaped at him. 'You mean I'd be a *suspect*?'

'If we didn't have all those witnesses, I suppose so.' Mike shrugged. 'Nothing personal, obviously.'

'Obviously.' Joe cupped his cup in his hands, trying to draw warmth from it. 'But as it happens, she quite spectacularly and gruesomely killed herself in front of half of Scratch Moss's children.'

Mike made a note in his little book. 'Good turn of phrase, that. Spectacularly and gruesomely. You always had your nose in a book, didn't you? I understand you write them now. You'll be going back to London, then? To your book-writing life. After the funeral and everything.'

'I suppose so,' said Joe. 'I mean, yes. Of course. After everything's sorted.'

'There'll have to be an inquest, obviously. But it all seems fairly cut and dried. The coroner will open proceedings tomorrow so you can get a death certificate. You won't have to attend the hearing. You might have to for the full inquest, though. I imagine it'll be a straight verdict that she took her own life.'

Joe said, 'Is that everything?'

'I think so. Your mother's body will be taken to Harty's Funeral Parlour after the coroner has finished with it.' He closed his notebook, but didn't make any move to leave. 'Joe... how was your mother before it happened?'

Joe thought about it. The thing was, he saw his mum so infrequently he didn't know whether the strange episodes she'd been having since he got back home were out of the ordinary, or if it was something that had been going on for a while. Eventually he settled on, 'A bit odd. I can't explain it any better than that.'

Mike leaned forward. 'And how are you feeling?'

Joe frowned. 'Well, my dad's died and my mum's just committed suicide in front of me, so I'm not exactly turning cartwheels.'

Mike put his notebook into his breast pocket. 'If you start to feel *odd*, if you have strange thoughts or... or violent feelings, will you let me know?'

'Violent feelings?' said Joe, frowning. 'Then I am suspected of something?'

'Not to do with your mother's death,' said Mike. 'Not to do with anything. It's just that... it's strange times, Joe. Things have been settled in Scratch Moss for a good many years. As long as I've been on the force. But some of the older people... well, they're talking.'

'Talking about what?'

'Talking about how things used to be. For a long time. Before your dad got banged up.'

Joe was at a loss to understand. 'You're saying my dad getting jailed for murder changed things around here?'

'For the better,' said Mike. 'And I don't mean because he was a danger to anyone, nothing like that. But your dad... he did a brave thing. For the community.'

Joe shook his head. 'You're a copper. You're not meant to be feting someone who committed murder.'

'Good word, that. Feting.' Mike took his notebook out and jotted it down, then put it back in his pocket. 'I don't mean him killing Johnny Crowe, Joe. I mean what he did afterwards.' Mike drained his tea and stood up. 'Anyway. Just think on what I said. If you start to feel in any way...'

'Odd,' said Joe.

'Odd,' agreed Mike. 'If you do, get in touch.' He dug into his pocket and pushed a card over the table. 'My mobile's on that. The forensics lot will come and get their stuff tomorrow. Then you can get on with organising a funeral.' He paused at the door. 'Another funeral. My condolences, Joe.'

Just before Mike went, Joe said, 'When I arrived here... there was a man. Hanged himself from a tree up the road.'

Mike frowned. 'You think it's relevant?'

Joe shook his head. 'No, I just wondered... who he was.'

'Not from round here,' said Mike. 'Manchester, I think.' He looked at Joe. 'Strangers don't come to Scratch Moss often, but if they do, it's rarely for any good reason.'

—

The next morning, Joe was visited by a chirpy, red-headed woman from Harty's undertakers. The company was based in

Scratch Moss, set back on the main road opposite the cemetery, and she announced herself as Cheryl and said that she had already organised his dad's forthcoming funeral.

'Do I get a two-for-one offer?' said Joe weakly, hating himself for it the moment the words left his mouth.

Cheryl seemed to find it uproariously funny. 'I always think laughter is the best way to cope,' she confided. She pulled out a clipboard from her briefcase and said, 'Now, you might not want this, but we could actually organise the funeral for the same day as your dad's. Do the double, as it were.'

'Really?' said Joe. 'But it's next Thursday.'

'I mean, you could have two funerals, if you wanted…'

'What about the… the church, and everything?'

Cheryl frowned. 'You wanted a Christian service for your mum? Did she specify that to you?'

'I…' Joe faltered. 'No, not really. I just assumed…'

'I mean, we could check availability at St Michael's at Hindleshaw, or Our Lady's at Platt Fields. It's not usual, though. Not for Scratch Moss.'

Joe peered at her. 'What is usual for Scratch Moss?' He realised he didn't even know what had been organised for his dad.

'Burial in the graveyard,' said Cheryl. 'A short ritual in the old church.'

'*Ritual?* You make it sound like…' Joe didn't know what it sounded like. Something off a film, maybe. 'And who leads this *ritual*?'

'The community, generally,' said Cheryl brightly. 'And then a wake at the Working Men's Club. That's usual.' She waited, her pen poised over her clipboard. 'So…?'

Joe shrugged. 'Fine. Whatever you think best. And you can do the burial and the… the ritual on the same day as my dad's?'

'I think it would be nice,' said Cheryl, smiling. 'We can get the headstone done this weekend. With both their names on it.'

'And... there'll be a magpie on it?' said Joe.

Cheryl gave him a querulous smile. 'Duh, of course.'

'Why is that?' said Joe. 'What is it about the magpies?'

Cheryl laughed, as though he was stupid for not knowing. She put her clipboard back into the briefcase. 'For safe passage of their souls, of course. Magpies are psychopomps, you see.'

'Psycho... what?'

'Psychopomps. They escort the spirits of the dead to their just rewards. And keep them out of the clutches of... well.' She gave a little tinkling laugh. 'You know who.'

'Do you mean... Red Clogs?'

Cheryl put on a mock stern face and gave him a playful slap on his knee. 'Now, now, Joe Collier. I know you've been away for a long time, but you know better to say that name at a time like this.'

'But it's just a silly old story,' said Joe, feeling suddenly frustrated and annoyed.

'Of course it is,' said Cheryl. 'Thanks for the tea. I'll be in touch when we've made all the necessary arrangements.'

And then Joe was alone, sitting on the sofa, staring at the cup of cold tea in his hands.

'What the actual fuck?' he eventually said, the words slicing into the thick stillness of the room. The very act of saying them seemed to anchor him to the floor beneath his feet, bring him back from wherever his mind was starting to unspool to.

He had watched his mum kill herself. In the most gruesome, grotesque, terrible way he could imagine. It was only just beginning to sink in. The image of her, just before she pushed the whirring drill bit deep into her brain, appeared in terrible clarity. He closed his eyes, but she was still there, the tears running down her face, just before she... she...

Joe opened his eyes, the room spinning. Momentarily, the window and walls were splatted with blood and gore, even though he knew they had been cleaned and scrubbed, the scent of bleach still lingering. Then it was gone. Joe felt like he was choking, that the air was too thick, and ran for the kitchen. He didn't make it. He vomited with such force that he fell to his knees, hands planted on the carpet, and continued to throw up until he felt utterly empty.

—

Joe awoke in darkness and a shrieking noise pummelling into his head. He was on the sofa, a blanket pulled over him. He fumbled for his phone on the floor but couldn't find it, and instead reached over to click on the lamp by the couch. Nothing happened. There were no pinprick lights on the satellite box, the TV's red standby glow was extinguished. The noise kept pulsing, and he dragged himself off the sofa and went to the open curtains. The houses across the road were in darkness. The streetlights were dead. The sound... it was a house alarm, somewhere, he realised. There had been a power cut.

Joe dropped to his knees and felt around on the carpet until he found his phone, half-under the sofa. It was a little after four in the morning. His mouth was bone dry and his head was throbbing, in rhythm with the distant house alarm. Flicking on the flashlight, he picked his way to the kitchen, across the wide damp patch where he'd cleaned up his vomit, and ran a glass of water from the tap. As he was drinking thirstily he paused. What was that? Joe waited, silent, his head on one side, listening. There it was again. A thump. From upstairs. As though someone had dropped something, or there was a slow, heavy footfall directly above him.

Joe swallowed and wondered what to do. A burglar? Or just an old house creaking? He was about to write it off as half-asleep imagination when it sounded again, this time a little further away, over the dining room.

Whoever it was, they were moving through the house. Joe tugged open the cutlery drawer and his fingers closed around the handle of a carving knife. His phone torch lighting the way, he crept through the dining room to the door that led to the hall and the stairs. He gripped the handle and opened it painfully slowly and quietly, wincing as the hinges creaked. The air in the hallway was cool, and he listened, his palm sweating where he tightly held the knife. Maybe he should just call the police. The house alarm whined on, streets away. Maybe he should just get out.

Joe took a deep breath, then put one foot on the bottom step, and crept up, each creaking step sounding thunderous. He reached the top and shone the flashlight around, listening. At the far end was his mum's room. Her door was ajar. He'd been up earlier, to find some papers for Cheryl from the undertakers. Birth certificate, some funeral insurance plan documents. He was sure he'd closed the door behind him. Cautiously, he padded along the carpet towards the door. A fresh breeze seemed to emanate from the room, colder than the rest of the house.

He's back.

That's what his mum had said, that first night, standing over his bed in the darkness.

He's back.

Who's back? Dad? thought Joe, almost laughing with fear and the craziness of it all. He paused at the door, listening. He suddenly whirled around, sure he was being observed, that there was a presence at his back, but there was just the darkness of the hall, his phone light casting shadows. Joe took a deep breath, and pushed open the door swiftly. His hand snaked in and clicked down the light switch, but the power was still off. Then his breath caught in his throat at a sudden, ragged movement ahead of him.

It was the curtains. Billowing inwards, swaying in the breeze from the open window.

He was certain the window hadn't been open earlier. But now it was, the small top window above the main pane, propped open on the metal arm. He stepped towards it to close it, shining his torch around the room, then stopped. There was something on the bed, several somethings, scattered around. And a box, a shoebox, upturned. He reached down and picked up one of the white squares, turned it over. A photograph. A Polaroid. In the light from his phone he saw it was a picture of him and Dad, when he was maybe seven or eight, on the seafront at Blackpool. But there was something wrong with the picture. Joe picked up another, and another. More holiday snaps, a relative's wedding, Christmas, playing in a paddling pool in the yard. Photos of Joe, aged anywhere between a baby and twelve, before he left Scratch Moss for Leeds.

And in every single photograph, Joe's eyes had been crossed out. He looked at every one, and then found, beside the upturned shoebox, a pen, a red-ink Biro. The slim plastic vein of ink inside it had burst, and the outside of the pen was slick with red. Joe rubbed his fingers and stared as it stained his skin.

The photos had definitely not been on the bed when he came to the room earlier, and he hadn't got them out. That he knew for a fact. He stared numbly at the sheaf of photos in his hand, wondering what it all meant, and then something rose up noisily from the other side of the bed, a shape at first as black as the darkness, but then displaying, caught in the spiralling beam of his phone flashlight as he leapt back, a flash of white and iridescent blue.

'Jesus fucking Christ,' yelled Joe. The bird squawked and flew to the open window, perching on the frame, considering him with a beady black eye. He caught it in the cold glare of his torch, staring at him, Joe staring back at it. And then the magpie ducked its head and dropped out of the window, wings spread like a parachute, and then the main bulb in the room suddenly blazed into life, and he could hear the clicking and beeping of appliances waking up, around the house. The distant house alarm wailed one last time, and fell silent, and the streetlights flickered on outside.

Joe went to close the window and turned to survey the bed. He quickly gathered up the photographs and stuffed them back in the box then, ensuring his mum's bedroom door was firmly closed, went to check the rest of the house and lock up. When he was satisfied there was nobody but him in the house, he decided he would call the police in the morning. For now, he needed to get some sleep.

Joe didn't hold out much hope of that happening.

9

Joe must have slept, at least a little, because when he opened his eyes in his old bedroom the sunlight was streaming in through the open curtains. And it brought with it more rational thoughts.

The window in Mum's room had been open, you just hadn't noticed, Joe told himself as he made coffee and toast. The box of photographs must have been on the chest of drawers by Mum's bed. The bird had got in through the window, flapped about, making the noises you heard downstairs. It had knocked the shoebox off the drawers, scattering the photographs across the bed.

And the angry red crosses slashed through young Joe's eyes on every single photo? Mum, he thought soberly. She must have been in a bad way for a while. God knows what had gone through her head when she did that, but what other explanation could there be?

The house felt cloying and claustrophobic, the shadows heavy. Joe needed to get out, have some fresh air. He started walking aimlessly along the main road, the Little Woods rearing up in front of him. He had no desire to go there again, nor down the Donkey Lane. Instead he veered up Hall Lane, before the woods, and walked past the former council houses. Most of them were privately owned now. He felt eyes on him from behind the curtains and blinds, and he tried not to stare back as his feet carried him over the railway bridge. He paused and peered over the soot-blackened wall as an express train thundered along the West Coast Main Line, heading south.

He wished he were on it, going back to London. It had been nothing but death since he arrived. His dad, then Shep — Joe had a sudden stab of sadness, imagining the old dog lying on some vet's table, the fatal injection being administered — and now his mum.

Beyond the bridge the road became a track and wound around to what had once been Scratch Moss pit. Where his dad worked, where most of the Scratch Moss men had worked, until it was closed in 1985. From where Joe stood now you were once able to see the pit-head gear rising up, the big winding wheel on top. Now it was just open land, bordered at the far end by the canal and lines of trees. At some point someone had laid in a labyrinth of paths, perhaps thinking that the former site might become some kind of leisure facility for dog walkers and children, but they were overgrown with tall grasses and the site was just scrubland.

Joe walked along the obscured paths, his memory mapping on to the empty grassland the old buildings and roads that used to be on here, forty years ago. A wind whipped up as he walked, and he pulled his jacket tighter about him. When he got to the middle of the site, he paused. This was where the pit-head gear used to be. It had all been dismantled, demolished and the mine covered over, after he had gone to Leeds.

Joe crouched down, his fingers grazing the fine grit of the path. Right below him would be the shaft down which the men were lowered in a steel cage, and deep down the network of tunnels from which they used to claw out the coal on which the country ran.

I'm talking about the devil of the pit, the god of dirty coal and hellfire. The spirit of the broken, blasted land.

Joe stood, the wind blowing harder and colder. He felt a *thrumming* in the soles of his feet, as though the pit were still working far beneath him, men lowered into the bowels of the earth, dragging out that dirty mixture of compounds that had been formed and compressed over millions of years. One time,

Joe's dad had brought home a piece of coal that had a perfect fossil of a leaf inside it. Joe had wondered over it for days, at the vast, impossible age of it, whether it had once grown on a tree or bush at which dinosaurs feasted.

Joe started to walk back towards the road and the bridge, and felt the merest tremor in the earth beneath his feet. Puzzled, he turned back. There was a crack in the field, running over the path where he had just squatted. He bent down again and ran his fingers over it. It was barely a couple of millimetres wide, but he was certain it hadn't been there before. He stood again, keen to be away. It had been thirty-five years or more since the site was cleared. It stood to reason that whatever they had filled the pit in with would shift and settle over time. He suddenly felt aware of the yawning chasm beneath him, and hurried back to the road, rubbing his fingers.

It was his imagination, he was sure, and a symptom of that cold wind that was blowing, but when he'd put his fingers over that narrow fissure, he had been sure he felt *warmth* emanating from within.

–

Joe sat in the living room, in darkness, staring at the window. The room had been thoroughly cleaned, but he could still see the splattered blood all over the window, even though he knew it wasn't there. *Is this what Mike meant by feeling odd?* he wondered. Then the doorbell went and he was never more grateful to see Ellen standing there with a plastic carrier bag that steamed and smelled delicious.

'Chippy tea,' she said, holding up the bag. 'I'm guessing you haven't eaten all day.'

'For two days,' said Joe, suddenly ravenous.

'Maybe this isn't a good idea, then,' she said, holding up another bag that clinked with the promise of wine bottles.

'Believe me, that's almost as good an idea as the fish and chips.'

They wolfed down the food straight from the paper on the dining room table, Joe glugging the red wine down thirstily. 'Easy, tiger,' said Ellen. 'So… how are you feeling?'

'Empty,' admitted Joe. 'Like… like I'm a two-dimensional character come to life.'

'Very authorial,' said Ellen as they took the wine into the living room. She stared at the window, just as Joe had been doing before she arrived.

'I'm sorry,' he said. 'I hope Korben is all right.'

'Firstly, there's nothing for you to be sorry about. You didn't know that was going to happen. And he saw nothing. I covered his eyes as soon as I could see what was going on. Some of the other kids, though…'

'Oh God,' said Joe, burying his head in his hands.

Ellen stood up and closed the curtains, cutting off the window, and then sat beside him on the sofa. He felt her arm go around his shoulders. 'Cry if you want. Let it out.'

'I can't,' he said in a small voice. 'I don't know why I can't.'

'People cope in different ways. It'll come. Eventually. And you won't be ready for it when it does.'

Joe inhaled Ellen's scent, and leaned into her further. She stroked his hair, and murmured into his ear that everything was going to be all right. Joe was a teenager again, except this was what he had always dreamed of when he was thirteen. A hug from Ellen Dowd. He turned his face towards her, and she let him brush his lips against hers. Almost instantly, Joe felt himself stiffen in his jeans, and Ellen laid a hand on his thigh. He kissed her properly, tasting the balm on her lips, and his hand snaked towards her middle.

'No,' she said gently, pushing him away.

'Sorry,' mumbled Joe. 'Shit.'

Ellen took his face in her hands, and kissed him softly on the forehead. 'I don't mean no, I don't want to. I mean no, not right now. Your head's all over the place. You don't know what you want or need.'

'I do,' said Joe. 'I want and need you. God, I have for forty years.'

'Then another couple of days won't matter,' she said. 'I want to be sure you're not just out of your mind with grief.' She kissed him lightly on the lips. 'Another couple of days, then let's see.' She smiled crookedly. 'Forty years?'

Joe sighed and sat back on the sofa, suddenly dog-tired. 'You broke my heart, Ellen Dowd. You wouldn't look twice at me. And then the day I left for Leeds, after my dad had been arrested... Daz Twist told me you'd been fingered by Neil Hall behind the Working Men's Club. I didn't even know what fingered meant, not really. But it broke my heart anyway.'

Joe felt Ellen stiffen beside him, and move slightly away. When he looked at her, she had her arms crossed, staring at the clock above the fireplace. 'He didn't do that to me.'

Joe laid a hand on her arm. 'Hey, it was a long time ago. I was only trying to make light—'

'He didn't do that to me!' Ellen said more fiercely. She sighed and said, 'Remember we talked about Julie and Jan, that gang? I was desperate to be one of the cool girls like them. They kept dangling carrots in front of me... do this and you can be in our group, skip school tomorrow, go out with him. I did everything and it was never quite enough. Then they said I had to go on a date with Neil Hall. He was... what, fifteen at the time?'

'Yeah, a couple of years above us at school.'

A faraway look came in Ellen's eyes. 'We just walked around for a bit, then he steered me behind the club. Kissed me so hard it hurt. Tried to get his hand down my jeans. Julie and Jan had told him I'd let him do anything. And I nearly did let him, Joe. Because I'd have done anything to be in their gang, properly a part of it. But not anything, as it turned out. I stopped and pushed him away. For a second I thought he was going to do it anyway, force me. But he just called me a dick-teaser and walked off. Then he told everyone he'd done that anyway, and nobody believed me when I said he hadn't.'

Joe took a drink of his wine. 'I'm sorry. That you had to put up with all that.'

'They got off on it, the power over me,' said Ellen. 'It was only when we left school that the spell was broken. They stopped caring. And so did I.'

'I still think you could have just left Scratch Moss,' said Joe gently. 'Could have gone away. Made a better life away from this place.'

Ellen shrugged. 'Nobody leaves Scratch Moss. Hardly ever. Apart from you, and that wasn't by choice.'

'Why not, though?' pressed Joe. 'Why don't people leave?'

She looked him in the eye. 'This life... being working class, it isn't something you have to escape from, you know. It's not a bad thing. Of course, people always want more money, but that doesn't mean they want to get away from where they're born, where they live. People just want to get on with their lives.'

'This place, though,' he said. 'Scratch Moss. It's fucked up. Everything's fucked up. The longer I'm here, the more I remember. It's always been fucked up. It's always been *wrong*. I don't understand why anyone would stay here.'

'You're just having a bad time right now,' said Ellen, softening, putting her hand on his thigh. 'You don't remember. You don't speak to older people here. We might have always been a working-class place, but we had prosperity. Until the pit closed, anyway.'

'Wait here,' said Joe, and ran upstairs. When he came down he was carrying the shoebox from his mum's room. Wordlessly, he handed it over and waited for Ellen to sort through the photographs.

'Who did this?' she said. 'Your mum?'

'I have no idea,' said Joe quietly. He told her what had happened, the noises from upstairs, the magpie in the room. She reached for him and at first he thought she was holding his hand, but she twisted it over and stared at the red stains there.

'The pen had burst,' he said, rubbing at the dried ink. 'That's what made me think it had... just been done.'

He waited for Ellen to tell him that was ridiculous, that grief and shock were making him imagine things, but she just sat, quietly and thoughtfully. Joe said, 'Those straw babies at the old church. The magpies. The way my mum had been in the last couple of days.' He shook his head. 'There's something wrong with this place, Ellen. Scratch Moss. There's something bad about it.'

'It is what it is,' said Ellen, pouring them both another glass of wine.

'Nobody knows what's going on here, or nobody wants to talk about it,' said Joe, accepting the glass. Then he paused. 'Wait. That's not true.' He put the glass on the coffee table and stood up. 'Get your coat.'

'What?' said Ellen. 'Where are we going? Another mad writer's adventure?'

Joe led her into the street behind the house, then across a patch of wasteland towards the start of the Avenues, lined with what used to be council houses. Now social housing, he supposed, or private homes bought during the big council house sell-off. 'Does he still live in the same place? I remember it. It was along here.'

'Who do you mean?' said Ellen, hurrying after him through the darkness. Then Joe stopped at a weathered gate hanging off its post on one rusted hinge. 'Oh, right. Joe, I'm not sure this is a great—'

But Joe was already up the garden path, hammering with his fist on the door. By the time Ellen joined him the door had been opened a crack, and a rheumy eye set deep into a gaunt face peered out at him.

'You said you knew everything about Scratch Moss,' said Joe.

'I do,' said Freddy Blackwood, opening the door wider.

'Then tell me,' said Joe, pushing inside past Freddy, not waiting to be asked. 'Tell me everything about Scratch Moss.'

'Are you sure about that?' said Freddy, an amused smile on his thin face, as Ellen followed Joe into the house, wrinkling her nose. 'You might not like what you hear.'

Joe turned in the doorway to the living room. 'This is about my dad, isn't it? And Red Clogs. You said Red Clogs was back.'

Freddy nodded. 'Red Clogs is back. He's been away for a long time, but now he's back.' He bared the stumps of his rotten teeth. 'And everyone's forgotten what that means.'

PART TWO

1985

10

'I'm starving,' said Keith. 'Absolutely bloody starving.'

'Well, you should have had your dinner before you came out,' said Colin with a grunt, pulling at a branch on the tree nearest to him, the supple wood bowing and bending but not snapping.

'Maybe Bob Geldof will make a charity record for you,' said Joe quietly.

'Haha, good one,' said Colin. The branch eventually gave way under the strain of his tugging and broke, landing him on his arse in the grass. He shouted, 'What do you reckon, Daz? Keith's starving and Bob Geldof should make a charity record for him.'

Daz was away ahead of them, lost in the trees. Joe sighed. He was always coming out with funny stuff but never had the confidence to say it loudly. Everyone else always repeated what he said and made out it was their own idea. At the same time, he felt bad about what he'd said. Keith's dad was dead and he lived with his mum and three brothers and everybody knew they were totally skint. He felt in his pocket where he'd squirrelled away a packet of Polos and tossed them at Keith, who tore into them and started stuffing them into his mouth.

'Shall we play *Return of the Jedi* or *Krull*?' said Colin, wielding the broken stick like it was either a lightsaber or a sword. He peered into the woods. 'Did you hear that?'

They all went quiet, save for Keith crunching the Polo mints. Joe definitely heard something. Like metal striking metal, distant and discordant. It was coming from ahead of them, along the old railway line that the pit didn't use any more. Colin hefted the stick, holding it at the bottom with two hands. 'Come on,' he said.

Keith dutifully followed Colin along the track, but Joe held back. He didn't like the Little Woods. Always felt uncomfortable here, like there was somebody watching him. The sound seemed to be getting closer. Colin and Keith stopped, looking around. Then a voice, harsh and croaking, issued from the darkness of the trees.

'Red Clogs is coming to get you.'

'Daz, that you?' said Colin a little doubtfully. Then a figure emerged from the trees ahead of them, Daz Twist, taller than the rest, his hair short at the front and long in a mullet at the back.

'What's up with you girls?' said Daz.

'Did you say something about Red Clogs?' said Colin. He tossed the Polo wrapper on the ground. Joe, who had caught up to them, quietly bent down and picked it up, shoving it in his pocket.

'Not me,' said Daz, feigning innocence. 'What did you hear?'

Then the clashing sound, metal on metal, came again, and Joe started to feel proper freaked out. Daz laughed, unable to keep up the pretence any longer, and they saw he was clicking the heel of his Kicker boot against the old track, the seg on his sole ringing against the metal.

'Your faces,' said Daz, shaking his head. 'Thought Collier was going to shit himself.'

Joe laughed it off. 'Good one, Daz.'

Colin held up his stick. 'I was saying, should we play *Return of the—*'

With sudden viciousness, Daz grabbed the stick from Colin's hands and threw it into the undergrowth. '*Playing?* Are you soft in the head? We're not *playing* anything. Christ. Grow up.'

'So what are we going to do then?' said Keith. 'I'm starving.'

'Bob Geldof might make a charity record for you,' said Colin, nudging Daz. 'Good one, eh? Like Band Aid.'

'I got it,' said Daz, reaching into the back pocket of his jeans. He pulled out a piece of shiny paper, folded over several times. They all crowded round to look as he unfolded it. 'What do you reckon to that, then?'

It was a page ripped out of a dirty magazine. Joe felt himself flushing, and glanced away, then looked again. There was a woman lying on her bed, totally naked, her legs wide open, displaying everything. She was clutching at her boobs and had her head thrown back, her eyes half-closed, her mouth open. 'Cheeky Cheryl,' said Daz, reading the caption. He looked at the rest of them. 'Does she give you a stiffy?'

Keith was already re-arranging himself in his jeans. Colin announced, 'I'd definitely bonk her.' Joe felt hot and uncomfortable, and it wasn't just the dry, July heat, but he couldn't drag his eyes away.

Daz said, 'Who would you like to see on her back like that from our year?'

'Julie Wishaw, definitely,' said Colin.

'Me too,' agreed Keith. Everybody fancied Julie Wishaw, or Jan Horton. Joe did too, because they were the fittest girls in school, but he didn't really like them very much. Not that he'd ever have a chance with them, or would any of them, except maybe Daz.

'What about you, Collier?' said Daz, waggling the page in front of him.

'Everybody knows Joe fancies Ellen Dowd.' Colin laughed.

'No I do not,' snapped Joe, his face burning hotter.

'Ellen Dowd,' said Daz, thoughtfully. 'Not much to look at but she's got big tits. Yeah, might agree with you there, Joe.' Daz folded up the page. 'Might see if she'll let me get the top off her after the disco next week.'

'Lend us that page until tomorrow,' said Colin.

'Fifty pence,' said Daz.

Colin thought about it, then dug into his pocket and counted out the coins. Daz took the money and handed the page over. 'Dinner time tomorrow. And I want it back clean, you dirty bastard.'

Joe didn't really know what Daz meant, but laughed along with everybody else. Colin put the page in his pocket and said, 'Well, if we're not playing, what are we doing?'

Daz nodded towards the woods. 'My dad said they might be sending the coppers down today so they can get into the pit and close it down. Let's go and have a look.'

—

'What's that mad bastard up to?' said Gary Grady, by Terry Collier's side in the tumult of miners gathered at the locked gates to the Scratch Moss pit site. Well, ex-miners, really, thought Terry. Given they were all officially unemployed as of today. He looked across to where Gary was pointing, at a lone figure standing on a slight rise overlooking the pit, his arms stretched up to the sky.

'Johnny fucking Crowe,' said Terry, and spat on the ground. 'Ignore him. We've got more on our plates.'

'I'm going to go and tell him to either fuck off or come and join us,' said Gary, starting to shoulder through the crowd.

Terry grabbed his arm. 'Ignore him, I said. He'll be neither use nor ornament either way.'

Gary was a hothead, but Terry liked that. He had balls. He was only eighteen, and Terry wished half of the miners here showed as much passion. Not to mention the bastards who'd stayed at home and not bothered turning out on a day like this. Terry had hoped that one day soon his lad Joe would be joining him at the pit, despite what Mary said. She thought the boy was clever, and should go and do A-levels and then even go to university. A couple of years ago, Terry would have said that was nonsense, men from Scratch Moss dug coal, and that was that, and nobody was going to take that away from them.

That was before Margaret Thatcher came along and decided to take on the miners. And won. The strike had been hard, and losing had been even harder. And now this was the result.

'Here they come,' said Gary, nudging Terry. Ahead of them, weaving along the road, were three coaches.

They were coming to close down Scratch Moss pit for good.

'It's all for nothing,' said the man in the yellow vest over his suit and white hard-hat, carrying a clipboard. His name was Roger White and he was from the National Coal Board. Terry knew him well; he was only from Platt Fields. Somebody had put his windows through during the strike. 'The decision's already been made.'

'Judas!' bellowed Terry. He looked around at the others, brandishing homemade placards that said *Coal Not Dole* and *Hands Off Scratch Moss*. Somebody had a scarecrow held aloft wearing a plastic Maggie Thatcher mask. The call was taken up by another man, and then more. 'Judas! Judas!'

Behind Roger White there were three rows of police officers, brandishing clear plastic riot shields. And in one of the coaches behind them, the engineers who were here to decommission Scratch Moss pit. Terry felt a pit of his own opening up inside his stomach. This was it. The real thing. The only work he'd ever known, that any of the men gathered here had ever known. And when they took it away from them, what was going to happen? How were they meant to pay their mortgages and feed their families.

'This pit's viable!' shouted someone. 'We know that and you know that and if fucking Thatcher doesn't know that, somebody should get her down here and I'll tell her myself.'

There was a volley of applause, and boos at the mention of the prime minister. Then a whoop went up and Terry glanced over to see the effigy of Thatcher had been set light to and was burning merrily on the ground in front of the gates.

The line of police moved forward a step. Terry scanned their faces. They weren't local. They'd been bussed in from another county. He could see they were up for a ruck, holding their truncheons, ready to wade it. They'd all seen what happened at Orgreave a year earlier, during the strike. It had been a massacre. The police had attacked like they were dealing with an occupying enemy. Terry could see these coppers were up for something like that, too. Put some men in a uniform, and they'd do anything they were told, and half of them would enjoy it.

'Scratch Moss coal is the best ever dug,' shouted someone else. 'There's miles of it down there. We know, we've worked the field all our bloody lives.'

'It might be the best, but it's not the cheapest,' said Roger White.

Everybody knew that Thatcher wanted to buy cheaper coal from Australia and South Africa, but that wasn't the only reason she was closing the pits. Terry felt his anger rising within him. Thatcher wanted to break the working classes. Wanted to break him and his family. She was punishing the unions, and was going to finish them, starting with the National Union of Miners. She called them 'the enemy within'.

Something made him glance over to where that mad bastard, Johnny Crowe, was now dancing on his little hill, arms spiralling. What *was* the stupid twat up to? The way he was staring at the pit, ignoring the drama playing out at the gates. It freaked Terry out a bit. Because there was something in all this that Thatcher and the National Coal Board and even the National Union of Miners could never guess, something in Scratch Moss, something in that pit, and if it was closed down… then nobody knew how that was going to play out, because there'd been coal mined on this site for a hundred and twenty years and in Scratch Moss, they knew how things were done, and—

Terry suddenly snapped back to the here and now as he felt himself jostled forward. Roger White was now flanked by three police officers on either side of him, the line of coppers with riot shields moving forward another step.

'Move aside, now,' said White. 'It's time to accept the inevitable. Let the engineers in to do their jobs. It's over.'

Terry felt Gary bend down beside him, and when he stood up, he had in his hand half a red house brick. Terry could have told him to drop it, but he didn't want to. He felt adrenaline rushing in his head. If this was what they wanted, this was what they'd get.

'All coppers are bastards!' yelled Gary, and he launched the house brick over the shields and into the midst of the police.

Terry braced himself as the police, banging their batons on their plastic shields, charged.

11

Joe sat on the sofa, reading the book he'd got out of the mobile library, but not taking it in. He'd just discovered Michael Moorcock, and had been hoovering up the slim paperbacks that were a dozen-strong on the shelves of the big, book-laden bus that parked up in the street every Thursday teatime. He was hopping between the series, reading the random books that the library had, *Elric* and *Hawkmoon*, the *Dancers at the End of Time*. This one was about time travel. *Behold The Man*. A man goes back two thousand years in search of Jesus. It was quite possibly the most mind-blowing thing Joe had ever read.

Except, he wasn't really reading it. He was looking over the pages of the open book at his mum, who was cleaning a cut on his dad's head with TCP, which caused him to wince, and then applying a big plaster.

'Well, was it all worth it?' said his mum to his dad, who also sported a black eye and a sprained wrist.

'You should see the other fella.'

'It's no joking matter, Terry,' admonished his mum. 'You might get charged with something. And the pit's still closed down. And you're out of work.' Her voice dropped to a whisper, but still audible. 'I'm worried. What about the mortgage? We can't survive on what I make part time from the shop, and the dole.'

'I'll find something,' sighed his dad. 'The dole won't be forever. Something will come up.' He shook his head. 'I've got to go to a Job Club next week. Show us how to apply for work. Fucking hell.'

'Sssh,' said his mum. 'Not in front of...' Joe saw her nod her head towards him. She took a deep breath. 'Besides. This is Scratch Moss. We've always been looked after here, haven't we, Terry? Haven't we?'

His dad said nothing.

They'd watched it from the edge of the woods, the police piling into the miners. It was messy and scrappy and only lasted ten minutes. Some ambulances came and took away some of the miners and a couple of the coppers. And then the gates opened and the police formed a line either side, facing out towards the subdued miners, as the coach full of engineers drove in. And that was that.

Joe put his finger into his place in the book and stood up. 'I'm going to my room to listen to my record,' he said, leaving them to it. He'd bought the record last week, *Misplaced Childhood* by Marillion. As he dropped the needle on it he studied the sleeve. A barefoot boy in a kind of old-fashioned military uniform stood against a backdrop of clouds and a rainbow. By his feet there grew a poppy. Perched on his right forearm there was a magpie. Joe played 'Kayleigh' and 'Lavender', which were really love songs, not rock songs. He played them over and over again and thought about Ellen Dowd. How he wanted to dance with her in the snow and lie with her in a park. Whenever he thought of Ellen he kept getting flashes of that page from the dirty mag that Daz had. In a secret notebook he hid between the mattress and the base of his bed, he tried to write songs like the ones Marillion wrote, about being in love with Ellen Dowd. He wrote lines about how their love was the greatest love the world had ever known, but was, for reasons which escaped him, doomed to failure, and the sadness that they had to part. He was getting ahead of himself. She'd never even looked twice at him.

He was so lost in the music that he didn't hear his mum knock on his bedroom door then push it open. 'Your mates have called for you,' she said.

Joe went downstairs to find Daz, Colin and Keith on the doorstep. 'All right?' said Daz.

'All right? What are you doing?'

Colin shrugged. 'Hanging about.'

They walked along the road towards the parade. When he was getting his trainers on, Joe had stolen a handful of biscuits from the tin. He was eating a chocolate digestive and Keith was looking at him, his mouth watering. Joe silently handed them all over to him. He'd nicked them for Keith anyway. He knew he wouldn't have had much for his tea.

They stood outside the newsagents for a bit, leaning on the window until Mr Benson came out and told them off. Then they walked over to the Working Men's Club and watched the delivery lorry rolling barrels into the hatch that led to the cellar. There was a poster up saying the club would be showing the Live Aid concert in a few weeks.

'We should come to that,' said Daz.

'We could go to the Black Diamond now and play the jukebox,' said Colin. 'Anybody got any money?'

They all emptied their pockets – except Keith, who had nothing – and pooled their change: enough to buy four glasses of Ribena and put five songs on the jukebox. They were walking back to the road when Daz said, 'Look who it is.'

It was Julie Wishaw and Jan Horton, with Ellen Dowd tagging behind. They all straightened up, and Joe subconsciously smoothed his hair. As they met on the pavement, Daz said, 'All right?'

'All right?' said Julie. 'What you doing?'

'Pub.' Daz sniffed casually.

'To drink pop,' Jan said, laughing. She had straight black hair where Julie had wavy blonde curls. Ellen hung back, her mousy brown hair over her face. She briefly caught Joe's eye then looked away.

'All right, Ellen?' said Daz, and Joe hated him briefly but fiercely.

A little smile played on Julie's lips. 'Ellen wants to go on a date with you, Daz. Don't you?'

A look of dismay flashed across Ellen's face, then she pushed it away. 'I never said—'

'All right,' agreed Daz quickly. 'Pictures? Want to see *The Breakfast Club*?'

Ellen shrugged and Julie said, 'Yeah, she does. Tomorrow night.' She leaned in and whispered theatrically, 'You're on a promise, Daz Twist.'

Daz grinned and Joe looked at Ellen again, who once again met his eyes, then looked down at her feet. Then Joe heard Jan groan. 'Oh God, look who it is.'

'What do you want, Freddy Krueger?' said Colin.

Freddy Blackwood limped up to them. He wore black school trousers two inches too short, showing his dirty white socks and his beaten-up Dunlop Green Flash trainers. Despite the July evening he wore a jumper, shoved into his waistband. His greasy hair framed a face pustulating with angry-looking acne.

'They shut the pit today,' said Freddy, a weird smile on his face.

'Duh, yeah,' said Daz. 'Like, all our dads work there. Does your dad work there, Freddy?' Daz grinned evilly. 'Oh, I forgot, he's dead.'

'Everybody dies at some point,' said Freddy, still smiling.

'Creep,' said Julie, crossing her arms.

'I wonder who's next?' said Freddy.

'Next for what?' said Joe, frowning.

'Somebody's got to die,' said Freddy, nodding. 'A kid's got to die. Haven't you noticed? A kid dies in Scratch Moss every year. Not yet this year.'

'What are you going on about?' said Daz, puffing up his chest and glancing at Ellen. Joe groaned internally. Why was Daz interested in Ellen all of a sudden?

'Remember that kid got run over last year?' said Freddy, counting off on his fingers. 'He was still alive when they took him away. Never saw him again.'

'Yeah, well, he died in hospital,' said Jan. 'He lived in the street behind us.'

'Then Tommy Freedland went missing the year before,' Freddy said, counting on his fingers.

'They reckon a child-molester had him,' agreed Keith.

Freddy looked at Ellen with interest. 'How's your cousin?'

She glared at him. 'What?'

'Your cousin. Little lad. What was his name?'

'His name *is* Jamie,' said Ellen.

'Jamie's very ill,' said Julie, fronting Freddy up, arms crossed. 'He's only a little kid. He had to go away to a special hospital.'

Freddy grinned. 'Is that what they told you? Three years ago, wasn't it?'

Then Daz interjected, pushing Freddy away from them with both hands planted in his bony chest. 'Why don't you fuck off, Freddy Krueger? Nobody wants you here. Nobody wants to hear this bullshit.'

Freddy shrugged and turned away without another word, limping away. They all watched him go then Daz went over to Ellen and said, 'All right?'

She shrugged, then smiled at him. Julie and Jan made *oooh* noises and started to sing 'Move Closer' by Phyllis Nelson, and Ellen started to burn up and moved away from Daz.

'Have a good time with your pop at the pub,' said Jan, looking at her watch.

'Ellen'll meet you outside the pictures at seven,' said Julie. 'We need to go and decide what she's going to wear for the big date.' She did her theatrical whisper again. 'It'll be a skirt, Daz.'

As the girls walked off, Daz punched Joe in the arm. 'Did you hear that? On a promise, she said. She'll be wearing a skirt.' He laughed giddily. 'Reckon I'll get tops *and* bottoms at least.' He turned to Colin. 'That reminds me. Where's Cheeky Cheryl?'

'Can I have her for another night?' said Colin, wheedling.

Daz thought about it, then held out his hand. 'Fifty pence.'

'But I put all my money in the kitty for the Black Diamond.'

Daz shrugged. 'Then I get your goes on the jukebox. Deal?'

—

Joe felt upset and angry and not in the mood, so after gulping down his Ribena in the upstairs room of the Black Diamond he said he was going home. Colin said, 'Your songs haven't even been on yet.'

'He's just jealous because I'm going on a date with Ellen Dowd,' said Daz.

Joe laughed it off and left, seething all the way home. When he got in his dad was asleep in his chair, gently snoring, and his mum was watching *The Little and Large Show*. 'They crack me up, these two,' she said. 'Want to watch it?'

'Think I'll just go to my room,' said Joe. 'Play my record.'

His mum smiled hesitantly at him. 'Joe? You know, with the pit closing for good now... well, money's going to be tight for a bit. So there'll be no more records for a while. Or anything like that. OK?'

Joe nodded and retreated upstairs, putting *Misplaced Childhood* on his little record player. He lay back on his bed and listened to the opening bars, eyes closed. He thought about Ellen Dowd, and he thought about Daz going on a date with her tomorrow, and anger and anxiety curled together in his gut. Then he thought about Freddy Blackwood, and what he'd said.

Somebody's got to die. A kid's got to die. Haven't you noticed? A kid dies every year. Not yet this year.

'Stupid freaky Freddy Krueger,' murmured Joe out loud.

Then he said, aping Daz's voice and commanding tone, 'Nobody wants to hear this bullshit.' He wished he were more like Daz. He wished he were going on a date with Ellen Dowd. He listened to the music, and started to drift off.

'I wonder who's next?' he heard Freddy say, before he fell asleep.

12

Terry was up at six, his body not yet having got the message that there would be no shift at Scratch Moss pit today, no shift at the pit ever again. He went for a walk in the already-hot morning, up to the pit to watch from the road. They hadn't started taking down the winding gear yet. When they did, it would be like a dagger to his heart. Once that was gone, then... well, what then? What now? What was he supposed to do with the rest of his life? Terry was 39, which meant he was too young to retire and probably too old to retrain. But he'd have to find something to keep the family afloat.

When he got home he found Mary at the dining room table, two bags of straw open on the floor beside her. He stared at her for a while from the kitchen door, until she said, 'If you're just going to stand there you might as well put the kettle on.'

'I've not seen you do that for a while,' said Terry, bringing her a cup of tea. He glanced towards the hall door. 'Joe...?'

'In bed still. He's a proper teenager now. Doubt we'll see him surface until eleven. By which time I'll be down the shop for my shift. Just need to finish this first.' Mary hefted up the straw figure, three feet tall, twine around its wrists and ankles and neck.

Terry inspected the effigy. 'Do you think this is necessary? I mean, Joe's thirteen...'

Mary looked up at him. 'Joe's a *child*, Terry. You forget that sometimes. Just because you left school at fourteen. It's different, these days. He's a child still. And that means... well. Better safe than sorry.'

Terry sat down at the table and watched her put the finishing touches to the straw figure. 'Do you want me to take that down to the old church? Before Joe gets up and sees it.'

'If you would,' said Mary, tightening the twine around its neck. 'Then it's done.'

'I wondered…' said Terry hesitantly. He took a drink of his tea. 'I wondered, with the pit closing now, whether that might mean… well, it might all be over. Do you think?'

Mary looked at him. 'It's never over, Terry. And the pit closing? I think that just means it's going to get worse.'

–

Terry wrapped the effigy in a black bin bag and walked over to the old church. There was no one there but the doors were open, and there were already five straw children propped up against the altar. So Mary wasn't the only one. Must be a woman thing, thought Terry. Female intuition or something. He unwrapped the effigy and placed it alongside the others. 'Not my lad,' he whispered. 'If you have to take somebody, don't take my lad.'

He turned to leave and saw a figure in the doorway, framed against the sunlight. It stepped into the shadows and Terry nodded. 'All right?'

'All right?' said Harry Doyle. Harry was one of the National Union of Mineworkers stewards for Scratch Moss. He looked hollowed out, empty in his eyes. Nobody had fought harder than Harry, and he was taking their defeat worse than anyone.

Terry nodded at the bulky newspaper-wrapped parcel under Harry's arm. Harry had twin girls, a couple of years younger than Joe. 'You too?'

'Well, the missus.' Harry sniffed. 'You know what they're like.'

Terry went outside and lit up a cigarette, leaving Harry to do what he had to do. He stared at the packet. More than two quid for twenty now. That was an expense that might have to go. If they hit £2.50 I'll definitely stop, he told himself. Harry came out and said, 'What are you up to now, then?'

Terry shrugged. 'Thought I might go into town, look at the Jobcentre.'

Harry grunted. 'Good luck with that. Three million unemployed and rising.' He looked to the heavens and bellowed. 'Fuck Thatcher!'

'Feel better for that?' said Terry.

'Not really.' Harry shrugged. 'I'll feel better after a pint, though. Black Diamond?'

Why not, thought Terry, falling into step beside him.

—

When Joe awoke, his mum had gone to work and his dad was nowhere to be seen. He ate some cornflakes but they made him feel sick; he had a ball of anxiety in his gut. When he looked out of the window he could see men just milling around. Walking up and down the main road. Leaning on their garden walls. Doing nothing. The end of coal mining in Scratch Moss seemed unthinkable, and yet here it was. They hardly bothered with careers advice at school for the Scratch Moss kids, because the expectation was that you would just go down the pit. Joe had been told by most of his teachers that he should do A-levels and then apply for universities. He had no idea whether that was even possible for someone like him. Would it cost money? Because that was going to be in short supply for everyone. He guessed he wouldn't be getting a ZX Spectrum this Christmas. Daz Twist had got one two years ago.

Joe had a shower and wondered what to do for the day. Hang about, he supposed. He was just getting dressed when he heard banging at the front door. Hopping along the hall to his mum and dad's room as he pulled on his jeans, Joe peered cautiously from behind the curtain. It was Daz, Colin and Keith. Joe hesitated, then stepped back. Maybe he wouldn't just go out to hang about today. He couldn't be doing with Daz crowing about his date with Ellen tonight. Joe loitered in the shadows until they wandered off towards the parade.

In his room, he put on *Misplaced Childhood* and listened to the hiss before the haunting bars of the opening track, 'Pseudo Silk Kimono', started. Daz had got a CD player last Christmas. Joe wanted one, because everybody was getting them, but he liked the act of putting the needle on the record, listening to it crackle before the music burst out of the speakers. He supposed nobody would listen to records in a few years. He wasn't sure he liked compact discs. He liked a record with a big gatefold sleeve with all the lyrics and liner notes that you could prop up on your knees while you sat on your bed and listened to the music. But you couldn't stop progress. That's what the people who had closed down Scratch Moss pit said. That's what Thatcher said.

Joe wished he could write like Fish, who was the singer and lyricist of Marillion. It was like poetry. Hard-edged, bitter poetry. He got a notepad from his pile of books and opened it, thinking what he would write to Ellen Dowd if he was Fish.

He put the Biro to the paper, then hesitated. Instead of poetry, he wrote *1984: Kid got run over*. Then underneath, *1983: Tommy Freedland*. And finally, *1982: Ellen's cousin Jamie*.

That's what Freddy Blackwood had said, hadn't he? Every year a kid dies or goes missing in Scratch Moss. And they were the last three years. Joe chewed his pen while he thought about it. In 1981 he would have been nine, going on ten. At Scratch Moss Primary. He thought about the kids in his class, most of whom had transferred to Platt Fields Comprehensive along with Joe. He closed his eyes and pictured each of their faces and their names. Something was bugging him, but he couldn't quite put his finger on what. Then he remembered the school photo, every summer just before they broke up for the holidays. They all had to stand in rows, class by class, on the field. His mum always bought a copy.

Joe went into his mum and dad's room, where there were big cardboard boxes full of photos on top of the wardrobe.

Balancing on a chair, he hauled them down, and in the second one were all his class photos from Scratch Moss Primary. He found the one from 1981, counting each child off. There were nineteen of them, Joe on the back row, grinning, his hair a mess. Standing in front of him was Ellen Dowd, her hair in a ponytail, her chubby face smiling. Then he found the one from 1982. There were eighteen children. One was missing. Joe held the photos side by side and compared them, mentally checking off each child, until he found who was missing. A scrawny, unsmiling girl with greasy hair was in the 1981 photo, but not the 1982 one. Joe screwed up his face and thought about her. Anne something. Anne Warner. Never seemed to have any friends, never took much part in lessons, always off sick. And after the summer break in 1981, she just didn't come back to school. Joe had never questioned it, had probably not even noticed the absence of this slight, almost invisible girl.

What had happened to Anne Warner? And if Freddy Blackwood was right and a child died or went missing in Scratch Moss every year... It was already summer. And as far as Joe knew, everybody was accounted for.

-

'Anne Warner?' said Ellen, once she had got over the surprise of Joe phoning her at home. 'God, yes, I remember her, now you've said.'

Joe sat on the stairs, where the phone was plugged into the wall, cradling the handset between ear and shoulder. 'I've got our school photos here. She was there in 1981 but not the following year.'

'Maybe she moved away?' suggested Ellen. 'Why do you want to know?'

'I don't really know why,' confessed Joe. 'Do you remember where she lived?'

He could hear Ellen clicking her tongue. 'I think I had to go to her house once to give her a card from school. She was always off sick, wasn't she? It was in the Avenues, definitely. Gloucester Place, I think. The cul-de-sac. Her house was right at the end, with a red door. Garden was like a jungle.' Ellen paused. 'Is this about what Freddy Blackwood said? About kids going missing and dying?'

'I'm sure it's nothing,' said Joe. 'Enjoy your date tonight.' Then he put the phone down and hurried out of the house.

—

Gloucester Place was tucked off Cheltenham Drive, just nine houses arranged in a frying-pan shape. Joe walked slowly along the pavement, not really knowing what he was doing. Straight ahead, flanked by two other houses in the circular bit of the frying pan, was number nine. It did indeed have a red door, the top half of it bubbled glass, and the garden was thick with weeds and tall grasses. Joe paused at the gate, his hand on the latch. Maybe he could just say he was looking for someone and didn't have the right address. Taking a deep breath, he pushed open the gate, which creaked on rusty hinges, and stepped on to the cracked concrete path.

The bell wasn't working so Joe knocked briskly, and waited. He was just about to walk away when he saw a shape on the other side of the glass, and the door opened a crack. A dull eye set in a shadowy hollow peered out at him. It was a woman, and Joe couldn't tell how old she was. She had grey hair, wild and uncombed, and her face was deeply lined. She pulled the door wider, her brow furrowing, her thin lips pursed.

'I'm sorry to bother you,' Joe said politely. 'I'm looking for someone but I don't have the full address.'

The woman just stared at him and Joe realised she was wearing a grubby white nightshirt with a thin cotton dressing gown over the top. He coughed and said, 'There used to be a girl in my class called Anne—'

The woman's eyes widened and Joe yelped as she flew at him, her bony hands grabbing the front of his Adidas T-shirt.

'What are you doing coming here asking about Anne?' she said, flecks of spittle showering Joe's face.

'I just want to know what happened to her,' said Joe, trying to wriggle free. Her grip was stronger than he'd have given her credit for. He looked around Gloucester Place for help but the cul-de-sac was deserted.

'You know what happened to her!' said the woman fiercely. 'You all know what happened to her! And you stood back and let it happen because it suited you.'

Joe eventually pulled free of her and stepped back. 'Mrs Warner? Anne was your daughter? I don't know what happened to Anne. Tell me, please.'

'He took her,' she shouted, pointing wildly over Joe's head. 'And they let him.'

'Who?' said Joe tremulously. He held his breath. She was going to say Red Clogs, wasn't she? She was going to say Red Clogs.

'Johnny Crowe,' hissed Mrs Warner. 'That's who took her, and you all just turned your backs and—'

And then there was a man standing behind Mrs Warner, thickset and bald, gently but firmly steering her back inside. 'That's enough, Winnie,' he said, glaring at Joe. 'Go back and have your dinner.'

The man pulled the door half-closed behind him and loomed over Joe. 'What are you doing, coming here asking questions about Anne?'

Joe shrank back. 'I just... I just wanted to know what happened...'

The man squinted at him. 'You're Terry Collier's lad, aren't you? Ask your dad. Ask your mates' dads. Ask any bloody sod in Scratch Moss what happened to our Anne, but nobody'll tell you anything. Because they'd rather close their eyes and pretend it doesn't happen, and when it does they just breathe a sigh of relief and thank their stars it wasn't their kid. Then they just get on with their lives, and reap the rewards.'

'What rewards?' said Joe, lost.

'Scratch Moss has made a good living out of that pit,' said Mr Warner, stepping back into the house. 'Me, your dad, every family here. But there was a cost, lad. A cost that everybody decided was worth paying. I don't know what's going to happen now they've closed us down, but I hope to all that's holy that your family never has to go through what we went through.'

Then he slammed the door, leaving Joe bewildered on the path.

13

Joe's dad came in at nine o'clock, rolling drunk, and his mum threw his plate of tea right at him. As the shouting started, Joe retreated to his room, playing *Misplaced Childhood* loud enough to drown out the row. At ten o'clock it quieted down, and Joe heard their bedroom door slam. From downstairs, he could hear his dad snoring loudly on the couch. Joe turned off the record player.

As long as Joe could remember, Red Clogs had been the bogeyman who haunted Scratch Moss. Parents would use him as a threat to get their children to go to bed. He roamed the Little Woods and the Donkey Lane and the fields around the mine. He was the ghost of a long-dead miner, some said, who earned his name for kicking his victims to death, soaking his feet in their blood. Other people said he was a demon, straight from Hell, who stole kids away for the devil himself.

But what if Red Clogs was just a man? A man called Johnny Crowe? Joe knew who Johnny Crowe was, everybody in Scratch Moss did. He must have been about sixty, lived in a tumbledown house up beyond the fields by the pit, and always had done. He was a loner and a weirdo, and dressed in blackened rags that flapped in the wind like the wings of his namesake. He had a long beard and wild hair and was to be avoided at all costs.

And Johnny Crowe had taken Anne Warner. At least, according to Anne's mum, whom Joe wasn't sure wasn't as mad as Johnny Crowe himself.

But that wasn't the most disturbing thing. That was what Mr Warner had said, who didn't seem mad at all. *Ask your dad. Ask your mates' dads. Ask any bloody sod in Scratch Moss what happened to our Anne, but nobody'll tell you anything. Because they'd rather close their eyes and pretend it doesn't happen, and when it does they just breathe a sigh of relief and thank their stars it wasn't their kid. Then they just get on with their lives, and reap the rewards.*

If Johnny Crowe was killing children, why wasn't anyone stopping him?

He jumped, his heart in his mouth, as something tinkled against his window. He listened, holding his breath, and there it was again. Cautiously, Joe went to the window and drew the curtains back a little. There was someone in the yard, someone throwing handfuls of gravel at his window. With a start and a leaping heart he realised it was Ellen Dowd.

Joe crept downstairs, checking in on his dad, dead to the world on the sofa, then unlocked the back door. Ellen stood there, in jeans and a tracksuit top. Joe couldn't think why. He said, 'How was *The Breakfast Club*?'

'I didn't go,' she said, pushing past him into the kitchen. Joe told her to whisper and pointed towards the living room.

'You stood Daz up?' he said, aghast and delighted all at the same time.

'I phoned Jan and told her I was on my period and she'd better tell him because I wasn't going out.'

'Are you?' said Joe.

'None of your business,' said Ellen. 'Can we talk somewhere? Your room?'

His heart pounding, Joe quietly led Ellen up the stairs and into his room, and closed the door. She looked around at his posters and his piles of books. She sat down on the bed and picked up a notebook, which Joe with a stricken start realised was the one he wrote his songs and poetry in. He snatched it off her and made out he was tidying up so she had more space.

'Was that poetry?' said Ellen. 'Was that my name?'

'Don't be daft.' Joe laughed.

'Oh.' She looked a little disappointed, and Joe wished he'd told the truth.

He looked at her curiously. 'So why did you cancel the date?'

Ellen sighed. 'After what Freddy Krueger said yesterday and then you on the phone... it got me thinking about our Jamie. I asked my mum why we never went to see him in hospital. Which hospital he was in. What exactly was wrong with him, and why had he been away for three years.'

'What did she say?'

Ellen pushed back her hair, revealing the bruise flowering on the side of her head, near her eye. Joe gasped. 'She hit you?'

'I don't think she meant to and she was crying for hours afterwards,' said Ellen quietly. 'She just flipped. Lost it. Said I'd never to ask about Jamie or any other kid that went missing. That I should just keep my head down and get on with life and when I was an adult I'd understand.' Ellen fell quiet, then said, 'Joe, I think Jamie's dead. I don't think he's away in hospital anywhere.'

Joe reached for his notepad – his other notepad – and showed Ellen his list of kids that had gone missing or died or gone away. He said, 'I went to Anne Warner's house today.'

She stared at him. 'Did you? Did you find out what happened to Anne?'

Joe told Ellen everything, and her eyes widened when he mentioned Johnny Crowe, and when he told her what Mr Warner had said. She seemed to think about it for a long time, then said, 'What does he mean? Everyone knows? And nobody does anything?'

'I don't know,' said Joe, helplessly.

'They're letting Johnny Crowe kill kids but nobody cares? Why would they do that? Our parents? Why, Joe?'

'I don't know,' he said again. 'But there's only Anne Warner's parents mentioned him.' He held up the list. 'I thought maybe we could...'

'Investigate!' said Ellen, her eyes shining. 'But where would we start?'

'The kid who was killed on the main road last year,' said Joe, excitement mounting. 'People must remember that. And don't they put these things in the papers? We could go to the library in town. They have all the newspapers there.'

'A proper investigation!' said Ellen, almost bouncing on the bed. 'It'll be like *Hart to Hart*.'

Joe blushed; the couple in *Hart to Hart* were married. He said, 'We could start tomorrow?'

'Yes! That accident happened on the main road, near the top of Scratch Moss. He was only eight or something. Lived near Jan. We could go to his house? Or see if there were witnesses! There's the old folks' bungalows up there. It was only last year. I bet somebody saw something. They're all nosy old bats in those bungalows.'

'Brilliant,' said Joe. 'Tomorrow, then? About eleven?'

'It's a date,' said Ellen, and Joe's heart soared as he crept down the stairs with her and let her back out into the yard.

—

Joe's mum and dad seemed to be talking again the next morning, and Joe wolfed his breakfast and had a shower, dousing himself with the Hai Karate aftershave he'd got at Christmas. At ten to eleven he was standing on the bend where the road headed out of Scratch Moss, his notebook in hand. At eleven he decided that Ellen wasn't coming and, crestfallen, decided to abandon the stupid idea. But at five past he saw her emerging from the street at the side of the Working Men's Club, and after waving frantically he decided to lounge nonchalantly against a lamppost.

She was wearing the same jeans and tracksuit top as last night. She sniffed the air as she approached. 'You smell nice,' she said. Joe shrugged and muttered something inaudible. Ellen glanced at his notepad. 'Made a start?'

'Well, I think it happened about here,' said Joe, pointing at the road. 'Which means that those two bungalows over there had a perfect view.'

Ellen followed his outstretched arm pointing at the two kitchen windows separated from the road by a grass verge and some low shrubs. 'OK, well, let's go and find out, then.'

At the first house they got no luck. The figure of a thin man in a cardigan appeared at the frosted glass door but didn't open it. 'We don't want any!' he bellowed.

At the adjacent bungalow, the door was answered by a tiny woman with platinum hair set as hard as a helmet, wearing a long-sleeved floral dress. She put on a pair of glasses hanging around her neck on a chain and peered at them. 'Yes? Is it bob-a-job week?'

Joe opened his mouth to speak but Ellen got in their first. 'We're doing a school project on road safety,' she said loudly. 'We wondered if we could ask you a couple of questions. We won't be long.'

'Oh,' said the woman. 'Well, you'd better come in then.'

They sat on the sofa while the woman, who said her name was Mrs Oldroyd, served them glasses of flat, warm dandelion and burdock. She said, 'So, how can I help you?'

'We wondered if you remember the accident that happened outside about a year ago,' said Ellen. 'Little boy called Peter Hodgson got knocked over. Think it was June.'

Joe gaped at her and she murmured, 'I did a bit of research this morning. Saw one of Jan's neighbours at the shop and she remembered the kid's name.'

'Oh, yes, I do remember that very well,' said Mrs Oldroyd. 'Awful, that was. In fact, I saw the whole thing. Not him actually being knocked over, but everything after that. I was in the kitchen and heard all the commotion.'

'And what time was this?' said Joe, taking notes.

'Let me see... must have been about a quarter to eight, because I was watching Coronation Street and the adverts had come on, and I always like to make a cup of tea when the adverts are on.' She smiled. 'They are daft, some of those adverts, aren't they? Oh, he really gets on my nerves. That man with the turkey. Bootiful.'

'A quarter to eight,' said Joe. 'And what did you hear?'

'Well, all this commotion, like I said,' Mrs Oldroyd said. 'There was this car stopped on the road and the driver and a lady had got out and if I stood on my tiptoes I could see the little laddie in the road. Then a couple of other people turned up, I don't know where from, maybe from the club or the houses. There was quite a crowd by the time the man came to take him away.'

'Was it an ambulance?' said Ellen.

Mrs Oldroyd frowned. 'No-o-o, I don't think there was an ambulance. Doreen, who lives down by the chemists, you know, she told me later that the little kiddie was at death's door, so I don't suppose there'd have been any call for an ambulance.'

Joe and Ellen looked at each other. He said, 'I'd have thought that was exactly when you'd need an ambulance.'

'You said a man took him,' said Ellen. 'Did he take him to hospital?'

'Well, I wouldn't have thought so. Like I said, the little mite was practically dead.' Mrs Oldroyd smiled. 'You see, when something like that happens, it's a gift really, isn't it? I mean, it's not very nice, of course, but it's too good an opportunity to pass up.'

Joe glanced at Ellen, who was frowning as hard as he was. He said, 'An opportunity? I'm not sure I—'

'It's quite simple, lovey,' she said. 'If it wasn't that poor kiddie, it would have to have been another one. Someone else's little boy or girl.'

'Mrs Oldroyd,' said Ellen slowly. 'Did you know the man who took Peter away?'

She sniffed a little. 'I wouldn't say *know* him. He's not the sort I'd associate with. But I knew who he was. *What* he was. I don't suppose it's his fault. It's like that old saying, it's a dirty job but someone's got to do it.'

'You know his name, though?' said Joe softly.

'Well, I should think so,' said Mrs Oldroyd. 'It was that Johnny Crowe, wasn't it?'

Joe and Ellen sat on the low wall beside the chip shop, reviewing the notes Joe had made. Their legs were touching and Joe tried to ignore it and the funny feeling it gave him in his stomach. He said, 'What do you think she meant when she said she knew *what* he was?'

'I don't know what to make of any of it,' said Ellen. 'But that's two people now who've said the name Johnny Crowe.' She looked at him. 'What are we going to do, Joe?'

'*What are we going to do, Joe?*' They both looked sharply at the voice mimicking Ellen. It was Daz Twist, and he did not look happy. 'Still on the rag? Or feeling better?'

'None of your business,' said Ellen, looking away.

Daz turned his attention to Joe. 'Didn't take you long to make a move,' he said, seething. 'You'll regret this, Collier. Snake in the grass.' He looked back at Ellen. 'Julie and Jan are not happy with you, either, so I'd watch your step. Both of you.'

As Daz stormed off, Joe looked at Ellen, who shrugged. 'It's not like I was actually going out with him or anything. He's just pissed off he didn't get to feel me up on the back row. I don't even like him. I'm done with going out with boys I don't like.'

'Julie and Jan though…'

Ellen shrugged again, and looked away at Daz's retreating back. 'Maybe that's something else I'm done with, as well.'

'So…' said Joe. 'What *are* we going to do?'

'I've got an idea,' said Ellen, standing up off the wall. 'Meet me outside the Working Men's Club tonight. Eight?'

'It's a date,' said Joe, then he groaned and wished he could reel the words back in. But Ellen didn't seem to mind.

'See you later,' she said.

14

Another morning dawned and Scratch Moss pit was still closed, and Terry Collier didn't know what to do with himself. After the big row with Mary when he let Harry Doyle talk him into drinking himself insensible in the Black Diamond, Terry had buckled down, heading off to the Jobcentre and even starting a few of the odd jobs around the house that he'd always promised her he'd get round to when he had time.

Well, he had time now, and lots of it. He'd been up since the crack of dawn, grouting tiles in the kitchen. He was handy enough, and reflected that maybe he could pick up a bit of work with a builder, or even set himself up in business. He'd need money for that, though. Tools and a van. The Cortina Estate was on its last legs. Maybe a job first, if he could find one, to build up some cash.

Terry suddenly felt the energy seep out of him. His shoulders slumped, the trowel dangling from his slack fingers. What was he going to do? How was he going to look after his family? By the time Mary got up and came into the kitchen, unnoticed by him, Terry was gently sobbing.

Wordlessly, she took him in her arms and hugged him. He spluttered out a formless apology but she stood on her tiptoes and kissed him. 'We'll work it out,' she said softly. 'We'll do what we need to. Tighten our belts and cut our cloth. Something will turn up.'

Would it, though? He didn't have as much confidence as she did. He'd worked down that pit for twenty-five years, and thought he'd have twenty-five more in him. It was all he knew. All he could do.

'Have you spoken to your dad?' said Mary suddenly. 'About the pit? He might not even know.'

'I was thinking of going over,' said Terry. 'Not seen him for a couple of weeks. Do you want to come?'

Mary wrinkled her nose. 'Do you mind if I don't? I'm not sure I'm in the right frame of mind for that hospice today, with everything that's going on. It would just upset me, seeing your dad like that, and I don't want to cry in front of him.'

'Think I should take Joe?' said Terry, washing the grout off his hands.

'I'd leave him in bed,' said Mary. 'We'll all go over and see Arthur in a week or two, yes, when things have calmed down a bit? But I think it would do you good to go over and talk to him on your own.'

'Was he out late last night? I didn't hear him come in. Is he knocking about with Carol Dowd's lass?'

'Ellen,' said Mary.

'He's growing up fast.'

'Not fast enough,' sighed Mary.

—

It was a half-hour drive to the hospice. Whenever Terry left Scratch Moss, which wasn't often, he always felt a strange sense of being where he wasn't supposed to be. Or perhaps, not being where he was meant to be. As he passed through the couple of miles of open fields between Scratch Moss and the edges of the next community, he thought that everywhere else looked the same as Scratch Moss, the same red-brick houses, the same fields, the same shops and schools and people. But they weren't the same as Scratch Moss. Nowhere was the same as Scratch Moss.

The hospice was housed in an old, blackened stone hospital building, set back from the road behind a row of trees. It had broad gardens, and in the sunshine he saw some of the patients sitting on chairs and loungers, the blue-uniformed nurses moving among them. At the reception desk he announced himself and said he was there to visit Arthur Collier.

'How is he?' said Terry as the young man led him to the lift to go up to the third floor.

'Comfortable,' said the nurse. That could mean any number of things, thought Terry. They normally said that about people who were just about to die. Which, being in a hospice, Arthur Collier was. Mary said they'd all come to see him in a week or two. Maybe that would be too late.

Terry's confidence in his dad's longevity wasn't improved when he was shown into his room. Arthur lay on the bed, a mask over his face, the oxygen tanks hissing and whirring by his bed. He looked pale and thin, thinner than he had when Terry was last here, and his eyes were dull and dark.

'Dad,' said Terry, putting the box of Maltesers he'd picked up from the petrol station on his bedside table. He sat down on a plastic chair by the bed. 'How are you?'

Arthur pulled the mask down under his chin. 'Shite,' he wheezed in his thick Glasgow accent. 'But all the better for seeing your ugly mug. Come here and give us a hug.'

Terry's dad had been known in Scratch Moss as Scotch Arthur ever since he'd arrived forty years ago. He was a novelty not just for being Scottish, but for coming to live in Scratch Moss. People rarely did that, even when the mine was booming and the coal was in demand across the world. People rarely left, and people didn't often come. And yet, Arthur Collier had. Terry gave him a cautious squeeze, feeling the frailty of his bones and his paper-thin skin beneath his touch, and sat down again.

Arthur put the mask back over his mouth, took three deep breaths, and removed it again. 'How's Mary? And Joe?' Just those four words seemed to take it out of him and he sucked at the oxygen again through the mask.

'Fine,' said Terry. 'As well as can be expected.' He leaned forward. 'They closed the pit, Dad.'

Arthur nodded. 'Saw it on the news. Fucking disgrace. That pit was as profitable as they come.' He stared at Terry for a moment. 'Scratch Moss men never had any fight in them.'

Terry took a deep breath, trying not to rise to the bait. He hadn't come here for a row. He said evenly, 'We fought, Dad. We fought like bloody hell. But it wasn't enough. It didn't save Scratch Moss and it won't save the rest of the pits. I just wish we weren't one of the first to be closed.'

'It was always going to be the case. Get Scratch Moss off the books. Then nobody has to ever think about the damned place ever again.'

Terry looked out of the window, at the lawned gardens. Perhaps it was being here, away from home, where people were dying but having *good* deaths, that made him think his dad was right. Scratch Moss was a damned place. A literally damned place.

As if reading his mind, his dad wheezed, 'If it had been up to me, I'd have taken your mother away from there as soon as I found out she was pregnant. I tried to. But she'd not have it. Not leave Scratch Moss. You'd have grown up somewhere else. You'd have never heard of it.' He sank back into his pillows. 'God knows, I wish I'd persuaded her.'

Half of Terry wished that had happened, that he'd grown up in Glasgow or Birmingham or anywhere but Scratch Moss. But then he'd never have met Mary, and never have had Joe.

'Why do we live like this?' he said, almost to himself. He looked at his dad. 'Why have we always lived like this?'

His dad chuckled, then lapsed into a coughing fit. When he recovered he said, 'Might as well ask yourself why you stood on a picket line and fought tooth and nail for the right to do a job that would have ended up with you like this. Dying in a bed, unable to catch your breath, lungs riddled with emphysema.'

'It's all we know.' Terry shrugged. 'It's our way of life.'

'Same answer, then,' said his dad. 'Scratch Moss isn't like other places. What happens there isn't *normal*. But it's all anybody ever knew. It's the way of life. And it was a good way of life for a long, long time. Provided you didn't think too much about the price, or who exacted it.' Arthur coughed again. 'Never underestimate the ability of even good men to look away from bad things when their livelihoods are under threat.'

Terry looked around. It felt wrong talking about Scratch Moss, about *that*, in this place. Like someone might hear. Like the dirty little secret might get out. 'But what happens now? The pit is shut. The way of life is gone. Does that mean it's all over?'

Arthur didn't answer, but instead leaned over, with great effort, and opened the drawer in the bedside cabinet. He took out a long white envelope and laid it on the bed, gasping for breath from the exertion. When his breathing slowed enough, he said, 'What are you going to do? For work?'

'I'm looking,' said Terry. 'There's not a lot about. I've got to sign on the dole while I'm job hunting.' Suddenly he felt tears prick his eyes. 'Jesus, Dad. The *dole*. I've never not worked for a living since I was fourteen.'

'How long have you got left on that mortgage?'

'Five years,' said Terry. Interest rates were above eleven percent, which was nothing compared to the seventeen percent when Thatcher came in, but they'd been creeping up again the last couple of years. Another big hike and the Colliers were sunk, and a lot of families with them.

Arthur handed over the envelope with a shaking hand. 'I've had a bit put away. It should help you out.'

Terry opened the envelope and his eyes widened. 'Dad. This is a lot of money.'

'It'd come to you anyway when I'm gone. Which won't be long. But you might as well have it now, while you need it.'

Terry stared at the cheque. That could actually pay off the mortgage, and there'd be enough left over maybe even to set himself up in business. And Joe could have that bloody games box thing for Christmas. 'Dad. I don't know what to say.'

'Say thank you, and bugger off to pay it in before the banks close for the day.'

Terry gave his dad another hug. 'Thank you. I can't wait to tell Mary. We'll all come and visit next week.'

As he got to the door, his dad waved at him and pulled his mask down again. 'You asked me if it was all over now that the pit was shut.'

Terry nodded. Arthur went on, 'If I were you, I'd use that money to get out of Scratch Moss. Because it's not over. The coal's gone, and the prosperity it brought, but the piper still wants paying. It'll never be over. Only now, it'll seem a lot worse.'

That was exactly what Mary had said. 'That doesn't seem fair.'

'Life's not fair, lad,' said Arthur. 'But think on this: just because something's always been done one way, because it's a way of life, because people don't know any other way… that doesn't mean things can't be different. It just needs somebody with a bit of bravery to make them different. It needs a Scratch Moss man to stand up and fight for a change.'

—

Terry stopped at the first bank he passed and paid the cheque in, not allowing himself to believe it was even real until the cashier gave him the receipt. He wouldn't really believe it until it cleared into his account in the next three days, but he couldn't wait until then to tell Mary. He'd been crying in the kitchen this morning. Now he was going home with good news. That new song came on the radio again, the one that seemed to be on twice an hour. Dire Straits, 'Money for Nothing'. It's not for nothing, though, is it, he told himself. Your dad's dying. But Arthur had been dying for three years now. Nothing was going to change that. This money, though. It could change everything.

When Terry got home he dashed in through the back yard, finding Mary pacing up and down in the dining room. 'You'll never guess—'

'Terry, where have you been?' she said, exasperatedly.

'To see dad. But you'll never—' He paused. Mary had been crying. 'What's up?' Whatever it was, he was sure the receipt in his pocket would make it right.

He was wrong.

'It's Joe,' she said hoarsely. 'It got to mid-day and I went to get him up. His room was empty. His bed wasn't slept in last night. Terry, Joe's gone missing.'

PART THREE

1945

15

'You're Scotch,' said the girl who signed him into his room at the Black Diamond pub. It wasn't the most salubrious lodgings he'd stayed in, but neither was Scratch Moss the nicest place he'd ever visited. Even for a mining village, there was something about it, something he couldn't quite put his finger on.

This lassie, on the other hand, she was a pretty little piece indeed. 'Scottish,' Arthur gently corrected her. 'Scotch is a drink. And I hope you have a few bottles behind the bar.' He took in her slightly faded tea-dress and her wavy curls. 'To whom do I have the pleasure?'

She giggled. 'I'm Nora. My dad runs the pub. How long will you be staying with us?'

'Two weeks or so,' said Arthur, taking the key when Nora offered it to him.

'Business, or pleasure?' Her eyes twinkled when she said it. 'Not that anyone comes to Scratch Moss for a holiday, so I expect business.'

'Aye.' Arthur nodded, hefting his case towards the stairs. 'Business at the pit. Hope to see you around, Nora.'

The room was small, but he'd endured more cramped quarters over the past five years. It was not yet five in the afternoon, but the view from his window offered a darkened vista of a cobbled main road lined with red-brick terraces, each home pumping thick black smoke from its chimney. They said Scratch Moss coal was the best in Britain, and it had certainly contributed to the war effort well enough. Arthur was here to see that it continued to play its part in Britain thriving now that the war was over and won.

At seven o'clock he took a dinner of lamb chops, potatoes and peas in the main bar of the pub, there being no separate dining room. It was a sumptuous plate of delicious food, which surprised Arthur a little, given rationing was still in full effect. Even more welcome than the food, though, was the fact that Nora was waiting on him, and he engaged her in pleasant chit-chat. She wanted to know all about him, how old he was (thirty-three), where he was from (Glasgow), whether he was married (no), firing questions at him with innocent enthusiasm. From her Arthur learned that Nora was twenty-seven, had worked in the pub since she left school, her father and mother being the licensees, and although there was no shortage of suitors in Scratch Moss, she remained without a sweetheart or any plans to get one.

'You should get away, see the world,' said Arthur, sipping an agreeable pint of beer. 'There's lots of it, and now that the war is over...'

'Oh, I doubt that,' said Nora, clearing away his plate. 'Nobody ever really leaves Scratch Moss.'

'Well, I daresay plenty of the young men had to leave to fight,' observed Arthur.

'Oh, no,' said Nora. 'Nobody went to war. What we do here is too important. Can I get you another pint, Arthur?'

He nursed his second beer and covertly watched the local men as they came and filled up the main bar and the snug, some of them casting curious glances towards him. He guessed they didn't get many strangers in Scratch Moss. Nora must have been mistaken, or she was particularly dull-witted; surely some of them must have volunteered or been called up. Of course he knew that Ernest Bevin, the Minister of Labour, had set up conscription to the coal mines two years ago, when it became apparent that Britain's coal reserves were being depleted by the war effort faster than it could be dug out. Arthur eyed these so-called Bevin Boys who had stayed behind to work the pits rather than go to war with suspicion and not a little disdain. Dirty work it might be and dangerous to boot, but not so perilous as facing German machine guns, he warranted. His right leg pulsed with sudden pain, almost as a reminder that he had done his duty in that regard, and had the shrapnel still in his thigh to prove it.

As he was finishing his beer, Nora walked through the bar holding the hand of a small child, a girl no more than four or five. She caught him looking and laughed. 'She's not mine. This is Elsa. Say hello to Arthur, Elsa.' The child burbled something in his direction. Nora dropped her voice low. 'She's my cousin's. Or was, I should say. Mabel died of polio last year. Elsa lives with us, now.'

The child stared at Arthur, then hid behind Nora's skirt. He felt in his jacket pocket and pulled out a new, unused pencil. 'Would you like this, Elsa?' he said. 'Perhaps you can draw something, or practise your letters.' Elsa nodded shyly, and Arthur handed it over. In a stage whisper he said, 'Property of the Coal Commission, so keep it under your hat.' He winked at her, and smiled at Nora, who was looking at him with a beaming grin.

Arthur announced he was retiring, as he had an early appointment with Lord Brody at nine o'clock sharp. Nora said that if he needed an early wake-up call, her room was next door to his, so she could knock him up for breakfast.

'I'm sure I'll manage,' said Arthur, feeling somewhat discombobulated, though unsure exactly why. 'But thank you.'

In the room he washed from the jug and bowl, and changed into his pyjamas, and lay on the hard mattress, listening to the sounds of the pub below until the landlord ran last orders for ten o'clock, and the clientele began to drift away. Half an hour later he heard movement in the next room, then the creak of bedsprings as, he surmised, Nora got into her bed. Arthur thought about her until he dropped off to sleep.

Scratch Moss Hall was a grand country house in the Palladian style, built on money – Arthur guessed – earned on the backs of slaves in the plantations of the West Indies in the 18th Century. A painting of the house made a century before showed it in grand isolation amid the rolling fields; a couple of decades later the Brody family had shifted their interests from cotton to coal, and now, sitting in the vast, wood-panelled drawing room, Arthur could see from the huge windows the winding gear of the Scratch Moss pit in the hall's grounds.

A servant brought tea while Arthur waited for Lord Brody, who emerged half an hour late for their appointment, apologising profusely. He was about Arthur's age, clad in an expensively cut suit and with a clipped moustache on chiselled features. 'Mr Collier,' said Lord Brody warmly. 'Do forgive my tardiness.' He sat on the couch opposite Arthur, and helped himself to tea. 'Collier. Rather a fitting name for a chap who works in coal.'

'A common name,' said Arthur, somewhat gruffly. Lord Brody had the air of a playboy about him. 'Mere coincidence. And I have only worked in coal since coming out of the army. Prior to the war I was a policeman.'

Lord Brody chuckled. 'Then I see I shall have to watch my step. And please, call me Walter. Lord Brody is so dashed formal. It's only a baronetcy, when all's said and done. I daresay I'll find it useful when I get to such a creaking, venerable age that I decide to spend my afternoons snoozing in the House of Lords.'

Arthur harrumphed. 'I think best to keep things on a formal footing, Lord Brody.'

Lord Brody shrugged. 'So, down to business then. You are here to take Scratch Moss pit away from me.'

'Not quite like that, Lord Brody,' said Arthur. 'As you have already been informed, the Coal Commission will next year, if Parliament allows, begin a process of taking all coal production facilities over a certain size into public ownership. The plan is to form a National Coal Board to oversee Britain's future coal provision.'

'All sounds dashed socialist.' Lord Brody sniffed. 'Scratch Moss pit was started by my great grandfather eighty years ago. I rather think he anticipated it would be in the family forever.'

'Things change, Lord Brody. The war taught us that. And with Mr Attlee's new Labour government in charge... well. We have to look to the future.'

'You have visited other mining operations?' said Lord Brody, standing and walking to the window to look out on the distant pit.

'Scratch Moss is my third,' said Arthur. 'I have another half-dozen to inspect by the end of the year. Needless to say, just as you were when the Coal Commission commandeered coal production at the start of the war, your family will be rather generously compensated for the putting of the mine into public ownership.'

'It's the men I worry about, Mr Collier,' mused Lord Brody. 'We treat our workers very well at Scratch Moss. What guarantees will there be that will continue?'

'There will be standardisation of pay and conditions under the new National Coal Board,' said Arthur. 'That will take some time, and the concerns are understandable. But it is anticipated that workers will be, by and large, better off.'

Even as he spoke, Arthur wondered if his well-rehearsed spiel was true, in the case of Scratch Moss. From what he'd seen so far it was a bit of an odd place. On the one hand, it seemed very prosperous indeed, and he wasn't in his heart absolutely certain that the National Coal Board could make that any better. The people seemed healthy and happy and while perhaps not wealthy to Lord Brody's standards, they at least seemed comfortable. On the other... Arthur couldn't quite put his finger on that. But there was *something* about this place he didn't quite understand.

'Hmm.' Lord Brody gazed out of the window, seemingly lost in thought. Arthur stood and joined him, and the other man turned and noticed his limp. 'You are injured?'

'I took some shrapnel at Gold Beach,' said Arthur, rubbing his thigh. He looked pointedly at Lord Brody. 'That was at Normandy. D-Day.'

'Yes, I am aware,' said Lord Brody. 'How awful for you.'

'Not as awful for my mate who was at the side of me,' said Arthur flatly. 'He got his head blown off.'

'Hmm,' said Lord Brody again, and turned back to the window.

'Did you serve?' said Arthur, perhaps more viciously than he intended. And this certainly wasn't in the Coal Commission script.

'No, I'm afraid not.' Lord Brody smiled.

'I was told no Scratch Moss man was called up. I can't believe that can be right.'

'Oh, it is, Mr Collier,' said Arthur. 'Reserved occupation and all that. Got to keep the wheels of industry – and war – turning. Scratch Moss coal played its part.'

'Bevin only introduced mine conscription in forty-three,' pushed Arthur. 'And in the four years before that...? Not one man volunteered, or was drafted?'

Lord Brody turned to him, smiling broadly. 'What can I say? We are somewhat blessed in Scratch Moss, Mr Collier. We live under a lucky star.'

Cowards, more like, thought Arthur. Lord Brody went on, 'So, what's say I get us some more tea and you can tell me more about this compensation, and what you require from us?'

—

After Arthur had outlined the Coal Commission's plans in more detail, Lord Brody handed him over to a phalanx of employees responsible for the direct running of the mine, managers and supervisors and foremen, with outdated titles and a structure that would have to be thoroughly brought into the nationalised system. Arthur said he would require all the accounts going back at least a decade, and plans of the current tunnel system, as well as the number of workers, the accident record, and any other documentation they had. He was installed in a library with a wide desk, and a procession of servants brought ledgers, files, books and stacks of papers to him.

Arthur caught the sleeve of one of the managers, a rotund chap by the name of Clarke. 'I shall also need to see the pit in operation. I like to do it twice, once when the men are working, but also once when it is in-operational. Let's see… it's Friday today. We could get down there on Sunday, when you're not working?'

'We works the pit Sundays,' said Clarke.

Arthur gaped at him. 'You work the Sabbath?'

Clarke shrugged. 'We tends to have Saturdays off.'

'But what about church?'

He smiled crookedly. 'No church in Scratch Moss. At least, not the sort you mean. I'll arrange for one of the lads to take you down tomorrow, then.'

No church in Scratch Moss, ruminated Arthur as he got down to inspecting the accounts ledgers. He had been brought up Presbyterian, but had lapsed himself in recent years. Watching your mates killed around you tended to send you one of two ways: into the arms of God or questioning why He allows such things to happen. Arthur dithered somewhere in the middle. But he was surprised that a working community the size of Scratch Moss didn't have several churches, let alone one.

A servant brought him sandwiches and a glass of beer, and he broke for lunch, walking around the library and inspecting the spines of the books. He guessed Lord Brody wasn't much of a reader, given the patina of dust on the books ranked on the higher shelves. He glanced at his pocket watch and decided he would do another hour. He fancied a walk around Scratch

Moss, get a feel for the community and the people. He was curious about them. This place was unlike anywhere else he'd been.

Arthur was just sitting down when there was a rapping at the door and a young man of about twenty, face blackened with coal dust and wringing his cap in his hands, stepped in.

'Mr Clarke sent me, sir,' said the chap. 'He's the foreman, like. Said I was to make arrangements to take you down the mine tomorrow, sir.'

'Excellent,' said Arthur. 'I'd need a good few hours down there, I'm afraid. Can you arrange for all the equipment? I'll make sure you're properly compensated.'

'I can do all that, sir. And it's no bother.'

Arthur nodded. 'Very good. Shall we say ten? I'll meet you at the pit.' The boy turned to go and Arthur said, 'Wait, what's your name, lad?'

'John,' he said, pausing at the door. 'Most folk call me Johnny, sir. Johnny Crowe.'

16

Arthur decided to spend the rest of the afternoon wandering around Scratch Moss. The doctors had said the best thing for his leg was exercise, and the more he did, the less it would hurt, after a while. They'd taken out as much of the shrapnel as they could, but there were still tiny pieces in there, a constant reminder of D-Day. Arthur wore his pain like a medal. He was proud to have landed on Gold Beach, proud to have survived when so many didn't. Proud to have done his duty.

It was a warm day for September, the sun doing its best to penetrate the haze of coal-smoke that hung over the community. From what he'd seen so far in the books, it seemed like every male in Scratch Moss worked at the pit. Over the course of the war, the Brodys had been running three eight-hour shifts a day, the pit operating round the clock. Now it was down to two again, but the reports suggested that the coal beneath the ground was both plentiful and extremely high quality. Lord Brody had been right when he said Scratch Moss was blessed, but not for the reasons he meant. Whatever geological factors had conspired to create the conditions for the coal under Scratch Moss, they were damn near perfect. It was little wonder he was reluctant to give it up, even for the generous compensation the government was paying.

Arthur counted five pubs, including the Black Diamond, and a parade of shops. Rationing was still in full effect but the shelves looked groaning with produce. He stopped outside the greengrocer's, marvelling at the bananas. The shopkeeper saw him looking and smiled from the doorway. 'Lord Brody's influence. We have a good life in Scratch Moss.'

Indeed they did. Despite the back-breaking toil of mine-work, the populace seemed healthy and content. Arthur almost felt a stab of guilt that he was here to facilitate change. Scratch Moss almost felt like an idyll that should not be tampered with, that should be left to its own devices.

As he started to move on, he almost bumped straight into Nora, carrying a basket laden with shopping. 'Scotch Arthur!' she exclaimed.

'It's Scotti—' he began and she laughed, and laid a hand on his arm.

'I know, I'm only joshing with you. Did you enjoy your visit to Scratch Moss Hall?'

'Well, it wasn't pleasure, Nora. I'm here to do a job.'

She tutted. 'But you must get some time off, surely.'

'Indeed,' agreed Arthur. He looked at Nora, in her dress, her bare feet in ballet pumps. 'Would you agree to let me buy you dinner? Do any of the other pubs serve food?'

'Not as good as ours,' said Nora. She tapped her chin with a painted nail thoughtfully. 'It's a lovely day. How about a picnic? I'll make some sandwiches and get a nice pie. Couple of bottles of beer from behind the bar. Shall we say in an hour? Meet me in the snug.'

—

'We call it the Little Woods,' said Nora.

'Original,' answered Arthur mildly. She slapped him playfully on the arm. They had walked along the main road from the Black Diamond in the teatime sun, and Nora had led him into a thicket of trees just beyond the railway track that ran from the mine to a branch line, over a bridge crossing the road. Beyond the treeline he could see the grey spire of a church.

Nora led him to a sun-dappled clearing and laid down the tartan blanket. 'Brought this to make you feel at home.'

'Och, aye,' he said, and she clapped, then laid out the beer and sandwiches.

'Bought you a banana as well, for pudding.'

'Not seen one for years before I came here,' said Arthur admiringly. 'Didn't expect to for a long time.'

They ate and chatted and Arthur tried not to look at Nora's long, brown legs as her tea-dress rode up over her thighs. She said airily, 'So, when you are not poring over dull old books full of facts and figures about coal mines, do you have a sweetheart at home?'

'No,' said Arthur curtly, then surprised himself by continuing, because he wasn't usually one to talk about his private life. 'I did have. I expected we'd get married after the war. But when I came home after Normandy... well. She'd taken up with someone else.' He looked away. 'Dockworker. Reserved occupation.' The words almost curdled on his lips.

'Ah,' said Nora. 'So that's why you're none too fond of Scratch Moss. Think we were just living it up while you were risking your life for King and Country.'

Arthur said nothing, and drank his beer. That was exactly what he thought, but he didn't want to sour the mood. He looked around and pointed his beer bottle at the tip of the church spire, just visible. 'Your Lord Brody said that the pits work on Sundays, and that there was no church in Scratch Moss. What's that, then?'

'The old church,' said Nora. 'Not been properly open for, gosh, forty years, I expect.' Somewhat obviously changing the subject, she said, 'So what does tomorrow hold? More ledgers and accounts? Or are you taking Saturday off?'

'Down the mine, while it's closed for the day,' said Arthur. 'I'm getting a tour of the working tunnels.' Something flapped and cried raucously to his left, startling him. At the sight of the magpie flying into the upper branches of the trees he saluted, and said, 'How's your wife, sir, and I hope your chicks are healthy.'

Nora burst out laughing. 'Why did you say that?'

Arthur gave her an amused frown. 'You've never heard that? One for sorrow, you see. It wards off the bad luck.'

'Bad luck!' exclaimed Nora, laughing again. 'Sorrow! Magpies? I've never heard the like. Magpies don't bring bad luck or sorrow!'

'Surely you've heard the rhyme,' said Arthur, counting off on his fingers. 'I thought everyone knew it, everywhere. One for sorrow, two for joy, three for a girl, four for a boy. Five for silver, six for gold. Seven for a secret, never to be told.'

She shook her head in wonder. 'No, I've never heard that in my life. Magpies are revered in Scratch Moss. We'd never say they bring misfortune.'

'I'm sure the farmers round here would disagree,' said Arthur. 'Revered? In what sense?'

'Come with me,' said Nora, packing into the basket the remains of their picnic.

—

Arthur crouched down by the headstone of the grave in the cemetery, running his fingertips over the carving of a magpie. Every stone had one, some more ornate than others. Sometimes the magpie was in flight, others perched on a branch. Some of the larger monuments had statues of magpies on them. He stood up and looked around at the tall trees bordering the graveyard; he could see the telltale signs of deep nests and spot the corvids resting on the swaying branches.

'I've never seen the like,' he said. 'It must be a highly local tradition.'

'It must,' agreed Nora. 'Certainly for as long as anyone can remember.'

Arthur looked around the cemetery again. 'No crucifixes, no words of Scripture engraved on any of the headstones. Just magpies.'

'Just magpies.' Nora glanced at her wristwatch. 'I should get back. I'm working in the pub this evening. Friday night is always a busy one. You'll have a drink in the bar?'

'I will,' said Arthur. 'I'll walk back with you. Thank you for the lovely picnic.'

As they left the graveyard and turned on to the road, the ratcheting cries of the magpies rose up in a cawing chorus behind them.

—

Arthur was a few minutes late meeting Johnny Crowe at the pit on Saturday morning, which put him in bad humour. He never liked to be late for anything. But he had stayed up later than he had meant to, drinking beer at the bar while Nora served, and had a thick head to boot. Johnny Crowe didn't seem to notice or mind, though. He had already got a pair of lamps from the lamp room and supplied Arthur with a helmet before ushering him into the cage, suspended over the deep, black shaft by the headstocks of the large winding wheel far above them.

Arthur had no great dislike for the depths of the mines, but no love of them either. He preferred to be where he could see the sky and feel the breeze. The cage rattled and jerked as it descended, presumably operated by a crew up above that had been brought in for the morning. It seemed to go down for a long, long time. Arthur looked at Crowe, his face painted a sickly yellow by the lamplight. 'How long have you worked the mines?'

Crowe shrugged. 'Since I were twelve, or something like that. Had no use for schooling after that. Not when there's coal to be dug.'

Eventually the cage ground to a halt with a shrieking of the cables that held them tight, and Crowe flung open the doors. Arthur took off his jacket and folded it over his arm; it was already almost unbearably hot down here. He started off by inspecting the timber pit props; they all seemed in good order and well maintained. When he'd finished making copious notes, sweat beading his brow, he nodded at Crowe, who had been impassively watching him the whole time.

'I'll take you inbye,' said the lad. Over the past year or so Arthur had got to know the jargon of the pits. Inbye meant away from the shaft and towards the coalface. There he'd see where the hewers had been loosening the coal with picks, loading into the tubs that were driven along the rails to the lift. It always felt eerie when he came down here while the men weren't working, but it helped Arthur get a sense of the scale and scope of a mine without the noise and clamour. He'd see that in the next few days, and get to talk to some of the men in confidence about their working conditions.

Arthur had a copy of the map of the various tunnels and faces, and instructed Crowe to take him along all of them. The Scratch Moss coalfield was vast, he realised. The coal glittered and sparkled in the walls. He was glad for Crowe's presence; even with the map, he was sure he'd be lost in these labyrinthine tunnels. On a whim, Arthur put out a hand to the coalface. It felt warm, and something else; it thrummed, no, more than that. It pulsed, as though he was taking the heartbeat of the earth, deep down and black. He'd never felt that before in any of the mines he'd visited. Never felt anything other than being beneath the ground, where back-breaking toil occurred. Some geological peculiarity, perhaps? Maybe even an underground watercourse? They were what his rational mind came up with. Down in the dark and the heat the voice of his rational mind seemed plaintive and desperate. Arthur Collier wasn't a man given to fancy, but he felt suddenly unnerved, and nodded for Crowe to move on. They had almost got to the end of the tunnel when Arthur noticed, down a slope off to his right, a boarded-up passageway. 'What's that?'

Crowe shrugged in the lamplight. 'Dead tunnel. Might have been a collapse at some point. Don't know.'

Arthur checked the plans. There was nothing indicating a tunnel, dead or otherwise, off the main road here. His foot nudged something and he bent down, holding his lamp near it. It was a corn dolly, half a foot tall. He surmised some miner had dropped it, perhaps a gift from his child, when he noticed another, a couple of feet away. And another. Squinting into the black, he saw a dozen, two dozen. Some evidently newly made, others old, almost falling apart. He looked at Crowe, who shrugged.

'You must know what this is all about, man!' said Arthur, hot and exasperated.

'Just something the men do,' muttered Crowe. 'Them as has children.'

Arthur felt doubly unnerved though he couldn't have said why. He'd seen enough, he reckoned, and instructed Crowe to take them outbye to the lift shaft. As the cage juddered and clanked on its ascent, Arthur felt he could breathe again, and was never so glad as to see the September afternoon sun over the mine site.

After he'd washed the coal dust off his face and cooled down a little, he pushed a few shillings in Crowe's hands. 'I'll get something in my wages for taking you down, sir,' he protested. Arthur waved him away and made him pocket the coins.

He was planning to go back to Scratch Moss Hall to do more work on the books, but his shirt was dripping and plastered to his back. He'd have to go back to the pub to change. He pointed towards the copse of trees where he'd picnicked with Nora earlier, at the edge of the site. 'Can I get back to the main road that way? Along the rail track.'

Crowe nodded and Arthur set off, drinking in the clear, fresh air. Of all the pits he'd been down, he'd never known one like Scratch Moss pit. Not just the bountiful, high-quality coal. But the feeling he had down there, the sense of being so deep, down so far. The darkness was thick and absolute, even in the lamplight. And the way the walls seemed to pulse, as though a living, breathing thing.

He cut through the woods, watching a magpie high in the trees, watching him. He saluted anyway, even though they didn't do that in Scratch Moss. Then something caught his eye on the path. He bent down to pick it up. It was his pencil, the one he had given to little Elsa. She must have been brought to the woods that morning, probably by Nora, and dropped it. He pocketed it. He would give it back to her when he got to the pub.

As he veered off on a rough path that led down from the bridge to the main road, he noticed people on the road, singly and in pairs, all heading the same way. In the direction of the spire.

Arthur knew he should get back to the Black Diamond, wash up and put on a fresh shirt, and get back to his work. But curiosity got the better of him, and he turned right on the road, towards the old church.

17

From the road and the shade of the overhanging trees, Arthur watched them go through the open doors of the church. It was a small but grand old building, he thought, looking up at the soot-blackened stone spire. Then he frowned. There was no cross at the zenith. Then he saw that the tall windows along the side of the building were clear, not the usual stained glass depicting Biblical scenes. Forty years, Nora had said, since it had last been a working church. He could scarcely credit that a community the size of Scratch Moss had no resident minister. And if the church was abandoned, why were all these people going in?

The doors had been closed behind the last people to enter, and Arthur didn't feel like disturbing them by opening them again. He stole around the side of the church and was able to pull himself up a foot or so by a rusting metal downpipe, to allow him to surreptitiously peer through the window.

There were perhaps thirty of them, all adults, ranged along the pews, as though at any normal church service. Arthur could even hear what at first he took to be singing, and strained to listen to identify the hymn. But it wasn't any hymn he recognised. It was more like chanting, guttural words he couldn't make out, intoned dully by the swaying congregation. *Shkod moll*, it sounded like. *Doo Preeth*. It wasn't English, that was for sure, nor Latin. It sounded old, earthy. They were saying it, over and over, and then Arthur noticed the altar at the front of the church. No cross stood there, but instead a shape, dark and black and glittering in the sunshine that filtered through the windows. It was a lump of coal, but immense; four feet tall. Of no discernible design, but angular and carved with rough planes. Hewn from the mine, he guessed, and mounted on the altar. What grotesque idolatry was this?

Arthur ducked as those on the front pews stood. He peeped more cautiously through the window as they made their way to the altar. Each of them placed a hand on the coal, head bowed, then placed something beside it at the altar. Corn dollies, a little larger than the ones he had seen in the mine. Straw effigies. As the Scratch Moss people filed up to the coal statue the mound of effigies grew. The chanting rose in volume, and Arthur craned his neck for a better look, as—

'What you doing, mister?'

He yelped at the voice, and lost his footing, scraping down the wall and landing heavily, his bad leg wincing. The boy was no more than five or six, dressed in ragged shorts and a tank-top, staring up at him with curiosity.

'What goes on here, boy?' demanded Arthur.

The child shrugged, and started to pick his nose. He said, 'It's what the mothers and fathers do.'

'But why?'

The boy raised his shoulders again. 'To keep us safe from Red Clogs.'

Arthur was about to ask him to explain himself when he heard the doors open at the front of the church, and the boy ran towards the sound without a by-your-leave. Discretion, decided Arthur, was the better part of valour in this instance, and he stole away as quickly as he could. But he would get answers, and he would get them from Nora at the Black Diamond.

—

Arthur burst into the pub, full of questions, but stopped in his tracks. There were half a dozen or so men sat in the snug, all quiet and morosely nursing pints. Nora's father was behind the bar, staring at his hands. Then Arthur heard gentle sobbing, and saw Nora, at the end of the bar, dabbing at her eyes with a handkerchief.

'What's happened?' he said.

Nora's father looked at him. 'Nothing to worry about, sir. Perhaps you should just go to your room. I can have some food sent up if you're hungry.'

'Nora?' said Arthur, addressing her directly.

She looked at him with red-rimmed eyes. 'It's Elsa. She's gone.'

'Nora…' said her father, a note of warning in his voice.

Arthur crossed the snug to Nora. 'Gone? Gone where?'

'Missing,' said Nora quietly. 'My father's right—'

'Since when?' said Arthur. 'You have informed the constabulary? We should get a search party together.'

'It's not how we do things in Scratch Moss,' said the landlord firmly, planting his hands on the bar. 'Now, sir, as I said—'

Arthur gaped at him. 'A child goes missing and you haven't told the police? The station is but two hundred yards up the road! And why are you all sitting here, doing nothing?'

'Please, Arthur,' begged Nora.

'I shall go and offer my services to the police at once,' declared Arthur, turning back to the door. As he did so he remembered and put his hand in the pocket of his jacket. His fingers closed around the pencil. 'Nora,' he called. 'Did you have Elsa out for a walk today?'

She shook her head, and recommenced crying. Arthur looked at the men gathered in the snug. 'I think I know where she is, or at least where she's been. If any of you men wish to accompany me, I am going there now.'

'Mr Collier,' said the landlord forcefully. 'This is not how—'

'Not how you do things in Scratch Moss,' said Arthur, shaking his head in disgust. 'But it's how I do things.'

As much as his leg pained him, Arthur ran all the way down the road and to the Little Woods, retracing his steps to where he had found the pencil. She had been here, but where was she now? He began to call her name, and hurried along the paths beside the railway track, emerging onto the mine site. The pit-head gear was silent and still, and he could see no movement. Arthur dug into his pocket and pulled out the folded, sweat-sodden map of the mine he had carried with him this morning. There was no way, surely, the child could have found her way down the main shaft, with the cage there. But there were other passages on a pit site. *Adits*, tunnels to the surface used for drainage or emergency access. The Scratch Moss pit must have half a dozen at least? He re-orientated the schematic and looked ahead at the winding gear. There was an adit over to the west. Arthur peered into the sun, starting to set, and saw them. Two figures, one tall, one tiny. Elsa.

He tossed the map to one side and set off at a run, gritting his teeth against the pain. They had their backs to him and did not see him running pell-mell along the path as they headed towards a slight hillock, in which he could see a gate as he neared them.

Barely thirty feet away, Arthur yelled Elsa's name, and the girl turned, holding the hand of the man. He turned also, and Arthur, adrenaline pumping in his veins, skidded to a halt. The man was fifty, perhaps, weathered and whiskered, a tweed waistcoat over his shirt.

'Unhand that child,' demanded Arthur, marching towards him.

Elsa smiled broadly as she saw him, and tried to tug her hand away from the man, but he held her firm. Arthur was about to tell him to let go once again, when his words faltered on his lips.

The man was staring at him with eyes as black as midnight, as black as coal. Not just his pupils, but the whole of his eyes, where the white should have been. Black and glittering. Arthur had never seen anything like it, and took an unwilling step back. The man opened his mouth, and hissed at Arthur as a cat might. It was as though he was not quite human. Every nerve in Arthur's body screamed at him to run away.

Just like it had on Gold Beach, as the bullets and shells flew. Just as it had when his mate got his head blown off. And Arthur had ignored every shrieking nerve, and fought on. Just as he would now.

He took a step forward, drew back his arm, and landed a jackhammer blow on the chin of the kidnapper.

—

The Scratch Moss police station was a small affair, barely the size of a terraced house, and the sergeant looked surprised, to say the least, when Arthur marched the half-conscious man in and slammed him face down on the desk.

'Here, I've done your job for you,' said Arthur, breathing heavily. He had walked the man along the road by the scruff of his neck, the Scratch Moss villagers shrinking back from him, with Elsa holding his other hand. 'Arrest this man.'

The policeman nodded at the man. 'William.'

'You know him?' gaped Arthur.

'William Maxwell, gamekeeper up at Scratch Moss Hall,' the sergeant said with a nod.

'Well, arrest him,' said Arthur, a little disconcerted. 'Child abduction. God knows what else.'

The man, William, straightened up and gave Arthur a baleful stare. Baleful, but normal. His eyes were no longer as black as coal, if they had ever been. Perhaps that had been the adrenaline pounding in Arthur's head. The sergeant nodded. 'We'll take it from here, Mr Collier. Thank you for your assistance.'

Word had got round, of course, about Arthur's presence in Scratch Moss. He leaned forward. 'For your information, Sergeant, it used to be Inspector Collier. Just so you know.'

The sergeant touched his forehead with his finger. Arthur wasn't quite sure whether he was being sardonic or not. 'Good to know, sir. And thank you again.'

'Come on, Elsa, let's get you back to your family,' said Arthur, taking the child's hand. He walked her along the main road, ignoring the stares of those who came to their windows or doors to watch. He pushed open the doors and triumphantly marched into the snug.

There was a stunned silence as the clientele, which had doubled since Arthur left, simply stared at him. Then he heard Nora issue a heart-rending sob, and she ran forward, dropping to her knees and embracing Elsa.

'She seems unhurt,' said Arthur. 'But you might want to check.' As Nora wiped her tears away and led Elsa to the stairs, Arthur called them back, and squatted down. 'I have something of yours,' he said, handing over the pencil. 'It's rather a good job you lost it or I might never have found you.'

When they'd gone, Arthur turned to the locals, who were all just staring at him. He addressed the landlord behind the bar. 'I daresay I deserve a pint on the house for that.'

The landlord seemed to think about it, then pulled the drink. 'Mr Collier. I know you think you did the right thing but...'

'I know I did the right thing,' said Arthur. 'What I cannot for the life of me fathom is how you do not. That child is your own flesh and blood.' He turned, meeting the eye of every man there, who watched him silently. 'I cannot fathom anything about this.'

'Things are done differently in Scratch Moss, Mr Collier,' said the landlord behind him.

Arthur shook his head. 'I shall drink this in my room, if you don't object. And I shall take dinner in there, if it's not too much trouble to have it sent up.'

'I think that would be best, Mr Collier,' said the landlord. It was only as Arthur began to ascend the stairs that he heard the snug rumble once more into conversation.

Arthur had just got into his pyjamas after spending the evening brooding until darkness fell about what he was going to do next when there was a knock at his door. He opened it a crack to see Nora. 'Can I come in?' she whispered.

'I'm in my night things,' said Arthur, but he opened the door. She crept in and closed it behind her and sat on his bed.

'You must think us awfully strange,' she said at last. Arthur couldn't find the words to disagree. She patted the bed. 'Sit with me.'

He did, and she turned to him, putting her hands on his arms. 'I want you to know how grateful I am. For bringing Elsa home. I wish I could explain why everyone acted the way they did. But I can't. Just know that I'm so happy.'

'I don't understand this place at all,' confessed Arthur.

'You don't need to understand us. Just do what you have to do, then leave, and never think of us again.'

Arthur said nothing for a moment, then looked at her. 'I doubt I shall never think of you again, Nora.'

Then, to his surprise, she kissed him, hard and fierce, her hands on his face. He felt himself stir in his pyjamas and she pushed him backwards until he was lying down, then began to unbutton her dress.

'Nora—' he began but she put a finger on his lips, shrugged off her dress, then tugged down his pyjama bottoms and straddled him. They both gasped as he entered her, and she rode him quietly and quickly until they both shuddered to a climax, then collapsed on him.

'Do what you need to, then leave Scratch Moss,' she whispered, as sleep began to overtake him. 'Leave while you can.'

'Who's Red Clogs?' was the last thing he remembered saying.

18

The next morning, Arthur went up to Scratch Moss Hall early, not engaging in conversation with the landlord or anyone he met along the way. There had been no sign of Nora when he woke, and he might have thought it all a dream, save for her scent lingering on his skin.

Leave while you can, she had said. Arthur Collier wasn't scared of any man in Scratch Moss, any man at all, but he admitted to feeling on edge as he walked along the high street and up the lane to the house. He had a sensation of being watched from behind net curtains, felt that as he passed people in the street they fell silent, staring at him, then commenced whispering behind his back. In truth, he would be glad to be away from Scratch Moss and forget about the place entirely. Well, not entirely; he would not forget the way Nora kissed him, or how it felt as he penetrated her and she dug her nails into his chest as she moved sensuously above him.

Arthur was shown to the library where he recommenced his study of the accounts and technical notations of the pit's workings since it had been instituted eighty years previously. He lost himself in the data until the door opened and Lord Brody let himself in. 'Might I have a word?'

Arthur put down his pen. 'If you have come to reprimand me for punching your gamekeeper's lights out and delivering him to the police, then don't bother. I was just doing my duty.'

Lord Brody glanced back through the door, as if being cautious he wasn't being observed, and closed it. 'Yes, I heard. Terrible business.' He took a cigarette case from his inside pocket and put one in his mouth before offering it to Arthur, who accepted, then lit both with a match.

'I've been giving what you said some thought,' said Lord Brody, blowing out smoke and perching on the edge of his desk. 'After due consideration, I think I'd like to accept whatever offer is on the table. And as quickly as possible.'

'Well, I still have to complete my report...' said Arthur. He scrutinised Lord Brody. 'Why the change of heart? You were quite resistant to the idea when I first arrived.'

Lord Brody sighed. 'The modern world is coming to Scratch Moss whether we like it or not. And believe me, Collier, there are many who don't like it. I've had representations from the men who do not want any part of this National Coal Board business. I've told them it's not as simple as that, but they don't seem to understand. Or choose not to.'

'But you understand, Lord Brody?'

He nodded. 'The mining business... it was the brainchild of my great grandfather, and has been passed down through the family ever since. But I don't want it, Collier, and this is my perfect opportunity to walk away.'

'Away from Scratch Moss? Your ancestral home?'

Lord Brody gave a mirthless laugh. 'It's the back of beyond, Collier. The arse end of nowhere. There's a whole world out there, and I'm young and rich enough to enjoy it. Have you ever been abroad?'

'Normandy,' said Arthur shortly. 'It wasn't much of a holiday.'

'Well, quite. But I do want to go on holiday, Collier. I want to go to France and Greece and New York. New York! I can go away and forget about all of this.' He waved his hand around. 'Forget Scratch Moss.'

Arthur hesitated, then said, 'It's a peculiar place, right enough. A very peculiar place.'

Lord Brody stubbed out his cigarette in Arthur's empty teacup and lit up another. 'You don't know the half of it. I want out, Collier, and this Coal Commission money can make that happen. The question is, how soon?'

Arthur thought about it, and what Nora had said. 'I would like to finish up as quickly as possible. But I have to do the job properly. Perhaps if I work into the evenings, I can be done in a week. Possibly less.'

Lord Brody nodded. 'As quick as you like, Collier. And if you'd be so good… this talk is strictly chap to chap.' He tapped the side of his nose. 'I don't want the natives getting restless.'

As Lord Brody made to leave, Arthur said, 'I saw something quite odd at the church yesterday. Some kind of… I don't know what you'd call it. Ritual, maybe. I find it quite extraordinary that there hasn't been a proper ministry here for forty years.'

'Not really surprised after what happened to the last fellow,' said Lord Brody. 'Before my time, but by all accounts he climbed the spire in a thunderstorm and was struck by lightning. You should ask my gamekeeper, Maxwell, about it. His father was there, I understand.'

'Well, your gamekeeper is in the cells awaiting an appearance before the magistrates to answer charges of child abduction,' said Arthur, turning back to the books. 'So I doubt he's in any position to talk.'

'Are you sure?' said Lord Brody. 'An hour ago he was up by the woods setting traps for the foxes.'

—

Arthur ran, along the drive in front of Scratch Moss Hall and across the fields and towards the woods that separated the estate from the mine. He ran though pain stabbed through his leg and his lungs burned. He ran until he saw the figure of William Maxwell, leaning on a tree with a spaniel by his side, having a smoke.

Arthur ran straight up to him and hit him again, knocking him to the long grasses. The dog barked and jumped up, and Arthur smacked it hard on the nose. It whimpered and ran behind a tree as Maxwell slowly began to pick himself up off the ground.

'I'd stay there or I'll just knock you down again,' said Arthur, his fists up. 'What are you doing out of police custody?'

Maxwell squinted up at him, shielding his eyes from the sun behind Arthur. 'They let me go about half an hour after you dropped me off.'

'Get up,' demanded Arthur.

'So you can hit me again?'

Arthur leaned forward and grabbed the front of Maxwell's shirt, hauling him to his feet. 'What did you tell them? Did you deny everything? Are you on bail? Aren't they putting you up before the magistrate?' He glared into the man's eyes. Normal eyes. Nothing there but fear. Certainly no glittering black depths.

'It isn't my fault,' Maxwell whined. 'It isn't me.'

'Who was it then,' said Arthur, brandishing his fist. 'Your twin brother?'

'I mean, it's not *me* that does it. It's what's *inside* of me.'

Arthur let him go and pushed him away from him in disgust. 'Then maybe you need a doctor, not a prison cell.'

'I'm not mad,' said Maxwell, and this time his eyes were full of tears. 'I never asked for this. But it has to be somebody, and since my daddy died, it's me.'

Arthur threw his hands in the air, and Maxwell flinched. 'You're talking in riddles, man. Did you snatch that poor little girl, or not? If you're not mad, then I'm starting to think I am.'

'I can't remember,' sobbed Maxwell snottily. 'I can never remember. But I know I did it. Every time.'

Arthur gaped at him. 'Every time? How many times have you done this? And what happens when you get caught?'

'I never get caught,' said Maxwell. 'Because nobody tries. It's the way it is, you see. The way it's always been. That's why they let me go. Because somebody has to be the one.'

Arthur felt lightheaded. He couldn't quite believe he was having this conversation. 'Be the one?'

'The one who carries *him*. So that the sacrifice can be made.'

'Sacrifice?' Arthur felt his blood run cold. 'And who's *him*?'

'We call him Red Clogs.'

—

The desk sergeant looked up from his newspaper as Arthur, sweating from his run, stormed into the police station. 'Ah, Mr Collier,' he said. 'Former Inspector Collier.'

'You let him go,' Arthur said, seething. 'Without charge. Don't deny it because I've just spoken to him. William Maxwell.'

The sergeant folded his paper. 'Indeed.'

'He was blathering about *sacrifices*.' Arthur looked around the station, at the posters on the walls still warning people that *careless talk costs lives*. 'Now either you're going to tell me what's going on in this godforsaken place or I'm going straight to the county headquarters to give it to them straight.'

The sergeant leaned on his desk. 'And what will you tell them, Mr Collier?'

'That... that...' He paused. What *would* he tell them? 'That I apprehended a man in the process of abducting a small child and you did nothing.'

'Ah.' The sergeant nodded. He reached for his mug of tea. 'There's the absence of *evidence*, you see. All I had to go on was the word of a man who's been in Scratch Moss for a matter of days against that of someone I've known all my life.'

'But *sacrifices*...' said Arthur helplessly.

'You fought at Normandy, didn't you?' said the sergeant.

Arthur frowned. 'Yes, but I don't see—'

'How many men died on those beaches, Mr Collier? How many boys?'

Arthur thought of his mate who had his head blown off right at the side of him. He'd been seventeen. The sergeant said, 'Those in power sent you away as sacrifices to die on foreign shores for what?'

'For freedom,' said Arthur uncertainly. 'For the prosperity of the nation.'

'Quite,' said the sergeant, turning back to the newspaper. 'Sacrifice for freedom and prosperity.'

'I shall report you,' Arthur announced. 'I shall go to the county headquarters immediately.'

'Very good, Mr Collier.' The sergeant looked up one last time. 'As I said, though, it's all a question of evidence, isn't it?'

–

Arthur stood on the street, seething. The sergeant was right. If Arthur went to the police raving about sacrifices and heathen rituals, they'd lock *him* up. He glanced around as people wandered past on their errands. Were they all complicit in this? Was it a conspiracy that touched every life in Scratch Moss, a secret kept by every single soul? Was even Nora in this up to her neck?

He thought about going to see her, putting it directly to her, then decided against it. The sergeant had challenged him for evidence. He didn't have any. But he was bloody well going to find some. Everyone in this cursed place might be involved in this today but they hadn't always been, had they? There had been a minister at that church, even if it was forty years ago. A minister who had died there. He set off with purpose towards the church.

When he got there, he walked around the building casually a couple of times, inspecting the stonework, until he was sure he wasn't being observed. Then he tried the door, which was unlocked, and slipped inside. In the cool interior he regarded the coal idol, which gave him a sick feeling in his stomach. The straw effigies were gathered around it, seemingly staring at him with featureless faces. At the far end of the nave, behind the altar, were two doors, one either side. Arthur tried the left one and it opened into a small kitchen area, obviously still in use. He rifled through the drawers and cupboards but found nothing of value.

The door to the right was locked. Looking round to make sure he was still alone, Arthur put his shoulder to it, and on the third go something splintered and it opened inward. He found himself in a room littered with prayer books and crucifixes, some broken, obviously torn from the walls and the altar. He felt his bile rise. What were these people? What devilry was afoot?

Arthur searched through the piles of Bibles and hymn books, not knowing what he was looking for. For an hour he searched, and was almost about to give up when his foot creaked on a floorboard. On a whim, he pushed back the faded rug and ran his fingers over the floorboard. It was loose, whereas the others were firmly nailed in. Arthur got out his penknife and prised up the board, which lifted easily. And there, beneath it, was a leather-bound book.

Arthur pulled it up and sat down on the floor, gingerly opening the cover. Inside on the yellowed flyleaf, written in a jittery, spidery hand, were the words *The Testament of Rev. George Ackman*.

He somehow did not feel he could take this back to the Black Diamond, did not trust anyone, even Nora. So he cast about until he found a candle, lit it with a match, and sat down on the floor to read, as the light outside began to fade.

PART FOUR

1905

19

The Bishop silently read through the papers on his desk while George Ackman sat up straight in the chair on the other side of the desk. It was a lovely day in Liverpool, and George glanced out of the office window at the tidy cathedral grounds.

'Theological training at Cranmer College,' said the Bishop. 'Durham's a lovely part of the world.' He ruminated some more as he read on. 'Ordained a deacon a year ago, spent your curacy with old Alfred Hearn at St Oswald's in Sheffield.' The Bishop looked over his glasses at George. 'A hard taskmaster, I should guess, but there's no better teacher.'

'Indeed, My Lord,' agreed George.

The Bishop put the papers down on his desk. 'I think it is time for your ordination, George. And for you to have a crack at your first parish.'

George tried to keep his glee from showing. 'I'm very grateful, My Lord. Dare I ask if you have yet selected a location…?'

The Bishop pushed himself up from his chair and walked to the window. He said, 'Tell me, George, have you ever heard of a place called Scratch Moss?'

'I must say I haven't, My Lord.'

'Small parish in Lancashire,' said the Bishop. 'Mining community.'

'Often the most Godly of people,' observed George.

The Bishop turned to him. 'Hmm, well. Scratch Moss is not Sheffield, and certainly not Durham. They dig coal there, but that's where the similarity ends.' He seemed to think for a moment, then went on. 'It's a difficult parish. Vicars tend not to stay very long. You do well in Scratch Moss, George, it could be the making of you. And to be quite frank with you, if you cannot make it work… the diocese is giving serious consideration to closing the parish completely.'

George could not hide the shock from his face. 'Close down the parish? Abandon the flock? Scratch Moss is so… challenging?'

The Bishop turned to the window again. 'The working classes are a mixed bag, George. Some are devoted to God, some pay lip service. Some are even opposed. And sometimes there are… elements that are unsavoury.'

'A wolf in sheep's clothing sort of situation, My Lord?'

'That's bad enough,' agreed the Bishop. 'But when you suspect the entire flock is comprised of wolves in disguise…' He looked back at George, a broad smile on his face. 'Anyway. Let's give it a go, shall we? The Reverend George Ackman, of St Mary's Church, Scratch Moss. Does have a lovely ring to it.'

—

George arrived in Scratch Moss on a Wednesday, his things delivered to a small but homely house embedded in a small woods to the side of St Mary's Church. The previous vicar had left some months before, but the buildings had been kept clean and well maintained. There was a tidy graveyard adjacent to the church building, which he planned to explore the next day. For now, once he was unpacked, it was time to familiarise himself with the parish and meet his flock. That began with Martin Maxwell and his wife, Sarah, she as rotund and florid as he was beanpole-thin and pale. There was no verger or sexton at St Mary's, nor a housekeeper at the vicarage. Maxwell had been seconded from the estate of Lord Brody, where he was gamekeeper, to tend the graveyard and do maintenance in the church, whenever it was required. Sarah was paid a modest stipend by the parish to keep the church in good order and clean the house once a week.

'I tends to make extra when I do our meals and send it over with the boy, if that suits,' she said. The boy was their son, William, perhaps ten years old. George told her it suited very well, and he looked forward to meeting them all properly on Sunday. The Maxwells left without saying anything.

Scratch Moss was built around the coal mine, which was owned by Lord Brody, whose family lived in Scratch Moss Hall, adjacent to the pit. The small community that had built up around it seemed healthy and prosperous enough, though a little... insular. George took a turn along the high street, stopping to talk to anyone he saw and introducing himself enthusiastically. He was met with, at best, indifference and, at worst, guarded hostility. Somewhat disgruntled, he stopped into a public house, the Black Diamond, and bought a glass of beer.

'You'll be the new vicar then,' noted the landlord.

'What gave it away?' said George, fingering his dog collar. He meant it to be humorous but it came out somewhat weary. He was quite deflated by the reception he had received so far. Well, the Bishop had warned him that Scratch Moss was a somewhat challenging parish.

'Is this your first posting?' asked the landlord. George nodded. The man said, 'Well, I daresay you'll find it interesting. We do things differently in Scratch Moss.'

'How so?'

The landlord shrugged. 'I daresay you'll find out.'

There was a perpetual haze over Scratch Moss from the chimneys of the neat terraced houses and the coal mine workings, and as the afternoon wore on that seemed to merge with looming grey clouds, as though an angry artist had painted an angry sky. Before the threatened rain arrived, George took a turn around the cemetery. The lawns had been cut recently by Maxwell in preparation for his arrival, he surmised, and were dotted with strutting magpies trying to coax worms and insects out of the turf. A mischief of magpies, they called a crew of them. It was apocryphal, of course, but it was said that when our Lord was crucified, two birds alighted on the cross, a dove and a magpie. The dove caught one of Christ's tears, but the magpie turned away and would offer no comfort to Jesus. Some said magpies were the bird of Satan himself, others that from that day forth they were eternally damned. George confessed he did not care for the birds; they exhibited a rare and, he thought, malign intelligence behind those black eyes. As he approached the mown grass where they gathered the birds rose up with a raucous cacophony and flapped towards the tall trees that bordered the graveyard.

It was then that he saw it.

Carved into the nearest headstone, above the name of the interred and the dates of their birth and passing, was a bird. A magpie. George frowned, and then looked at the one beside it. It was the same. And the next. Then he was running along the gravel paths, stopping to check every gravestone. And every one had, in some form, an engraving of a magpie.

George spent Saturday preparing his inaugural sermon. He was troubled, both by the indifferent reception he had received in Scratch Moss and the proliferation of magpies in the cemetery. He had never seen anything like that before. And not a crucifix or Bible verse on any single grave marker. He pondered awhile before settling on the Book of Chronicles, specifically chapter two, verse fifteen.

The Lord is with you, while ye be with him; and if ye seek him, he will be found of you; but if ye forsake him, he will forsake you.

Perhaps not the lesson he anticipated having to impart upon his first ever Sunday, but maybe it was the stall that needed setting out to the people of Scratch Moss.

At five o'clock sharp, the Maxwell's boy, William, arrived with a dish of stew and some thick bread. 'Rabbit, sir,' he said politely. 'My father caught it fresh this morning.'

'Tell me, William,' said George. 'Do you intend to go down the mine when you are of age?'

William shook his head. 'My father says I'm to follow him and learn the ropes at Scratch Moss Hall, then I can be gamekeeper there when he's too old for it. I'm already learning.'

'And what about school, William? What form does your learning take there?'

William shrugged. 'Letters. Numbers.'

'And God? What do they teach you of God?'

The boy hesitated. 'Which god, sir?'

George stared at him. 'Why, God, boy! The only God! He who sacrificed his Son to save humanity.'

'Nothing, sir,' said William quietly, and went away.

—

By the time ten o'clock arrived on Sunday morning, George had wound himself up into an almost righteous fury. He would have his work cut out for him in Scratch Moss, and no mistake. He did not know what mealy-mouthed appeasement the previous vicar had practised, but George felt that he had to get off on a strong footing with these people. They have lost their way, he told himself. That is all. They merely need to be shown the right path. That is why you are here. He stood at the pulpit, reviewing his sermon, and waited.

Nobody came.

George waited until a half past the hour then stormed outside. There was no one around, no congregation waiting to be let in. He frowned, then listened. That noise... it carried on the wind, the distinct and quite clear sound of the pit-head gear turning. The mine was working. On a Sunday. No wonder he had no congregation if they were forced to work on the

Sabbath. George set out for Scratch Moss Hall to have it out with their master.

The venerable servant who opened the doors at the grand house to George's constant hammering regarded him with a baleful eye when he demanded to see Lord Brody.

'His Lordship is of an advanced age and not in good health,' said the man, who was no spring chicken himself. 'The estate and the mine is managed by his son, Peter. Is it him you want to speak to?'

'If he's in charge, yes,' said George. He allowed himself to be shown into a sitting room and waited. Eventually a man of around fifty years of age, wearing plus-fours and a hunting jacket, entered the room, looking George up and down.

'I understand you wanted to see my father. You've probably been told he's extremely infirm. Are you here to deliver the Last Rites?'

'Erm,' said George. 'That would a Catholic—'

'Just having you on, old chap,' said Peter Brody, pouring himself a glass of brandy from a decanter. He paused. 'What time is it? The sun's over the yard-arm, isn't it? Not that there's much sunshine today. You'll have one?'

'Not for me,' said George. 'I'm the new vicar of St Mary's and—'

'Ah, good bloody luck with that.' Peter Brody chuckled. 'Come for a donation for the church roof fund?'

'No,' said George, gritting his teeth. 'I came because I held my first sermon today, but it seems that my congregation was largely working. On the Sabbath, which I can barely credit.'

'Hmm, yes.' Peter Brody nodded. 'Bit of an oddity, that. They tend to take Saturdays as their rest day here.'

'But Sunday is God's day, sir!' said George, outraged.

Peter Brody winked at him. 'Some gods have Saturdays off, Reverend.'

George gaped at him, and was about to demand he explain himself when there was a terrible racket from outside. George stood and peered through the window to see a motor-car chugging up the drive. It was a shiny black thing with white tyres, a young man of around twenty sitting upright in front of a steering wheel on a long column. Peter Brody clapped his hands.

'Oh, it's my son, Michael. He's just taken delivery of that beauty. Brotherhood 20 HP Tourer. Quite the little mover.' He shook his head. 'The world's changing, Reverend. Come and look at it. I'm sure Michael will give you a spin around the grounds. You can see the mines close up, if you like.'

Peter Brody dashed out and left George alone. His audience, it seemed, was over. He got up to find his way out, and in the large entrance hall noticed a door open by the stairs. Through it he could see a bed, in which was a wizened, almost desiccated old man, as thin as a bundle of sticks. This must be Lord Brody, George surmised. The old man seemed to notice him, and half raised a hand as though in greeting. Then the manservant appeared from behind George, went to close the door, and showed George out.

20

George spent the next few days at something of a loss. Should he tell the diocese what was occurring in Scratch Moss? But, presumably, they were aware. According to the church records, no one seemed to stay at St Mary's above a year, and the Bishop himself had suggested that it was a difficult parish. That, thought George, was somewhat understating the matter. It had twice been hinted at him now about other gods. Were these people heathens? Pagans, even? It was the twentieth century. George could not countenance such a thing, right here in the heart of England.

When he had been there a week, and the young Maxwell boy brought him his dinner at five, as usual, George asked him if he might run an errand and see if the Post Office was still open. He would like a copy of that day's Manchester Guardian if they still had one. He had been meaning to organise a delivery, but had not felt the appetite to go mingling with the Scratch Moss community overly much.

William hesitated, then said, 'I'm to go straight home, sir. Mother says. I'm not allowed out. None of the children are.'

'Why ever not?'

'Robert Taylor, sir. He didn't come to school today. Nobody's seen him.'

George was perplexed. 'He's unwell? Something contagious?'

'He's missing, sir. He's been took.'

'He's been taken,' corrected George. 'But taken where? By who?'

'By Red Clogs, sir. I've got to go home.'

'Wait!' George held the boy's arm fast. 'What is this Red Clogs?'

'It's a man, sir. But not really. It's inside a man. I've got to go now.'

'This Taylor boy,' George said quickly as William ran to the door. 'Where does he live?'

—

George found the Taylor household easily enough, a family living in one of the narrow terraces off the main road. The Brody family had built rather superior housing for their workers when they opened the mine forty years before. Scratch Moss could be something of a model village, industrialism with progress and humanity, were it not for the altogether strange nature of the place.

George was let into the house by a girl of twelve or so, who silently showed him into a room packed with people. A woman he surmised to be Mrs Taylor sat on a high-backed chair surrounded by children and other adults. It was very much an atmosphere of mourning.

'I apologise for the disturbance, but I understand you might have need of God's comfort,' said George softly. 'You have had news? About your son?'

The woman looked at him with red-rimmed eyes and shook her head. George said, 'Then there is still hope. I take it a search party is combing the area? Let me sit with you and we can pray for success.'

A man with deep, coal-lined crevices in his face stepped between George and Mrs Taylor. 'We've no need of prayers.'

'You are the boy's father?' said George, looking up at him. 'Why are you not out with the searchers?'

'There are no searchers,' said Mr Taylor brusquely. 'I thank you for your time, Reverend, but I think we'd all prefer it if you left now.'

'No search party? For a missing child?'

'This is Scratch Moss, Reverend. You wouldn't understand. Go back to your church.' Mr Taylor put a polite but firm hand on George's arm.

As he was being steered back to the door, George said, on impulse more than anything, 'Who is Red Clogs? What has he done with your son?'

There was an audible drawing of breath, and a silence so sharp it could have cut glass. George shook his arm free of Mr Taylor's spade-like hand and turned back to the room. 'Well? Who is it? And if you know he has the child, why aren't the constabulary arresting him?'

'Red Clogs is a children's story, nothing more,' said Mr Taylor quietly. 'Now, we thank you for your time.'

—

George spent Friday composing a letter to the diocese, suggesting that Scratch Moss was in dire need of help that might well be beyond a vicar in his first posting. Then he re-read it, and threw it on the fire. If he admitted defeat a week into the job, then he might as well throw his dog collar in the flames as well. Instead he wrote another sermon, about God's love for children and how they must be cherished and cared for.

A sermon which, on Sunday, nobody came to hear.

William had taken to putting George's meals on the doorstep and knocking, and disappearing by the time George opened the door. He guessed that word had got out of his visit to the Taylors, and Mrs Maxwell did not want him quizzing her son any further.

Who was Red Clogs? A children's bogeyman, as Mr Taylor had suggested? A local legend, like Black Shuck, the fire-eyed dog said to roam East Anglia? A phantom like Spring-Heeled Jack? Or a real murderer, a Jack the Ripper who stole away children?

George was standing in the window, pondering, when he noticed movement in the graveyard. He couldn't make out what, but decided to go and investigate, for want of something to do more than anything else. He was crossing the road towards the cemetery gates when he realised what was going on.

It was a burial. George ran through the gates and towards the knot of people, who were starting to walk away from a plot near the centre of the graveyard. He could see Maxwell, stripped to his shirt sleeves, nearing the end of filling in a grave.

What on earth? A burial? On consecrated ground? Without a Christian ceremony? Without the knowledge of the local vicar?

Rage building inside him, George stalked towards the mourners who were drifting away, only to realise who it was. A tall, broad man with his arm around the shoulders of a thin, frail woman. It was the Taylors.

'What is the meaning of this?' he gasped.

Mr Taylor regarded him coolly. 'We have laid our son to rest, Reverend.'

George could scarcely believe it. 'He has been found, then? But this... a burial without a Christian funeral? Without prayers? Without the necessary reconciliation with God?'

'It's how we do things in Scratch Moss,' said Mr Taylor. 'Now, you are upsetting my wife. Please let us grieve in peace, and our own way.'

George watched them go, his fists balled in fury.

—

He stalked around his living room until it grew dark, then he lit candles and paced some more. It was a test, that's what it was. Not just from the Bishop, the diocese, to see if he could handle a difficult parish. It was a test from God. To see if he was worthy.

'What do you want of me?' he begged. 'What do you want me to do?'

He read from the Bible, seeking guidance, craving solace. There was none. A burial without the necessary prayers and preparations... it was vile. It was an affront not just to God, but to the soul of that poor child. How could he ascend to the kingdom of heaven without a proper service? His soul would wither and fade in the absence of God's love.

And in the absence of God's love, without that armour to protect him, Robert Taylor would be dragged screaming to hell.

'They shall suffer the punishment of eternal destruction and exclusion from the presence of the Lord and from the glory of his might, when he comes on that day to be glorified by his saints,' whispered George.

He could not allow that to happen. Fat raindrops began to smack against the windowpane in the darkness. He *would* not allow that to happen.

—

Maxwell had left the spade he had used to fill in the grave leaning against the church wall. The night was black and dark clouds hung low, sluicing the cemetery with driving rain. His coat tight about him, George grabbed the spade and marched to the new grave, not yet marked with a headstone. No doubt the cursed magpie was being carved into one at that very moment.

The mound of earth on the grave was still soft, even more so as the rain soaked it. George drove the spade into it and tossed the soil to one side. 'Saints of God come to this child's aid!' said George, pushing the spade in with his foot. 'Hasten to meet him, angels of the Lord.' Another spade-full was thrown to the side. 'With God there is mercy and fullness of redemption; let us pray as Jesus taught us.'

Within minutes George was soaked, his coat heavy and sodden with rain. He sloughed it off and threw it to the ground, digging his spade in again and again. He recited the Lord's Prayer as he dug, the words giving strength to his arms, putting iron in his resolve, armour-plating his soul. Robert Taylor would have a proper blessing. Robert Taylor would ascend to the waiting arms of God. Then, Robert Taylor would have justice. George would see to that.

'May almighty God bless us with his peace and strength, the Father and the Son and the Holy Spirit,' gasped George. His arms were tiring and rain was pounding his face. His shoes, his trousers, even his shirt, were black with mud. Yet still he dug, still he persisted. He would not fail Robert Taylor and he would not fail God. And George would not fail himself. This was a test, he was sure of that now. God would not find him wanting.

George was waist deep in the plot, and he kept on digging, though his muscles burned. Close, so close. Then the edge of his spade hit something solid, and he dropped to his knees in the hole, clearing the last of the soil away by hand. George felt the smooth, damp wood beneath his hands, and he almost keeled forward with relief. Standing up, he felt for his coat, and the Bible in the pocket. It was drenched and soggy, and there was no light to read by, but he needed it more for comfort and the strength it imparted than as a guide as to what to say.

George Ackman knew what words were required. He closed his eyes and took a deep breath. 'In the name of the Father, and of the Son, and of the Holy Spirit. Amen. I commend you, my dear brother, to almighty God, and entrust you to your Creator.'

He needed to see. To see the child, to deliver the blessing properly. Pushing himself back in the hole, George tried to prise the lid from the coffin, but it was shut tight. He reached out of the grave for the spade, and in the confined space managed to get the edge of the tool under the lip of the coffin, levering it down until it came apart. With a grunt he tossed the spade up and out of the grave, and dragged the lid away.

'May you return to him who formed you from the dust of the earth,' said George, his voice rising to be heard over the pounding rain and the gale. 'May holy Mary, the angels, and all the saints come to meet you as you go forth from this life.'

George braced himself, and looked down, to bless the poor child, to send Robert Taylor on his way in the proper Christian tradition.

'May Christ who was crucified for you bring you freedom and peace...' he began, but the words tailed off and died on his lips.

Robert Taylor was not in the coffin. In his place was a grotesque effigy of a human child, made out of straw.

21

George sat shivering in the vicarage, wrapped in a blanket with his feet in a steaming bowl of hot water. Mrs Maxwell held up his trousers and shirt, wet through and caked with mud. 'These are ruined,' she said. 'I'll try my best.'

'I don't care about the clothes,' said George flatly. 'I care about why that grotesque abomination was buried in the place of that poor child, and the actual whereabouts of Robert Taylor.'

The rain pattered against the window in the darkness. Mrs Maxwell had lit the gas lamps and her husband poured the pot of tea she had made. George caught them looking at each other.

'Is there not one Godly man or woman in this entire cursed place?' moaned George.

'We are,' said Maxwell hesitantly. 'Possibly the last, or at least, the only ones who might admit it to you.'

'But why?'

'There are older gods,' said Mrs Maxwell. 'Especially in Scratch Moss. Darker gods. Dirty gods.'

'What has happened to Robert Taylor?' said George, accepting the cup of tea from Maxwell. 'Why pretend he is dead and buried?'

'He's dead all right,' said Maxwell. 'And buried. But not in the Christian fashion. He's been left as an offering to the god beneath the land. His body rots in the darkness below.'

'Satan?' whispered George. 'The Devil himself? His family has sacrificed their own child to the Fallen?'

'Not his family,' said Mrs Maxwell. 'They'd never do that. They are good people, the Taylors.'

'And not to Satan,' said Maxwell. 'The god who brings prosperity to this place lived in the earth long before the word of Jesus was brought to these isles. Most here don't even know his name, but the Ancient Britons called him *Duiw Prið*.'

The words Maxwell spoke sounded like *Doo Preeth*. The gamekeeper said, 'It means the god of the earth, or dirt, as far as I can make out.'

George looked at him curiously. 'How do you know all this?'

'My father was gamekeeper at Scratch Moss Hall before me. When Lord Brody – the old Lord, who clings on to life – discovered coal on his land and founded the pit. That was forty years ago. Before that, there were only a smattering of houses here, mainly for the servants and staff of the family. Lord Brody built up Scratch Moss as it is today to house the families who came in to work the mine.' Maxwell hesitated. 'My father had Lord Brody's ear, and heard a lot of what happened in that time. With the pit came riches and prosperity. You have seen this place, Reverend. Good food is plentiful, houses are solid, we have sanitation and good health. But there was a price to be paid. A price to he who dwelt in the coal far below.'

'Duiw Prið,' said George, scarcely believing what he was hearing. 'And this price to be paid... the lives of children?'

'Perhaps once a year,' agreed Maxwell. 'It was decided back then it was a price worth paying, as painful as it was. One innocent, a year. Many children would not reach adulthood anyway, especially those who worked in the pit in its early days.'

'A price worth paying,' repeated George dully. 'And the families... what? Draw lots? Offer up a sick child? They murder their own? Or this Duiw Prið himself walks the earth, taking innocents?'

Maxwell shook his head. 'There is what you might call a representative of Duiw Prið. The god himself cannot emerge from the deep earth. As far as I understand from my father, that was the work of old Lord Brody. But some of his... essence is up here. It lodges in the soul of a man, or woman. They call it—'

'Red Clogs,' said George, remembering what young William had said. 'But if the townsfolk know who this is, why not arrest him? Drive him out of Scratch Moss?'

'He who carries Red Clogs within him cannot easily leave Scratch Moss,' said Mrs Maxwell. 'And sometimes nobody knows who it is. Or if they do, they turn a blind eye.'

'My father told me that in the early days, the miners tried to kill Red Clogs, to break the curse,' said Maxwell. 'But this essence... it sits in a man as long as he lives, and when he dies, it transfers to another.'

'You know who it is now?' asked George. 'Who carries Red Clogs in his soul?'

'I have my suspicions,' said Maxwell.

George fell into silent contemplation. The diocese could not know any of this, or they would not have sent a raw recruit like George Ackman to do the Lord's work in such a place. 'I think I need to speak to Lord Brody,' George said decidedly. He had but half a story here, and the word of two who could just be superstitious yokels, or even feeding him a pack of fantastical lies to put him off the scent of something else. 'Do you think you can effect a meeting, Maxwell?'

Maxwell frowned. 'His Lordship is ailing, and old. His son Peter is waiting to take the mantle when the old man dies, and I doubt he would countenance such a meeting, Reverend.'

'But you'll try?' pressed George.

'I'll try,' said Maxwell.

-

Maxwell had been reticent to give George the name of the man he suspected of murdering Robert Taylor, and apparently several other children over as many years, but eventually he gave it up. Party by the name of Herbert Timmins, who worked not as a miner but as a gardener at the Scratch Moss Hall. He lived alone in a small cottage on the edge of the estate, and the next day George resolved to go and confront him.

Timmins was a slight, nervy-looking fellow, perhaps in his thirties, though it was difficult to tell with his shock of prematurely white hair. He answered George's authoritative knocking with a cautious eye at the crack of the door, and asked what he wanted.

'I am the new vicar of St Mary's,' said George. 'I'm working my way round the parish, meeting people.'

'I've no call for the church,' said Timmins shortly, and made to close the door. George stuck his foot in it.

'Perhaps the church has call for you, Mr Timmins.'

The cottage was cold and damp, not a shred of comfort in it. Timmins had the rough hands of a lifelong gardener, his nails black with soil. He consented to put a kettle on and made George a weak coffee, and they sat on the hard chairs in the one living room of the hovel.

George talked airily of this first week or so at the parish, mentioning that there had been no congregation for two Sundays running, and saying that he hoped to encourage the people of Scratch Moss back to his services. He talked of things he had read in the Manchester Guardian, mentioned the weather and how foul it had been yesterday, and complimented Timmins on the quality of his coffee. When he saw the man starting to relax a little, he said casually, 'Why did you kill young Robert Taylor, Mr Timmins?'

Timmins started, then stared into his cup. 'I didn't, Reverend.'

'Ah, my information must be wrong,' said George cheerfully, as though he was still discussing the weather. 'Have you killed any other children, Mr Timmins?'

'I never killed anybody in my life, Reverend,' said Timmins miserably.

'Ah, I see,' said George, putting down his cup. Then he grabbed Timmins by the arm, shocking the man, and shook him hard. 'You're lying, Timmins. To a man of God.'

And then Timmins looked at him, and George's grip faltered. The man stared at him with black eyes, as black as midnight, his entire orbs seemingly with a total absence of any light at all. Timmins snarled, or rather hissed at him, and George's resolve gave way and he leapt to his feet.

'I don't kill 'em,' said Timmins thickly. 'I just takes 'em. *He* kills 'em.'

George backed towards the door, but Timmins seemed entirely normal now, his eyes back to how they were, how they should be. He looked querulously at George. 'Reverend? Are you well? You look pale.'

'What did you just say?' stammered George.

The man frowned. 'I said I never killed anybody in my life, sir.'

'*After* that,' demanded George, trying to quell the turmoil in his head. 'What did you say after that? And what happened to your eyes?'

Timmins shook his head. 'I said nothing, Reverend. And my eyes are fine. Are you sure you're not ill?'

George made some excuse and left the cottage, drinking in the clear air as soon as he was outside. Was Timmins right? Was he ill? Had he picked up a fever in the rain last night? No, he had seen it. He was sure of it. He *had* seen it, and heard Timmins utter those awful words. Either that, or he was bound for the asylum.

-

Three days later, Maxwell called to say that he had spoken to Lord Brody and the old man wished to see him. But it had to be necessarily covert, cautioned the gamekeeper. Peter Brody and his family were taking a weekend away and would leave on Friday afternoon. Maxwell suggested he take George up to

Scratch Moss Hall on Saturday morning, when the mine was not in operation and some of the estate staff would have the day off. There would only be a couple of servants and Lord Brody's nurse at the hall.

At the appointed time, Maxwell called for him and they walked up to Scratch Moss Hall. The weather was more clement, though a cold wind whipped across the quiet mine workings. Maxwell took George in through a side entrance, and they padded silently through the corridors until they came to the main entrance hall and the side room in which the aged Lord Brody was installed. Maxwell knocked and went inside, and after a brief conversation showed George in.

Lord Brody was almost skeletally thin, a few wisps of white hair on his mottled skull, his eyes sunken and hollow. A chair had been placed by his bed and he waved for George to sit, then flicked his hand at Maxwell, who said quietly, 'I'll be back for you in half an hour.'

When the door had been closed Lord Brody closed his eyes, and George listened to his rasping breathing, wondering if the old man had fallen asleep. Then he said, his voice dry and papery, 'The new vicar. You won't last.'

'What makes you say that, Lord Brody?' said George.

'Your lot never do.' The old man gazed out of the window. 'But you are here for now, and my time is short. I wish to make my peace with God before I die.'

'Then you are a Christian?' said George, relief flooding through him. 'You do not subscribe to these bizarre tales of old gods beneath the earth?'

'The two things... are not necessarily incompatible,' wheezed Lord Brody. He indicated for George to come closer. 'I wish to tell you.'

'Tell me what, Lord Brody?'

'Tell you everything,' said the old man.

: : *PART FIVE*

1865

22

There was a fire roaring in the hearth of the sitting room at Scratch Moss Hall, despite it being July. Lord Brody stood with two men, plans and diagrams spread out on the table behind them, and watched the flames licking at the chimney opening.

'It's very good coal, Lord Brody,' said the younger of the two men. 'Very good indeed.'

Lord Brody turned to the older man, who he had known for a good long while. 'Edward?'

'Jackson's right, Henry. You have prime-quality coal beneath the land here. And Britain has much need of it.' As if on cue, a distant train whistled and they all looked out of the window at the plume of white smoke far beyond the trees that bordered the estate.

Henry made a show of thinking about it. In truth, his mind was already made up. He was thirty-nine years old and had inherited the title of Lord Brody upon the death of his father a year ago. Inherited the title, and also the balance sheets and accounts. Scratch Moss Hall was not a profitable enterprise. The family were on their uppers. He said, 'And your financial projections are correct?'

'Modest, if truth be known,' said Jackson. He and Edward had been carrying out surveys of the land over by what they used to call the grove for some weeks now, digging deep and sampling the coal that lay beneath the surface. 'We're not even sure how far or how deep the coalfield goes. But it's big, and as we have seen here, the quality is extremely high. Possibly the best we have ever seen.'

Edward's engineering company would see to the sinking of pit shafts and construction of tunnels, and erect the necessary pit-head gear. There would be no upfront expense to the Brody family, which was just as well. Edward predicted his company would make back their investment, with interest, in three years, and then the pit would be handed over lock, stock and barrel to the Brodys.

'What of a workforce?' said Henry.

'They shall be banging at your door to work here.' Edward nodded. 'They will come from far and wide. That small village outside your land? In five years it will have grown tenfold. It will be a town in its own right, I should say. And they will all work for you.' He wagged a finger at Henry. 'But not women or girls, at least not underground, and not boys under twelve, as of five years ago.'

'I must say,' added Jackson, 'that odd stone structure up there came in very useful. It already had rather deep tunnels sunk from it. What is it, anyhow?'

'A barrow,' mused Henry thoughtfully. 'An ancient burial chamber. Was on the land long before Scratch Moss Hall was built a century ago. For thousands of years, some say.'

'Does it have importance to the family?' said Edward. He tapped the arm of his spectacles on the plan unfurled on the table. 'It would be a rather suitable spot to sink the main shaft. But if it is of sentimental or archaeological value…'

'Neither,' said Henry briskly. 'Do what you need to.'

'Then we should begin? And draw up the necessary contracts…?' said Jackson. 'You wish to discuss with your brother first?'

Henry smiled tightly. 'Oh, I doubt Sebastian will show much interest in the endeavour until profits begin to roll in.' He nodded, his mind made up. 'Draw up the papers. Let us begin as soon as practical.'

Edward and Jackson had been gone scarcely an hour, and it was such a lovely day and Henry was in such a buoyant mood that he was considering telling Elizabeth to get their son, Peter, out of his lessons for the day and taking them all for a picnic in the grounds, when his venerable butler, Mallory, let himself into the sitting room.

'Sir, there appears to be a... contingent from the village,' said Mallory, distaste turning down his mouth. 'Mr Maxwell has tried to see them off but they are quite insistent. They are at the doors now.'

'Well, let's see what they want,' said Henry with jollity. Perhaps word had got out about the coal mining operation already and they were petitioning him for work.

Mallory opened the doors to reveal a dozen or so of the village men, shabby and somewhat exercised in their demeanour. They mostly found work as labourers on surrounding farms, those that worked at all. Oscar Maxwell, Henry's trusted gamekeeper, was standing on the step, facing off against them with the 12-bore he generally used for bringing down pheasant and rabbits loosely in his hands. Not here for work, then.

'How can I help you gentlemen?' said Henry pleasantly.

Their leader, a rough-looking, unshaven fellow, stepped forward. 'It's not you we want to speak to, Lord Brody,' he said. 'It's your brother.'

'Sebastian? Why ever would you want to speak to him?'

The men muttered and jostled and their spokesman said again, 'There's been an incident, sir.' He nodded his head to a thin man with a vacant stare, his eyes rheumy and red. 'Involving Whitaker's daughter, Anne.'

'I believe the girl in question is a common prostitute,' murmured Mallory at Henry's ear, but quietly enough for the villagers not to hear. They commenced much muttering and pressed forward.

Henry held up his hands. 'And what does my brother have to do with any of this?'

'She's dead, Lord Brody,' said the leader. 'Most horribly. Kicked to death in her home. And that's not the worst of it. Her son, who is only an infant of three, has gone missing. He's taken.'

Henry frowned. 'It sounds quite horrible, and you all have my sympathies, but—'

'He was seen, sir. Master Sebastian.' The man turned and dragged another man forward by the sleeve, this one even shabbier and less prepossessing than the others. 'Llewellyn saw him. He was outside the inn, and he saw Master Sebastian walk past, his clogs dripping with blood. Red as poppies, Lord Brody.'

Henry frowned again and rubbed his chin. 'And what time did this all occur?'

The men conferred, and their leader said, 'About ten o'clock, sir. Llewellyn had just been asked to leave the inn, on account of, uh...'

'On account he was drunk, no doubt,' said Henry, his voice suddenly hard. 'And on the say-so of a drunkard lying in the dirt you have marched up here slinging about accusations about your betters. I see. Well, I am very sorry for your loss, and I do hope the child is recovered safely, but my brother Sebastian was playing cards with me all night, and at ten o'clock we had just started on our second bottle of brandy. And I'm quite certain he would never be seen around the village in something so pedestrian as *clogs*. So, you see, you are all mistaken. I bid you good day.'

As Maxwell began to usher the grumbling men down the drive Mallory closed the doors on them. Henry glared at him. 'Where is my brother?' he said coldly.

'Still in his rooms, I believe, sir. He has not breakfasted to my knowledge. Would you like me to have him sent for?'

'No,' said Henry, heading towards the sweeping staircase. 'I think I shall give Sebastian a wake-up call myself.'

'Sebastian!' roared Henry, flinging open the drapes in his brother's room.

His younger sibling, just turned thirty, groaned in the pit of his bed and tried to pull the covers over his head. Henry tore them off him with as much fury as he had thrown wide the curtains. 'What time is it?' said Sebastian through a dry mouth, rising and shielding his face from the sun with his hand.

'Almost noon,' said Henry, standing with his fists on his hips at the foot of the bed. 'And not ten minutes since I had a crew of ruffians at the door, baying for your blood.'

'Oh,' said Sebastian, sinking back into his pillow. He ran his hand through his blond hair. 'Can this wait, Henry? I am feeling sorely under the weather.'

'What time did you get in? And where were you last night?'

Sebastian looked at him through one eye, and still managed to convey an air of amusement. 'So it's not true what they say. You are your brother's keeper.'

'Sebastian!'

The younger man groaned and attempted to sit up again. 'Very well. I went to the village. I'm deathly bored here, Henry. I just wanted a little amusement.'

Henry picked up a frayed, grimy shirt from the rug. 'And you went dressed as one of the lower classes?'

Sebastian smirked. 'Well, I didn't want to draw attention to myself. I'd heard some of the staff talking. About a young filly down there who was quite pretty, by their standards, and would have a tumble for a few pennies.'

'Anne Whitaker, was it?' said Henry.

Sebastian raised an eyebrow. 'You know her? Had a ride yourself?'

Henry threw the shirt at Sebastian angrily. 'No, but I've just had her father on the doorstep, accusing you of her murder.'

Sebastian blinked, and sat up properly. 'Murder? Henry, no—'

'And her child, an infant, has been stolen.' Henry cast around, as though he might see the youngster in the room, discarded as carelessly as Sebastian had abandoned his clothing.

'Henry, no!' said Sebastian more forcefully. A cloud of fear seemed to pass over his face. 'What did you tell them?'

'That you had been here with me all night,' said Henry. He stared at Sebastian coldly. 'I do not know what happened and I do not much care. But I do not want ruffians on my doorstep, and I do not want Elizabeth or Peter to be troubled by any of this. And I certainly do not want to be put in a position where I have to lie for you again. Is that understood?'

Sebastian nodded and Henry turned to leave. As he stalked out of his brother's bedroom, something caught his eye by the wardrobe. A pair of labourer's clogs, kicked off haphazardly. And they were dark, stained almost black.

23

Over the coming weeks, work began in earnest on creating what would become known as Scratch Moss pit. Henry watched the pit-head gear taking shape as Edward's engineering company's men dug down to create the initial tunnels from which the coal would be dug. Coal that would make the Brody family rich once again, and ease the pressure of the bills that were mounting up on Henry's desk.

As such, he was somewhat distracted from Sebastian's activities. His brother seemed to be spending more and more evenings away from Scratch Moss Hall, and spent his days in laconic recovery from his over-indulgence wherever he went. When Henry did think of Sebastian, he wondered about those dirty clogs he saw in his rooms, and put out of his mind just what the dark stains might possibly be.

Then, one day in September, work halted on the site. Henry was summoned and went to the main shaft that had been dug on the site of the now-removed barrow, to find young Jackson addressing the workers. And then he was shown the cause of the consternation. When the men began their work that morning they were greeted with a gruesome sight: the body of a young boy, aged nine or ten, though it was difficult to tell due to his terrible injuries. About the same age as his son, Peter, Henry realised.

'He'd been dumped down the shaft at some point in the night,' Jackson confided to Henry.

'Perhaps he'd been involved in a carriage accident?' mused Henry. 'The perpetrator sought to dispose of the body to avoid trouble with the law?'

Jackson shook his head. 'We think the boy was alive, just about, when he was put down there. There's evidence he tried to claw his way up the shaft, to no avail of course, before he expired.'

'Then he'd been messing about on the site, and fallen down there,' suggested Henry.

Again, Jackson looked doubtful. 'His injuries were not compatible with a fall, Lord Brody. He appeared to have been viciously attacked and then deposited down there while still clinging to life.'

'It's Red Clogs, sir,' called one of the men.

'Quiet!' called Jackson sternly.

But Henry held up his hand. 'Wait. What do you mean by that?'

The men muttered and stared at their feet, and the one who had spoken cleared his throat and said, 'Red Clogs, sir. That's what they call him. They don't know if he's a man or a devil. Seven children lost in as many weeks. We've found bodies before, here.'

Henry tugged at his whiskers. Red Clogs. Wasn't that what the men had said when they came to Scratch Moss Hall demanding to see Sebastian? The man who had kicked that poor girl to death and stolen her child was said to have been wearing red clogs. And those boots he found in Sebastian's room that day...

'I shall put a guard on the site,' Henry said decidedly. 'I'll have my gamekeeper Maxwell organise it. If this man of yours tries this again, we'll catch him.'

That seemed to mollify the engineers, and they got back to work. Henry rushed back to the hall to find Sebastian, and instead found Mallory.

'I was just coming to find you, sir. It's Master Sebastian.'

'What of him?' said Henry. He hadn't seen his brother all day, though that was not unusual now.

'He's been arrested.'

—

By mutual agreement with his brother, Sebastian had taken to carousing not in the village but in the nearby towns of Wigan and Warrington. The former was a mill-town, the latter had made its name as a producer of wire, for everything from fences to bridges. Between them were dotted the mining communities. Both towns had a surfeit of inns and public houses, and plenty of opportunity for Sebastian to sate his thirst… and his hunger.

Henry strode through the streets of the mill-town, bound for the police station to pay his brother's bail money. Sebastian had been arrested for brawling in the street after apparently harassing a young woman who not only had with her a sweetheart, but several of the sweetheart's friends. Henry would smooth it over and get whatever charges were looming dropped. But he really despaired. Sebastian was becoming a problem.

Henry passed a newspaper seller hollering the headlines of the Wigan Observer and District Advertiser, and stopped. The man nodded at him and repeated his call. 'Red Clogs at it again; two girls missing in a week.'

Henry bought a newspaper off the man and scanned the columns right there until he saw the item. *Is he a phantom or is he a man? Red Clogs strikes again!* Then he hurried on to the police station.

In the carriage on the way back to Scratch Moss Hall Henry flung the newspaper at Sebastian, who was leaning against the window, much the worse for wear. 'What do you know about this?'

Sebastian batted the paper away. 'I am in no fit state to read, brother. What is it?'

Henry snatched back the newspaper and read the item in full. Sebastian stared out of the window at the countryside. 'Ghost stories, Henry?'

'You tell me, Sebastian.'

Sebastian shrugged and closed his eyes. Henry shook him violently. 'Children, Sebastian. Children are going missing. That day those men came... I saw in your room a pair of clogs, stained with something.'

'Mud, I should imagine,' muttered Sebastian. 'If you are to build more houses in that village for the men you want to work in your mine you should think about investing in some cobbles. It's a swamp ten months out of twelve.'

'Tell me you know nothing of this Red Clogs,' demanded Henry furiously.

'I know nothing,' said Sebastian, and they continued their journey in silence.

Then, one month later, Henry's son Peter went missing.

Henry and Elizabeth didn't even know anything about it until Oscar Maxwell opened the door, holding the boy's hand. It was after midnight, and though Elizabeth had retired Henry was up, reading with a brandy the latest progress reports on the mine construction. Peter was in his night things, looking confused.

'Where on earth have you been at this time?' demanded Henry, shaking his head at the boy's filthy feet. Elizabeth came running down the stairs, taking Peter in her arms.

'I just went for a walk,' said Peter, yawning. 'It's all fine, though. I was with Uncle Sebastian.'

As Elizabeth took the boy upstairs to be washed and put back to bed, Henry said to Maxwell, 'He was with Sebastian? But where is my brother now?'

Maxwell looked sheepish. 'He's in my cottage, sir.'

'Drunk, no doubt!'

'Unconscious,' admitted Maxwell. 'I'm afraid I had to knock him out, Lord Brody. With the butt of my shotgun. And then tie him up.'

Henry gaped at him. 'What? Why would you do that? Where did you find him?'

Maxwell swallowed. 'At the edge of the mine shaft, Lord Brody. I for all the world believed your brother meant to throw Master Peter right down it.'

'You must be mistaken,' said Henry, though doubt shook his voice.

'I think you had better come and see him, Lord Brody, before you make that judgement.'

—

Sebastian was strapped to a dining chair in Maxwell's cottage. The gamekeeper's wife and his son, Martin, had been despatched to the bedrooms so as not to see what was occurring. When Henry arrived, he realised why.

Sebastian was raving, as though with some kind of mania. Spitting and slavering like a dog, hissing like a wildcat. And his *eyes*… they were completely black, no pupils, no whites, just dark orbs rolling in his head as he gnashed and tore at his bonds.

'Brother?' he said uncertainly, crouching by Sebastian.

'He doesn't know you, Lord Brody,' said Maxwell, standing with his shotgun cocked. 'He's… not himself.'

'An illness?' frowned Henry. 'Bitten by a rabid dog?'

Maxwell shook his head tightly. 'Possessed, sir.'

Henry stared at him, then back at Sebastian. Possessed. And he had sought to murder his own nephew. Henry's son. And had killed all those other children…

'Red Clogs,' whispered Henry, his heart pounding, his stomach in knots. 'My own brother.' He stood up. 'Then we need a priest.'

'Might I suggest another course of action, Lord Brody?' said Maxwell hesitantly. 'There's a woman lives over the hill. They say… well, round here, they say she's a witch. That she traces her lineage all the way back to the druids which legend says used to mark this place as a sacred grove.'

'I'll not consort with those claimed to be witches,' said Henry shortly. 'It's not the sixteenth century, Maxwell. We live in more enlightened times.'

Maxwell bit his lip. 'It's just, Lord Brody... there are stories. About this place. And this woman, Old Mother Pye, they call her... sir, I just think it wouldn't hurt to speak to her first.'

Henry considered it, while Sebastian gnashed his teeth and strained at the ropes Maxwell had wrapped around him. 'What about my brother?'

'Lock him in his rooms, sir. Under guard. Until this passes.'

After a moment's thought, Henry nodded. 'Then arrange for this woman to come here. Discreetly, though. Not at the house. I'll meet her here.'

'And Master Sebastian?'

Henry looked into his brother's black eyes. 'Knock him out.'

Maxwell raised the butt of his shotgun and hit Sebastian once, hard, and Henry's brother slumped in the chair.

—

The next morning, Sebastian seemed back to normal, though Henry had taken the precaution of having him firmly strapped to his bed. His eyes were as they should be, and he claimed no knowledge of what had occurred the previous night. Sebastian begged to be set free, and sobbed at the accusations Henry levelled at him. Henry ordered that he remain bound until he had met with this Old Mother Pye.

She was exactly as Henry would have expected a witch to look, two hundred years previously. Of advanced age, stooped and thin, her nose and chin protruding, her teeth long gone. She wore a grey shift dress and a grimy bonnet, and leaned upon a dry, weathered stick for support. She was waiting in Maxwell's cottage when Henry arrived, alone.

'Maxwell thinks you can help,' Henry said, sitting on a chair facing her.

Old Mother Pye's lined face remained impassive. 'Perhaps. Perhaps it's too late for help.'

'What do you mean?' said Henry.

'All your digging up yonder,' said Old Mother Pye, nodding her wizened head in the direction of the coal mine. 'You've woken it. And once it's awake, it's hungry.'

'What exactly is it?' said Henry carefully.

The old woman ruminated for a moment, then said, 'A long time ago, before anybody lived here but for the Brigante tribe, this place was called *Skǫd Mol*. Over the centuries that became Scratch Moss. You can change the name of something, but you can't change its nature.'

'And what *is* the nature of Scratch Moss?'

'They used to believe, a long time ago,' said Old Mother Pye, 'that the gods lived in the land, or the air, or the woods. The most powerful of all was the god of the sun.' She sucked her gums for a moment. 'The Romans called them *genius loci*.'

'Spirits of place,' said Henry, impressed. 'You know Latin.'

'As much as I need to, which ain't much.' Old Mother Pye sniffed. 'Anyway, Skǫd Mol, or Scratch Moss as was, it had its genius loci. But it wasn't a god of the air or the woods and certainly not a god of the sun. It was the god of the dark, dank, dirty places below the earth.' She tapped her cane on the wooden floor of Maxwell's cottage. 'Below *this* earth. And they called it Duɨw Prið.'

PART SIX

AD85

24

Skọd Mol, whose name means the place where they praise shadows, lay almost exactly between the two settlements the invaders had named Coccium and Veratinum, and might have remained unnoticed by either except for the damn fool Brigantes who thought it was a fine idea to try to sell coal to the Romans. Pie sat on the stump of a tree in the barrow glade, leaning on his staff. He'd cut it himself from a rowan tree when he was young, and it was smoothed with many years of use. *Pie* was what they called him here in Skọd Mol, though in other places they knew him by other names, because his white robes were half-blackened from years on the road, travelling between the tribes, and ragged too, and they thought he looked like one of the birds that proliferated in the grove, the ones that chattered and cawed incessantly, the ones like ravens, or crows, but black and white. It was not Pie's chattering that had brought this ruination on Skọd Mol, though. It was those assembled in front of him.

They'd taken cartloads of coal to the Romans, who found it burned long and clean, and had wanted more. But not to barter for. They would take Skọd Mol and all its coal for themselves. A cohort was marching towards them even as they sat there. A hammer to crack a walnut, perhaps, but the Romans really wanted Skọd Mol. Pie might have simply shrugged off the Brigantes' pleas but for one thing.

The coal had been dug from the bowels of the long barrow behind him. The walls and roof of stone had been constructed who knew when. Hundreds and hundreds of lifetimes ago. It had been a burial chamber, once, but the Skǫd Mol tribes had not utilised it so for a long time. The dry bones of those interred there cracked underfoot if you walked through. The barrow sloped downwards, and at the end even more sharply, and led deep into the earth, where it was hot and dark. And there, glittering in the walls, was coal. The Brigantes had been burning it for generations.

But it was not just the coal that caused Pie to help. It was that which suffused the land all around the barrow grove. Pie was Setantii, and chief among his gods was the life-giver, the sun. But there were plenty of other gods, and one of them was the spirit of this place. Darker and dirtier. The antithesis of the sun.

Duiw Prið, Pie and the druids called him. The god of the dirt. He wasn't sure these idiots even knew what coal was. A rock that burned, nothing more. They didn't know that coal was dead things, from aeons ago. The sacred trees and plants of this grove, the animals that once roamed here. Dead and rotted and compressed. Nothing truly died, nothing ceased to exist. It just became something else. And in the dead, rotted things that became the coal, Duiw Prið resided. A dark and terrible spirit, forever interred in the black earth. But dreaming of the sun and the wind and the rain that he could never again feel.

And that was why Duiw Prið was now their only hope. But that hope would come at a price.

Pie named it, and there was much wailing and shouting and denial. He waited. There were perhaps a hundred men and women who could fight. The Romans would massacre them in an hour. Duiw Prið, though, could make each of the Brigantes fight like ten men. Like twenty. It was their only chance.

One of the elders banged the heel of his stick on a rock. There would be no compact with Duiw Prið, he declared. The black god lived beneath the earth and they lived above it, and that was that. Ah, said Pie, but the coal you dig is from beneath the earth, from Duiw Prið's domain. Now and forever, the Brigantes and Duɨw Prið were entwined, like the ancient symbols etched into the walls of the barrow. The dark god had been munificent up to now, but this was something else.

The elder banged his stick again. The cost was too high. The Brigantes sounded their approval.

Then you die, Pie had said. The clamour faded to mutterings, and they thought about it.

Eventually, they agreed. The price would be paid. A woman fell to the earth, screaming and pounding the grass with her fists, as her baby was brought forth. The Brigantes fell silent as Pie took it, and turned to the barrow.

His feet crunched on the long-dried bones as he ventured to the far reaches of the barrow. He walked with the baby in his arms, down the slope, down, down, down into the earth, into the domain of Duɨw Prið. Then he laid the child down, and left it mewling as he walked a little way back and began to blindly chip coal from the walls with his sickle, then arranged the twigs and kindling he had brought, and set to with his flint.

When the fire sprang into life, he could see the baby wriggling. It issued a full-throated wail, then began to cry as Pie picked his way in the dancing shadows back to the surface. He closed his ears to the plaintive cries as they became more distant and choked, and then mercifully ceased altogether.

–

A boy ran up breathlessly and said the cohort had been sighted. The tribe turned to Pie, demanding to know what they should do. He told those who could not fight, the children and the old, to go and hide in the rowan trees of the grove. They dragged the baby's mother, almost insensible with grief, with them. The child's distant cries could still be heard.

And then, they stopped. Duɨw Prið had taken it. Innocence and blood, fresh and young, a reminder of sunshine and life, a taste of something long lost to the god of the dirt. Something young, for something old. The tribe fell silent. Distantly, the marching of the cohort's regimented feet was carried on the warm breeze.

At first, nothing happened. Then smoke, thick and black, began to issue from the entrance to the barrow. It writhed like a serpent tasting the crisp, fresh air, and wound around the Brigantes, tendrils exploring and probing, and then it was as though each man and woman assembled there sucked the smoke into them, and it dissipated.

They turned to Pie, and each one had eyes as black as the coal in the barrow, blacker than the smoke which had issued from the dark god's domain. Duɨw Prið could not walk the earth, but his essence was in them now, suffusing each man and woman. The god could taste the sun and the wind, smell the grove's sweet aromas, if just for a short time, through them. And he could lend them his power, his strength, his rage. The Brigantes, dark eyes shining, took up their shields and weapons, and roared, and ran to meet the approaching cohort.

They would win, Pie knew, but not without loss. And that child, the price that had been paid... alone in the grove, he threw back his head and commenced a chattering and ratcheting, mimicking the cries of the birds the Brigantes likened him to. They flapped down from the trees, then, two dozen of them, perching on his outstretched arms, alighting on the stone roof of the barrow.

Take the souls of the dead, he instructed the pies. Take the spirits of those who fall in battle, and the child whose life was forfeit for this victory, and ensure they are escorted to their just rewards, become one with the trees and animals and land, and are not further sustenance for the dread Duɨw Prið. He has had his price; let him take no more than he needs.

But now Duɨw Prið was awakened, would one taste of the world above be enough? That was for the Brigantes to concern themselves with, decided Pie. He had played his part. He had saved Skǫd Mol and the sacred grove and the sleeping place of the dark and dirty god. What happened next was up to the people.

PART SEVEN

1865

25

There was a long silence in Maxwell's cottage when Old Mother Pye finished her tale. Henry had listened in silence; for the latter part of the story gazing out of the window towards Scratch Moss Hall.

'It's just too fantastical for words,' he said eventually, when the old woman had fallen quiet.

'Maybe it's just a story,' she said, shrugging. 'Maybe you don't want to pay any mind to it.'

Henry peered at her, narrow-eyed. 'Is it just a story?'

'Maybe. But that don't mean it ain't true.'

'So this... druid. Awoke an old evil beneath the land. Beneath my land. Almost two millennia ago. And since then it has walked the Earth?'

Old Mother Pye shook her head. 'Weren't you listening? Duiw Prið cannot walk the Earth. He's tied to the land beneath the barrow. But his essence has been out there for all this time, lodging in the souls of weak men. Doing his bidding. Bringing him offerings.'

Weak men. Henry thought of Sebastian. 'And these... offerings. Always infants?'

Old Mother Pye showed her gums in a grotesque smile. 'Children remind him of what he's lost, or never had. Life. Innocence. Sunlight and smiles. That's why the people round here, they make the effigies. You never seen them?'

Henry frowned. 'The small figures I see propped up in fields and on lanes? Made of straw, in old clothing? I took them to be scarecrows.'

Old Mother Pye laughed. 'Not scarecrows. They think they can fool Duiw Prið. Keep their children safe by confusing him with these straw babies.' She shrugged. 'It never works, but it makes them feel less helpless, like they're doing something.'

'But why?' Henry was at a loss. 'Why would anyone live in a place where such a foul entity exacted such a price from them?'

'Children die all the time.' Old Mother Pye shrugged. 'If one of them sates Duiw Prið's hungers, then so be it. It is an occasional thing, and people learns to live with such.' She regarded Henry mildly. 'This mine you want to sink, though. Right into Duiw Prið's domain. To take the coal from him. That'd be a different matter, I think. That'd need a price on it, and I think we both know what that would be. A price that had to be paid a lot more regular.'

Henry sat down again. 'Let's say I believe you. Let's say this isn't just some dark and fearful fairy tale. What can be done? How would one get this... essence... out of its host?'

The old woman shrugged. 'I daresay you can't. Not short of killing him that carries it. But then it just flits and flies like a bird to the next one. Always has done, ever since it was released. When it went into those Brigantes and made them fight like demons, it got a taste for it, you see. Freedom. It's been here ever since, sometimes all quiet and sleepy, sometimes not.'

Henry threw up his hands in frustration. 'Then there's no hope! The genie is out of the bottle and can never be put back in!'

Old Mother Pye looked at him slyly. 'That's not exactly the case.'

Henry leaned forward. 'There is a way? A way to end this?'

'I reckon. Old Duiw Prið, he's a spirit of darkness, of dirt, of the coal made from long-dead things. Ask yourself why he don't come up himself? It's the sun god, ain't it? That's who Duiw Prið fears and respects, and will never walk the land in his presence.' Old Mother Pye scratched the thin skin at her temples. 'Now, a clever man who wanted to put an end to this, he'd employ the services of the sun god, wouldn't he?'

'And how would one do that?' said Henry carefully.

'Well, a man who is already digging tunnels in Duiw Prið's domain might think to himself, what if I dug a certain type of tunnel?' Old Mother Pye waved at Maxwell, and he brought over the stub of a pencil and an old letter. She turned it over to the blank side and commenced to draw upon it, a circular band with six rectangular shapes protruding from it at intervals, like a child's drawing of the sun. 'He might think to himself, what if I dug a tunnel shaped like the sun, right underneath that old barrow where Duiw Prið snoozes.'

Henry took the sheet of paper from her and inspected it. 'And you think this would do the trick?'

'Not just that,' said Old Mother Pye. 'That's just a tunnel, and naught else. But if you were to fill it with the sun...'

Henry shook his head. 'No riddles, I beg of you. Please, just tell me.'

Old Mother Pye ruminated. 'I've heard tell the sun is made of fire. A huge ball of fire in the heavens. Now, suppose you filled that tunnel with oil? And set fire to it? Be like the sun, that would. The sun underground. That'd trap him, for good and proper.'

Henry stared at her. 'Light a fire underground? But all that coal... it would burn up. For years, probably.'

'And probably send old Duiw Prið packing.' She nodded. 'Looking for somewhere else to rest his head.' She leaned forward and took back the paper. At the centre of the ring she drew a square. 'But there's also the matter of his essence, isn't there? See, what you'd need to do is find out where its lodged, whose soul carries it. And put him down there before you light your fire. Not kill him first, mind, or that essence'll just hop, skip and jump into someone else. Lock him in there, then let the sun do its job.'

'That would be inhumane,' whispered Henry, imagining locking his brother in a cage deep inside the earth, to slowly die. 'And you implied in your story that it was this creature's presence that gave the coal its... richness. Its value. If he was driven away...'

Old Mother Pye shrugged. 'I suppose you'd have to decide what was more important to you. Your coal and what it's worth, or ridding the land of this terror that's plagued it for centuries. And inhumane? Yes, it would be. But think how many more children will have to die if it isn't done?'

-

Henry returned to Scratch Moss Hall, and went to see his brother, still bound to his bed. Sebastian glared at Henry as he let himself into his room. 'Hasn't this foolishness gone on quite long enough?'

Henry sat on the edge of the bed, scrutinising Sebastian. There was no hint of the darkness that had flooded him before. He said, 'Do you remember kidnapping Peter?'

Sebastian at first frowned, and then shook his head violently. 'Henry, you lie! I never touched a hair on that boy's head! You know I simply cannot stand children.'

Henry leaned over and hit him. He didn't intend to, but the full force of what might have happened if Sebastian hadn't been caught suddenly hit him. He slapped Sebastian hard across the face. 'It is not I who lies, Sebastian,' he hissed. 'You took Peter and intended to do away with him. To serve your dark god.'

Sebastian shook his head again. 'Henry, no, please, for God's sake—'

'Do not invoke God to me, Sebastian,' spat Henry. 'Unless it is the one who lies sleeping beneath the barrow.'

Sebastian fell silent, his eyes on Henry. 'Brother, one of us is mad, and though good sense would suggest it is I, having been strapped to my bed, I honestly insist that I have no idea—'

Henry slapped him hard again. Then his heart softened as he saw the tears in his brother's eyes. 'Sebastian,' he said softly. 'Do you remember nothing? What of all those other times? When you were drinking in the village, or in the towns? The violence.

The children.' He dropped his voice to a whisper. 'They call you Red Clogs, Sebastian.'

'I don't remember,' sobbed Sebastian. 'I know... I feel, sometimes, something rising within me, some darkness... but then it takes hold of me, and I have no thought of my own. I awake and sense dark deeds have been done, but I know not what.' He looked pleadingly at Henry. 'Help me, brother. Help me. Put an end to this.'

'I intend to,' said Henry, standing. He left the room and told the servants to free Sebastian. Then he went to study the plans for the Scratch Moss pit.

–

Edward and Jackson listened to Henry in silence in the drawing room, occasionally glancing at each other as Lord Brody outlined his proposals. When he'd finished, Edward blew out a long plume of cigar smoke. 'Henry, this is madness.'

'But it can be done? A circular tunnel? Beneath the main mine workings? And a room at the centre, made of iron or steel, and lockable?'

'It can be done,' admitted Edward. 'At great cost and diversion of manpower, and thus causing huge delays to the opening of the mine. What I cannot understand is why it would be done.'

Henry walked to the window and gazed out. 'Please don't ask me, Edward. Please just trust me. You'll do it? Starting immediately?'

'The only thing I cannot countenance is this idea of flooding the tunnel with oil and setting fire to it,' said Edward. 'There are gases down there, Henry. The whole mine could explode. And if it didn't, once that fire got into the coal face... it could burn for centuries. And the mine would be useless before it even opens.'

'Useless?'

'You would never make a penny from that coal, Henry. Not a penny,' said Edward. 'What do you want more? This insane venture or more money than your family has ever seen before?'

Henry sighed. Jackson said hesitantly, 'To what purpose is this burning, Lord Brody?'

Henry could not tell him. He said lamely, 'To flood the mine with sunlight. Even just for a few moments. Could it not be extinguished almost immediately? Once it has circled the tunnel?'

'It's too dangerous and too risky and too mad,' declared Edward. 'And you haven't given a good reason for any of it.'

'Flood the tunnel with sunlight,' mused Jackson.

Edward smiled at him indulgently. 'See, Henry? You've posed the boy a problem and he likes nothing better than solving the unsolvable.'

'You have an idea, Jackson?' asked Henry curiously.

'Possibly...' said Jackson, then set to scribbling in his notebook with his pencil. Edward stood up and joined Henry at the window.

'Tell me, old friend. What's this all about? If you've had second thoughts about opening the mine just say so. There's no need to continue with this elaborate charade pretending you've gone cuckoo.'

'I wish I could explain it adequately,' said Henry forlornly. 'Let's just say... local sensibilities. It would greatly be to the benefit of the workforce and the community I hope to build in Scratch Moss if we could see a way around this problem.'

'Good Lord,' Jackson said behind them. 'I think I've got it.'

Henry and Edward walked over to where Jackson was clearing space on the desk, finding a blank sheet of paper. 'Flood the tunnel with sunlight,' he said gleefully, and started to sketch.

Henry waited until he'd finished and explained his plan, then looked at Edward, hope rising inside of him. 'This could work?'

Edward inspected the work with a frown, then straightened up. 'Henry, I am going to pretend I never heard your harebrained scheme to set fire to our precious coal mine, and I am not going to press you on what local sensibilities means, because whatever they are, Mr Jackson – and science – has just found you a solution. A solution that means you can pander to your strange whim and still be as rich as Croesus.'

26

It took six months but Edward came up to Scratch Moss Hall to tell Henry that it was done.

'We managed to get more men in,' said Edward over a glass of brandy. 'We have not fallen too far behind with the main works. The mine could be open in the next two months. Now, what do you intend to do with this little underground folly of yours?'

'Show me how it works,' said Henry. 'And then give all the men the day off on Saturday. I need to handle this alone.'

'Saturday?' Edward frowned. 'Why not Sunday, when they are usually on their rest?'

'Because that is God's day and this is nothing to do with Him,' said Henry shortly. 'Nothing to do with Him at all.'

Edward shrugged. 'As you wish.' He presented Henry with a large black key. 'For your little room underground, whatever you intend to do with it. Now, come and let Jackson show you how it all works. He's terribly proud of it.'

—

Henry had informed Elizabeth and Peter that, with much regret, Sebastian was to be taken away to a sanatorium as his ongoing treatment at Scratch Moss Hall was proving inadequate. He informed his wife and son that there was every chance Sebastian would not be able to effect a full recovery, and they should prepare themselves to never see him again, but they must have hope. It was not that onerous a thought for either of them; Elizabeth hated Sebastian with a passion for the disrepute he brought on the Brody family and Peter feared him intensely after Sebastian had taken him to the mine that day, though the boy had no inkling what fate had been in store for him. They both just knew that Sebastian was a bad lot, and were both relieved when Henry said he was going away, perhaps for good.

For the past six months Henry had kept Sebastian locked in his quarters, on an enforced diet of laudanum. It was during this period that Henry truly began to believe what Old Mother Pye had told him in Maxwell's cottage. His brother seemed to have lost his mind… no, that wasn't quite true. He had lost his *body*, rented it out to another. A dark force that glared at him with black eyes and spoke in tongues, not all of them recognisable. It was as though even the natural world knew what an abomination Sebastian was. Houseplants placed in his rooms withered and died in days, even with copious watering. On one instance, a trio of magpies crashed into the window while Henry was watching over his brother, throwing themselves frenziedly at the glass repeatedly until it cracked and their bloodied bodies fell in a tangled, broken heap on the ground below. Occasionally Sebastian would surface, the Sebastian he knew of old, and beg him to release him, to help him.

'Release will come,' said Henry gently to his brother. 'And soon.'

When Saturday came, Henry made a big show of putting Sebastian and his baggage in a carriage, driven by Maxwell. The plan was that Henry would accompany Sebastian by carriage and train to the outskirts of London, where he would be admitted to a sanatorium for his continued treatment and good health. With a bit of good luck and the best medicine money could buy, perhaps they could all hope to have him back at Scratch Moss Hall before very long. That was what he cheerily told the family, at any rate. But the carriage was not bound for any sanatorium.

'The mine?' murmured Maxwell as Henry climbed into the coach with his heavily sedated and sleeping brother.

'The mine,' agreed Henry, with a heavy heart.

Jackson's design and the engineers' realisation of it was astonishing. A little way from the main shaft over the now long-gone barrow another, thinner pipe had been dug, straight down, to some twenty feet below the main mining chambers that had been prepared below. It was capped with a circular wooden cover, some five feet across, and as instructed Henry removed the cap and looked up at the faultless blue sky. The sun would be directly overhead within an hour. They had no time to waste.

In the absence of any workmen, who had all been instructed to take Saturday off and not go anywhere near the site, Maxwell operated the series of pulleys and gears that allowed Henry and his bulky, heavy package to descend into the dark depths below. With the light from his lamp he traversed the dark hall, its coalface walls glittering, and found a tunnel that veered off to the right and sharply down. Henry followed the instructions from Edward, the tunnel turning and becoming so steep that Henry's boots almost went out from under him, until it began to level off. He held up his lamp and saw the tunnel curving away in front of him, and behind. A perfect circle. And far above him, a disc of brilliant blue, where the thin shaft opened into the fresh air. The sun would be overhead in moments. Henry was sweating from the heat of the mine and the exertion of dragging his heavy burden. He longed to be up there in the cool breeze.

A further tunnel turned off to the left, towards what would be the centre of the circle. And at the end of it was a steel door.

But there's also the matter of his essence, isn't there? See, what you'd need to do is find out where its lodged, whose soul carries it. And put him down there before you light your fire. Not kill him first, mind, or that essence'll just hop, skip and jump into someone else. Lock him in there, then let the sun do its job.

'God forgive me,' whispered Henry. With some effort he dragged the dead weight into the tiny box, walls, ceiling and floor of hard steel, and dumped it in the centre. 'There is no other way.'

Without a look back he left the infernally hot cell and locked it with the key Edward had given him. Then he found his way back to where the small shaft opened to the sky, just as the spring sun began to move into position.

Henry stepped back as the light filled the shaft, and hit the carefully positioned mirror at the bottom of it. He held his breath, not daring to believe it could work. But the lens retracted and magnified, sending a beam of bright, brilliant sunlight onto the next mirror, which intensified it yet more and passed it on. Henry ran, hugging the rough wall of the tunnel, all around the circle, eventually coming back to the beginning and finally seeing it. A continuous band of light. Jackson was a genius. He had flooded the mine with sunlight.

Henry stumbled, and held the wall for support. No, not stumbled. The ground was moving beneath his feet, shuddering, shaking. An earthquake? Or something else? Something older and angry and darker? The coal wall seemed to pulse and move under his hand, like something vast and unknowable breathing. He pulled his hand away, and felt a trickle of coal dust fall from the low ceiling. Panicked, Henry turned to run back to the main shaft, but then the shaking subsided, just as the sun passed over and the light dimmed, then faded to nothingness. He held up his lamp, now his only source of light, and hesitantly touched the tunnel wall. It was solid, and still.

Let the sun do its job, the old woman had said.

Whatever lay in the ground, whatever haunted the fissures and seams, it was asleep, at last.

It was over.

Though, not quite yet. When Maxwell let him up, Henry fell to the ground, gasping, his fingers knotting in the cool grasses, gulping lungfuls of fresh air. He would never set foot in that mine again, if he could avoid it.

'Is it done, Lord Brody?' asked Maxwell.

'It's done,' said Henry, getting to his feet and walking to the waiting carriage. He opened the door and beheld his sleeping brother. 'Now to get Sebastian to London.'

They had been driving barely ten minutes when Henry heard Maxwell call to the horses and pull them up. They were on the road that would take them to Warrington and the train station. Henry opened the window and stuck his head out, meaning to ask what the delay was, when he saw her.

Old Mother Pye stood on the dirt road, leaning heavily on her stick. 'Out of the way, please,' called Maxwell.

She just stood there, and stared, and Henry sighed and opened the door. 'It's done,' he said as he walked towards her. Up in the sunlight, the prospect of Sebastian receiving actual medical care, he had started to feel a little foolish about his terror down the mine. Daylight and logic were becoming ascendant in his mind now, not silly superstition.

'You didn't burn it, like I said,' called Old Mother Pye.

'No, we wrought another solution,' said Henry. 'It worked.'

She pointed with her stick to the carriage. 'Your brother. He carries the essence. If he's not down there, it's not done.'

Henry smiled. 'I took your advice, Old Mother Pye. A straw effigy, in Sebastian's clothes, with his personal effects in the pockets. Fool the damn thing, whatever it is.'

She smirked. 'I also said it never works. Just makes the folks feel better.'

'Well, we're on our way to London. Sebastian and whatever is within him will be away from Scratch Moss. However you slice it, and whatever you say, it's over.'

'It'll not let you leave,' said Old Mother Pye. 'Not in a host as weak-minded as your brother.'

Henry was about to protest most strongly when he heard a shout from Maxwell and then a low, formless growl, as though issued from an animal. He turned to see Sebastian, awake and out of the carriage, crouching on the track, sniffing the air and looking wildly around.

Even at that distance, Henry could see his eyes were completely black. And then he saw what Sebastian held in his hand. Henry swore. 'Where did he get that bloody knife?'

Maxwell had climbed down from the carriage and was backing away. The horses were whinnying and stamping the ground, as though they could sense the presence of something not natural. 'Looks like a bread-knife, Lord Brody. He must have squirrelled it away somehow.'

Henry walked slowly towards his brother, hands held out placatingly. 'Sebastian. It's me. Henry. Lay down the knife. Get back in the carriage. We're going to London, brother. We're going to make you well again.'

'You might take his body to London, but not that which rides within,' said Old Mother Pye behind him.

Sebastian waved the knife, as a wind suddenly whipped up, bending the grasses by the side of the road and ruffling Sebastian's hair. Grit flew into Henry's eyes, and as he paused to wipe them his brother started to back off, looking around as though preparing to flee.

'Mr Brody, back in the carriage,' said Maxwell loudly. He had emerged from behind the vehicle, brandishing his shotgun. 'Please, sir. It's for your own good.'

Sebastian hissed, his eyes blacker than ever, and he cast around, like a trapped animal.

And then he plunged the knife into his right eye, up to the hilt.

'Sebastian!' cried Henry, rushing forward. The wind intensified almost to a gale, to a hurricane, and the trees bent in its force, dust swirling on the track. Sebastian crumpled and fell, blood gouting from his eye. Then, with what was surely his final breath, he threw back his head and screamed.

Henry skidded to a halt. Sebastian's scream died away, but there was something else issuing from the lifeless body. Smoke, coal-smoke, black as night, pouring out of Sebastian's open mouth as he lay bent on the ground. A plume of thick smoke that took shape in the air, a cloud, hovering above the body, even in the roaring wind.

Henry ducked involuntarily as the black smoke seemed to lunge for him, passing over his head. He turned to see Old Mother Pye, standing upright with her arms outstretched, head turned upwards, as though in supplication. He watched in horror as the smoke cloud gathered above her, and then plunged down, into her mouth and nostrils, as though she was sucking it inside her with a superhuman effort. Then Old Mother Pye collapsed to her knees.

Henry turned to Sebastian but Maxwell was already there, feeling his neck for a pulse. The gamekeeper shook his head solemnly. Henry ran to the old woman, who was pulling herself to her feet on her ancient stick. 'I told you,' she said. 'I told you it wouldn't let you take it away from here.'

'Where is it now?' whispered Henry, horrified.

Old Mother Pye looked at him, and smiled, and her eyes slowly filled with utter and total blackness.

–

A little over a year later, Henry finished his lunch in the drawing room, with Elizabeth and Peter, as Mallory brought in the post. He sorted through the envelopes and said, 'Ah, a letter from Uncle Sebastian, Peter.'

Henry read out the letter, which was brief but positive, saying that Sebastian was responding well to the treatment and hoped to be able to come home soon. He hoped that Peter was being a good boy and that the mine was working well.

Henry had written the letter himself and had Maxwell post it in Scratch Moss a few days ago. Only the two of them knew that Sebastian was buried in an unmarked grave at the far reaches of the estate.

The mine was working well, though. Better than anyone could have hoped. Scratch Moss coal was in much demand, and workers had flocked there to take up residence in the village that, with the aid of the new cottages being built, was fast becoming a small town. Henry had even had a church built, though just a few days ago he'd had a visit from the vicar, who was most perturbed at the lack of Godliness in the new town.

'They have an obsession with magpies,' confided the old man. 'And a most heathen way about them. Why, just last week they filled the nave with straw children. I am quite at a loss, Lord Brody. Perhaps if you would reconsider your decision to open the mine on the Sabbath, with a Saturday off? It's most irregular.'

'They work hard, Reverend,' Henry had said. 'And they have become used to their Saturdays off. Scratch Moss isn't like other places, but it works for us.'

For the Brodys it was certainly working well, better than Henry could ever have hoped. Coal from other mines was eighteen shillings a tonne; Scratch Moss coal was fetching almost twice that. Industry could not get enough of it, and they were clamouring for it in France and even the Americas. He was already making plans for a new wing for Scratch Moss Hall, and after attending a party at Elvaston Castle he had already begun negotiations with the landscape gardener William Barron to transform the grounds at Scratch Moss. Henry had a fancy to construct something to replace the barrow, perhaps a temple or some such thing, maybe as a way of mollifying the thing in the ground that provided all this prosperity, the thing he didn't like to think about too much.

Henry took the rest of the correspondence into the study. He had been informed some six months ago that Old Mother

Pye had finally died. When she had taken the presence into her upon Sebastian's death, Henry had briefly thought about locking *her* in the metal room below the ground and fulfilling his original plan. But he was afeared that such meddling might drive away the force which was going to make him rich, and he let Old Mother Pye be. She had come to see him once since it all happened, and said that his plan had worked, at least partially. The dark god in the ground slept, and his presence still infused the land, making Scratch Moss coal the best in the country. He still needed sustenance, though, just not as regularly. Perhaps one child a year, she said. It was something the people of Scratch Moss were going to have to get used to.

As he looked at the balance sheet for the previous month, Henry briefly wondered who carried the god's essence now. But then he got lost in the figures, and calculating how much money he was making. Yes, the people of Scratch Moss were going to have to get used to it, because it was most definitely a price worth paying.

PART EIGHT

1905

27

'You have heard my confession,' said Lord Brody, his lips dry. Henry passed him a glass of water from the bedside table. 'Am I damned, Reverend? Or can I yet ascend to the Kingdom of God?'

'You could have ended it forty years ago,' whispered George, scarcely able to understand the tale he had just been told. 'And yet you put profit first.'

'If I had sacrificed my own brother,' said Lord Brody, 'you would have countenanced that, had you been here?'

'Of course not,' said George. 'But... the old woman... she told you to burn it out. Drive it away. You did not. You put business first.'

'I beg you, tell no one of that. Tell no one that I could have ended this. Give me this redemption, vicar, please. I could not sacrifice my own brother.'

'And yet you have damned countless children to the same fate,' said George coldly. 'I would bid you read, if you are able, the Bible to make your proper amends. I should point you to Mark, chapter eight, to begin with. *For what shall it profit a man, if he shall gain the whole world, and lose his own soul?*'

Lord Brody sank back into his pillows. 'Then I am damned.'

Martin Maxwell appeared at the door, and George stood. 'I will pray for your soul, Lord Brody. I suggest you do the same.'

-

Maxwell walked with George down from the hall back to the church. George strode mostly in silence, ruminating on Lord

Brody's story, until they reached the town. He looked at the gamekeeper. 'Your father was complicit in everything,' he said flatly. 'Did you know?'

Maxwell shrugged. 'He didn't talk about it much. I remember, vaguely, being a boy and Sebastian being in our cottage, but I was kept out of the way. My father died five years ago. Whatever Lord Brody told you about his involvement, he mostly took it to the grave.'

'The entire town has lived under the cloak of a conspiracy of silence for four decades,' said George, as they turned on the road towards the vicarage. 'I can barely believe such heathen beliefs and practices are going on in this day and age.'

'Then you believe it all?' said Maxwell, hesitantly.

George thought about it for a moment. 'All this talk of Duiw Pri∂ and Red Clogs. It is nonsense, embellishments. I believe that the people of Scratch Moss have created a legend, constructed a myth, to explain away what is obvious.'

'Which is, Reverend?'

George looked at him. 'That Satan himself has claimed Scratch Moss for his own. It is not the avatar of some ancient god that has lodged in men's souls here, Maxwell, but the Devil himself.'

Maxwell nodded. 'And what do you intend to do, Reverend?'

George gritted his teeth. 'Drive out the Devil, Maxwell, and reclaim this land, these souls, for the one true God.'

-

Another Sunday came and went with no congregation. George was no longer shocked, but his anger deepened. The people of Scratch Moss had been sold a lie to justify the riches their masters amassed. They had been persuaded to let Satan into their lives, to accept the unacceptable, to justify the unforgivable. It was not their fault. They had merely been led from the true path of righteousness, and just had to be shown the way back.

George considered asking the diocese for assistance, but decided against it. He was unsure that anyone would believe him about what was happening in Scratch Moss. Better that he resolve the problem himself, and inform the Bishop later. In the meantime, he resolved to keep a log of everything that happened. He found a leather-bound notebook in his trunk and meticulously recorded everything that had happened in Scratch Moss since he had arrived, including a detailed account of his conversation with Lord Brody. Should, God forbid, any misfortune befall George, then at least there would be this record for the next vicar to take up post in this unfortunate parish. He paused when he had written down Lord Brody's account of what happened in 1865. Did the old man deserve a chance at redemption, as he had begged? Didn't everyone? George looked at the notes where Brody had been told by Old Mother Pye to lock Sebastian away, but he had not. The most damning evidence, George decided, and tore out the pages. Perhaps Lord Brody did deserve a chance, if he was truly repentant.

A day or so later, it being fine weather, George was in the church grounds, looking up at the huge metal cross on the spire framed against the blue sky, and taking much comfort and strength from it. God had not deserted this place. He had not. And George would prove it.

A high-pitched, almost comical-sounding horn blasted from behind him, and George turned to see the motor-car he had first observed at Scratch Moss Hall, trundling along the cobbled road. It was driven by Michael, the son of Peter Brody, who sat in the passenger seat. The younger man pulled the vehicle up outside the church and Peter Brody waved at him to come over.

'Thought I'd better let you know,' said Peter. 'The old man snuffed it last night.'

'Your father? Lord Brody?' said George.

'My father, yes,' said Peter. 'Which makes me Lord Brody now.' He squinted up at the church in the sunlight. 'I understand you visited my father a few days ago.'

George could not lie, of course. 'He wished to see me.'

Peter nodded. 'Well, I suppose that scratches whatever itch he had.'

'Your father is a deeply Christian man,' said George.

'Was,' corrected Peter.

'Indeed. There will be a funeral? When should I attend? You wish to hold it at the church?'

Peter sniffed. 'Private affair, family and friends. Up at the hall, I think. Burial in the grounds.'

'Christian burial,' pressed George.

Peter looked up at the church again. The shadow of the cross on the spire was cast on the grass at the front of the building. 'Thing is, old chap, with dear papa gone... there's not much point in any of this any more.'

'Any of... this?' George frowned.

Peter waved his hand. 'All this church business. Not really our thing in Scratch Moss, sure you've noticed.'

George stared at him wordlessly. Peter went on, 'So I suppose what I'm saying is, we no longer have need of your services. Thought it best to tell you in person. We're letting you go.'

George barked a laugh despite himself. 'Letting me go? Mr... Lord Brody, I am not one of your employees, to be hired and fired at your discretion. I am employed by the diocese of Liverpool and I am a servant of God. They are my masters, not you.'

Peter gave him a penetrating stare. 'Shall we say we'll give you to the end of the week to put your affairs in order? I can send a few chaps over next Saturday to make sure you've moved everything out. We'll put on some transport for you and your things.'

'This is intolerable,' said George. 'It is not your decision, sir! I shall have to inform the diocese and—'

'Look, old chap,' said Peter, a note of steel entering his voice. 'You wouldn't really want to be where you're not wanted, would you?'

George held his gaze. 'Are you talking about me or the Church, Lord Brody?'

Peter shrugged. 'Either of you. I understand you had a jolly good chat with my father. Perhaps you understand how differently things are done round here, now.'

'I understand that profit is put before God, and the lives of innocent children are considered a fair price to pay for industry.' George seethed, his fists balling by his side. 'I understand that you have opened your hearts to the Devil himself and soiled your souls in the process.'

Peter smiled thinly. 'Reverend, one man's devil is just another man's god. It's all a matter of perspective, you see. And my perspective, from where I'm sitting, is that you are on a hiding to nothing in Scratch Moss. Best to get out while you still can, don't you agree?'

'That, sir, sounds like a threat.'

Peter laughed. 'Threat? Oh, no, no, no, Reverend. Merely just a bit of friendly advice.' He nodded at his son. 'Now, it's a lovely day and we are going for a pootle around. Toodle-pip, Reverend. End of the week, as I said.'

Incandescent with fury, George watched the motor-car pull away from the side of the road and thunder along the road until it was out of sight.

–

George sat in the gathering gloom of the vicarage, noting down in his book everything Peter Brody had said to him. The man was serious. He meant to throw George out of St Mary's, out of Scratch Moss. Surely the diocese would not countenance that. Then he recalled the words of the Bishop, about this being the last chance for Scratch Moss, how they were considering abandoning the parish altogether.

He had failed. Barely weeks into the job, and he was to be run out of town like a dog, whimpering with his tail between his legs. What future for him now? The Bishop would not trust him with another parish. His career in the Church was over practically as soon as it had begun. He had dithered about writing to the Bishop, but that would be an admission of failure. Things seemed bleak, but perhaps they were not yet completely lost. Perhaps this was a test from God.

And George Ackman would not go down without a fight. He would not turn away from these people, not in their darkest hour. They knew not what they did, nor why they did it. This life was something they had grown accustomed to over the years, not just since Lord Brody had opened the mine and created this town, though that had intensified and accelerated matters. Scratch Moss, and the land it had been for centuries before it was known by that name, was a cursed, benighted place that had fallen under the shadow of the Fallen Angel. It may be the last thing George ever did as a representative of the Church, but he would do what he could to save them before he was forced out.

He knew what he had to do. He had to drive the Devil out of the possessed man. He had to exorcise Herbert Timmins.

28

George had told old Lord Brody to look to the Gospel of Mark for guidance, but it was there that George now turned for strength and succour. Because nowhere else in the Bible were detailed as many exorcisms as in Mark's Gospel. Jesus knew the demonic and the possessed, and he knew how to deal with them. And thanks to Mark, George knew that he, too, had the fortitude to follow Christ into the darkness of men's souls and cast out that which lodged there, and bring in the light.

For three days George read the Scriptures and prayed, ignoring the food left on the doorstep by William, paying no heed to the knocks on the door from Maxwell and his wife. He had to be pure of mind and of body, and though his stomach yawned and contracted with hunger, he took only water. He did not wash or shave, nor attended to any business other than making copious notes in his book.

At last, on Friday – though the days had lost all meaning to him – George Ackman was ready. Gathering his crucifix and vials of holy water he had blessed in the church font into a small leather bag, he set off for Herbert Timmins' cottage just as the sun was going down.

–

George was unsurprised to see that Timmins did not want him there. Once again, he was forced to shove his foot into the door to prevent the man closing it, and insist most forcefully that he let him in.

'I don't want no part of anything you've got to say,' said Timmins. 'Besides, I heard you was taking your leave tomorrow.'

He tried to kick George's foot out of the door so he could close it. George was not a big man, nor of course a violent one, but at Cranmer College he had enjoyed a bit of boxing. His right fist darted out and landed Timmins a good jab on the chin, putting the man on his back, and when his head hit the bare floorboards he was knocked out cold.

By the time Timmins awoke a half hour later George had him tied to a chair in the cold, tumbledown cottage the man lived in alone. He'd found some lengths of rope and twine among the gardener's effects, and sat him in a chair in the middle of the living room. Timmins groaned and opened one eye, and braced himself against his bonds, but George had tied them tight.

'What's the meaning of this?' said Timmins when he had come fully back to consciousness.

George began by reading the Lord's Prayer, his own voice shaking and hoarse from his constant praying and lack of food. But the only sustenance he needed right now was God's strength. Timmins began to loudly protest but George simply prayed louder than him, and by the time he reached the end of the prayer he was bellowing in the man's face.

'O God, whose nature and property it is ever to have mercy and to forgive, grant that the chains of evil binding this person may, by your mercy, be loosed, and let no evil power harm any one. Through Jesus Christ your Son our Lord. Amen,' he cried, his Bible in one hand, his crucifix in the other.

Timmins strained at the ropes. 'You're mad. I'm not possessed. Let me free. There'll be hell to pay when Lord Brody hears of this.'

'Aye, Hell will pay!' shouted George. 'Hell will forfeit your soul and return it to the loving embrace of God!' He sprinkled a vial of holy water over Timmins, and pressed his Bible against the man's forehead, though he tried to twist away from the vicar. George held his cross high and said, 'I command you, every evil spirit, in the Name of God the Father Almighty, in the Name of Jesus Christ his only Son, and in the Name of the Holy Spirit, that harming no one you depart from this creature of God, Herbert Timmins, and return to the place appointed you, there to remain for ever.'

Timmins swore and strained, twisting and snarling, and at last George began to see the true nature of the demon that possessed him bubbling to the surface, like marsh-gas. Timmins spat, and his eyes widened, and then darkened as George had seen them do before. The demon was fighting, but God gave strength to George's arm, and to his resolve. He pressed the Bible to Timmins' forehead again and looked to Heaven.

'O Holy Lord, Almighty Father, who hast sent your only begotten Son into the world that he might destroy the works of the devil, speedily hear us we pray you,' cried George. 'Grant strength to your servants to fight valiantly against the evil one. May the strength of your right hand make Satan loose thy servant Herbert Timmins, so that he no longer dares to hold captive him whom you have made in your image and redeemed in your Son: who lives and reigns with you in the unity of the Holy Spirit, world without end. Amen.'

George felt faint and somewhat lightheaded, and stepped back from Timmins. The man regarded him slyly, his black eyes narrowed.

'You're barking up the wrong tree, priest,' he said thickly. 'What lives in me has nothing to do with your paltry little God. He's as old as the hills, he is.'

'The hills God created!' shrieked George. Why wasn't it working? Why could he not compel the evil entity to flee Herbert Timmins? He placed the cross on the man's forehead and recited the prayer again.

Timmins just laughed at him.

George hit him. A sharp right hook, connecting with his chin. Timmins' head snapped back and he cried out.

'I command you, every evil spirit, in the Name of God the Father Almighty, in the Name of Jesus Christ his only Son, and in the Name of the Holy Spirit,' said George again, then he hit Timmins square in the jaw with his fist. Timmins' head lolled forward, blood dribbling down his chin.

'Get out!' screamed George, and hit Timmins again. And again. If prayer would not work, then he would smite the demon out of this man, knock it straight back to Hell.

'Please...' said Timmins, spitting blood and teeth down the front of his stained shirt. 'Please, Reverend...'

George glared at the man in fury. The demon would not depart. It had its hooks too deep into him. George's eyes widened. Perhaps it was Satan himself. The Lord of the Flies. He would never let go, just to spite George.

And then it came to him, like a flash of lightning, like a bolt from the blue. Timmins was too weak. The black soil of his soul was too fertile for Satan to let go of. He had planted himself there, his roots had taken hold. He would never give up Herbert Timmins.

George thought of the story Lord Brody had told him, of when the demon had lived in his brother, Sebastian. Only death could be a release for one so possessed. And then the devil would simply move to another host. Another weak soul, like all the despoiled souls of Scratch Moss. And then George would never find him again before he was cast out by Lord Brody.

But what if... what if the only way George could defeat the demon was on the battlefield of his own soul? For surely there he would have the advantage. God's armies would stand at his back.

He had to take the demon inside him, and defeat it there. And the only way to do that...

George hit Timmins again. Then he cast his Bible and cross down and grabbed hold of the man's hair, holding his head steady, and resumed punching him. Timmins lost consciousness but George remained steadfast. The man's face became a bloodied pulp, his features unrecognisable, and George's knuckles were cut and bruised but he kept punching, kept hitting Timmins until…

The man's had lolled back and his mouth, a bloody, gory maw, fell open. George stepped back, gathering up his Bible in his bloody hands. And there it was. Just a wisp at first, as though from a guttered candle. Smoke, curling and wreathing out of Timmins' open mouth. Smoke that gathered in volume and blackness, bringing with it the smell of Hell itself, coal and firedamp and sulphur.

The smoke billowed out and hovered above the dead body of Timmins like a raincloud. George had freed him. At last, George had driven the demon out of Herbert Timmins. Now he could go to his just reward.

'Come on, you bastard,' said George, opening his arms wide, throwing back his head. 'Let's really see what you're made of.'

He began to chant the Lord's Prayer as the smoke gathered above him, and then plunged like a serpent right into George's face.

-

It had begun to rain as George staggered out of Timmins' hovel. He had no recollection of the journey back to the vicarage but when he got there he was exhausted, soaked and famished. He dropped to his knees and cast around for the last lot of food young William Maxwell had laid on the doorstep, finding in the dark a dish covered with a tea-towel. It was soaked and smelled spoiled, and had probably already been sampled by vermin. George didn't care. He scooped handfuls of the stew and forced them into his mouth, the food hitting his empty stomach and momentarily easing the gnawing pain there.

George climbed to his feet and pushed into the vicarage, lighting the gas lamps with shaking hands. He had done it. He had exorcised Herbert Timmins and taken the demon into himself. He started to shake, whether from the drenching he had got from the rain or from the parasite that he had willingly planted in his own soul, he didn't know. He didn't care. George Ackman was not a failure. He had freed Scratch Moss of the terror that assailed it. Red Clogs, demon, Satan himself. George had the power of God at his elbow and he had triumphed.

He stared at his hands, his knuckles bruised and swelling, blood staining his palms. His blood, and Timmins' blood. Then he felt his stomach convulse, and he bent over, and spewed the spoiled stew out, right there on the rug. George staggered against the mantle, and looked at himself in the mirror above it. He was gaunt, and pale, his hair plastered to his head, a patchwork of vomit and blood colouring his face. His eyes were as black as midnight, as black as the pits of Hell.

He threw back his head and laughed.

29

George must have slept, because he came awake to a hammering at the door. The clock said it was a little after six in the morning. He pushed himself up from the sofa, his limbs stiff and aching, and peered out of the window. It was Martin Maxwell, with his shotgun in the crook of his arm. The clouds above were black and roiling, the rain driving. George heard a distant rumble of thunder.

When George opened the door Maxwell looked at him and took a step back. 'Good God.'

'Indeed,' croaked George, his mouth dry. 'Good God. He has saved you. He has saved Scratch Moss.'

'Well, you need to think about saving yourself,' said Maxwell, looking around and scanning the road. 'They just discovered Herbert Timmins' body in his cottage. You left your crucifix behind. You need to get out of here.'

'They've already told me I have to leave today,' said George, stepping back so Maxwell could come into the vicarage.

'I'm not sure a jolly farewell is on the cards any more, Reverend. They'll be on their way imminently. If you come with me now I can get you over the fields, away from Scratch Moss. You might be able to pick up a bus from Platt Fields, if we're sharp.' The gamekeeper glanced around. 'You haven't packed.'

'They mean me harm?' said George.

Maxwell looked at him levelly. 'I saw what you did to Timmins. Lord Brody... his blood is up. He's despatching several men to detain you. Reverend, I fear for your life. We need to get you out of here. I can't be seen to be helping you, but if we leave now...'

George bent down to pick up a cardigan and his notebook. Maxwell sighed. 'There isn't time to pack. Leave it. We need to go.'

'Five minutes, that's all I ask. Do we have that?'

Maxwell looked stricken. 'I'd prefer four. Three would be better.'

'I just need to do something in the church.'

Maxwell bit his lip, then grabbed George's shoulder. 'Quickly, then. Come on.'

Maxwell waited outside the church as George stood by the altar, looking up at the cross on the wall, rainwater mixing with the dried blood on him and pooling at his feet.

He had the demon inside of him. It was like... it was like nothing he could even find the words to describe. Like an infinite space within him. As though all the stars in the sky were glittering in his every cell. Ancient tides on seas long since dried to nothing ebbed and flowed in his veins. He fancied he could hear the cries of birds gone extinct millennia ago, creatures that only existed in picture books and displays in museums. George was a religious man but also a modern one; he knew of the vast age of the Earth and how it had changed over the many, many years, since long before man walked its hills and glades. He felt a connection to those long-gone days, saw flashes behind his eyes of impossible landscapes.

Those plants, those creatures, long, long dead, were in the coal. Compacted and fossilised. Death upon death upon death, giving life to something that drew its power from these strata of prehistory.

No, he told himself. It is Satan, or one of his demons.

Duiw Prið, came from somewhere.

Same thing, thought George. Just names men give to things they do not understand, or fear. Or worship.

'Please, Lord, give me strength,' begged George to the cross. Within him, something laughed. He felt hungry, but not for food. Thirsty, but not for drink. He hungered and thirsted to please his master, to bring him an offering while he slept in the dark, hot coal beneath the land.

I could just find a child and take it, just one, just one child, leave it battered and broken in the mine, give my god succour and and and

'No!' Screamed George, hitting himself in the forehead with his first. 'No! There is only one God and that is the true God and I beseech you now, O Lord, I beg of you, give me the strength to fight this thing within me.'

Outside, he could hear voices.

–

'Maxwell,' said Peter Brody. 'Where is he?'

Maxwell hesitated. The vicar had wanted five minutes; he had been inside for ten or more. The jig was up. Maxwell was a man of God, privately, but he also knew on which side his bread was buttered. If he was to remain in Scratch Moss – and what alternative did he have? – then he had to be careful.

'Inside,' said Maxwell eventually, sending up a silent prayer for forgiveness. 'I followed him across the road from the vicarage. Thought I'd keep an eye on him until you got here.'

Brody was accompanied by seven men from the estate, all of whom Maxwell knew. Workers and housekeeping staff. They stood in the pouring rain as thunder rumbled close by. 'Sir... Lord Brody...' began Maxwell.

Lord Brody smiled at him. 'Maxwell. I understand. You still heave to the Christian ways, as your father did. You are indulged in that, as he was, because your family has always been good servants to mine. But you saw what he did to Timmins, yes?'

Maxwell nodded wretchedly.

'Such violence. Such needless violence. He cannot expect to walk away unpunished. You do understand that, Maxwell? And if he did walk away... what trouble could he visit upon us? It's for the best, Maxwell.'

Maxwell stood for a moment more in front of the door, weighing it all up. If he had been right, it was Timmins who carried the essence, who was Red Clogs. And if the vicar had killed him... then that meant...

Trying to take him out of Scratch Moss would almost certainly be futile, anyway. Better it ends now, in whatever way Lord Brody sees fit, he decided.

He stepped aside. Then a shout went up from one of the men. 'The vicar, Lord Brody! He's on the roof!'

—

George knew he wasn't leaving Scratch Moss. He didn't dare to even try. With that thing inside him... who knows what might happen? Once he entered that *fugue state*, the demon ascendant, George no longer in control of himself, who knows what harm he could cause? To innocents. To children. Better to exorcise himself here, in the house of God, even in this blasted place.

Upon hearing the voices, and realising Brody and his men had arrived, George had first gone to the room to the right of the altar. It was an office, though he'd never had call to use it. But he'd noticed a loose floorboard beneath the rug, and bending down he prised it up. Inside he put his notebook, praying it would not be found. Whoever came after him to St Mary's, if indeed the diocese sent another vicar, needed to know the truth about this place. Then he hurried to the staircase behind the door to the left of the kitchen. He could fend Brody's men off from the upper storey, which was merely a storeroom in the eaves, but for how long? He needed to take action, and he needed to do it now. He could feel the demon within him, scratching and clawing, trying to take over his mind.

In the roof space there was a ladder that led to a trapdoor in the roof, and then to a further ladder fixed to the outside of the spire. He needed to be closer to God, to better draw his strength, to fight the monster within. George climbed the ladder and pushed open the trapdoor, immediately assaulted by the rain and wind. The spire towered above him and seemed to be scraping the underside of the low black clouds that hung over Scratch Moss, dumping their rain on the town. Worms of light flickered in the clouds, and thunder rumbled directly overhead.

Bracing himself, George gripped the narrow ladder fixed to the outside of the spire and began to climb. As he did, he began to sing, in defiance of the storm. 'Nearer, my God, to thee, nearer to thee! E'en though it be a cross that raiseth me, still all my song shall be, nearer, my God, to thee; nearer, my God, to thee, nearer to thee!'

He chanced a look down, the height dizzying, the ground so far away, and saw Lord Brody, and Maxwell, and the men from the estate pointing at him. He redoubled his efforts, his foot slipping on the rain-slick rung of the ladder, and sang all the more loudly. 'Though like the wanderer, the sun gone down, darkness be over me, my rest a stone; yet in my dreams I'd be nearer, my God, to thee; nearer, my God, to thee, nearer to thee!'

A crack of thunder directly overhead almost deafened him. George smiled broadly, his face sluiced by the pounding rain. It was a sign. A sign from God. His Lord was with him, was giving him strength. Above him, the large cross on top of the spire almost shone against the black clouds.

George pressed on, and the ladder ended at the zenith of the spire, the cross above taller than him. George gripped it with two hands, hauling himself up, the wind buffeting him, the rain driving almost sideways, thunder rumbling above. He held on to the cross and closed his eyes.

'Come to me in my hour of need, O Lord,' he murmured, his face against the cold metal of the cross. 'Drive this demon from my body, free Scratch Moss from the foul serpent's coils.'

Another crack of thunder, then a flash of lightning that lit up the inside of George's tight-closed eyes. He opened them and tried to turn so he was standing on the tiny platform the cross was fixed to, and pressed his back against it.

'Our Father, who art in heaven, hallowed be thy name,' cried George. 'Thy kingdom come; thy will be done; on earth as it is in heaven.' He felt warm even though the wind howled and the rain lashed him. He felt warm from within.

It was God's love.

'Give us this day our daily bread. And forgive us our trespasses, as we forgive those who trespass against us,' said George. He smiled. He felt the demon ebbing away. He was sure of it. He risked throwing his right arm against the horizontal patibulum, and resumed his prayer.

'And lead us not into temptation; but deliver us from evil. For thine is the kingdom.'

He pushed back against the upright stipe, his left arm now spread out.

'The power and the glory.'

George's ears popped as the pressure of the rumbling thunder grew and grew. He stood stock still, against the giant cross, just as Christ might have been, looking to Heaven, praying for Our Heavenly Father to come to his aid.

'For ever and ever,' cried George as the storm gathered its strength. 'Amen.'

—

'Well,' said Lord Brody, looking up through the rain at the figure of George pressed against the cross on top of the spire. 'I think the damned fool is going to do our job for us.'

The thunder cracked like an explosion, directly above, and Maxwell flinched. The sky lit up, and a jagged fork of white-hot lightning speared down from the black clouds, straight to the cross. Maxwell stared open-mouthed as the vicar was illuminated by a fizzing electric halo all around his body, head thrown back, mouth open in a scream lost to the storm.

'It's coming down!' yelled one of the men. He was right. There was a terrible creaking sound, and the cross shifted visibly on the spire.

'Everyone back to the road!' called Brody. Maxwell was aware of the men around him fleeing, but felt rooted to the spot, forced to stare upwards as the cross, the vicar spread-eagled against it, leaned over, and then with a shriek of rending metal and brickwork, plummeted off the spire.

It landed but twenty feet away from him, the right-hand patibulum embedded in the grass, the cross on its side. He ran over then cautiously crept towards the smoking crucifix. The vicar was dead, of course, his body seemingly fused by the lightning to the metal cross. His corpse was blackened and charred, his mouth open in his final scream.

Maxwell looked around. He was alone. He crouched down by the embedded cross and said a silent prayer for George Ackman. He had to be quick, not only because he did not want the others to see him, but because he had heard the tales of how Red Clogs moved once its host had died. He wanted to be away from here before... Maxwell stopped. The burned corpse was hot and smoking... but not just that. From the vicar's mouth there seemed to issue a cloud of black smoke, driving up in defiance of the rain, gathering above the grotesque tableau.

Too late, Maxwell realised what it was as it plunged into him, filling his mouth and nostrils.

-

It was but minutes until Lord Brody returned with the men, joining Maxwell at the side of the cross and the blackened body of George Ackman. 'Well,' said Brody eventually. 'Damn fool.'

Maxwell looked at Lord Brody. All his life, Martin Maxwell had fallen between two gods. The one his father brought him up to worship, and the one the people of Scratch Moss believed in. Up to now they had both been merely stories, a question of choice of belief. Now he knew with damning uncertainty that one of them was real. And it wasn't the god to whom this church had been built, for whom George Ackman had died. He felt power rippling through him. Strength. Hunger. Desire to kill. He dampened it down, looking at the church. 'We should make sure they never send us another priest,' he said thickly.

'How?' said Lord Brody.

Maxwell stalked forward towards the church, and kicked open the door. He turned and beckoned to the others. 'Wreck it all. Wreck everything.'

They followed him inside as he lifted his shotgun, took aim at the crucifix over the altar, and blasted it to splinters.

PART NINE

1945

30

It was fully dark by the time Arthur Collier had finished reading the notebook of George Ackman. It ended with the vicar seemingly quite mad, detailing how he had taken a demon inside him by killing a man. Nora had told Arthur that the last vicar at St Mary's had died after being struck by lightning on top of the spire. He could only assume that was Ackman, and that the church had lain abandoned by the diocese ever since 1905. He had come in search of evidence of the dark goings-on in Scratch Moss, but this account by Ackman was bordering on insanity. Some kind of... spirit, sleeping beneath the earth, at the heart of the coal mine? A spirit that demanded sacrifice, and sent its essence to possess men and bring it children? Arthur shook his head. He could not countenance such a fairy story. And yet... he recalled the way the eyes of William Maxwell – the son of Martin Maxwell, who was mentioned by Ackman – had darkened to utter blackness when Arthur confronted him. A phenomenon mentioned by the vicar in both his own experiences of attempting to exorcise Herbert Timmins, and in his relaying of the story told to him by the former Lord Brody.

In truth, Arthur didn't know quite what to believe any more. But he was certain that, while illuminating, Ackman's book could not really be construed as the sort of evidence he needed to take this case to the district police headquarters. There were some pages ripped out of the journal, around where Ackman was relating Lord Brody's confession, and Arthur puzzled over what they might have contained, and why the vicar had removed them. Well, he would take the book with him, just in case. But he would have to find harder, firmer proof.

As he left the room, holding the candle, and stepped into the main body of the church, Arthur saw the misshapen lump of coal standing on the altar. It disgusted him, suddenly; this town, these people... they were complicit in everything that had happened. They turned their backs even as their own children were taken and sacrificed to an ancient god. And they thought straw effigies and paying tribute to a piece of coal would keep them safe. Arthur put down the candle and stalked over to the altar, putting his hands flat against the coal, and pushing it with all his strength. It hit the stone floor and shattered into a thousand pieces. Good, he thought. Your prayers to this graven idol do not work. Do what no man has done in Scratch Moss before, and stand up and fight to save your children.

Arthur had hoped to be finished within a week and be away from here, but he knew the evidence he required was likely to be found down in the mine. Which meant staying to at least Saturday again, when the workers had their day off, and gaining access to the tunnels. For now, he was famished, and he headed back to the Black Diamond.

Arthur had been expecting to take his meal in his room again at the pub, but when he stepped in to the lounge there was an almost palpable sense of what he could only call relief among the clientele. The landlord greeted him warmly, pulled him a pint, and told him to take a seat and he'd have Nora bring his meal over to him shortly. Somewhat nonplussed, Arthur sat down at a round table, returning the nods of two or three of the miners who were assembled in the bar.

When Nora appeared, gripping his hot plate of pork chops, potatoes and carrots with a tea-towel, Arthur stared at the tabletop, as though it had suddenly become intensely interesting to him. He was, in truth, not used to dealing with matters of the heart, and he did not quite know how to properly handle women, especially ones as forthright and confident as Nora. He supposed this was the modern world now, and attitudes were different now the war had ended. People had six years of wasted time to make up, those who had survived, at least. It was hardly surprising that the old mores and ways of doing things were being swept aside.

Still, all that said, he didn't quite know where to look and certainly didn't know what to say as Nora put the plate in front of him. He settled on asking how Elsa was.

'None the worse for her ordeal,' said Nora. 'She's very taken with you, though. Been asking all day after the nice man who gave her a pencil.'

Arthur harrumphed and nodded. He glanced around the bar and said quietly, 'I must say, the reception I've got this evening is somewhat different to yesterday. I was expecting to be *persona non grata* again.'

'Would you like to take a walk after your dinner?' said Nora suddenly.

'In the dark?' said Arthur.

Nora smiled and pinched his arm playfully. 'Don't worry. I'll hold your hand if you get frightened.'

-

Arthur and Nora walked along the main road, and at first he thought she was taking him to the old church. He felt slightly panicked; had he been seen smashing the coal? Was there going to be a delegation of townsfolk waiting for him? But before they got there she turned off to the left, alongside the railway track that ran down from the pit and over the road and up to the branch line.

'We call this the Donkey Lane,' said Nora. Arthur felt her arm brush his as they walked along the dark track. 'I don't know why.'

'Probably at one point donkeys used to haul the coal buckets along here,' he suggested.

Nora laughed lightly. 'That makes sense.'

It was dark but there was a full moon, and the sky was clear. Stars twinkled in the black, and reminded Arthur of the coal face glittering down the pit. They passed a dark pond, and something splashed in it. Arthur and Nora began to speak at the same time.

'You first,' said Arthur. 'I insist.'

She took a deep breath. 'I just didn't want you to think... well. When I came to your room. I didn't want you to think I made a habit of it, that's all. I'm not easy, Arthur.'

'I didn't think you were,' he stuttered. 'I don't make a habit of it either.' He was glad it was dark so Nora couldn't see him blushing.

'I like you,' she said, and it hung between them as they walked. They crossed the railway line and Nora pointed to a black shape rearing up against the night ahead of them. 'The Rabbit Rocks. I don't think rabbits used to pull the coal buckets up it, though.'

Arthur laughed. He'd never quite met anyone like Nora. Confident but not brassy. Funny but dry. And very beautiful. He wished he had met her anywhere but Scratch Moss, then wondered why he'd thought that.

She said, 'Up for a walk to the top? You can see for miles.'

Arthur didn't mention the shrapnel in his leg, but swallowed the pain and headed up the steep but mercifully not-too-long path behind Nora, her dress swishing as she stalked upwards. At the top Arthur was surprised to find a concrete pill-box, its slit windows looking out from all sides. In case the Germans invaded, to protect the coal supplies. Thankfully it had never been needed and, hoped Arthur, everyone had learned enough of a lesson now that it never would. Nora had been right, though. Even at night, the views were incredible. He could see the distant lights of Warrington in one direction, Wigan in the other. And looking back the way they had come he could see the Little Woods and, beyond, the pit-head gear and Scratch Moss Hall.

'I like to come up here, find out how far I can see,' said Nora. 'All those places. Sometimes on a really clear day you can see Manchester.'

'You could go to Manchester,' said Arthur quietly. 'You could go anywhere.'

'I suppose,' said Nora. She looked at him. 'People rarely leave. I'm not sure why. It's like this place has a hold on you. As though once you know its secrets, you owe it to Scratch Moss to keep them, and keep them here.'

'Secrets?'

She put a hand on his arm. 'What were you going to say, down there, when we spoke at the same time?'

Arthur looked out towards the distant lights. No blackout, no air-raid wardens, no fear of bombers droning overhead. The world was a different place than it had been just a few short months ago. Safe. Free. And yet... not here. Not in Scratch Moss. For reasons he didn't fully understand.

'When I brought Elsa back yesterday, everyone seemed angry,' said Arthur slowly. 'And this evening... your father, the locals, they couldn't have been more friendly. I wondered what had changed.'

Nora held out her hand. 'Let's walk back.' Arthur took it and she led him down the path from the Rabbit Rocks, back the way they'd came. When they got to the bottom and followed the train track she said, 'Mrs Dowd's daughter died of diphtheria this afternoon.' Nora kept hold of Arthur's hand.

He said, 'And that was cause for... celebration?'

'Not really,' said Nora as they turned back onto the Donkey Lane. 'Not at all. It's just... I can't explain it, Arthur. But little Bess dying means it's all right that you saved Elsa. Please don't ask me why. It just is. It's sad and everything, but she was going to die anyway.' She squeezed his hand tighter. 'It makes everything all right.'

Arthur didn't say anything, just walked along the track, holding Nora's hand. The night was warm and he could smell her scent. He thought about what he'd read in George Ackman's notebook, about the tradition of child sacrifice going back hundreds of years. He did not want to believe Nora was caught up in all this.

She filled the void of his silence and murmured, 'I meant what I said before. About not making a habit of... of what happened.' Her pace slowed as the track passed through a particularly thick copse of trees.

'I know,' said Arthur. 'I believe you.'

She slowed further, almost to a halt. 'But that doesn't mean I wouldn't want it to happen again.'

Nora stepped back, and leaned against a thick tree trunk. Somewhere, an owl hooted, and close by, another answered. She reached out a hand and took hold of the lapel of Arthur's jacket, and dragged him towards her. Before he knew what he was doing, Arthur was kissing Nora fiercely, his hands gripping the hem of her dress and dragging it up, over her waist. Without ceremony she pushed down her underwear, stepping out of it, and her hands went to the buttons of Arthur's trousers. He kissed her deeply as she guided him into her, gasping as his hands went to her hips, holding her firm.

'Come with me,' Arthur whispered into her ear. 'Come away with me. When I leave.'

'Stay with me,' she whispered back, biting his earlobe. 'Stay here with me.'

31

Arthur was served his breakfast by the landlord, who informed him Nora had gone out to the weekly market to procure fresh produce. He was in equal parts relieved and disappointed. He wasn't quite sure what he was allowing himself to get into, here. It could only end badly. He was, of course, not going to stay in Scratch Moss, and Nora was never going to leave. Perhaps Arthur had been caught up in it all, everything moving so quickly, and the strange discombobulation he felt at being in this strange place. Maybe once he did actually go, in a week's time, it would all be put into proper perspective, and the heightened feelings he was experiencing would fade with the miles he put between himself and Scratch Moss.

He was due at Scratch Moss Hall again today, but he had another motive as well as inspecting the accounts and logs. George Ackman's diary had referred in detail to his conversation with the old Lord Brody, the current incumbent's great grandfather, who had built Scratch Moss pit. There were one or two things Arthur wanted to check out.

Fortunately, the young Lord Brody, Walter, was waiting in the drawing room when Arthur arrived just after ten. He seemed somewhat exercised and distracted at the same time. Arthur frowned at him. 'Are you quite well, Lord Brody?'

'Yes, of course,' said Walter, looking around as though they might be being observed, then closed the door. 'No, not really, Mr Collier. I wondered… might you expedite your work? Perhaps get it completed in the next day or two?'

Speeding up the work would mean getting away from Scratch Moss more quickly, and saying goodbye to Nora. Arthur made a show of thinking about it. 'I might be able to shave off a bit of time here and there, but I'm not sure the next day or two is strictly doable.' He looked at Walter. 'You are keen to have me away from here?'

'Not that,' said Walter, his voice dropping to little more than a whisper. 'I'm keen to be away myself. I've been making arrangements, over the last few days. Travel itineraries, that sort of thing. I think word has leaked out from some of the household staff. There are mutterings, Mr Collier.'

'Mutterings, Lord Brody?'

Walter sighed. 'Look, old fellow, don't tell me you haven't noticed what a strange place this is. And I know you've been directly involved, as well. Taking Maxwell down to the coppers, punching him onto his arse.' He dropped his voice low again. 'Thing is, there's always been a Brody at Scratch Moss Hall, longer than anyone still alive can remember. Word's got out I'm planning to up sticks. Coupled with this National Coal Board business, folks are getting rather cheesed off.'

Arthur considered it. 'I can see why there might be some consternation about the nationalisation programme. If you like I can speak to the miners directly about the positives we feel it is going to bring. But I fail to really understand why the townsfolk would be perturbed about you potentially leaving Scratch Moss Hall.'

'Thing is, Collier, it's more than just being the local landed gentry, carrying the Lord Brody title,' confided Walter. 'These people, they seem to think there are certain... responsibilities that go with it.'

'You mean being the nominal head of some kind of pagan cult that sacrifices its own children to some dark god sleeping in the earth beneath your land?' said Arthur, almost casually.

Walter stared at him, then blinked slowly, his mouth falling open. When he had recovered, he said, 'Yes, Collier. Yes. Exactly that. My, you have done your research, haven't you?'

'And would you be willing to testify in court, or at least in a police statement, about any of that?' asked Arthur.

Walter gaped at him. 'Are you mad? No, of course I wouldn't. Why would I even have to?'

'Because what is happening here is not right, even though it might have been happening for hundreds of years, Lord Brody.'

'And that's why I need to get away,' said Walter. 'Put it all behind me. Take your Coal Board money, sell the hall, and steer bloody clear of Scratch Moss for the rest of my life.' He looked around again fearfully. 'But I don't think they're keen on that idea, Collier. I feel they think having a Lord Brody at Scratch Moss Hall is part and parcel of the whole shooting match. As though we're some sort of curator of this mad ghost they believe in.'

'If you're that frightened, Lord Brody, why not just leave right now?'

Walter looked at him and said quietly, 'I'm afraid they might not let me, old chap.'

Arthur nodded. 'Right. Then we best get on, then. Something I need from you today is the plans of the mine workings.'

'I thought you had them all?'

Arthur shook his head. 'I need you to look through the old documents from when your great grandfather set up the pit. I believe there are some tunnels in the mine that don't appear on the current diagrams.'

Walter nodded. 'I'll see what I can turn up.'

—

Just as Arthur was going to break for lunch, Walter bustled back into the drawing room, laden with rolled plans and blueprints. 'I went through some drawers in the old study and found these,' he said. 'Not sure if they're what you're after.'

Arthur spread the plans out on the desk until he found the one he was looking for. Designs for a circular tunnel, built some thirty or forty feet below the main tunnels, and not listed on any other plans.

'Well, I'll be damned,' said Walter wonderingly. 'This was underneath the pit all this time, and nobody knew?' He looked at Arthur. 'But what does it mean?'

What it meant, as far as Arthur was concerned, was his best chance at finding evidence yet. Because despite what had happened with Nora, Arthur could not shirk his duty. He had not shied away from duty during the war, and he had never failed in his duty as a policeman before that. He would fulfil his duty to the Coal Commission and complete his work here. But he also had a duty to expose to the proper authorities what was going on in Scratch Moss. And that meant evidence. And *that* meant going back down the mine. Alone.

–

The Scratch Moss pit ran two shifts, one from six in the morning to two in the afternoon, then an hour's handover and the second from three until eleven. The site was generally clear of people by midnight. That afternoon, Arthur visited the pit and said he wanted to see the equipment rooms. While under the guise of an inspection and inventory, he secured himself a lamp, a helmet and a length of rope, and secreted in the leather bag he had taken with him. Then he returned to the Black Diamond to eat, but not to drink; he needed a clear head for what was to come.

Nora brought him his dinner, and when he declined a pint she asked him if he was quite well. He dropped his voice low and said that he had to go out to do a late-night assessment of the mine's perimeter workings and test how secure it was when closed, but would be grateful if she didn't mention it as he did not want to alert anyone to the fact, instead requiring to do a spot-check, as it were. Nora nodded and tapped the side of her nose conspiratorially, and Arthur felt a little sickened at having to lie to her. But he could not tell her the real reason why he needed to be let out of the pub gone eleven-thirty. She was from Scratch Moss, and he knew where her loyalties must ultimately lie.

Arthur stole along the darkened road towards the Little Woods, having decided it would be better to approach the site surreptitiously through the trees rather than along Hall Lane which led to the works. As he started off along the path that ran alongside the railway track, he noticed through the trees a light in the old church. No doubt someone had discovered his vandalism of the coal idol; he wondered if they suspected him, or thought it was a mere accident, perhaps knocked off the altar by a fox or other vermin.

It was pitch black in the woods, the clear, starry night of the previous evening replaced by a dull night of low-lying cloud. He didn't dare light his lamp though, even though he could barely pick out the path in front of him. It would not do to alert anyone to his presence at the pit so late at night. He had taken a risk by even saying what he had to Nora, but somehow he felt slightly less awful for lying to her if he could dress it up in at least some half-truths.

Arthur was rather beginning to fall for Nora. He wondered how much more he would see of her before his time in Scratch Moss came to an end. He might fancy he could see her again when he left, persuade her to come away, perhaps for a weekend or so. But if he succeeded in his plans to expose the wrongdoing in the town, he expected she would not want anything more to do with him, and he could scarcely say he would blame her.

Arthur swore as he stumbled on a tree root, the lamp and helmet clanking in his bag. He thought he heard something and stopped, falling silent, slowing his breathing. It sounded like someone pushing through the undergrowth, snapping twigs or branches as they moved. He listened in the darkness, his head cocked to one side. But there was only the gentle swaying of the trees in the breeze, the occasional cry of a night bird.

Arthur forged on, the pit-head gear rising up blackly ahead of him. Scratch Moss pit was not secured by a fence around its perimeter; nobody had ever thought there was such a need. Once the National Coal Board came into effect and took charge of the mine, doubtless they would want to ramp up security, especially given the prized nature of Scratch Moss coal.

As if anyone would ever dare try to steal from here. The thought rose unbidden in his mind, but it was true. It would be a foolish man who came to Scratch Moss and tried to take away the coal they believed was blessed by a dark god. What, then, did that make Arthur Collier, if not a foolish man? For when he took his findings to the authorities, that's exactly what he would be doing. Stealing the living made by Scratch Moss right away from them.

Arthur stood at the treeline for a moment, surveying the site. It was dark and silent; nothing moved. Of course, he couldn't go down the main shaft; he'd need someone to operate the lift, first of all, and the noise it would make would have people running over in minutes. But there were other ways into the pit, and he'd seen one almost used with his own eyes.

Arthur had memorised the plans of the pit and in the darkness tried to locate the place where he'd seen William Maxwell taking Elsa. The adit to the west, an air tunnel that ran out of the main chamber below, and doubled up as emergency access if needed, say in the event of a collapse. Staying low, Arthur ran across the site as best as his bad leg would allow him, and followed the land as it sloped downwards, hiding him from view of the main workings, on the off chance that there was anyone still there. As he had seen when he had accosted Maxwell, there was an iron gate set in a raised hillock, giving access to the adit. Arthur got out his oil lamp and lit it, certain he was shielded from the main pit. The light it cast pierced a little way into the blackness through the bars of the gate, showing a rough, tight tunnel sloping downwards sharply.

The gate was unlocked, and swung open towards him easily. Arthur put on the helmet, and ducked inside. There wasn't room to stand up straight, and holding the lamp up in front of him, he walked forward as quickly as he could, bent almost double as he was, into the dark, hot bowels of Scratch Moss pit.

32

Arthur's leg began to hurt, shooting pains all up his right thigh. It was from walking downwards in a crouched position, he knew. But he also felt as though it was his body trying to tell him that what his brain was doing was stupid beyond words. It was as if the sharp stabbing in his thigh was a reminder of D-Day. *At least you had a chance on Gold Beach*, he thought. *At least you were only facing men with guns.* He looked downwards at the infinite blackness beyond the pale reach of the lamp's glow. *You have no idea what's down here.*

If Arthur's study of the plans of the pit were right, then this adit should intersect somewhere around where he had seen that blocked-off tunnel on his first visit down the shaft. That's right, he told himself. Concentrate on the plans. Remember that everything down here is made by man; every tunnel is planned and engineered. This is all the work of sane, rational men. *Can you be any less?*

He took deep breaths of the stale air as the tunnel turned and descended more sharply. He remembered this dog-leg from the blueprints; he should be getting close. Just a few more minutes and...

His light suddenly showed a larger black space ahead of him, the walls glittering with pinprick reflected light. The path levelled and Arthur found he could stand up. He was down in the pit. And there, to his right, was the boarded-up section he had seen, the ground around it littered with those little straw figures. The lad who brought him down the pit, Johnny Crowe, had said that the boards must have blocked off a dead tunnel, possibly due to a collapse. Arthur knew better, now. That way led to the circular tunnel some thirty feet below that Lord Brody had built back in 1865. Arthur dumped his bag on the ground and wiped the sweat from his brow with a handkerchief. In the bag he had a stoppered bottle containing water, and drunk eagerly of it. He'd also brought a crowbar, and setting the lamp on a shelf carved into the coalface he set about the wooden boards with it, pulling them out of the frame in which they'd been nailed with loud cracks. No doubt the men would puzzle over the damage when they came down for the morning shift, and report it to the supervisors, but by then Arthur hoped he might have the evidence he was looking for, and whatever the gruesome jig was in Scratch Moss, it would be up.

Arthur grabbed his bag and slipped through the gap in the boards, into a narrow tunnel that sloped sharply down. He estimated that it was a 1:3 gradient, falling a foot for every three, which meant in thirty long strides he would be at the circular tunnel. He was right, and he could see by lamplight as the slope levelled off that the tunnel curved ahead and behind him. And there was more; on a wooden frame set at an angle there was a mirror, its surface cracked and mottled. Which meant above him... He held the lamp high and could see the slim shaft that went straight to the surface, where the sunlight had once penetrated and created the ring of sunlight that Lord Brody had been sure had captured and caused to sleep the god he believed was below the earth.

The tunnel smelled badly, not of gases but of rot. Something crunched under Arthur's boots, then his toe nudged something soft and yielding. He bent forward with the lamp, seeing first the dried, brittle bones, some covered in rags, that littered the ground. Then he gasped and stepped back, almost dropping the lamp.

The thing his foot had touched was a body. An infant's body. Battered and bloodied and relatively fresh. Arthur covered his mouth as he felt his bile rise, then he turned and vomited loudly against the wall. His conversation with Nora on the Rabbit Rocks came back to him.

'*Mrs Dowd's daughter died of diphtheria this afternoon.*'

'*And that was cause for... celebration?*'

'*Not really. Not at all. It's just... I can't explain it, Arthur. But little Bess dying means it's all right that you saved Elsa. Please don't ask me why. It just is. It's sad and everything, but she was going to die anyway. It makes everything all right.*'

'Little Bess,' croaked Arthur, his bile rising again. He could hear his own breathing, his own heartbeat, down there in the depths of the earth. A child had died. Not from diphtheria, though that was doubtless her fate. She had been taken and thrown down that shaft, dying broken and alone in the blackness. By William Maxwell, no doubt.

She had been sacrificed to the dark pagan god they called Duiw Prið. Tossed into the pit like a rag-doll, still breathing.

'You fucking monsters,' said Arthur out loud. His heartbeat was almost deafening now, his breathing like the howl of a train horn. 'Every one of you in this accursed place. Every single one of you.'

It's sad and everything, but she was going to die anyway. It makes everything all right.

Even you, Nora, he thought. Even you. How could that be in any way *all right*? A scared, hurt child, breathing her last in the darkness. But because she was going to die anyway that was *all right*.

He had his evidence. He would see them all hang for this. All of them. Arthur threw up again, steadying himself on the wall. The coal face was warm to the touch, almost pulsing, like a living thing. It was then he realised it wasn't his own breathing he could hear, not his own heartbeat.

Something shuffled ahead of him and he held up the lamp in panic, just in time to see a vast mouth, lined with razor-sharp teeth, snapping at him out of the darkness, a reptilian thing, an impossible, long-dead beast. Arthur yelled out and fell backwards, and when he landed...

...it was not on the hard surface of the tunnel, but on a bed of springy moss, impossibly huge leaves rising up around him from the thick trunks of plants he could not recognise. The air was hot and humid and bright; up ahead the sky was blue and the sun shone straight down on him. In front of him there was some... creature. Like a lizard, perhaps, but monstrous, bigger than a cow, a waving, spiny sail on its back, its jaws snapping at the air. It was just like the bones of the vast, unknowable giants that were displayed in the museums, which the scientists said once walked the earth, but made flesh.

'Where am I?' Arthur managed to utter, as the beast crashed on through the undergrowth. It was like some jungle, grunting and chattering with life. Overhead wheeled vast birds with reptilian wings, and the unfamiliar trees swarmed with insects and bugs, some of them bigger than his hand.

Arthur shrank back into the moss, and felt himself sinking into it, deeper and deeper, so deep he thought he might drown in it. The sun wheeled overhead at an impossible pace, night falling and bringing with it sounds and roars, then the sun was there again, moving faster and faster before Arthur's uncomprehending eyes. Night and day flickered by in the time it took Arthur to blink, the trees and plants growing and growing then dying and rotting around him, strange beasts falling, their bodies stripped of flesh and reduced to bones in seconds. Time was flying like a speeded-up picture at the cinema, years, centuries, millennia squeezed into seconds, and all through it he could sense the thundering heartbeat of *something*, a presence that seemed to infuse the trees and the plants and the ground beneath him, as though it was part of everything around here, and everything was a part of it.

Then there was a blinding flash and the ground rippled beneath Arthur and he felt a hot wind scorch him. Then there was darkness and he felt himself sinking further, the dead plants and animals compacted around him like mulch, the earth closing over his head as he screamed and screamed and...

...screamed, falling back on to the hard floor of the tunnel, surrounded by the bones of dead children.

'Duiw Prið sleeps and I have journeyed in his dream,' Arthur whispered to himself.

It was true. It was all true. The god that had dwelt here since the dawn of time. Arthur had seen what it had seen, felt what it had felt. Such joy as it beheld the seedlings pushing through the soul, as it watched the tiny creatures breaking out of their shells, as a cocoon cracked open and an insect unfurled iridescent wings. Such joy in life. And then... a cataclysm, darkness, howling winds, the earth heaving and shaking and then Duiw Prið was forced down, down, down into the deep earth, his domain gone, his only company the dead remains of that which once gave him such succour, compacted into peat and then into hard, flinty coal, all that he now held sway over. And that joy in life fermented into a sour, sharp bitterness, as millennia rolled on and on and on under the deep, dark ground.

And as he inhabited Duiw Prið's dream, so Duiw Prið sent dark, smoky tendrils into the depths of Arthur's mind, dragging out memories and thoughts and—

A cow bellowed into the night as her calf, barely able to stand on its legs, was taken away from her, its throat cut within her sight. A trio of mewling kittens was tied into a hessian sack weighted with bricks and thrown into a river. A tiny boy breathed his last in the bombed-out remains of a house, the broken bodies of his family dead around him. And Jimmy Collins, only seventeen, gave Arthur a tremulous smile as their boat beached at Normandy, and Arthur told him gruffly to keep his head down and keep running, and everything would be all right. And minutes later Arthur turned to him, to tell him to keep running, just as an enemy bullet ripped into the boy's forehead and splattered his brains all over Gold Beach.

Duiw Prið's thoughts mingled with Arthur's, like oil and water, and Arthur tasted what Duiw Prið tasted, joy at the images plucked from Arthur's mind. No longer joy at new life, but bitter, angry, sad joy at young life being snuffed out, and the more he tasted, the more he hungered for it, even in sleep.

Arthur felt his mind shatter like a window, and as the cracks spread like a spider web and the pieces of his sanity began to fall, tinkling, to the bone-strewn ground at his feet, he grabbed his lamp and ran shrieking into the darkness.

He ran and ran, up up up, up towards the air and the night and away from the cloying, heavy darkness below, away from Duiw Prið's awful black hunger, and by the time he found the tunnel from the adit he was crawling on his hands and knees, stones ripping his palms and the fabric of his trousers. He thought about just collapsing, giving in to the darkness, dying there and then, but forged onwards, just as he had forged on at Gold Beach, bits of Jimmy Collins's skull and brains spattered all over his shoulder. He forged and fought and crawled until he thought he smelled fresh air and his mind switched itself off like an electric lightbulb, and Arthur Collier embraced the merciful darkness.

33

When Arthur awoke he was in his bed in the Black Diamond. His hands and knees were bandaged, and he had a thumping headache. His mouth was dry and his lips chapped and cracked. Pale, late-afternoon sunlight filtered through the curtains. There was a glass of water on his bedside table. Arthur reached weakly for it, but the bandages across his palms made him clumsy and unable to grip it, and it crashed to the floor, shattering on the boards. Within seconds he heard thumping feet on the landing and his door was flung open. It was Nora.

'Arthur! Oh, thank goodness!'

'Water,' he croaked. Nora ran out of the room again and in moments returned with a jug and a glass. She perched on the side of the bed and supported his head as she put the glass to his lips.

'What happened?' he said as he sank back into the pillow. He looked at his bandaged hands. 'What happened to me?'

'You were found at the pit,' said Nora slowly. 'Unconscious, when the men came on for the first shift. Near one of the adits. They thought you were dead.' She looked at him. 'Arthur, had you been down into the mine?'

He thought about the darkness, the blackness, the utter terror. Images of impossible things, of jungles and war, interspersed the memories, to the point where he could not separate what was real and what was not. He had gone down into the pit, he remembered that much. He had broken the barrier to the closed tunnel, he had found... what had he found? A memory of something crunching under his feet, of a rotten stench, of blood...

'I think so,' he said, laying his hand on Nora's arm. 'But I cannot recall...' He looked at the window. 'What time is it? They found me this morning?'

Nora smiled and stroked his forehead. 'Arthur, you have been unconscious for three days.'

He stared at her and struggled to sit up, his head pounding. 'No wonder I'm famished. Three days?'

'When you did come awake, you were raving like a madman. The doctor gave you a little morphine to help with the pain and to encourage you to sleep. Your hands and knees were ripped to ribbons, Arthur.' She put her head on one side. 'What... what did you see down there?'

An image of a cow bellowing as its calf was killed in front of it rose in Arthur's mind. 'I'm... not sure,' he said, doubtfully. Not cows, surely. But then... what? He looked down at his left shoulder, for some reason expecting to see Jimmy Collins's brains splattered over his pyjamas.

'I'll get you some tea and toast, perhaps a couple of eggs,' said Nora decidedly. 'Then we'll see if you're well enough to get out of bed.'

When she was gone, Arthur racked his brains to remember what had happened down the pit. All he could recall were feelings of abject terror, which shamed him. He had gone looking for evidence, but even that seemed to recede into some kind of insignificance. He grew angry at himself. 'Children are dying,' he whispered. But somewhere in his head, a little voice seemed to whisper, *That's just the way it is in Scratch Moss.*

He intended to get up and catch up with his work, but when he'd eaten the fried eggs and toast and drunk the tea, he started to drift off into sleep again. He was dimly aware of Nora lying on the bed beside him, holding him tight as he slipped back into unconsciousness and strange, formless dreams.

Arthur awoke early and refreshed the next day. He unwound the bandages and found the cuts on his palms mostly closed and healing, so he washed and dressed, and finally began to feel human again. He was just about to head down to see if he could get breakfast when there was a knock at his door. It was Nora, looking somewhat perturbed.

'There's someone to see you from the pit,' she said. 'Johnny Crowe.'

Arthur met Crowe in the snug of the pub, which was yet to open to the public. The lad hopped about from foot to foot, looking anxious. He said, 'Mr Clarke, the foreman, sent me. The lads at the pit... they're going up to Scratch Moss Hall.'

Arthur shrugged. 'For what purpose?'

'All this Coal Board business,' said Crowe. 'They're not happy. Word is that Lord Brody's been packing up and has plans to abandon Scratch Moss.'

'Hmm,' said Arthur. Lord Brody had said as much to him, and had been keen to make sure the miners didn't find out about it. 'So, Mr Clarke would like me to... what? Have a meeting with the workforce? Explain what the proposed National Coal Board is, and what the benefits are?'

'I reckon Mr Clarke thinks it's gone beyond all that,' said Crowe. 'He says the lads are out for blood.'

Arthur glanced at Nora. 'I think I shall skip breakfast and go and see what all this is about.'

'I'm coming with you,' said Nora.

When they got to Scratch Moss Hall there were almost a hundred men gathered on the gravel drive. Mr Clarke the foreman was standing on the steps, seemingly attempting to calm them down.

'This thing's coming whether we like it or not, this National Coal Board,' Arthur heard Clarke saying. 'We just need to make sure it works for us, not against us.'

'Things are fine as they are!' shouted someone from the crowd. 'We don't need this bloody Coal Board.'

There were shouts of assent and Clarke suddenly spied Arthur, Nora and Crowe approaching. 'Look, lads, here's Mr Collier from the Coal Commission. He can explain it to you better than I can.' Clarke shot Arthur a desperate look.

The crowd of men turned to watch Arthur approaching. Someone cried, 'We don't need outsiders telling us what to do in Scratch Moss.'

Nora put a hand on Arthur's arm. 'Perhaps it would be better if you left, Arthur,' she murmured. The crowd did seem to be getting ugly, but Arthur wasn't going to be cowed by them. He pushed through towards the steps in front of the house and joined Clarke.

'Now, see here,' he said in a commanding tone. 'I can quite understand you might be feeling a bit unsure of what's happening, but getting a mob up like this isn't the way we do things. There are certain assurances I can give you—'

'Stick your assurances up your arse!' came a shout, and there was a volley of laughs and catcalls.

Arthur raised his hands for quiet. 'No matter how you cut it, Lord Brody isn't going to be in charge of Scratch Moss pit for much longer. So there's no point coming up here, see? Let's all go back down to the mine and I can give you the proper information in a meeting.'

'We heard Lord Brody's buggering off,' said someone.

'Well, what he does isn't any concern of the National Coal Board,' said Arthur.

'But it's a concern to us! There's always been a Brody at Scratch Moss Hall. There always has to be. It's the way things are.'

Arthur was about to speak when he heard the door unlock behind them. There was loud murmuring from the crowd and

Arthur turned to see Walter Brody emerge, flanked by his butler and by William Maxwell, the gamekeeper, who carried his shotgun in the crook of his arm. Arthur glared at Maxwell, not quite sure how he could show his face after Arthur had tried to have him arrested, but the man seemed impassive, normal-looking, even. A memory of his black eyes bobbed into Arthur's mind, and he had a sudden vision of being down in the dark earth, the terror he felt. There was something else, as well, at the periphery of his remembrance. A child, broken, bloodied, battered, in the darkness… But there was no time for that now.

'Look here, you men,' said Walter Brody in what Arthur thought was quite the wrong tone of voice to be addressing an angry mob. 'Things are going to change around here, and it's no fault of mine. But you're all going to have to get used to it.'

'You're running away from your responsibilities,' shouted a man at the front.

Brody shrugged. 'Not my responsibilities any more, old chap.' He clapped Arthur on the shoulder. 'I suggest you address any concerns to Mr Collier here, and the Coal Commission that's setting up this National Coal Board.'

'Judas!' called a man, and the cry was taken up by the rest of them, becoming a chant aimed at Brody. 'Judas! Judas! Judas!'

'You're all mad!' cried Brody, losing his composure. 'Believe in what silly folk tales you want to, but you'll be doing it without me or any future Lord Brody!'

The mob surged forward, and Maxwell stepped in front of Brody, brandishing his shotgun. 'Get back, all of you!' called the gamekeeper.

Then there was a crash, and Arthur turned to see one of the tall sash windows flanking the door shatter, the glass falling to the ground. Someone had thrown a rock. He ducked as another one skimmed over his head, smashing the glass above the double doors.

There was a deafening crack as Maxwell fired his shotgun into the air. The mob paused, but their blood was up. Arthur felt Clarke grab his arm and drag him to one side as the miners poured forward. Maxwell and Brody retreated into the hall and the gamekeeper tried to close the doors, but the force of the crowd was too strong, and they let out a triumphant cheer as the doors flung open inwards, and they poured into Scratch Moss Hall.

'I'll see them all sacked for this!' gasped Arthur, picking himself up from the gravel where Clarke had dragged him away from the advancing miners. Nora and Crowe ran to his side, as the sounds of violence and destruction issued from the open doors.

'You sack them, you've no pit,' said Clarke, brushing gravel off his suit. 'You'll struggle to get anyone from outside Scratch Moss to come and work here.'

There was a cacophony of smashing glass and splintering wood as the mob rampaged through the hall. Arthur said, 'Get the police, for God's sake! What do they hope to gain by this vandalism?'

Nora put a hand on his arm. 'They feel they're being abandoned, Arthur. All their lives they've worked that pit, and lined the Brody family's pockets. Now Lord Brody wants to wash his hands of them.'

'It's just progress,' said Arthur, exasperatedly. He ducked as the window beside them shattered from the inside.

'They're frightened,' said Nora softly. 'All this time, there's been a Brody running the pit. At least with the family here, the Scratch Moss people didn't feel alone. With… with everything. With what else is down the mine. Now…'

There was a screaming and Arthur turned to see the household staff fleeing from the far side of the hall, emerging from the tradesman's entrance around the corner. 'What now?' he said, as the miners began to pour out of the doors again, some of them carrying trophies: vases, cigar boxes, small statuettes.

Then he smelled the smoke.

'Good God, they've set fire to the place!' he said.

Wherever the blaze had been started, it took hold quickly, and thick smoke began to pour out of the broken windows and through the door. The mob streamed out, fleeing back towards Scratch Moss along with the household staff and servants.

'Did anyone see Lord Brody come out?' said Arthur.

No one had, and Arthur grabbed the jacket of young Johnny Crowe. 'You, in with me!'

Arthur and Crowe headed through the doors to see the staircase already ablaze, the sound of cracking timbers creaking above them. The smoke was already making Arthur's eyes smart, and he pointed to the drawing room, where he had met with Lord Brody several times, and dragged Crowe along with him. Smoke and heat billowed out as they pushed open the door, and Arthur could make out two figures, one crouched by the other. Holding his breath, he plunged into the thickening smoke, where he found the gamekeeper, Maxwell, prone on the rug, Lord Brody kneeling beside him.

Arthur pointed to Crowe to get Maxwell, unable to speak for the choking smoke. Crowe shook his head, his eyes wild. 'I'll not go near him!' he coughed.

Arthur grabbed Crowe's jacket and pushed him roughly towards Maxwell, then he grabbed hold of Lord Brody, pulling him up to his feet. Brody lolled against him, almost unconscious, and Arthur battled back through the smoke and licking flames to the entrance hall, pushing out and gasping for air as he stumbled out onto the steps.

Arthur and Nora dragged Brody out into the drive as Crowe pulled Maxwell out of the hall. The entire building was on fire now, flames licking out of the windows and through the roof, and Arthur heard the distant, urgent sound of fire engine horns. Brody coughed and sat up, looking at the blazing Scratch Moss Hall almost uncomprehendingly.

'You saved my life,' he said, looking at Arthur. 'That rabble… they'd have done for me.'

Brody dragged himself to his feet. Arthur said, 'Wait for the ambulances.'

Brody shook his head. 'No, I'm getting out of here, on bloody foot if I have to. And I'll never even think about Scratch Moss again, let alone come back here. I'll be in touch about where to send my money, Collier.' Then he limped off towards the fields, away from the hall and the mine.

Arthur turned to see Crowe standing back from Maxwell, lying on his back in the gravel. Clarke stood up, 'I'm going to go down to the main gates, see if I can see the fire engines.'

Arthur said, 'Crowe! Is Maxwell breathing?'

Crowe shook his head. 'I think he's done for, Mr Collier. I think...'

'Don't think, get closer and check, man!' cried Arthur in exasperation. Crowe looked pained, then crouched down, approaching the unmoving gamekeeper cautiously.

Then Maxwell seemed to convulse, his back arching, throwing back his head. And from his mouth issued what Arthur at first took to be a gasp of smoke. But it seemed to writhe and turn in the air, almost like something alive.

'No,' whispered Crowe, skittering away on his hands and knees. 'No. Not me. Please, not me. I don't want Red Clogs.'

Arthur watched in horror as the smoke seemed to gather itself, then plunged into Crowe's mouth.

Crowe twisted and turned, throwing himself backwards, but to no avail. He fell silent, so quiet that Arthur thought he, too, was dead, then he stirred and climbed to his feet. He gave Arthur a long, glowering look, then turned and ran.

'Arthur?' Nora pressed against his side, and he put his arm around her shoulder. Together they watched Scratch Moss Hall burning, the sirens of the fire engines sounding behind them. They would be too late. Nora said, 'There's something I need to tell you.'

Arthur looked at her. 'What?'

'I'm pregnant.'

He gaped at her. 'What? But... you know? So soon? Have you seen a doctor?'

'I know,' she nodded. 'I don't need a doctor to tell me. I can feel it inside me. It's Scratch Moss, Arthur. It rejoices when a child is conceived.'

Arthur felt sick. Another potential victim for Duiw Prið. No wonder the land celebrated. 'Then you are coming away with me after all,' said Arthur. 'I'll not shirk my responsibilities. We'll be married.'

'I'm not leaving Scratch Moss,' said Nora quietly.

Arthur stared at her. 'You would bring up your child here? Our child? When you have the chance to leave?'

'Nobody really leaves,' she said.

'But you *could*,' pressed Arthur. 'We could.'

Nora turned her face away from him. 'But I won't. I can't explain it. It's just the way it is.'

He turned back to the blazing building. Those windows which had not been smashed cracked and broke with the heat. Arthur Collier did not shy away from doing his duty. Not once in his life. And he would not start now. If Nora was set on staying in Scratch Moss, then so would he. He would give notice at the Coal Commission, and he would find work here. Well, there was always the pit. There would always be the pit. Besides… he did not quite understand what he'd just seen happen to Johnny Crowe, but he knew enough to realise that William Maxwell's death did not mean children were safe in Scratch Moss now. And if he was going to be a father, he would damn well make sure his child was safe.

As the firemen started to train their hoses on Scratch Moss Hall, Arthur steered Nora back towards the town. His new home. She said, 'I think it'll be a boy. What should we call him? What's your father called?'

'He was called Terrence,' said Arthur, watching Scratch Moss Hall burn.

PART TEN

1985

34

'Missing?' said Terry Collier, staring at Mary. 'When you say Joe's gone *missing*...'

There were two kinds of missing in Scratch Moss. There was when you just didn't know where someone was for a temporary period of time, and then there was *missing*...

As Mary dissolved into tears, Terry knew which one she meant. The one where you were supposed to just accept it, because that was how things were done in Scratch Moss. The one where you lost your child to a story, a shadow, a thing they called Red Clogs.

...just because something's always been done one way, because it's a way of life, because people don't know any other way... that doesn't mean things can't be different. It just needs somebody with a bit of bravery to make them different. It needs a Scratch Moss man to stand up and fight for a change...

Terry didn't know it yet, but those were the last words he'd ever hear his dad speak. He said, 'Joe's been hanging around with Ellen Dowd, hasn't he? I'll try there first.'

He could tell that Mary was about to tell him there was no point, that they just had to accept it, but he silenced her with a warning stare. 'I'm going out,' he said.

-

Brian Dowd was a thickset man with a moustache who Terry had been to school with and down the pit with ever since. He answered the door and nodded at Terry. 'All right?'

'All right?' said Terry. 'Listen, Brian, you haven't seen our Joe, have you? I know he's been knocking around with your Ellen a bit.'

Brian glanced down the road. 'Sniffing around, do you mean?'

Terry frowned at him. 'What?'

'You know what lads are like, Terry. We were young ourselves, once. Our Ellen... she's growing up. Got all sorts sniffing around her. Your lad Joe's one of them.'

'No, I don't think it's like that, they're just kids,' said Terry. 'Anyway, I wondered if he'd been round or Ellen had been out with him last night or anything?'

Brian shook his head. 'Not let our Ellen out since yesterday. She's not been with your Joe last night. She was at home.'

Terry looked at him curiously. 'Why are you not letting your Ellen out?'

Brian shrugged. 'Ran into Alan Warner yesterday. They lost their Anne—'

'I know who Alan Warner is,' interrupted Terry. 'That was years ago. What's that got to do with letting your Ellen go out right now?'

'Alan said your Joe had been round, asking questions about their Anne. Going *missing*. You know how it is, Terry. That sort of thing, you don't want to attract attention, do you? So I told our Ellen she couldn't knock about with your Joe. Not for a bit. Nothing personal.' Suddenly, Brian frowned. 'Why are you asking anyway? Your Joe... he's not *missing* is he...?'

Terry said nothing, just turned on his heel and headed for the Avenues.

Alan Warner peered around the flaking red-painted door at Terry, standing on the path in their overgrown front garden. Terry got right to the point, 'I heard our Joe was round here.'

Alan nodded. 'He was. Proper upset Liz, asking questions about Anne.'

'Sorry, I'll have a word with him,' said Terry. 'Why was he asking about your Anne?'

Alan shrugged. 'Search me.'

'What did you tell him?'

Alan's shoulders raised and fell again. 'I didn't tell him anything. Except that nobody did anything when Anne went missing, even though you all knew why.'

Terry remembered the girl, vaguely. Not so much what she looked like, other than the sense of guilty relief that his own child was safe for another year. 'Alan, you know how things are, how they've always been. Did Liz say anything to our Joe?'

Alan made to shut the door. 'Just what everybody knows but nobody talks about. That Johnny Crowe took our Anne away from us.'

—

Johnny Crowe lived in a big, ramshackle old house up above the pit, standing on its own at the edge of some fields that stretched on to the next community. His family had lived there for generations. Johnny Crowe had always been a weirdo, a loner, even when Terry was a lad. He was around twenty years or so older than Terry, which made him about sixty now, though he looked older; it was that beard and those ragged clothes he wore. Made him look like *Catweazle*, or that wizard on that poster Joe had on his wall, that *Lord of the Rings* thing. Alan Warner was right; everybody suspected it was Johnny Crowe. But it was one of those things you didn't talk about, as if just by thinking it you might draw attention on yourself.

When he was about ten, his dad had beaten him hard for playing knock-a-door-run on the Crowe place. He'd told Terry he never had to go anywhere near that old house, nor Johnny Crowe. There were rumours when Terry was young that Johnny was a kiddy-fiddler, that he liked children. He'd worked down the pit, once, in his dad's time, but after Johnny's parents died he just took to living in the old house like a hermit, getting increasingly more ragged and wild-looking. Even Joe and his mates had grown up knowing you didn't go near the Crowe place.

The summer afternoon sunshine lent an even eerier atmosphere to the Crowe place as Terry approached along the overgrown path that ran across the field. It was as though the bright light gave even more depth to the shadows, highlighted the grime on the windows and the crumbling brickwork and loose roof tiles. The Crowe house was in its element at night, in the dark, when it seemed more at home.

Terry veered off before he got to the overgrown front garden bordered by a falling-down wooden picket fence, and circumnavigated the house, all around the brick wall at the rear that enclosed the back garden and a couple of outbuildings. It had been a farm, once, probably before he was born. No doubt Crowe's father had abandoned farming in favour of working in the mine when the Scratch Moss pit was opened, as most people had who lived here on the scattered small-holdings before the coming of coal mining.

Terry didn't know what he was looking for, but just wanted to get a proper feel of the place before he knocked on the door. The upstairs windows were all draped with grimy net curtains, and there wasn't a door or window open, despite the heat. The Crowe place could easily have been taken for a derelict, abandoned house. Terry couldn't even remember the last time he'd seen Johnny Crowe; months ago? Longer? He didn't even know how Crowe got his food; he never saw him at the shops on the parade. Maybe he grew it all behind those tall brick walls at the back.

Coming full circle, Terry pushed open the gate, which was hanging on one hinge, and paused. A primal memory, childhood conditioning, caused him to hesitate. The bruises raised on his arm when his dad gripped him in his vice-like fist and smacked him one for playing at the Crowe place thirty years ago. You don't go near the Crowe place. Everybody knew that. You just don't.

Terry took a deep breath and stalked up the broken slabs of the path, banging his fist on the door. He waited, and then banged again. When there was still nothing, he considered slipping around the side of the house to take a good look at the back yard and those outbuildings, when he heard a scuffle of movement behind the door, and numerous latches being slid back.

The door opened a crack and Johnny Crowe's rheumy eye appeared in the shadow, above a security chain, looking impassively at Terry. He didn't say anything, so Terry went first.

'Crowe. Has my lad been here?'

'Who's your lad?' said Crowe eventually, his voice hoarse.

'Joe. Joe Collier.'

'Who said he'd been here?'

Terry took a deep breath. He didn't know what happened if you said the unspoken thing, didn't know if anything happened should people talk about the thing they never talked about, but he did it anyway.

'Nobody. But when kids go missing, people talk about Red Clogs. And when they talk about Red Clogs, they sometimes talk about you.'

The door closed and Terry prepared to bang his fist on it again, but then he heard the security chain being taken off. Crowe opened the door again, wider this time. His beard was down to his chest, and he wore a moth-eaten jumper and baggy, shapeless jeans, all filthy. Terry wrinkled his nose at the stench of the man, sour sweat and unwashed hair.

'Come in, if you want,' said Crowe, turning away from Terry and walking away from the open door, down a dark corridor.

Terry hesitated for a moment, then stepped across the threshold of the Crowe place. It smelled damp and musty, and the threadbare carpet stuck to the soles of Terry's boots. At the end of the corridor Crowe opened a door and some light flooded in from what appeared to be the kitchen, though when Terry got to the door he could see the windows were thick with grime and grease, creating a diffuse illumination from the afternoon sun. The windowsills were dotted with the corpses of dead flies.

Terry watched as Crowe took a battered kettle from the hob of an ancient cooker range and filled it with water from a clanking tap. He put it on the hob and lit it, and turned to Terry, leaning back on the wide sink, framed by the thin light leaking in through the grimy windows.

'Do you want a cup of tea? Or coffee?' Crowe nodded at a door set into the kitchen wall. 'If you want tea I've got it here but if you want coffee you'll have to get the jar from the pantry. I don't drink coffee. It's on the top shelf but I can't reach it because I've hurt my arm.'

'How did you hurt your arm?' said Terry, keeping his eyes on Crowe. Behind him, the kettle started to gently steam.

'Chopping wood in the yard,' said Crowe. 'I think I pulled a muscle.' He nodded to a green bottle on the worktop, beside the range. 'I take the special mixture. My mother used to make it from poppy seeds and gin. It takes the pain away. Makes you go sleepy. That's why I didn't hear you banging at the door at first.'

'Poppy seeds?' said Terry. Through the grimy kitchen window he could see the vague outlines of red flowers, swaying in the breeze.

'I grow them,' said Crowe, seeing Terry looking behind him. 'To make the special mixture.' The kettle started to whistle and Crowe took it off the hob. 'Did you want tea? If you want coffee, you'll need to get it from the pantry. It's over there.' He pointed at the door in the wall again.

'I don't want tea or coffee,' said Terry testily. 'I just want to know if you've seen my son.'

Crowe blinked, as though he was about to fall asleep, then said, 'Collier? Your father was Arthur Collier.'

'What of it?'

'I was there when Scratch Moss Hall burned down,' said Crowe, gazing into the middle distance of memory. 'So was your father. That was the day he decided to stay.' His eyes suddenly snapped into sharp focus. 'I've not seen your son. I'll send him home if he comes here. Do you want coffee? Because if you do, you'll have to—'

'I don't want anything,' snapped Terry. 'Do you want me to get you the coffee? Is that what you're asking?'

'No,' said Crowe, and turned to unwrap a newspaper packet tied up with twine, in which there were dark tealeaves. 'I only drink tea.'

He began to whistle tunelessly as he made a pot of tea. Terry waited, but Crowe didn't turn back to him. Casting one last look around the filthy kitchen, he turned on his heel and walked out of the oppressive gloom of the house, and back into the welcome sunlight.

—

When Terry Collier had gone, and the pot of tea was brewing, Johnny went to close the front door and slide all the locks and latches back into place. Then he went back to the kitchen and picked up the bottle of special mixture. The special mixture cured all ills. That was what his mother had said, and she was right. When Johnny was a little boy he had watched her mashing up the seeds from the bright red poppy plants into a paste then soaked it in gin. He had learned to do the same. The special mixture made him warm and woozy, and gave him funny dreams. Not all of them nice. But the dreams were strong and when he had the special mixture he could sometimes drown out the dark, black voice in his head. For a time, at least. Not forever. Never forever.

Johnny got a tarnished metal spoon from the drawer and went to the pantry. Part of him had wanted Terry Collier to open the door and look inside. The part of him that felt warm and woozy after he'd had big slugs of the special mixture earlier. The part of him that wanted all this to be over.

But it wasn't over, not yet. One more at the very least. It had been a long, long time that Johnny had been doing the work of the dark god beneath the coal. A long, long time. He was weary of it, but there was nothing he could do.

Johnny opened the pantry and looked at the boy, tied to a chair with ropes, a filthy handkerchief gagging his mouth. The cut over his right eye had stopped bleeding and started to scab over. His eyes were fluttering as he came to. A few minutes earlier he'd have heard his father's voice in the kitchen, and maybe made a ruckus, trying to call for help through the gag, perhaps knocking over tins and bottles. Johnny pulled down the gag and the boy gasped, still not fully awake.

'Time for your medicine,' said Johnny, pouring the special mixture onto the spoon. 'Open wide.'

35

Joe had waited outside the Working Men's Club from ten minutes to eight, constantly checking his digital watch and watching the men drift into the club, drinking the dregs of their money, pondering what they would do without the pit in order to get more money. He waited until half past, then shouldered his backpack and walked over to Ellen Dowd's house. On her street he dithered, then walked straight past. He couldn't just go and knock on the door, could he? Or could he? Joe casually walked back again, on the other side of the road, glancing in the downstairs window. The TV was off and he couldn't see anyone. Ellen's room was at the front, and he bent down to pick up a small stone, and flung it at her window. The first one missed, but the second pinged off the glass, and within seconds he saw Ellen's face appear.

She opened her window and beckoned him to come forward, putting her finger to her lips to tell him to be quiet. 'I'm sorry, my dad won't let me out,' she said in a stage whisper.

'Why not?' mouthed Joe.

'He's a twat,' said Ellen. She looked around then turned back to the window. 'They're in the garden, getting pissed. He says I've not to go out in the evenings.' She rolled her eyes.

'What was your plan?' whispered Joe as loudly as he dared.

'Let's do it next week,' she said, looking over her shoulder again. 'I'll work on him. Look, I think they're coming in. You'd better go.'

Ellen closed the window and disappeared, and Joe walked back towards the main road. The sun was dipping but it wouldn't go down properly for another hour. He should just go home, and hope Ellen persuaded her dad to let her out. He wondered what she'd done. Or maybe her dad was worried about Red Clogs. Grown-ups never said they were, at least not in front of their kids. But maybe they did worry.

Joe was interested in Ellen's plan, but he had one of his own he wanted to tell her. And there was no reason he couldn't do it himself. Think how impressed she'd be if the next time she saw him he had actual evidence of Red Clogs.

–

The sun was setting as Joe lay in the long grass, scrutinising the ramshackle old house standing alone at the edge of the fields. When he'd strolled nonchalantly along the path through the field he'd seen a man walking a big Alsatian, which he cursed at and dragged on the chain lead as the dog frenziedly barked in the direction of the old house. The man had shaken his head as he pulled the dog past Joe. 'Always goes fucking bonkers when he sees that place.'

In his rucksack Joe had his notebook, some pens, a torch and a can of pop. He took out the book and began to scrawl a note on one of the blank pages. Then he tore it out, folded it, and crept towards the Crowe house. There were no lights in the windows and he didn't know if he was being observed or not, so he walked as casually as possible up the broken paving stones of the path, shoved the note through the stiff letter box, banged on the door three times, and ran away, back to the long grass, where he lay down to observe.

Two minutes later the door opened a crack, then wider, and Johnny Crowe stepped out, looking suspiciously around. In his hand was the note, and Joe watched him open it up and read it, his eyes screwed up. Would he fall for it, or would he just think it was some prank? The note said, *Thought you might want to know, there's a young lad come off his bike down the Hollows and banged his head on a rock, looks close to death.*

The Hollows was a collection of hillocks just a little way behind the Crowe house, where kids rode their BMXs and sometimes scramble bikes, up and down the steep trails.

It was quite conceivable that some kid had fallen off his bike and hurt himself. The question was, was this the sort of thing people would do? Tip off Johnny Crowe about an injured child? Maybe if they had kids themselves they would. Let Crowe take a child that was almost dead, it might save their own.

Crowe looked around again, then went back in the house and closed the door. Joe sighed. It hadn't worked. He was glad Ellen wasn't here now. But then the door opened again, and Crowe came out, this time wearing a big, shabby overcoat, and carrying a rough, hessian sack in one hand. He looked down at the note again, shoved it in his pocket, then let himself out of the gate and turned to go on the path that led behind his house.

Joe dithered again. He could just turn around and run home. Nobody would be any the wiser. Or he could do what he set out to… and have something to impress Ellen with. His stomach churned. He just wanted to go home. He pushed himself to a crouching position, took a deep breath, and ran. Towards the Crowe house.

Crowe had not bothered locking the door, which both delighted and dismayed Joe. He pushed it and peered into the dark hall, the paper peeling off the walls, a long rug threadbare on the floorboards. The whole place smelled of damp and smoke, and other things Joe couldn't identify. He looked at his watch. It would take Crowe five minutes to walk to the Hollows, maybe five minutes to search and find nothing, and five minutes to come back. Less if he suspected some kind of wind-up, and wanted to get back to the house quickly. So Joe reckoned he had to be in and out within ten minutes at the absolute tops.

He left the door open and ran straight down the hall, which opened into a kitchen. Flies were buzzing over an overflowing pedal bin, and the sink was full of dirty dishes. The place smelled bad. Joe covered his nose and mouth with his sleeve and looked around. He didn't quite know what he was looking for. Some kind of evidence. On the films they'd watched on video at Keith's house, the serial killers always kept some kind of trophy from their victims. Clothes, or ears, or something. If Johnny Crowe was killing kids, he'd surely be one of those murderers. There was a big old fridge in the corner, rattling and humming, and Joe pulled it open, and almost gagged. There was a lump of steak on a plate, almost green, and crawling with maggots. He slammed the fridge and checked his watch, then rifled through the cutlery drawers. Crowe had a lot of big knives. A lot. More than anybody normal would need. Joe held up a carving knife, its blade shiny, like a mirror. On a whim he stuffed it in his backpack. Just in case.

There was nothing in the kitchen, and he was running out of time. Back in the corridor there were two doors, and then a staircase leading up to the black, dark recesses of the next floor. Joe didn't want to go up there if he could avoid it. He opened the first door, which led to a kind of second living room, piled high with yellowing newspapers and dog-eared books. Something rustled among the papers, and Joe backed out and shut the door. Place was probably crawling with mice, or even worse, rats.

The next door opened into a main living room, at the front of the house. It was a jumble of mismatched furniture and cabinets, a small portable TV balanced on a table under the grimy window, at which hung filthy net curtains. Joe looked at his watch. Three minutes gone. If there was going to be evidence, it was surely going to be in this mess of a room, one of those cabinets, maybe. Joe started to open drawers and sort through the aged letters and bills, but it was just ordinary, mundane stuff.

And then he heard it.

A thumping noise, from upstairs. Joe paused, holding his breath, and looked up to the yellowing ceiling. It had come from directly above him. Just a single noise. Probably something falling off a table or—

And there it was again. And again. There was somebody upstairs, in the room above him.

Maybe it was a kid. Maybe it was Johnny Crowe's next victim.

Joe looked at his watch. He had five minutes.

He could just go, run home and tell his parents. Call the police. But then Anne Warner's dad's words floated into his mind.

Ask your dad. Ask your mates' dads. Ask any bloody sod in Scratch Moss what happened to our Anne, but nobody'll tell you anything. Because they'd rather close their eyes and pretend it doesn't happen, and when it does they just breathe a sigh of relief and thank their stars it wasn't their kid. Then they just get on with their lives, and reap the rewards.

If Joe was going to get evidence about Johnny Crowe, he was going to have to do it himself. And he'd never get another opportunity like this again. He dug into the backpack for the knife and headed down the corridor to the staircase, taking one cautious look up into the blackness before creeping up the creaking stairs, the kitchen knife held out in one hand, his flashlight in the other.

Joe followed the yellow beam of the torch as it picked out faded photographs on the peeling wallpaper, seemingly of old people, long dead. There were five doors on the upper landing, all closed, contributing to the blackness on the first floor. Joe took a second to work out which door led to the room that had been directly above him when he heard the thump, then he stopped outside it, holding his breath and listening. At first there was nothing, and then there the noise was again.

Joe gripped the handle and flung open the door.

It was a small bedroom, the setting sun casting an angry red glow through the window. Joe was expecting to see a child, or children, maybe tied up, awaiting Johnny Crowe's vile ministrations. What he saw was a magpie.

There was some kind of perch, just a wooden stand with a crossbar, really, that had fallen over. The magpie was tied to it by a length of cord attached to its leg. It was flying against the window, thumping against the glass, and every time it did so the cord was pulled tight and the fallen perch knocked on the bare floorboards.

There was a bowl upended on the floor, birdseed scattered on the boards, and another with water in it, feathers floating on the surface. The magpie paused on the windowsill, cocking its head at Joe and giving a ratcheting cry.

It wanted to get out. Joe crossed the floor slowly, holding his hands out to the bird to calm it. He laid his torch on the floor and took hold of the taut cord holding the magpie prisoner, and cut it with one stroke of the kitchen knife. Still holding the cord, he gingerly lifted the latch on the window. The woodwork was rotten and soft, and he pushed against the glass with his shoulder until it creaked open. The magpie cawed again, tasting the fresh air from outside. Joe opened the window fully, and let go of the cord, and the magpie leapt from the sill, spreading its wings and taking flight, crying out as it gained its freedom.

Joe looked at his watch. Two minutes to get out, tops. Evidence would have to wait for another day. At least he had something interesting to tell Ellen. He turned to leave, and ran straight into Johnny Crowe.

'That were your magpie,' said Crowe, baring his rotten teeth. Joe shrank back, and dropped the knife clattering to the floorboards. 'That were for you.'

Johnny Crowe caught the dropped knife and lifted it high, and the red sun glinting off its blade was the last thing Joe saw before everything went black.

36

The first time he killed a child, Johnny Crowe wanted to die himself.

It got a little easier after that, though. After he had dragged William Maxwell out of the fire at Scratch Moss Hall, and taken the thick, oily smoke into himself, he knew he had it. He knew what he had become. Red Clogs. That wasn't its *name*, of course. Not its real name. It didn't have one, nor did the thing it was a part of, and which it served, which lived under the ground. Duɨw Prið, they called that. But they were just names that men had given to things they didn't understand. They were older than men, older than names.

Still, for want of better names... Red Clogs and Duɨw Prið. The one was part of the other, but separate from it. Johnny liked to think of it as though an ember had fallen from the coal fire and lay there, fizzing and popping, on the hearth. The ember was a piece of the fire, but it had become its own thing. That was how Johnny saw Red Clogs. It was its own thing. And it had lived inside him, now, for forty years.

Most of the time, you didn't really notice it. Like a dull, constant headache that you got used to, a slight weight in your soul. Except when the god beneath the ground stirred in his sleep, and started to hunger... then the headache became sharp and stabbing, the weight dragged your soul down, and his hunger became your hunger, and you knew you had to go hunting.

It was generally spring and summer when the hunger descended, and he who carried Red Clogs felt his blood thicken, head buzzing like a hive of bees. Spring and summer were easier to find children, because they were outside more, easily taken. In the early days, Johnny had thought about trying to get a child from outside Scratch Moss, but Red Clogs didn't like to stray too far from Duiw Prið. On the few occasions he'd tried to leave, thinking of perhaps taking a child from Platt Fields, or Hindleshaw, or even further afield in Warrington or Wigan, the pull to stay in Scratch Moss was almost magnetic. And thoughts of harming himself had buoyed in his mind. It was as though Red Clogs would rather his host die, so he could find another soul to lodge in, than leave Scratch Moss. Besides, Scratch Moss... the people had grown used to it. They accepted it. It was all part and parcel of life. Of course, they did that thing, with the straw effigies, some old, remembered thing. They thought they could fool old Red Clogs, confuse him, so he wouldn't take their children. It was a daft thing to do, and it would never have worked, but they did it anyway. Just like they accepted it when a child was eventually taken by Red Clogs. By Johnny.

He tried to do right, he really did. It was easier in the early days. Kids got sick a lot, and he would take one that was going to die anyway. Or there were accidents with cars as the roads got busier. Duiw Prið didn't care one way or the other, so long as the offering breathed its last in his domain. But lately... children didn't get ill as much as they had, and they were more careful. Sometimes there was no choice but to take a healthy child.

In truth, Johnny had thought about killing himself anyway, those first couple of years. When the hunger descended on him it sickened him to his core. He could never remember the actual act of taking the children, it was as though Red Clogs ceased being a passenger in his body and took the wheel, pushing Johnny into the background, darkness falling over his eyes. It was only when the job was done that Red Clogs receded, and the hunger waned, and Johnny was left with blood on his hands and the broken body of a child at the bottom of the mine shaft.

In the end, he hadn't, of course. Killed himself. Red Clogs wouldn't countenance those thoughts, and Johnny was sure if he'd actually tried, put a noose around his neck from a tree branch in the Hollows, or taken a knife to his throat, then Red Clogs would have taken over once more, and forbidden it.

Johnny sat cross-legged on the cold tile floor of the pantry, watching Joe Collier sleeping fitfully, full of special mixture. Joe was older than most of the children Johnny had taken, but he was still a child, nonetheless. He would do. And the hunger that burned in him would ebb away, for another year.

When the boy's father came round, Johnny had almost wanted him to look in the pantry. He had felt the bubbling anger of Red Clogs inside him every time he pointed to the door. Part of Johnny wanted it to be over, wanted it to stop. But the only way that would happen was if he died. He wasn't ready to die yet. The hunger was like a drug that flooded his system. It made him ecstatic. And when it receded, Johnny missed it. Even as the act of killing made him sick to his stomach, a part of him longed for the time when he could do it again. That's why he made the special mixture, to keep him warm and happy until spring came again.

Joe Collier groaned behind the gag, and his head lolled a little. He was coming awake. Time for some more medicine. Not too much, though. When it got dark enough, and late enough, Johnny would take him to the pit, and deliver him unto Duiw Prið. He didn't want to be dragging the dead weight of an unconscious teenage boy across the fields.

Johnny studied Joe's face. He had committed to memory the faces of all the children he'd killed. Sometimes, as he hovered between wakefulness and sleep late at night, or early in the morning, he saw them all, crowded around his bed, dozens of them, silently staring at him.

'I'm sorry,' Johnny would croak. 'I'm sorry. I tried to do right by you.'

Their bloodied, bruised faces just stared back at him silently.

The thing was, Johnny did try to help. That was why he caught the magpies. One for every child he delivered to the dark god. He would send the infants, bleeding and dying, down the hole, and he would release the magpie, willing it to take the child's soul onwards. Duiw Prið could take his fill of the ebbing life-force, and be sated, and sink back into sleep, and Johnny would have tried in his own small way to save their souls.

Joe Collier had buggered that up. It wasn't Johnny's fault. Now Duiw Prið would eat the boy, soul and all. It wasn't Johnny's fault. He'd tried his best.

The boy murmured, and his eyelids fluttered. Johnny reached for the bottle of special mixture and the spoon beside him. He climbed to a crouch in front of Joe and pulled off the gag. The boy dribbled, and opened his eyes, trying to focus on Johnny.

'Soon be over,' said Johnny tenderly. 'Take your medicine. It'll make it as painless as possible.' He held the spoon, just half a dose, to Joe's mouth and forced it in. The boy seemed to come more awake, his eyes widening, and spat it out.

'Shouldn't waste the special mixture,' murmured Johnny, filling the spoon half-full again.

'Where am I?' said Joe, looking around the pantry, then down at the bonds holding him fast to the chair. Fear filled his eyes. He looked at Johnny, his nostrils flaring. 'My head hurts.'

'You should remember. You came into my house, didn't you? I didn't tell you to. I wouldn't have taken you otherwise. Big strapping teenage lad like you. No, no, no. You'd have been safe. But you came into my house.' Johnny gave him a rotten-toothed smile. 'Can't look a gift horse in the mouth, can you? And your head hurts because I hit you with the handle of that knife you stole from my kitchen.'

'Are you going to bum me?' whispered the boy, his voice trembling.

Johnny stared at him, affronted. 'What? What? Why would you say that?' He'd never, not once, been what you might call inappropriate with any of the children. Never done anything like *that*. His face curled in a frown. 'Why would you say that?'

'They say you're a child-molester,' said Joe. 'Please don't—'

'I'd never!' said Johnny angrily, throwing the spoon down on the tiles so it clattered loudly. 'I'd never do that! Why do they say that about me?'

The boy fell silent again, then looked at Johnny. 'Are you going to kill me?'

'Not me,' said Johnny gently. He picked up the spoon. 'That what's inside me. Now, take your medicine. It'll make it all easier for both of us.'

'Inside you?' said Joe, his eyes widening. 'You mean Red Clogs.'

The hunger was almost unbearable now. The pounding in Johnny's head. The heavy blackness in his soul. He could feel Red Clogs surging through him, every nerve, every fibre, and sensed that he was being pushed back, into the passenger seat of his own body.

'Take your medicine,' he said thickly, and clamped open the boy's mouth with one hand while forcing the spoon in with the other. Joe gagged, then looked at Johnny, and tears burst from him. Johnny knew why. It was the eyes. His eyes, all dark like the blackest coal, the surest sign that Red Clogs was in the driving seat.

Joe began to scream until Johnny forced the gag back into his mouth. It was time. It would soon be over.

—

Johnny had stopped working in the Scratch Moss pit when he was in his thirties. The lads didn't like him any more, not since he'd taken Red Clogs into him. They never said, but they could sense it. Nobody wanted to work with him. Johnny had a bit of an accident, hurt his hand in one of the conveyor belts. It wasn't bad, but the mine pensioned him off. They were glad to be shot of him. Johnny was sad, though. He'd liked working in the pit. It had been all he'd known since he was not much older than Joe Collier.

'You know,' said Johnny conversationally as he steered the stumbling, drugged Joe through the fields towards the darkened pit, their path lit by moonlight. 'It's all your grandad's fault, this. If Scotch Arthur hadn't sent me into Scratch Moss Hall when it was on fire, I'd never have dragged William Maxwell out. Never have got Red Clogs.'

Maybe it was quite fitting, that Johnny was putting Scotch Arthur's grandson down the hole now. Had a bit of neatness to it. As he walked towards the wire fence surrounding the mine site, Joe leaning heavily on him, half-insensible, Johnny began to sing a song they used to sing down in the pit.

'I am a jovial collier lad, as blithe as blithe can be, and let the times be good or bad, it's all the same to me.'

There was a gap in the fence, right at the back of the site, one that Johnny had ripped with wire cutters himself, years ago, and nobody had ever bothered fixing. He put his hand on Joe's head and pushed the boy through. Joe stumbled and fell onto the grass, and Johnny hefted him up by his armpits when he'd climbed inside.

'It's little of the world I know, and care less for its ways. For where the Dog Star never glows, it's there I spend my days.'

Johnny liked to sing when he was working. Even though he was almost buried inside his own body, Red Clogs working his arms and legs, he liked to sing. It anchored him to what was going on, even if he wouldn't remember it properly. His eyes black and shining, he marched Joe across the quiet, deserted site, past the winding gear which they'd already started to dismantle, and off to the hidden shaft only he knew about.

He was breathing heavily when he got there and heaved off the wooden board that lidded the shaft. Down at the bottom were the bones of all the children he'd thrown down in the past forty years. He could feel the ground thrumming beneath his feet, as though his dark god and master was stirring in his endless sleep, awaiting his next meal.

'Down in the coal mine, underneath the ground, where a gleam of sunshine never can be found,' sang Johnny. Joe Collier was a bigger child than he was used to, and Johnny didn't know if the fall would kill him, like it usually did with the smaller kids. He had to be alive when he was at the bottom, though, so he could breathe his last in the presence of Duiw Prið. But not so alive that he might be able to shout for help, or somehow climb his way back up the narrow shaft.

Joe Collier would have to be half-dead when he hit the bottom. Johnny looked at the boy, stirring in the grass where he lay, his eyes rolling, trying to speak.

'Digging up the dusky diamonds all the seasons round,' sang Johnny. 'Deep down in the coal mine, underneath the ground.'

Then he lifted up his booted foot and readied himself to stamp on Joe Collier, right in the head.

37

'Where have you been?' said Mary when Terry finally got back home. 'You've been gone hours.'

It was almost dark out, and after visiting Johnny Crowe Terry had just walked and walked and walked around Scratch Moss, thinking. Mary was a mess; her eyes were red and her face blotchy from crying, her hair unkempt as though she'd been pulling it. Terry said, 'I was looking for Joe.'

Mary started to sob again, and sank to her knees against the living room wall. He said, 'I went to the Crowe place.'

Mary blinked at him, and said, 'Why?'

'Because it's him, isn't it?' said Terry fiercely. 'Johnny Crowe. He's Red Clogs.'

Mary looked stricken. 'Don't say that name.'

'Why?' said Terry, anger rising inside him. 'Why bloody not? Are we supposed to just sit here and do nothing?'

'Did you find Crowe?' Mary said in a small voice.

Terry began to pace up and down the small room. 'He said he didn't know anything. He was lying. I should have torn that place apart. I should have kicked down every door and ransacked every room.' He stopped. 'Why didn't I? Why didn't I do that?'

'Because it's not what we do,' said Mary. 'I always thought… once Joe got to being a teenager… I thought he was safe. Nearly safe. Thought we'd nearly made it.'

'It's not what we do,' echoed Terry dully. 'What we do is close our curtains and lock our doors and grieve for our children but never say a word. Never stand up and complain. Because that's the way things are done in Scratch Moss.' He looked at Mary, his own eyes suddenly full of tears. 'It's our son, Mary. It's Joe.'

Then the phone trilled into life in the hallway and Terry sighed. 'Who the hell is that?'

'Leave it,' begged Mary.

'It might be important. It might be about Joe.'

It wasn't about Joe, but it was important. It was the manager of the hospice. Arthur Collier had died suddenly an hour ago.

'It was really quick,' she said. 'We didn't have time to call you. He was very comfortable when it happened. He went within seconds.'

'Did he… did he say anything at all? Before he died?'

The manager hesitated. 'He was on a lot of medication. He'd been in a lot of pain these past couple of days. He was just rambling, really.'

'Tell me.'

The woman took a deep breath. 'He seemed to be talking about something that happened years ago. Decades ago. Said he went down the pit, and saw them. The bones of the children. Saw a little girl. Said they'd all been thrown down the hole. I'm sorry. It was horrible. It was the medication, I'm sure of it.'

'Did he say anything else?' demanded Terry.

'Just that… well, he said he should have done something. Taken Nora away before you were born, and done something. And that pile of bones was so much bigger now. Because nobody did anything. Nobody ever did anything.'

'Who was it?' said Mary when Terry went back into the living room. She was sitting on the sofa, dabbing her eyes with a scrunched-up tissue.

'The hospice,' said Terry. His own voice sounded far away to him. 'Dad's died.'

'Oh, God,' said Mary, and lapsed into sobs again. 'No. Not now. Oh, Terry, I'm so sorry.'

'He said nobody ever did anything. I have to do something, Mary. I have to.'

'What can you do?' she suddenly screamed at him. 'Don't you think I want to do something? Don't you think I want Joe back?'

'Then I'll get him back,' said Terry, turning to leave.

Mary stood and grabbed his arm. 'You can't, Terry. You can't.'

He looked at her. 'This place, this fucking town. It took my job and it took my dad and I'll be damned if it's going to take my son.'

—

Terry stalked along the pavements, lit by orange street-lamps. Where would he go? Back to the Crowe place? What had that woman from the hospice said? About his dad's final words?

Bones. The bones of children. Down the pit. Terry had worked every inch of that coalface, and there were no bones of children down there. And Arthur wouldn't have said *thrown down the hole* if he meant the mine shaft. And it obviously wasn't the mine shaft. Except… there was that tunnel that was boarded off, the dead tunnel. Scene of a collapse years ago, they said. Everybody avoided that place. So what was the hole, if not the shaft? Not one of the adits that ran off the pit, for air and drainage. They weren't *holes*. They were tunnels. Then Terry remembered. Up and away from the winding gear and shaft there was something boarded up, in the ground, with a circular wooden cap. He'd always assumed it was an aborted shaft, or dated back to when they had started to build the pit more than a century before. Terry turned off on Hall Lane, not to take him up to the Crowe place, but to get to the pit.

—

The mine was deserted and dark, almost derelict now, the life sucked out of it. They'd started taking down the winding gear and before long they'd fill in the shaft and cover it all over with turf and it would be like Scratch Moss pit had never existed. But it was like his dad had said at the hospice. The piper still wants paying. No pit, no prosperity, no jobs. But children would still die.

Unless Terry did something about it now. Unless he ended it. Unless, like his dad had said, he was the Scratch Moss man who decided to stand up and fight.

The main gate was locked and Terry hauled himself up the wire fence and over the top. That wooden cap in the ground was over to the left somewhere, quite a way from the main shaft. He crossed the tarmac, passing the once-mighty mountains of coal now dwindled to almost nothing, and picked up the pace. Then he paused, and slowed. He could hear something, the breeze carrying it to him in the dark night.

It sounded like singing. He stopped, and listened, holding his breath. Yes, definitely singing. And coming from dead ahead. Terry began to run, not caring about how his heart pounded and his legs hurt, and then he crested the slight rise and stopped. There was a figure two hundred feet away, hauling the wooden disc away from the disused shaft. A rangy figure dressed in rags. Johnny Crowe. And at his feet... the unmoving body of Joe. Then the singing stopped, and he saw Crowe take a step back, and raise his foot.

'Crowe!' bellowed Terry as he ran down the hill. 'Crowe! Back off! Now.'

Crowe turned, and put down his foot and stepped back as Terry, panting and with a sharp stitch in his side, ran up. Terry held up his hand. 'Crowe. Please. Move away from my son.'

Crowe bared his rotten teeth at Terry, and in the moonlight he could see the man's eyes were dark, almost entirely black. Crowe hissed. 'You're too late, Collier. He hungers. He must be sated.'

'Not my boy,' said Terry, holding up both hands placatingly. 'Not my boy, Crowe.'

'Someone else's, then?' said Crowe. 'Another child? You want to choose one for me? In place of Joe?'

Crowe was toying with him, in a way that he hadn't when Terry went round to his house. He seemed… different. Sly. Evil. Terry narrowed his eyes. 'Crowe?'

'Mostly,' said Crowe. 'Not all. You know what they call me, Collier. What they've always called me. And before they gave me a name, I was here. And I'll always be here. Feeding *his* hunger.'

Terry stepped forward. 'No. It ends. Now. Here.'

Crowe laughed unpleasantly. 'It never ends, Collier. You kill me, then Red Clogs rides in someone else. It never ends.'

Terry punched Crowe once, hard, in the chest, knocking him on his back. He kept his fists up and looked down at Joe. He seemed unharmed, thank God. He was stirring, murmuring, pushing himself up a little. Terry said, 'Get behind me, Joe.'

'Dad?' slurred Joe, then collapsed again.

'What have you done to him?'

'Just a little of my special mixture I told you about.' Crowe grinned. 'It would have made it all easier for him.'

Joe shook his head, as though clearing away cobwebs, and pushed himself up again. He looked at Terry, but seemed to find it difficult to focus on him. 'Dad?'

'Go home, Joe,' said Terry. 'Run.'

'Dad?'

'Go!' hissed Terry, and Joe climbed uncertainly to his feet, stumbled, and then began to unsteadily run into the darkness. Terry turned to Crowe, who was climbing to a crouch.

'What now, Collier?'

'Stand up,' said Terry, his fists still up.

Crowe did, and Terry knocked him down again, this time with a solid blow to his nose. Blood splattered all over the man's face. He grinned through it, and Terry dragged him up by his ragged shirt and punched him again.

Terry threw Crowe to the ground, and he propped himself up on one elbow, and spat a yellow tooth out of his bloodied mouth. 'Are you just going to keep hitting me until you kill me?'

'If I have to.'

Crowe smiled a bloody smile. 'And what do you think will happen then? Do you think that will end it? Red Clogs will just hitch a ride with someone else, Collier. And it goes on and on.' He gave Terry a sly look. 'Maybe he'll go into you, Collier. How would you like that? Then it'll be you killing children. Oh, it's horrible at first, but you grow to quite like it.'

Terry hit Crowe again. 'Stand up,' he demanded.

Crowe waved a hand in defeat. 'I can't,' he said, blood bubbling from his mouth.

'I'd never be like you,' said Terry. 'I'd never do what you do.'

Crowe nodded. 'You would. You'd have to.'

Terry shook his head. 'I'd fight.'

Crowe laughed. 'Nobody ever fights in Scratch Moss. They've forgotten how to.'

Just because something's always been done one way, because it's a way of life, because people don't know any other way... that doesn't mean things can't be different. It just needs somebody with a bit of bravery to make them different. It needs a Scratch Moss man to stand up and fight for a change.

'I'm going to fight,' said Terry, and he wasn't sure if he was talking to Crowe or his dad, but he did know one thing. He knew what he had to do. He drew back his right foot and kicked Crowe's head as hard as he could. Crowe's head snapped back, and just like that he was dead.

Terry suddenly felt so exhausted he could have just lied down and gone to sleep there and then. He stared at the battered body of Crowe, looked down at the blood on his own fists and his boots. Crowe had been right, though, hadn't he? It never ended. Nobody ever fought.

Then Crowe's corpse seemed to twitch, and Terry took a step back. Out of Crowe's open mouth there appeared what at first looked like wisps of smoke, gathering and thickening until a dark cloud issued from him, hanging in the air above the body, writhing and turning in on itself like a black snake. Terry could smell coal fire.

Maybe he'll go into you, Collier. How would you like that?

The thing, the cloud, hovered and turned, almost blacker than the night. Terry stared at it. It seemed to be thinking, considering, deciding. It rolled and coiled, extending an almost tentacular extrusion that seemed to sway hypnotically in front of him.

Crowe was wrong. It could end. And Terry knew how.

'Go on, then,' he said, putting up his bloodied fists to the darkness. 'Come and have a go if you think you're hard enough.'

Then the blackness gathered itself and struck, like a cobra.

38

Joe ran through the darkness. His legs felt like jelly and there was a fog in his head, wrapped around the wires of his mind that had been pulled taut and felt like they were about to snap. He didn't know where he'd been or why, all he knew was that his dad had been there, and told him to go home.

He must have been asleep, he thought. He couldn't remember anything other than being in his house and thinking he was going out to meet Ellen Dowd. Where was she? Where had he been? Where was his dad and who was that man on the ground?

Joe ran. He ran across the mine site and climbed over the fence and then ran again, down Hall Lane and to the main road, then turned and ran to his house. Breathless he let himself in through the back gate and stood, swaying, in the yard, unsure of what he was meant to do. Get help? For who?

Joe felt thirsty and hungry and sick. He stood in the moonlight, and thought he might faint. He put out his hand to steady himself on the bin, and stared at the words embossed on it. *No hot ashes*. He slumped against the brick wall, and slid down it, sitting heavily between the two bins. He drew his legs up and hugged his knees and closed his eyes, whimpering softly to himself.

He didn't know how long he'd sat there when he heard the latch click on the back gate. He tried to shrink into himself, make himself smaller, and held his breath. He heard laboured breathing and someone walking down the flagged yard. He saw feet walking past him. Booted feet, slick with blood. Then his dad passed, and Joe heard the back door open, and the sound of his mum's voice.

'It's done,' he heard his dad say.

'Done? What do you mean done? Did you find him? Did you find Joe?'

'It's done,' said his dad again. 'Crowe's gone. You know how it works, Mary. Everybody knows how it works.'

'Terry I... oh. Oh, God. Terry. You... it's *in* you, isn't it? It's in *you*.'

Then Joe pushed himself up and walked unsteadily to the open door. He stood there, framed in the doorway, painted in the light of the full moon. His dad turned to look at him and his mum's eyes widened.

'Joe,' she said, and he fell to the ground in a dead faint.

-

Mary sat on the sofa, and when Terry tried to sit next to her she shrank away from him, eyes full of fear.

'I'd never hurt you, you know. Or Joe.'

'You took it into yourself,' said Mary. 'Is this what you meant by sorting it out? Do you think this is going to help anyone?'

Terry looked up to the ceiling. 'It's helped Joe. I brought him back.'

'But at what cost?' said Mary through gritted teeth. 'It's you now, Terry. It's you. That... that...'

'Say it,' said Terry. 'Red Clogs.'

Mary put her head into her hands. 'What am I supposed to do? Just look away when it begins? Pretend I don't know what's going on when another child goes missing?'

'That's what everyone does. That's what everyone's always done.'

'I feel sick.' Mary stood and began to pace the living room. 'I feel properly sick. I always knew it was... it was *someone*. It had to be someone. But not my own husband.'

'No more children are going to go missing. Not like that, anyway. Not in Scratch Moss.'

Mary shook her head. 'You can't fight it, Terry. I know you think you can, but you can't. It never ends. You know that. It never ends.'

'It does now,' said Terry. And then he told her what was going to happen.

—

She cried and shouted and fell to the floor, sobbing, but Terry would not, could not change his mind. He went up to see Joe, who was sleeping fitfully in his bed. He sat on the edge of the mattress, and stroked his son's hair, and then the tears came as the enormity of what he was doing hit him. Joe stirred a little, and Terry said softly, 'I've got to go, Joe. I'm sorry, lad. I'm sorry.'

Mary was standing in the kitchen, smoking, her eyes flinty-hard when he came downstairs. Joe tried to take her in his arms, and she resisted, then let him. 'I love you, Mary. I've always loved you and I always will.'

'If you loved me you wouldn't be doing this,' she said into his chest. 'You could have just brought Joe home and left it at that.'

'And then it would have been someone else's child next. Or he might even have come for Joe again. This is the only way to be sure.'

'But why you? Why does it have to be you? What about your life? Our life?'

Terry took a deep breath and kissed her hair. 'When I stood on the picket line in the strikes, it wasn't just to keep Scratch Moss open, or to save my job. It was for every pit, every job. Sometimes you have to see the bigger picture, and fight for what's right for everyone, not just yourself.'

'My husband, the hero,' said Mary, and collapsed into tears again.

Terry set off driving at midnight. Any longer at home, in Mary's quiet embrace in their bed, he could have been persuaded to stay. He wondered how much of that was Red Clogs working on him from the inside. He felt different, somehow, but nothing he could properly put his finger on. He just knew it was there, like when you've got a bad cold coming on but before it came out properly.

He had to do this before the symptoms showed.

There was no point going to the small Scratch Moss police station. They knew too much about Scratch Moss. They would have quietly gone to get Johnny Crowe's body and disposed of it, and sent Terry home with no more said about it.

He decided to drive to Wigan. As he approached the edges of Scratch Moss, it began. A whispering in his mind, a tickling at the base of his neck, a shivering along his spine. He wanted to turn the car around and go home. He wanted to. He gripped the steering wheel and kept driving.

Drive into that wall, the voice whispered.

Drive into the canal, it wheedled.

Put your foot down. Turn the wheel. Smash into that lorry coming towards you.

Fight, Terry told himself. Fight for Joe, fight for your dad, fight for Scratch Moss, fight for you. You couldn't save your dad. You couldn't save the pit. You couldn't save your job. You saved Joe. Now save yourself.

Die, said the voice. *Die, die, die.*

Terry kept driving. He kept driving until he saw the ugly concrete edifice of the police station, and pulled his car up outside, in a no-parking zone. He left it unlocked and walked through the glass doors of the police station. The desk sergeant looked at him over his glasses.

'Sir, is that your car outside? You can't park it th—'

'Arrest me,' said Terry, tossing his keys on the desk. 'Lock me up.'

The officer raised an eyebrow. 'Why, sir, what have you done?'

Terry looked at him coolly. There was a cacophony in his head, a storm, a whirling chaos of blackness and noise. He could do this. He could fight. He was strong enough.

'I kicked a man to death,' said Terry. 'Now, lock me up.'

Joe lay in bed, staring at the record going around on his portable player. *Misplaced Childhood*. He'd lifted the arm so that when the needle got to the end of side one it jerked back and started again. He'd been listening to it for hours. A doctor had been and taken his temperature and looked into his eyes with a thin torch. He heard her talking to his mum outside the bedroom door. *No lasting ill effects from the drugs he was fed. But... we think there's intense trauma from whatever he experienced. It could take a long time to get over.*

Joe couldn't remember anything from that night a week ago. He'd barely got out of bed since. His mum had told him that Dad had been arrested for the murder of Johnny Crowe. He'd appeared in the magistrates' court and was going to a hearing at the crown court in Liverpool. He was admitting everything, and it was likely he would go to jail for a very long time.

People had been to see him. Joe had heard their voices at the front door. Daz and Keith and Colin. Even Ellen Dowd. His mum had sent them all away and said that she would get Joe to ring them when he felt better. Joe didn't care. He didn't care about anything. He reached out from the bed and dragged the needle on the record back to 'Kayleigh'. He thought about Ellen Dowd and was surprised to feel tears on his cheeks.

On the eighth or ninth day, Joe's mum came into his room and sat on his bed. 'I've got something to ask you,' she said. She looked like she'd been crying. She always looked like she'd been crying, recently. 'I've been on the phone to your Auntie Linda. We think it would be a good idea if you went to live with her and your Uncle Bob. In Leeds. Just for a bit. Get you out of Scratch Moss.'

'Why?' said Joe.

His mum sighed. 'Joe, you don't realise it yet, and it's possible you never will, but you've been given a second chance. Thanks to your dad. I want you to make the best of it. And I don't think you can do that here.'

'School starts soon,' said Joe.

'You could go to school in Leeds. For a bit. Auntie Linda says there's a good one near her. You're a bright lad, you could do really well. Maybe even get to university.'

People didn't leave Scratch Moss, not usually. Auntie Linda had, about ten years ago. Joe had only been little, but he remembered her going, and what she'd said to his mum as she left. *If you've any sense you'll do the same thing. This place is no good. Think of Joe.*

'What do you think?' said his mum. 'It wouldn't have to be forever.'

Joe watched the needle as it hissed around the dead grooves at the end of the record. 'OK,' he said.

—

It took a few more days, and Joe found himself one bright afternoon sitting in the rear seat of his Uncle Bob and Auntie Linda's Volvo on the side street by his house, the window rolled down. The back was piled up with his clothes, books and records. Auntie Linda had never been able to have children, so there was plenty of room for him at their house. Only for a bit, his mum had said. The way she was crying in the street, Auntie Linda hugging her, it felt more final than that.

Things felt… different in Scratch Moss. A few of the neighbours had gathered, as though to watch Joe off. Children played with balls and on scooters. There was music coming from somewhere. It was like a weight had been lifted, a curtain had been pulled back. Joe wasn't sure why he had to leave, if things were better, but his mum and Auntie Linda insisted.

Joe blinked as a figure rode up on a BMX. Daz Twist. He looked in at Joe. 'All right?'

Joe shrugged. Daz said, 'You off to Leeds, then?'

'Yeah.'

'How long for?'

'A bit.'

Daz nodded. 'Your dad's going down for life, my dad says.' Joe looked away. Daz said, 'Everybody says your dad's a hero.'

Joe didn't know what to say to that. He looked over and saw Auntie Linda and Uncle Bob walking towards the car. Joe had already had a tearful farewell with his mum. Well, she was tearful. Joe just felt... nothing.

'Anyway,' said Daz. 'Neil Hall says he fingered Ellen Dowd behind the Working Men's Club last night.' He waited for Joe to say something, and when he didn't, said, 'Think I might see if she wants to go to the pictures. *The Breakfast Club* is still on at the Ritz.'

Then Uncle Bob and Auntie Linda got in the car and Joe waved dutifully at his crying mum as they pulled away and on to the main road. As they drove through Scratch Moss, Joe saw Ellen Dowd standing by the side of the road near the shops. She raised a hand to wave at him, but he just stared at her. Stared through her. And then Uncle Bob gunned the engine, as though he couldn't wait to be out of Scratch Moss, and Joe settled back and listened to *Steve Wright in the Afternoon* on Radio 1, and waited to start his new life in Leeds. For a bit.

PART ELEVEN

2025

39

There was a thin streak of dawn in the distant east by the time they'd finished. Joe and Ellen had been up practically all night in Freddy Blackwood's house, sifting through the papers, notebooks and printouts he had assembled over many years. They sat in the living room, surrounded by boxes and piles of documents, no longer noticing the smell of damp and grime in the home. Freddy had been right, thought Joe. He really did know everything about Scratch Moss.

'I don't know,' said Joe eventually. He stretched, his back stiff from sitting in the lumpy armchair and poring over the papers all night. 'It just seems so... fantastic.'

Ellen picked up the battered leather-bound notebook that had once belonged to the Reverend George Ackman, its cover stiff and cracked, its pages yellowed and brittle. 'Seeing it all written down like this... I don't know. I mean, we lived with this thing when we were kids, but... but nobody talked about it. Not like this.' She pointed at the unfamiliar words in the diary. Duiw Prið. 'How do you even say that?'

'*Doo Preeth* is the nearest I can work out,' said Freddy.

'How did you get all this stuff?' asked Joe.

Freddy shrugged. 'It's my life's work, you might say. Searching Scratch Moss and all its buildings. Finding things on the internet. Putting all the pieces of the puzzle together.'

Joe's writer's mind was turning over. The thing was, if you stepped back from the impossibility of it all, then it kind of made sense. Freddy had joined the dots and filled in the gaps between the evidence, and it all sort of worked.

'It feels like Scratch Moss is cursed,' said Ellen. 'If you believe what the vicar wrote, the story he was told by Lord Brody by the old woman, then this goes back nearly two thousand years. Scratch Moss never had a chance, did it?'

Freddy rummaged in the piles of papers and pulled out a brittle envelope. 'That's not strictly true. It did have a chance, once, to end all this.' He told Ellen to flick through Reverend Ackman's book. 'See where those pages have been ripped out? They're right in the middle of Lord Brody's deathbed confession to Ackman. I wondered why he'd torn them out, so I went looking. I found them in the old vicarage, before it was knocked down twenty years or so back.'

Freddy gingerly opened the envelope and smoothed out the handwritten pages. 'I don't know why Ackman tore them out. To protect Lord Brody, perhaps, or the family reputation. But these detail the instructions that Old Mother Pye gave to Lord Brody about trapping Duiw Prið, sending it to sleep.'

'Which he did with the mirrors and the sunlight,' said Joe.

'Ah, but that wasn't what she said to do. She said he should fill the tunnel with fire. And, most importantly, that whoever carried Red Clogs should be locked inside, so that the avatar, the piece of Duiw Prið that was Red Clogs, would be trapped as well.' Freddy reached for the old plans of the circular tunnel that Lord Brody had had drawn up in 1865. 'See? He had a kind of metal cell built at the centre of the circle.'

'But he didn't follow her instructions,' said Ellen.

Freddy shook his head. 'Because Red Clogs was in his brother, Sebastian. He couldn't do it. Couldn't lock his brother away to die.'

'That would have ended it,' said Joe slowly. 'The killings would have stopped.'

'But Duiw Prið might have fled,' said Freddy.

'Then it was all for profit and greed,' said Joe, shaking his head.

Ellen shrugged. 'What else is new?'

After a pause, Freddy said to Joe, 'You don't remember anything from that night when Johnny Crowe died?'

Joe shook his head. 'I had a lot of therapy when I went to Leeds. I still do, to be honest. I'd been through a huge trauma. My mind just kind of shut down and blanked out a lot of what happened.' He paused thoughtfully. 'Sometimes I get flashes though, like dreams. And all this has sort of brought things back to me.'

'I remember that night well,' said Ellen. 'My dad wouldn't let me out. Do you remember me talking to you from my bedroom window, Joe?'

He screwed up his face. 'A bit, yes.'

'And what happened? Where did you go?'

Joe took a ragged breath. 'I think I went to the Crowe house. And I think he kept me there. Then I remember it being night, and being at the mine, and seeing my dad, and then nothing.'

Freddy produced a typewritten sheet. 'This is the arrest report for your father. He told the police that he'd murdered Johnny Crowe and led them to the body.' Freddy switched to an aerial photograph of the Scratch Moss pit site, long after it had been closed down. He jabbed at a landscaped, grassed point with a long fingernail. 'Which was here.'

Joe studied the photograph. It wasn't too far from where he'd been walking the other day, when he noticed the cracks in the dry ground. Freddy said, 'Nobody remembers Red Clogs any more. Not properly. Nobody talks about Duiw Prið. Not for a long time. But they're starting to again. You saw the straw children they put in the church.'

'But why?' said Ellen. 'Why now?'

'Isn't it obvious?' said Freddy. He passed another sheet of paper to Joe. It was a list of occasions in prison when his father had been placed on suicide watch.

Joe frowned at him. 'Why are you showing me this? Answer Ellen's question.'

'Because it's part of the answer. Can't you see? Can't you see what happened? Johnny Crowe was Red Clogs, and had been since 1945. Then your father killed him, and Red Clogs went into Terry Collier. Then Terry turned himself in to the police and went to jail.' Freddy picked up a sheaf of papers. 'These are his parole reports. Your dad would never go for parole, never asked to be let out. If there was any danger of him being considered for parole, he'd start a fight or assault a prison officer. He showed no remorse. Time after time he said to the parole officers that he had no regrets about what he'd done and he'd do it again in a heartbeat.'

Joe's mum had said as much. Freddy went on, 'This is why people in Scratch Moss think your dad was a hero, Joe. He did what nobody else had ever done, ever thought of doing. He took Red Clogs into himself then he got himself locked up. He made Scratch Moss safe. But don't think it was easy for him. Red Clogs must have worked on his mind every day. Every single day. That's why he was on suicide watch half the time.' Freddy shook his head. 'I can't imagine how strong he had to be to resist that voice in his head, constantly whispering to him, telling him to kill himself so Red Clogs could be free.'

'We'd all forgotten,' said Ellen slowly. 'Anyone born in the last forty years has never had to live with all this. Those of us who were kids at the time... we grew up and forgot about it all.'

'Mostly,' said Joe, patting Ellen on the arm, where her tattoo was. 'Some things still hang on. The magpies. The fact there's still no church in Scratch Moss.'

Freddy shrugged. 'Local traditions that nobody really remembers any more. But now they're starting to again.'

'Because my dad died at last,' said Joe. 'And Red Clogs is free.'

Freddy selected another piece of paper. 'A few days ago a man hanged himself from a tree in Scratch Moss.'

'I saw it!' said Joe. 'Drove past it on the way here from the station.'

Freddy had a coroner's report. 'He was from Manchester. No connections to Scratch Moss. No real reason he should come all the way here just to kill himself. Apart from one.' Freddy looked at Joe. 'He was a prison officer in the same jail your dad was in.'

'Red Clogs hitched a ride in him,' said Ellen slowly. 'And made him come to Scratch Moss. Then kill himself.' She glanced at Joe and then Freddy. 'But where is he now?'

'I think we know where Red Clogs went next,' said Freddy softly.

Joe was about to ask him where, and then shut his mouth as it hit him. 'Mum. That day... she told me she'd been for a walk. She'd seen the hanged man.'

'Oh, Joe.' Ellen put her hand on his arm.

He said, 'That's why she was so weird when she saw the kids. Why she killed the magpie. Why Shep went for her. And why she killed herself.' Joe felt sick. 'She knew what it was. Knew what Dad had been forced to do. And wasn't going to be the one to bring the horror back to Scratch Moss.'

'But it is back,' said Freddy. Was there a note of almost excitement in his voice? 'For forty years Scratch Moss has started to think it's a normal sort of place, but here's where we get reminded that it's not.'

'The question is,' said Joe slowly. 'Where is Red Clogs now? *Who* is Red Clogs?'

'It could be anyone,' said Ellen, pulling her cardigan tight around her. 'It could be absolutely anyone.'

'Who saw her die?' said Freddy.

'Me,' said Joe.

'And me,' said Ellen. 'We were outside the house. Half the parents from school were walking past.'

'It could be anyone,' said Joe, echoing Ellen's words. He couldn't help glancing at her, wondering if there was anything different about her.

'I suppose we might find out,' said Freddy, 'when the killings start.'

In the pale dawn light Joe walked Ellen back to her house. She said, 'I can't believe we've been up all night. What do you make of it all?'

Joe stared at the distant sunrise. 'I don't know. In the light of day it all seems a bit… insane. But at the same time, it all makes sense.'

'Speaking of insane…' said Ellen, stopping at her gate. 'Do you think Freddy seemed a little… I don't know. Kind of *delighted* it was all kicking off again?'

Joe nodded. 'He's certainly obsessed with the whole thing. He's made it his life's work.' He looked around. 'What I don't get is, why none of this came to anyone's attention. Outside Scratch Moss. I get that people here accepted it, but surely…'

'Because they ignore communities like Scratch Moss,' said Ellen. 'They let us get on with our lives, and turn a blind eye so long as we don't bother them directly.'

'How depressing.' Joe yawned. 'God. I need to get some sleep.'

'Me too. I'm picking Korben up from school later and then working nights at the home.'

'It's the funeral tomorrow,' said Joe suddenly. 'Bloody hell.' He looked at Ellen. 'You'll come?'

'Of course,' she said. 'I've already rearranged my shifts. Go and get some rest. You'll need it for the funeral.' She hesitated, then said, 'And afterwards? You'll be going back to London?'

'That was the plan,' said Joe.

'Is it still the plan?'

He looked up and around at Scratch Moss as it started to come awake. Behind one of those windows, someone was waking up with Red Clogs lodged like a splinter in their soul. 'I don't know,' said Joe. 'I really don't know.'

Well, of course he was going back to London. What else would he do? Move into the old house permanently? Live in Scratch Moss? Joe lay on the bed, staring at the crack of light between the curtains. On the other hand, why not? He could be an unsuccessful author just as easily in Scratch Moss as he could in London. And live a lot cheaper, too.

Joe picked up his phone and scrolled through it. Yesterday he'd emailed his agent to find out if his latest book idea had got any traction among editors. His agent had sent it out three months ago, or so she'd said. She hadn't replied to the email. He wandered through his various social media feeds, feeling a growing hatred of everyone and everything. Other authors were crowing about book deals and film options and posting pictures of their latest cover designs. Joe's follower count seemed to be plummeting, as though simply by going back to Scratch Moss he'd somehow started to erase himself from everyone's thoughts. He thought about when he was arriving by train, and his vague idea that he could write a book about his childhood. It wasn't what he was thinking about then, but perhaps he could? Write something about Red Clogs? He flipped back to his emails and fired a brief message off to his agent. *What do you think about me writing a horror novel?*

Joe tossed the phone onto the carpet and turned over, trying to get some sleep, though he felt wired and jumpy. What had Ellen meant when she asked if it was still the plan that he return to London? Did she think all this, everything Freddy told them, had changed everything? *Had* it changed everything? If Red Clogs and Duiw Prið were indeed real, then it wasn't anything to do with Joe, was it? His dad had gone to prison for forty years until he died, and his mum had killed herself because of it. Surely that was enough from one family. What could Joe do about anything? He'd stay long enough to get the house on the market and wrap up any outstanding financial affairs that might need seeing to, then he'd get back to London. Scratch Moss wasn't his home, and it wasn't his responsibility, and he looked forward to forgetting all about it once again, just as he had in 1985.

He stared at the wallpaper, his eyes following the patterns as though they were intricate mazes, until he finally fell asleep.

40

At ten o'clock on the morning of the funeral, Cheryl from Harty's called for Joe, who was dressed in his black suit and tie, shoes polished, pacing anxiously up and down the living room. Cheryl was wearing a black frock coat and a top hat, and on her lapel was pinned a vinyl magpie badge. She gave him an encouraging smile and said, 'Ready?'

Joe wasn't sure if he was. He'd not got to the age of fifty-three without attending a few funerals, but he had no idea how a Scratch Moss funeral was going to look. Outside there was a hearse with two coffins in the back, and parked behind a car. There was no other family apart from Joe. Mum's sister, Auntie Linda, had died five years ago.

As Cheryl let Joe into the back of the black car, rain started to spot from the darkening clouds. Suitable funeral weather, he thought. Couldn't have written it better myself. Cheryl smiled at him again and went to stand in front of the hearse. Then, as though marching to a silent drumbeat she set off walking, along the road, towards the old church. The hearse pulled out behind her, and the driver of Joe's car behind that, in a sombre procession.

Joe didn't know what to expect from the funeral, but there was one thing he hadn't been prepared for. As the cortège passed slowly down the road, people started to come out of their houses. The stood at their doors, in their front gardens, on the pavement. More filtered out of the side streets. And they all stood, silently watching the hearse pass. Some people bowed their heads. Old men took off their caps. Women held their children close. And finally, the enormity of it all hit Joe like a brick. His parents were dead. Terry and Mary Collier were dead. And though he had put Scratch Moss behind him, though he had forgotten about it a long time ago, though he had barely thought about his father, locked up in prison, everything suddenly came crashing down on Joe.

His dad had saved Joe's life. He got a flash of darkness, of the pit, of Johnny Crowe, singing an old song. A vision of his dad, dragging Joe off the ground, telling him to run. He was back in his Uncle Bob's Volvo, staring numbly through the window as he was driven away from Scratch Moss for the last time. Terry Collier had gone to prison, for the rest of his life, to save Joe. To save everyone in Scratch Moss. And in every face he passed, he saw. Saw that they knew. And saw that they were thankful.

Finally, finally, Joe wept.

—

The rain was coming down hard by the time they got to the old church, but Joe didn't care. He stood there, almost oblivious to the fact someone was holding an umbrella over him, as the coffins were carried inside the building and placed on stands before the altar. Ellen was waiting for him, and Joe indicated with a nod of her head for her to come to his side. Joe walked in with her, and the crowds who had fallen in behind the procession followed, taking seats where there were any, standing at the back once they were all taken.

Joe and Ellen sat on folding chairs at the front of the church, and he wondered what was going to happen next. Then a thin, white-haired woman in her seventies, wearing a neat black skirt suit, walked along the aisle to stand in front of the two coffins.

Joe recognised her. It was Auntie Elsa, though not his real aunt. She had been a child of a cousin to his Nana Nora, his dad's mother. Auntie Elsa used to come round the house when Joe was younger, amid a welter of other not-real-aunties and family friends. Joe missed those days, suddenly, when people used to call around on a whim, and stay as long as they liked.

Elsa stood, and waited for the subdued chatter in the old church to subside. She gave Joe a smile, and cleared her throat.

'When I was a small girl,' began Elsa, 'I was taken.'

There was a collective murmuring that quickly died down. Joe hadn't known this. Elsa said, 'You all know what I mean by that. I went missing. In the way that we didn't often talk about in Scratch Moss.' She paused, appearing to gather her thoughts. 'The fact I'm standing here talking to you today was down to the actions of one man.' She smiled again. 'He was known to everyone in Scratch Moss as Scotch Arthur.'

There was a ripple of warm laughter. Elsa went on, 'Scotch Arthur was a stranger here, he didn't know how things were supposed to be. When I went missing, he came looking for me. And he brought me home.' She looked around the gathering. 'Perhaps that was the start of it. The start of things changing in Scratch Moss. Because Scotch Arthur decided to stay, and he married a local girl, Nora, and they had a little baby boy.'

Elsa turned to the coffins behind her. 'Terry Collier, who we are here to lay to rest, along with his wife, Mary Clarke. Now, you'll all know the name Terry Collier. He hasn't been with us in Scratch Moss for a long, long time. But you know him. You know what he did.'

Joe glanced around to see people nodding and voicing their assent. Elsa said, 'You might say the apple didn't fall far from the tree with Terry Collier. Just as his father Arthur had gone against the grain in Scratch Moss, so did Terry. And, we suspect, so did Mary.'

Elsa walked forward, strolling slowly up the aisle, looking at every face gathered there. When she reached the end she turned around and walked back towards the altar. 'Terry changed things in Scratch Moss. There are people here who have grown up not knowing what the rest of us lived through, not knowing why we have some of the funny little traditions we have here.' Elsa paused, looking around. 'But those times, the times we might have been forgiven for thinking were long gone... they're back. Those of us who are old enough, we always knew they would be.'

Elsa smiled again. 'But let us not think of that right now. Let us instead celebrate the lives of Terry Collier and Mary Clarke, and all they did for Scratch Moss. Let us think about Terry, and his father Arthur, and the stands they took, when everyone told them that it wasn't how things were done, that they should just let Scratch Moss be Scratch Moss.' Elsa held out her hand. 'And let us think of Joe, son of Terry and Mary, grandson of Scotch Arthur.'

Elsa nodded, and went to sit down. Joe glanced around. Was it over? Then the pall-bearers returned and lifted up the coffins, and Cheryl nodded to Joe to follow them along the aisle and outside.

The rain had slackened somewhat, and Joe followed the coffins into the graveyard, where two rectangular holes, side by side, were waiting. A shiny new headstone was propped up by the graves, waiting for the ground to settle so it could be installed. It bore the names of his parents and two engravings of magpies. No one spoke as the coffins were lowered into the graves. Then Cheryl took Joe by the arm, and led him to the foot of the holes, and nodded to him to take a handful of earth. He did, throwing the dirt into each grave, hearing it slap onto the coffins. Cheryl led him away as the mourners filed up to do the same.

'Is it over?' he murmured.

'Not quite,' said Cheryl, scanning the graveyard. Then she smiled.

There was a sudden cacophony of cawing and squawking, and just a little way away a flock of magpies rose up from the grass, a cloud of white and black and iridescent blue, taking to the wing and flapping noisily into the sky. Everyone stopped what they were doing and watched, then the crowd broke out into spontaneous applause.

'It's over now,' said Cheryl. 'Well done. There's a spread laid on at the Working Men's Club. I imagine you could do with a drink.'

—

Joe had a drink, and then another drink, and then several more. He had been to many wakes, and they always seemed like a release of the pressure that had built up during the day, a way for people to finally come to terms with what had happened, and grieve properly, and perhaps start to move forward.

This was different, though. There was music and laughter and people telling stories about Terry and Mary, but there was an undercurrent of sombreness, of anxiety even. With the death of Terry Collier, people in Scratch Moss weren't looking at moving forwards. They were thinking about things going back. Back to how they were. And nobody seemed to be relishing that.

Joe sighed and put his head on Ellen's shoulder, sitting at a table in the corner of the big function room. 'I'm exhausted,' he said.

'You're also drunk,' said Ellen.

'Exhausted and drunk,' agreed Joe. He put his hand on her thigh. She didn't move it. 'I think you're a bit drunk, too.'

'Maybe you need to get to bed,' said Ellen.

Joe hesitated, then replied, 'Maybe you need to get to bed, too.'

Ellen put her hand on Joe's leg. 'Maybe we both need to get to bed.'

They went to Ellen's house, because Joe didn't want to take her back to the still oppressive atmosphere of his. Inside the front door, Ellen pushed him against the wall and kissed him. They moved slowly up the stairs, shedding clothes as they went, until they got to Ellen's bedroom, cosy and dimly lit by lamps, and he steered her to the bed and removed the remainder of their clothes.

They made quiet, slow love and afterwards Ellen lay in his arms, head resting on his chest.

'Come away with me,' he said sleepily. 'Come to London with me.'

'Stay with me,' she replied. 'Stay in Scratch Moss with me.'

Joe was going to say more, but couldn't stop himself sliding into the most peaceful, unfractured, dreamless sleep he'd had for days.

—

The next morning, Joe went downstairs to retrieve his scattered clothes while Ellen got in the shower. He had a thumping headache, but also felt lighter of heart, and there was almost a spring in his step. He picked up Ellen's bra from halfway up the stairs where it had been abandoned. *Well*, he said to himself. *It took forty years, but you made it in the end.*

Joe made a big mug of instant coffee and found some ibuprofen in Ellen's kitchen cabinet. He glugged the hot coffee and made another, and one for Ellen when he heard her creaking down the stairs.

'How are you feeling?' she said. She wore a fluffy dressing gown and was towelling her wet hair.

Joe held up her bra and grinned. 'Bloody brilliant.'

'Idiot.' She laughed and snatched it off him. 'Is one of those coffees for me? No sugar.'

'Sweet enough,' said Joe with a nod, handing the mug to her. 'I guessed.'

Ellen put her head on one side and considered him for a moment. 'Are you... all right with everything? You were drunk last night.'

'Not that drunk,' countered Joe. 'Are *you* all right with everything?'

She smiled. 'Yes, I am. You were pretty good for an old bloke, Joe Collier. Don't know why I waited so long.'

Ellen pulled her phone from her dressing gown pocket and plugged it in at a socket in the kitchen wall. 'If you're still feeling in a domesticated mood, there's some bacon and eggs and stuff in the fridge.'

Joe saluted. 'Consider it done.'

'Excellent. I'll go and dry my hair and get dressed. I look forward to sampling your culinary skills.'

Joe started to fry the bacon and sausages, whistling a tune. He realised it was 'Kayleigh' by Marillion. God, he hadn't listened to that album for decades. He considered his musical tastes a little more refined now than Eighties prog rock. Still, it was a good tune. A good album.

As he was cracking the eggs in the pan Ellen's phone buzzed on the worktop. The display said HANNAH, Ellen's daughter. He hesitated, wondering if he should take it up to Ellen, but then it clicked on to voicemail. A moment later a text message flashed up on the screen.

> Did I tell you that Korben's going to a swimming gala after school? I can't pick him up because I've got a double shift at the warehouse. Can you get him? About five? From the pool in Wigan? I'll give you the money for an Uber. I know you never check your voicemails.

Joe started to plate up the food as he heard Ellen descending the stairs again. As she popped her head around the kitchen doorway, he announced, 'Breakfast is served.' Then he paused, and looked at her, his heart feeling fit to burst. 'Wow. You look amazing.'

'I'd say the same to you, but I only have eyes for that fry-up,' said Ellen, settling down at the small table in the corner. She picked up the bottle of ketchup he'd put out with the cutlery and condiments. 'Joe, come on. I know you've been in London a long time but brown sauce please, yes?'

41

They'd made love again, in the kitchen, up against the fridge-freezer, before Ellen had to be off to her shift at the care home. Joe went back to the old house, and wondered what he was going to do.

He supposed he'd have to start by packing up the house in preparation for selling it. He went to the shop and bought a couple of rolls of black bin bags; he'd begin with clothing and soft furnishings, then go and find some big cardboard boxes for everything else. Joe started in his mum's bedroom, getting her clothes out of the wardrobe and laying them on the bed, sifting through to see what needed to be thrown and what was in good-enough condition to go to a charity shop. The other wardrobe was still full of his dad's clothes, pressed and hanged as though Mum was at some point expecting him to come back. A collection of clothing frozen in the mid-1980s. Joe piled it all into bin bags for the tip. Nobody wanted any of that stuff.

He worked for a couple of hours then took a break for a coffee, standing in the kitchen, sizing up how many boxes he'd need for the plates and utensils. They could all go to the dump. Joe wandered through the house. The dining table could go to charity, as could the sofa and chairs. In the living room he found the photos, the ones with his eyes crossed out in angry red ink. 'Oh, Mum,' he said aloud. What sort of pain must she have been going through? He wondered if she'd known that Red Clogs was in her from the off, or if it came to her gradually. It must have been that very day he came home, he realised, when he saw the hanging man. Why his mum? Because of her connection to Dad? Was Red Clogs that... sentient? That vengeful?

And where was it now?

It's not my problem, Joe decided, heading back up to the bedrooms. He thought about what he'd said to Ellen, and what she'd said back to him. Come with me, he'd said. Stay here, she'd replied. He knew she wasn't going to leave, though he didn't understand why. Not if it was all starting up again, and she had her grandson to worry about. But she must know that he wasn't going to stay. Not here. Not in Scratch Moss. Not after everything that had happened, and now this... this *pall* hanging over the town once more.

Joe worked until the late afternoon, then called it a day. He'd pop out on a couple of errands, he decided. He'd been cooped up too long in the oppressive atmosphere of the house. He needed some fresh air.

–

Joe had walked along the Donkey Lane, and across to the Rabbit Rocks. He stood on top, near the old pill-box, gazing out at the views. White clouds scudded across blue skies, the distant hills green, the ribbons of roads winding across the landscape. He'd got an Uber into town and registered his details with a couple of estate agents, who were going to come round and inspect the house in the next couple of days. A charity had said they would come and pick up the big furniture. He felt accomplished. He was getting things done. It would soon be time to start looking at trains back to London, and think about easing himself back into his old life.

Joe glanced at his watch. Just after six. He wondered whether Ellen was home from work yet, and just as the thought crossed his mind his phone vibrated, displaying her name.

'Joe Collier, mid-list author and middle-aged love god—' he began, then stopped. Ellen was crying; no, more than that, she was wailing. 'Ellen?' he said.

'Joe, it's Korben,' sobbed Ellen's muffled voice. 'He's gone *missing*.'

Joe raced around to Ellen's to find the house full of people. Hannah was there, sobbing in the living room, while Mike Speed, the local police officer, tried to take a statement from her. Ellen, her eyes red from crying, answered the door and ushered Joe into the kitchen.

'What happened?' he whispered.

'Oh, God, Joe, it's awful,' said Ellen, tears springing from her eyes again. 'It's all my fault.'

'Shush, I'm sure it's not.' Joe took Ellen in his arms. 'So when was he last seen?'

'He was taken to a swimming gala after school. I was supposed to pick him up. Our Hannah left me a message but I didn't get it.' She collapsed into sobs again.

'Surely the organisers know who collected Korben,' said Joe.

Ellen shook her head. 'It's not a school thing. It sounded a bit chaotic. The guy from the swimming club said all the kids were milling about outside, being picked up, and he was sure he saw Korben walking away holding a man's hand, and just thought someone else had signed him out as being collected.'

'In Wigan, though,' said Joe thoughtfully. 'Outside of Scratch Moss. I mean, if it was... if it was...'

'Red Clogs,' said Ellen flatly.

'If it was *him*... he can't leave Scratch Moss, can he?'

Ellen looked into Joe's eyes. 'Then that might make it even worse, Joe. Anybody could have him. At least if we knew he was here...'

There was a cough and Mike Speed came into the kitchen, holding his helmet. 'Ellen. I've spoken to Hannah. We'll do what we can.'

'Will you, though?' said Joe suddenly.

Mike Speed gave him a cool look. 'What do you mean by that, Joe?'

'If this is it starting up again, in Scratch Moss... you won't do anything, will you? Nobody ever does anything.'

Ellen choked back a wail. Mike Speed nodded to her. 'We'll be in touch as soon as we know something.'

When he'd gone, Ellen turned back to Joe. 'Do you think that's true? They just won't do anything? Things have gone back to how they always were?' Anger tightened her face. 'But why? The mine's gone. The coal's gone. What do we get in return, if Red Clogs is giving children to that thing? What do we get now?'

Joe was at a loss to answer, and then his phone buzzed. A withheld number. He was about to kill it when Hannah came into the kitchen, dissolved into tears, and Ellen went to comfort her. He picked up the call and said, 'Hello? It's not really a good time.'

'Joe?'

'Who's this?'

'Freddy Blackwood.'

Joe frowned at the phone. 'How did you get this number?'

'It doesn't matter. What matters is, it's started again.'

Joe glanced at Ellen and Hannah and turned away, dropping his voice. 'What do you know, Freddy?'

'I told you. I know everything. Haven't you worked it out, yet?'

The call went dead. Ellen saw him staring at the phone and said, 'Who was that?'

'I just need to go and do something,' said Joe. 'I'll come back in a bit, see if I can help.'

With Ellen calling behind him, asking where he was going, Joe went through the house and out of the front door.

'Freddy! Open up!' Joe banged on the door with his fist. 'Let me in!'

Freddy opened the door and Joe pushed in past him, into the living room piled high with papers and boxes. He rounded on Freddy as he followed him in, and said, 'Ellen's grandson Korben is missing.'

'I know,' said Freddy.

'Does Red Clogs have him?'

'What do you think? I told you. It's started again.'

Joe snarled and grabbed the front of Freddy's grubby shirt. 'And what are you *not* telling me, Freddy? What do you know? Do you know who Red Clogs is?'

Freddy smirked maddeningly. 'Don't you?'

Joe stared at him. 'It's you, isn't it?' He looked around the living room, waved his hand. 'All this stuff, all these records, papers, documents… you're fucking obsessed, aren't you? You always have been.'

Freddy said nothing, just watched Joe, silently waiting for him to go on. Joe grabbed a lump of coal off the mantelpiece and brandished it at Freddy. 'You worship the fucking thing, don't you?'

'That piece of coal used to be part of an idol in the old church. Your grandad smashed it.' He bared his teeth. 'What is it about the Collier men, always thinking they can save Scratch Moss? Have you ever thought that maybe Scratch Moss doesn't want to be saved?'

'What are you talking about?' shouted Joe angrily. 'Why would anyone want this? Why would anyone worship such a black, dark thing?'

'Might as well ask why men worked down the pit.' Freddy shrugged. 'Why your dad stood on a picket line and tried to stop them closing down the mine. Why he fought to carry on doing a job that was more than likely going to kill him.

'It's the same reason, Joe. Because it's ours, and because it's what we've always known in Scratch Moss. Same with the pit, same with Duiw Prið.'

'Stop with this bullshit,' warned Joe.

'Duiw Prið is a god that delivers,' said Freddy. 'How many religions can say that? He made Scratch Moss prosperous once, and he will again. There's no coal, not any more, but there are other ways. There have to be. Windfarms and solar panels and who knows what else? Call centres. Anything. Duiw Prið will find a way to repay Scratch Moss for its loyalty. Glory days are here again, Joe. And it's not that big a price he exacts, not really. One little child, just once a year.'

Joe grabbed his shirt again. 'Enough. What have you done with Korben? Have you killed him already?'

'He's still alive,' said Freddy. 'For how long, who knows?'

Growling with rage, Joe slammed Freddy against the wall, then punched him hard in the gut. He was going to hit him again, then he paused. If it was all true, if Freddy had Red Clogs in him... Joe couldn't risk killing him. Then Red Clogs would be free again, and he might never find him. He might never get this chance to end this. But he had to contain Freddy somehow... Joe stuck his hand in his jacket pocket where the big roll of duct tape sat that he'd bought when he went out earlier, to fasten up the boxes containing his mum's things. Joe stalked into the filthy kitchen and dragged a chair into the living room. 'Sit there,' he demanded, and when Freddy complied he wrapped the duct tape tight around him several times, fastening him to the chair.

'What are you going to do, Joe? Torture me?'

'No,' said Joe, breathing heavily. 'I just want to make sure I know where you are when I've found Korben. Now, last chance, Freddy. Where is he?'

Freddy, smiling slyly, told Joe to come closer, and whispered in his ear.

42

Joe staggered out of Freddy's house and ran straight into Ellen on the doorstep. She said, 'I knew you'd have come here. Does Freddy know something?'

She looked through the open door to where Joe had left Freddy, tied to the chair with a strip of duct tape over his mouth. 'Joe? Why...' Then her eyes widened. 'Freddy's taken Korben.' She surged forward. 'I'll murder the cunt.'

Joe grabbed her wrist. 'Wait. Stop. If you kill him... you know what that means.'

Ellen stared through the door and whispered, 'Red Clogs. Freddy was Red Clogs all along.' She looked at Joe, her eyes brimming with tears. 'Has he... Korben... has he...'

'I think I know where he is,' said Joe. 'Come on.'

Joe ran as fast as he could, not looking back to see if Ellen was following. He ran to the main road and then towards the Little Woods, up the Donkey Lane, over the old train track and finally stopped at the foot of the Rabbit Rocks, catching his breath, waiting for Ellen to catch him up.

He pointed up the hill. 'Up there.'

Ellen set off in front of him, and Joe followed, until they reached the summit. The sun was setting in the distance, and a cold wind had whipped up. Ellen cast around on the hill. 'Where? Joe, where is he?'

Then her eyes fell on the old pill-box. She looked at Joe and he nodded. Ellen began to pull at the rotten boards over the concrete structure's entrance, then stopped and cocked her head. 'Did you hear that?'

Joe joined her and listened. A faint, muffled noise. He began to tear at the wooden boards, ripping one off, and Ellen peered in. 'Oh, fuck. Oh, God. He's in there. Joe.'

They both heaved at the boards until they came clear and Ellen dropped to her hands and knees and crawled into the dark, damp space. In the last of the daylight Joe could see a tiny figure, against the back wall, wrists and ankles bound, tape over his mouth. It was Korben. He was alive.

—

Ellen dragged Korben out of the pill-box, the boy's face streaked with dirt and tears. 'Oh, my baby boy,' she said. 'My baby, baby boy. Your mummy is going to be so happy to see you.'

Ellen pulled at the grey tape around Korben's wrists, freeing him, while Joe unwound it from his ankles. Then she pulled it off his mouth and he took in a deep breath and wailed. 'Nana! Nana! The bad man took me!'

'Sshh,' said Ellen, holding him close. 'Sshh, Korben. Nana's here.' She pulled out her phone and dialled Hannah's number. 'I'm going to tell your mummy that you're safe. Nana's here. Don't worry, baby. The bad man can't get you. The bad man's not here.'

'Yes he is!' cried Korben. 'He's here! He's right there!'

Ellen looked round in a panic, then at Joe. 'Freddy? Has he followed us?'

'Not Freddy!' shouted Korben. 'The bad man! He's *there*.'

And he pointed right at Joe.

Joe just stared at Korben, and Ellen stared at Joe. The only sound was Hannah's tinny voice issuing from the phone. Ellen put it to her ear, not taking her eyes off Joe. 'We've found him. He's all right. Rabbit Rocks. Now.'

Joe took a step back. Ellen frowned. 'Korben. This is Joe.'

'Nana's boyfriend.' Korben nodded. 'The bad man.'

'Joe,' she said. 'What is he talking about?'

Joe frowned, and opened his mouth to protest, and then he remembered.

He remembered everything.

—

The day after his mum had died, Joe had slept on the sofa, unable to clear the image of her putting that drill into her nose. He remembered waking up, the room spinning, the air thick, as though he was choking, and ran to the kitchen, dropping to his knees in the dining room and throwing up. But it wasn't about what came out of him… it was what had gone in. While he lay there, trying to sleep. The thick, cloying smoke that had choked his throat and filled his lungs. And lodged in his soul. He didn't know if Red Clogs had chosen him, and bided his time after his mum's death, or whether the presence just lingered, still sluggish after its long incarceration, and he happened to be in the wrong place at the right time. Either way, it was in him.

He saw himself sitting on his mum's bed, sorting through the photographs he had found. And with a red pen, he took every picture of himself he could find and drew a cross over the eyes. Then he threw back his head and laughed and laughed and laughed. Red Clogs had been held prisoner, along with Terry Collier, for forty years. Now he was free and inside Terry's son. What sweet, sweet revenge.

There was a crack in the ground, right above where the old mine shaft used to be. Joe had crouched down, running his fingers across it in the cold wind that had whipped up. And he had felt it. Felt it far below, sleeping in the earth. The thing he was a part of. Reaching out to him in his dreams. He'd hissed, his eyes darkening.

Joe hungered. Hungered for a child. He watched them from the window, his eyes a veil of night, imagining taking one to the mine, almost killing it, throwing it down to sate the appetites of the dark god who dwelt there. Who Joe was now a part of, at the same time a separate thing. Joe, or at least the thing that lived within him, lived to serve Duɨw Prið. 'Doo Preeth,' he crooned, watching the children. 'Doo Preeth.' But he would have to bide his time. He would have to wait. Duɨw Prið was patient, and Red Clogs had waited a long time. A little while longer would not hurt. Red Clogs nestled at the back of Joe's mind, unseen, unnoticed, and bided his time.

In Ellen's kitchen, cooking bacon, cracking eggs. Her phone buzzing on the worktop. Joe opening her phone – one nine seven two – and listening as Hannah asked her mother to pick up Korben. Then Joe quietly deleted the voicemail and the text message that followed, and got on with cooking breakfast.

In an Uber, heading out of Scratch Moss, Red Clogs awake and writhing in his head. No leaving Scratch Moss. No leaving Scratch Moss. Kill yourself. Force your fingers into your eyes. Grab the driver's pen. Stab yourself in the throat. Die. Die. Die.

Hush, Joe had said. Hush now. We're coming back. We're coming back with a feast for Duɨw Prið. Patience.

Then Joe was standing on the concrete apron outside the swimming baths, watching the children milling around, scanning the crowd until he saw Korben, standing alone, and waved at him. Korben waved back. Joe beckoned him over.

'Do you remember me?'

'Nana's boyfriend!'

'That's right. Nana's boyfriend. She asked me to collect you because she's working. Shall I take you home to your mummy?'

Joe held out his hand. Korben frowned a little and said, 'What's wrong with your eyes?'

'A magic trick,' said Joe. 'I can show you how to do it, if you like. Let's get an Uber back.'

Korben hesitated, then nodded. 'All right.' He put his tiny hand in Joe's. Unnoticed, they walked away.

The child whimpering as Joe bound his legs and hands with the duct tape he'd bought before picking up Korben, the same duct tape he would later use on Freddy Blackwood. Tears streaming down the boy's face as Joe forced him into the darkness of the pill-box interior.

'You're a lucky boy,' said Joe, his voice thick and not really his. Joe was a passenger in his own head, had been every time Red Clogs took over. 'Not got a way to get you down to Duiw Prið yet. But don't worry, I'll work it out. Find a way into the mine.'

Joe put a strip of duct tape over the boy's mouth and smiled at him, a horrible smile, then fastened the boards back over the entrance, plunging the mewling Korben into pitch blackness.

Joe holding Freddy Blackwood by his shirt, snarling and demanding, 'And what are you *not* telling me, Freddy? What do you know? Do you know who Red Clogs is?'

Then Freddy smirking and saying, 'Don't you?'

No, he did not know, because Red Clogs wanted it that way. Wanted to savour the moment, wanted to ride in Joe Collier's soul.

Joe had said, 'Now, last chance, Freddy. Where is he?'

And Freddy had whispered in his ear.

'You know, Joe Collier. You know exactly where he is. You put him there.'

Then Joe was reeling away from Freddy, out of the house, and by the time he had run straight into Ellen, he didn't know how he knew, or why he knew, just that he knew exactly where little Korben was.

And now he remembered everything.

—

'It's you,' said Ellen, pushing Korben behind her. 'Red Clogs. It's *you*, Joe. How long?' She bent down, not taking her eyes off him, and her hand closed around a short stick, a length of tree branch.

'Since my mum died.'

Ellen looked like she was going to throw up. 'You made love to me, Joe. With that *thing* inside you.'

Joe took a step forward and Ellen backed off, pushing Korben with one hand and raising the stick with her other. 'Stop, Joe, or whatever you are. Stop. Or I'll hit you with this, and I swear to god, I won't care if I kill you.'

Joe stopped and raised his hands. Ellen peered into his eyes. 'Are you in there, Joe? Or is it just Red Clogs now?'

'It's both of us,' said Joe, baring his teeth in a smile. 'It's Joe and Red Clogs. Forever and ever. Until death do us part. That's just how it is in Scratch Moss.'

Then Joe convulsed, and bent forward as though he was going to vomit. He felt like his insides were tied in knots, his head was on fire. But he was doing it. He was pushing Red Clogs down. He could never get rid of him, but he was forcing him out of the driving seat, even if just for a moment.

'Go,' he gasped at Ellen. 'Take Korben. Go. I'm sorry.'

Then Joe turned and ran into the gathering gloom.

43

On the train journey all the way back to London, Joe wrestled with Red Clogs, who at first whispered to him to get off, to go back to Scratch Moss, then urged him to grab the knife with which the woman across from him was buttering bread, and then finally screamed at him to just die, die, die.

Joe must have looked like someone insane, writhing and gurning in his seat, closing his eyes tight and muttering. But he did it. He made it all the way back to London without caving in to Red Clogs's cajoling and hectoring and screeching inside his head, and as he staggered out of Euston the presence within him seemed to suddenly subside. But it wasn't gone, as fervently as Joe hoped it might be. He could feel it inside him, like a parasite coiled in his gut, like a cancer in his blood. It thrummed at the back of his head, waiting. Biding its time.

Ellen had phoned him several times while he was on the train, but he'd killed every call. He didn't know if she wanted to rage and rant at him, which would be understandable, or whether she was concerned after he'd just taken off and started running into the dusk. He'd run and run, straight to Wigan, and bought a ticket for the next train to London. He had just his phone and wallet and the clothes he stood up in.

Once back at his flat, Joe sat in the darkness and tried to calm down. His heart was hammering so hard he thought he might just keel over and die. He wondered what might happen if he did. Would Red Clogs hop into a random soul and direct them back to Scratch Moss, there to resume his duties to Duiw Prið?

Even as he pondered, he found he was suddenly in his kitchen, the cutlery drawer open, and was stroking the knives.

—

Over the coming days, Joe tried to slot back into his old life. He finally got a response from his agent, who said that his last book proposal had not really garnered much interest. She wanted to know more about his horror novel idea, and suggested if it was a good one he might want to consider writing it under a pen name. It seemed the Joe Collier name was the literary equivalent of box office poison among the publishing houses.

Joe sat at his laptop and tried to draft some ideas. On his phone he found some rough notes he'd made while on the train back home, which felt like a million years ago. *There was something in the earth beneath Scratch Moss, something darker than the coal they dug there for more than a century, something that burned with the malevolent glow of the fires of Hell. Something that just wouldn't let you go...* Where had that come from? Almost like a premonition of what was to come. Or something dredged up from the trauma-blanketed recollections of youth.

Could he write about it? About Scratch Moss, Red Clogs, everything? But even as he began to tap away, putting his thoughts into some kind of order, he felt his mind dulling, his eyesight fogging over.

The next thing he knew he was standing on Waterloo Bridge, traffic thundering behind him, staring down at the sluggish grey waters of the Thames.

No, Red Clogs would not have him writing the story of Scratch Moss. It was a secret to stay there, hidden away like the tunnels of the long-closed coal mine, landscaped over as though it had never existed.

That evening Joe saw on Jenna's social media that her ten-years-younger personal trainer had proposed to her, in Dubai. She was insanely happy, as the endless pictures on her Instagram showed. Joe drank half a bottle of whisky in the flat and then went out to a bar, where at some point in the evening he began a conversation with a young woman. He remembered telling her about his books, and the state of the publishing industry, and his life, and the fact he'd just lost both his parents. The next morning he couldn't remember her name or anything about her, or if he'd even asked. All he remembered was at some point, in a darkened street, she'd torn her hand away from his, telling him to stop, that he was hurting her. Then she'd looked at him, horrified, staring into his eyes, and fled.

He knew his eyes must have been as black as night.

Joe went for a walk to clear his head, just walking and brooding, letting his feet take him where they would. Maybe Red Clogs was right. Maybe he should just end it all. Put a stop to all this pain. It wasn't like his life was worth living, anyway. Joe was merely existing. His phone pinged. It was an email from his agent. A literary festival in Devon he was due to attend next month had been in touch and had regretfully decided that due to some programming adjustments he would no longer be appearing there. They hoped to work with him in future. His agent had forwarded the email on without comment, as though she was worried that even conversing with Joe would somehow infect her with the malaise of failure that surrounded him.

Joe wasn't sure what happened next, only that he found himself outside the gates of a school, holding the hand of a trusting, innocent child of no more than four or five years old. He looked down in horror as a shout went up behind him, and a terrified woman ran up and grabbed the child, glaring at him. He stared numbly at her as she cast about her wildly and began to scream, 'Police! Police! Call the police! Someone's just tried to snatch my child!'

On the way back to his flat, Joe drew as much money out of the cash machine as his card would let him. He dumped his phone and wallet in a waste-bin and went straight to Euston station, stopping only at a shop with used mobile phones arranged in the window in a garish display. This had to stop, and it had to stop now. And there was only one place that could happen.

Scratch Moss.

—

It had been a week since Joe had taken Korben and fled into the falling night when they found him up the Rabbit Rocks. Ellen had tried to call him, but she was just quickly sent to voicemail every time.

She hadn't left any messages. Korben wasn't in good shape. Physically, he was uninjured, thank God. But he kept waking up with night terrors, and twice he had wet the bed. One day, when Ellen was looking after him while Hannah worked, he had stood cautiously on the doorstep, peering inside the house. 'Nana's boyfriend's not here, is he?'

'He's not Nana's boyfriend,' said Ellen, hugging her grandson. 'And he's not here, he's gone away from Scratch Moss and he's never coming back.'

She did wonder, though, where Joe had gone, and what he was doing. She tried to tell herself that it wasn't his fault, that it was the thing inside him that had made him act like he had. But then she thought of them in bed, of Joe inside her, and her skin crawled. How could he not have known?

When her phone buzzed with an unknown number, she almost didn't answer it. It was usually a scammer or cold-caller. But she did, and her breath caught in her throat as she heard the voice.

'Ellen? It's Joe.'

'Where are you?' she said.

'Scratch Moss.'

'Oh, God.' Ellen had to sit down. He was back. And the thing inside him was back. She took a deep breath. 'I swear, Joe, if you've come back for Korben I'll not hesitate. I'll tear you apart and I don't care what that means.'

'I've not come back for Korben. Or any child,' he said. 'I've come back to end it. Properly. And for good.'

'And how are you going to do that?'

She heard Joe pause, as though gathering his thoughts. 'The same way it should have been ended a hundred and sixty years ago. When Lord Brody should have locked his brother away in the mine. Locked Red Clogs away with Duiw Prið. And freed Scratch Moss once and for all.'

Suddenly, tears came unbidden to Ellen's eyes. 'Do you mean what I think you mean?'

'It's the only way.'

Ellen wanted there to be another way. She wanted there to be a way to get Red Clogs out of Joe, and she wanted there to be a way for them to be together. Her heart suddenly ached. She said angrily, 'More fucking sacrifice. Hasn't this town seen enough of that?'

'Not meaningful sacrifice,' said Joe. There was wind whistling around him. Ellen thought she knew where he was. 'Not willing sacrifice. Those little children, for all those years... they never deserved what happened to them. Sacrifice is only worth anything if it means something. If it makes a difference.' Joe took a deep breath. 'My grandad sacrificed his life outside to stay in Scratch Moss with my nan when she got pregnant. My dad sacrificed his freedom to go to jail for the rest of his life. Now it's my turn to do something.'

'There must be another way,' said Ellen, even though she knew there wasn't.

Joe was silent for a long time. Then he said, 'All my life, I only ever thought about myself, Ellen. I never did anything for anyone else. I was always just so wrapped up in my own life, my own career, my own needs, my own wants. The only time that ever changed... the only time that ever changed was when I met you again.'

'You bastard,' she whispered. 'I think I could have loved you, Joe.'

'I could have loved you, too,' said Joe back. 'Which is why I have to do this. I have to do this for you. For everyone in Scratch Moss.'

Then the phone went dead.

44

Joe took the SIM card out of the burner phone and snapped it in two, then crushed the cheap phone between a rock and his heel. He picked up the debris and scattered it down the hole in front of him.

It had taken a while to find it, from the memory of the plans he'd seen at Freddy's that night. But once he did, he was almost overcome with a sudden rush of memories that had been subdued for so long. This is where it had happened. This is where Johnny Crowe had tried to kill him, all those years ago.

When he'd got off the train, late at night, Joe had wandered around until morning, fighting with the passenger in his head, who knew what he was planning. When the shops had opened he had bought everything he needed, packed into a rucksack that he'd dumped on the ground while he dug with a shiny new spade. There were three big plastic containers sloshing with liquid. The taxi driver had been unwilling at first, until Joe had said he wanted to go to Scratch Moss. Then the driver had shrugged. Whatever happened in Scratch Moss, he didn't want to know any more about it.

Joe dug until he'd hit something solid, scraping away the dirt until he exposed an aged, weathered circular wooden lid. And when he dragged it off a deep, dark shaft descended into blackness.

The shaft seemed to exhale, as though it had been holding its breath all these years, a dry sigh scented with the bones of children and the dreams of a sleeping god.

From the same hardware store that he'd got the spade Joe had a coil of rope and a hook fastened to one end. One by one he gingerly let the heavy containers down, then the rucksack. When everything was down there he let one end of the rope down the shaft then tied the other securely to the spade, which he lay across the hole. He sat for a moment on the edge, his legs dangling down. Perhaps... perhaps there was something that could be done. Something else. Maybe if he just went to Ellen, talked about it, thought about it...

No. That wasn't him. It was Red Clogs, wheedling and whispering in his head. Joe was doing what should have been done a long, long time ago, returning the essence of Duiw Prið back to him, reuniting them. But Red Clogs had tasted freedom for so long, been separated from the god for so long... he didn't want to go back. He began to fight, tried to take control of Joe's mind, his body. *The shaft is open*, murmured Red Clogs. *All we need to do is find a child. Feed our master. That's all. One child. Then I'll do what you want...*

'No,' Joe said aloud. 'No more children.' Red Clogs raged in his head, and Joe closed his eyes, willing the spirits of his dad and grandad to come to him, to let him be as strong as they were. Red Clogs quieted, a little.

Joe looked up, shielding his eyes from the bright sun in the cloudless blue sky, fixing the image in his mind. A good memory, he thought. A good memory of a good day to die.

Then he took hold of the rope, and started to let himself down into the depths.

Joe had never been anywhere so dark. Even with the disc of blue sky far above him, it felt as though the blackness was total and infinite. The beam of the head-flashlight he'd bought picked out the circular tunnel, its coal walls smooth and unseen for decades. Alone in the bowels of the earth, he felt the weight of the world pressing down on him.

Except, no, not quite alone. If he was very quiet it was almost as if something was breathing down there, as if the walls subtly moved under his hand, as if he was surrounded by a thing that slept fitfully. Duɨw Prið. Infused in the coal, all around him, dreaming of the sunlight, trapped in the compacted remains of dead things.

Joe's feet crunched on brittle bones. Every nerve in his body screamed for him to climb back up that rope, to gulp in the fresh air, to lie in the sunshine. Instead, he opened one of the big containers, and began to slosh the contents on the ground, walking forwards, his head-torch lighting his way, the pungent smell of paraffin scorching his nostrils.

It took the best part of an hour, but Joe emptied the contents of the three containers all along the circular tunnel, ending up back where he started. In the beam of his torch, the ground shone slickly. He felt exhausted, but he'd done it. Now he just had to finish it.

Joe grabbed the rucksack and walked along the tunnel, feeling the wall with his left hand until he found the opening, a narrow tunnel that led to the centre of the circle. And there it was, just a few feet inside. A metal door, hanging slightly ajar on its hinges. Joe struggled to force it open after more than a century and a half of never being used, but he eventually did.

It was a metal box, with a bench fitted to one side. Never occupied, never set foot in. The place where Sebastian Brody and the spirit inside him should have died, ending the reign of terror in Scratch Moss. But Lord Brody had refused to sacrifice his brother, fearing that the prosperity of his mine would suffer. Instead, he'd sought to cheat Duɨw Prið. Tossed in a straw man, thinking that would fool the god of the dirt. It still lay there, brittle and dry in the darkness. Lord Brody could have ended it, but swore his fealty to a bigger god than Duɨw Prið. Money and profit, at any cost. This could have been over a hundred and sixty years ago.

'Better late than never,' said Joe aloud, his words heavy in the still, dark air.

Something beneath him rumbled, and the floor of the tunnel shuddered. Red Clogs laughed with glee in his head.

Duiw Prið seemed to sense that something was happening, something that might prove more final than the measures taken long ago that had lulled him into slumber. Something that might force him to flee, or even kill him. Duiw Prið was waking up.

Joe jumped at a swift movement behind him. A rat, perhaps? He turned and scanned the tunnel with his head-torch. There was nothing there, save for the shining trail of paraffin.

Then a voice, not his, not Red Clogs's, said, *Let me show you.*

Joe whirled around, suddenly not deep underground any more, but in the open, the air humid and thick, buzzing with insects. His feet were no longer on the carved-out coal face but in springy moss, surrounded by thickets of trees and plants with enormous leaves, shaking as animals scurried beneath them. Distantly, something roared, and far above winged creatures wheeled in the skies.

Then Joe was sinking, down, down, down into the blackness, dirt falling in on him, obscuring his view of the skies and the blazing sun, and it was cold, so cold, and dark, and the earth filled his eyes and his nose and his mouth and all around was blackness, deep, dark blackness, cloying and suffocating and—

Joe staggered against the coal wall. 'I'm sorry,' he said softly. 'I'm sorry that happened. But it's no one's fault. No one deserves to be punished for it.'

Then the walls shook and the ground trembled and trickles of coal dust fell on Joe from above, as Duiw Prið vented his anger, his fury. He was waking. He was waking and he would not be mollified, not be subdued by mirrors and tricks of the light. Joe dodged to one side as a lump of coal as big as his head crashed to the ground.

He didn't have much time.

Joe forced himself through the gap in the open metal door and steadied himself inside the metal box, as the earth shook and shuddered all around him. It had to be now.

He opened his rucksack and took out the final items. A Zippo lighter and an old portable CD player he'd found in a charity shop. The CD he'd bought was already inside.

This was it. This was the end. Of Joe Collier, of Red Clogs, and of the horror that Scratch Moss had endured for too long. Duiw Prið and his essence would be placed back together, like the long-separated pieces of a puzzle, and the sun would be brought down to his domain, to either send him into deeper, endless sleep, or force him to flee.

Joe put the headphones on and pressed play, and thumbed the Zippo, watching the yellow flame spring into life and dance on the metal lighter.

As the first bars of *Misplaced Childhood* sounded in his ears, Joe threw the lighter out of the metal room and on to the paraffin-soaked ground, and closed his eyes.

—

In the following days, they decided it was an earthquake that had shaken the earth beneath Scratch Moss. There had been an explosion, perhaps caused by old mine equipment left down there. There were gases, trapped far below ground that had ignited. All that Ellen Dowd knew was that she was sitting in her kitchen, nursing a cup of tea and thinking about Joe Collier, when it felt like her house was about to fall down around her ears.

She ran outside into the street, looking at her neighbours, feeling the dull vibrations in her feet, from deep below. Far off, from where the mine used to be, she saw a thin column of smoke rising into the blue sky.

House alarms sounded, and in the distance Ellen heard the wail of sirens. Her phone buzzed and she answered it.

'Hannah? Are you all right? Is Korben?'

'We're fine,' Hannah said. 'But what the fuck was that? Next door's chimney just came down.'

Ellen watched the smoke rising into the air from what used to be Scratch Moss pit. But just smoke, she knew. Nothing else. Just smoke.

'It was an ending,' she said quietly, tears flowing down her face. 'He finally got to write a proper ending.'

PART TWELVE

2026

45

It was strange, getting used to life away from Scratch Moss. Ellen looked out of the window of her little house in Platt Fields as she washed up, at Korben and Hannah playing in the garden. Only a few miles from Scratch Moss, and yet a world away. No magpies on the headstones in the local graveyard, attached to a church that while not exactly thriving, was still in use. No fear of children going missing – apart from the usual anxieties, of course, but at least if it did happen, something would be done about it.

After the earthquake a year ago, pretty much the entirety of Scratch Moss had been deemed unsuitable and unsafe for human habitation. There was a fire burning deep below the earth, and the coalfields that still ran underneath the entire area were vast and fertile ground for the flames. An expert had been on the TV and said that it could burn for years, decades. The network of tunnels had become unstable, and put the whole town at risk of collapsing.

There was swift government action, and a generous compensation scheme put in place. New homes were built in the surrounding areas, Platt Fields and Hindleshaw. The once tightly knit Scratch Moss community was scattered, became a diaspora. You would always be from Scratch Moss, in your own eyes and those of others, but the place itself? Deserted, now. Largely demolished.

Ellen wondered whether, in time, it would be declared safe. Whether someone would come along and build new homes on it. Or whether its reputation would precede it, and people would just stay away, as they'd always done.

She supposed it all rather depended on whether the thing that lived down there was still present, asleep and whole now, no avatar or representative walking the earth, or whether it had fled, somehow, deep underground, as Old Mother Pye had suggested it might do. Ellen wondered if Duiw Prið had taken root somewhere else, and whether, now awake, he exerted his influence on some other community. Depended on that, and whether someone thought they could make a profit out of what had once been Scratch Moss. There was always someone, somewhere who wanted to make money. Whatever the cost.

She thought about Joe a lot, about what might have been. There wasn't much point doing that, but she couldn't help it. In another world, in another town that wasn't Scratch Moss, they might have got together sooner, not wasted all those years. But they had been born in Scratch Moss, and that was what it was. And now it was over, thanks to Joe. Ellen looked at Korben, laughing as he kicked a ball to Hannah in the sunshine. It was over.

The doorbell chimed, and Ellen wiped her hands on the tea-towel and went to answer it. No, not a lot of point thinking and wishing and hoping. Joe Collier was gone. Scratch Moss was gone. It was time to put it all behind them, and move on.

There was a woman on the doorstep, smartly dressed in a trouser suit, with nicely cut hair. She looked to be in her thirties. Probably selling something. Still, even that was a pleasant change. You never got door-to-door salesmen in Scratch Moss.

'Ellen Dowd?' said the woman. She had a southern accent, south-west, thought Ellen. Devon or Cornwall or something like that.

'Depends who wants to know, love.'

The woman held out a business card. Ellen couldn't help noticing she was missing the little finger on her left hand. She took the card and looked at it. One side was blank, the other had a single word. The woman said, 'I wanted to talk to you about Scratch Moss.'

'What about it?' said Ellen.

'About what happened there a year ago. About what had been happening there for a long time.'

'Are you a reporter or something?' Ellen made to shut the door. 'I don't think so, love. There's nothing I want to say.'

The woman put her hand on the door, the hand with the missing finger. 'Please, Ellen. Just a few minutes of your time. I understand, I really do. I'm from a town called Scuttler's Cove. Have you ever heard of it?'

Ellen frowned. It did ring a bell. Then it came to her. 'Oh. That place where they had the tsunami?'

The woman smiled. 'Which was no more a tsunami than what happened in Scratch Moss was an earthquake. I know, Ellen. I've been through similar to what you've been through. And there are others.' She paused. 'Something's coming, Ellen. Something big. And we're going to need people like you. People who understand. People who know what we're up against.'

'Who are *we*?' said Ellen, looking at the card again, and the single word there.

'Gemini,' said the woman. 'And my name is Merrin Moon.'

Ellen sighed. Maybe it wasn't over, after all. Maybe it was never over. She said, 'You'd better come in, then, Merrin Moon.' As Ellen was closing the door, a magpie alighted on the fence, threw back its black head, and gave a long, ratcheting cry.

AFTERWORD

I grew up in Scratch Moss. It wasn't called that, of course; it was Ince, a small community just outside of Wigan town centre. But it was the Scratch Moss presented in this book in all but name.

I lived on the main road, just like Joe, and we were surrounded by either cemeteries – there were three, and big municipal ones at that, not just churchyards – or old pits. These places were my playground. You can still find the Little Woods there, next to the abandoned St Mary's Church, and across the road you can walk up the Donkey Lane, and find the old concrete pill-box.

Ince Moss Colliery, on which Scratch Moss is loosely based, closed down in the early 1960s, but the remnants of it were still there as I grew up. There was still some open-cast mining, and we played on the grey, dusty slag-heaps as though they were sand-dunes. Right behind my childhood house there was a filled-in pit shaft, capped with a small concrete pyramid and fenced off with signs to keep away, which of course we roundly ignored.

We also had our folklore in Ince, though we didn't use the term then. Folklore, still to me, speaks of rural areas, of the countryside, of small villages. Not the red-brick urban sprawl of Britain's industrial north.

Yet, we had our folklore. In the Little Woods, there dwelt a spirit we called White Eyes, and at dusk every shadow in the trees seemed to be him, coming for us. In the concrete ponds by the Westwood Power Station, where my grandad worked after the war, lurked a water-witch, Granny Green-Grotch, who would reach out one wiry arm and pull a child beneath the still surface. One cold autumn, there was what I suppose these days we'd call a moral panic: the mad monks. They were devil worshippers, we surmised, and gathered in one of the local cemeteries late at night for their nefarious, occult rituals. We were banned from going to the cemeteries after dark by our parents, but still we went, droves of us, in search of the mad monks, equally terrified and joyous at our illicit adventures.

And, of course, there was Red Clogs. Rumour had it that Red Clogs was the ghost of a miner, who kicked his victims to death, hence his blood-stained footwear. It was a local legend known across Wigan, with some slight variations in each community.

The Red Clogs of Scratch Moss is not the Red Clogs I grew up with, but my own variation of him. For another, you can check out fellow Wigan author Paul Finch's excellent spooky novella, *Season of Mist*. But when I came to write the book that would be *Scratch Moss*, I knew I had to use Red Clogs in some form.

When I wrote my previous folk horror novels, *Withered Hill* and *Scuttler's Cove*, I was ploughing a well-worn furrow; the classic folk horror tropes of isolated, rural communities where the old ways had never quite been consigned to the local history books. When it came to *Scratch Moss*, I wanted to do something a little different. I wondered whether folk horror could work in an industrial/post-industrial setting? If it could work in the place where I grew up?

And that got me thinking about the old gods, and why people would worship them still. Allied to that, I was pondering mining communities. My grandad Charlie, before he went off to Burma in the Second World War, worked down the pit that Scratch Moss is loosely based on, and there were collieries across that part of Wigan. As a reporter working for the *Wigan Evening Post*, I reported on the final closure of the last deep mine in the Lancashire coalfield, Parkside Colliery at Newton-le-Willows.

I saw the dedication of the miners' wives who occupied the Women Against Pit Closures camp at the gates for months. I saw the despair in the eyes of the men when the battle was finally lost in the early 1990s.

Mining coal was a dirty, dangerous job. At Ince Moss pit, in 1871, 60 miners were lost when there was an explosion and fire deep below the earth. And if you got to retirement age unscathed, there was every chance your lungs and body would be wrecked by your years underground.

Why fight against the pit closures in the 1980s? Why battle to save a job that was probably going to kill you?

Why worship a terrible god?

The answer to both questions is the same, really, for those communities: it's ours. It's all we have.

Thank you for visiting Scratch Moss. If you haven't yet read its predecessors, *Withered Hill* and *Scuttler's Cove*, I should tell you that while all three books can be read independently of each other, or in any order, they do all take place in the same universe.

The next novel in the sequence is *Twisted Pike*, due out in autumn. And for that one I'd like to welcome you back to Withered Hill... be prepared.

Finally, thank you to everyone involved in every stage of the production of these books, including my fabulous agent Laura Williams and the Canelo team of Louise, Alicia, Kate and cover designer extraordinaire Sarah. Thanks especially to everyone who's taken this little folk horror universe to their hearts, and to my wife Claire and children Charlie and Alice for unwavering support.

David Barnett